Alice Sharpe met her husband-to-be on a cold, foggy beach in Northern California. Their union has survived the rearing of two children, a handful of earthquakes, numerous cats and a few special dogs, the latest of which is a yellow Lab named Annie Rose. Alice and her husband now live in a small rural town in Oregon, where she devotes the majority of her time to pursuing her second love, writing. You can write to her c/o Harlequin Books, 195 Broadway, 24th Floor, New York, NY 10007. An SASE for reply is appreciated.

Cassie Miles, a *USA TODAY* bestselling author, lives in Colorado. After raising two daughters and cooking tons of macaroni and cheese for her family, Cassie is trying to be more adventurous in her culinary efforts. She's discovered that almost anything tastes better with wine. When she's not plotting Mills & Boon Heroes books, Cassie likes to hang out at the Denver Botanic Gardens near her high-rise home.

HIDDEN IDENTITY

ALICE SHARPE

THE GIRL WHO COULDN'T FORGET

CASSIE MILES

MILLS & BOON

First Published in Great Britain 2019
by Mills & Boon, an imprint of HarperCollins*Publishers*
1 London Bridge Street, London, SE1 9GF

Hidden Identity © 2019 Alice Sharpe
The Girl Who Couldn't Forget © 2019 Kay Bergstrom

ISBN: 978-0-263-27407-3

0319

MIX
Paper from
responsible sources
FSC˚ C007454

Printed and bound in Spain
by CPI, Barcelona

HIDDEN IDENTITY

ALICE SHARPE

This book is dedicated, with love,
to Annabelle Marie Zi-Ling Yu.

Chapter One

It squatted on the tarmac like a bloated dragonfly, a little bigger and a lot older than she'd expected. Painted a drab green with half a dozen random splashes of other colors, it had obviously been in service for decades.

Chelsea had never flown in a helicopter before. She would have thought the stress of the past few weeks might have left her too worn-out for nerves, but nope, turned out that wasn't the case. She held the bouquet of roses closer to her body and approached a man she took to be the pilot, who, wrench in hand, was peering into the open engine compartment. Was that a bad omen?

He looked up at the sound of her footsteps and broke into a welcoming grin. "You must be Ms. Pierce," he said as he closed the cover and secured it.

"Chelsea, please. And you're Mr. Black?"

"Heck, call me Bobby. Everyone does except my ex-wife and you don't want to know the words she uses." He tucked the wrench into his pocket, stuck out his hand, apparently noticed all the grease smudges and plucked a rag from his belt instead. Tall and rangy with a touch of gray in his hair, it was impossible not to hear the lingering drawl of Texas in his voice. Chelsea opened her purse and withdrew the requested money order, made out for the amount he'd specified. It was a lot of money for her, and now, as she peered over his shoulder at the aging chopper, she second-guessed her decision to hire him.

Really, would that thing fly? Was it safe?

He apparently sensed her hesitation. "Don't underestimate old Gertie," he said, patting the drab metal. "She's been around, sure—heck, so have I—but we're both fit as a fiddle. I have our route mapped out. I'll get close enough to drop those roses." His gaze darted from the flowers to the money order.

For a second, she contemplated walking away but her peace of mind was at stake and that was no small matter.

Chelsea had found this guy on the internet—he was the only one she could afford—and had spoken to him on the phone. She'd outlined her plan and been assured it was a piece of easy-peasy pie. Then she'd asked her sister, Lindy, to run the food truck for a few days and driven from San Francisco toward Nevada, spent the night in a motel where the cockroaches were bigger than her shoes, counted out fifty dollars for flowers and allowed her heart to embrace the possibility of closure.

And now she was going to give up because the helicopter looked a little…tired?

Steven's face floated through her mind. Gray eyes that ranged in shade from hazy morning dawn to early evening twilight, lips that caused her heart to flutter, a killer body topped off by a soul as deep as the sea. With him, she'd embraced the concept of forever. And now he was gone.

How did a relationship that lasted only a few weeks produce such profound fallout including so many unanswered questions? Police found evidence of a struggle and gunshots in his empty house but no victims. She'd been frantic at first, then informed by various "officials" that Steven had driven to a small out-of-town airport, retrieved his plane and flown away.

Flown away? He had a plane? Where did he go? And why didn't he take her with him?

One of the officials, a fifty-year-old guy named Ballard, managed to insinuate Steven was not who he said he was and she was better off without him. She'd already guessed the first part, and she adamantly denied the latter, then told him to get out and not come back.

But where did Steven get an airplane? Why had he never mentioned it or that he was a pilot?

Authorities then located the downed aircraft in the extreme depths of a glacial lake located in a designated wilderness area in the Sierra Nevada mountains. Ballard had shown up again, this time with a smirk on his face. He'd casually informed her that due to a host of reasons, from EPA regulations down to cost effectiveness, the plane was unsalvageable. Gear from the crash had floated to the surface, but Steven's body remained underwater, probably strapped into his seat from now until time's end.

There was no turning back, not for Steven, and not for her, either. She extended the money order to the pilot.

Bobby's smudged hand reached for it as a taxi pulled up. It stopped with a squeal of brakes and the passenger door flew open. A man hit the ground running.

"I caught you, thank God," he said as he ground to a stop in front of the pilot. He didn't spare Chelsea so much as a glance. "I need to rent that helicopter," he added. "I need to get to my house outside of Elko, Nevada. There's a private airstrip there you can use. I'll pay whatever you want. Just hurry."

Greed stole into Bobby's eyes. He licked his lips as he glanced at Chelsea and for a second she was sure he was about to send her packing. The panic of that possibility cemented the importance she'd placed on this sojourn and any lingering doubts fled. If Bobby thought he could ditch her for Mr. Money Pockets, he was in for a fight.

Before she could plead her case, Bobby turned back to the newcomer and sighed. "Sorry," he said with obvious regret. "I'm already booked. This little lady here, well, me and Gertie are all hers for as long as she needs."

The newcomer turned the force of his attention to Chelsea. Standing face-to-face with her, he appeared younger than she'd originally thought, closer to forty than fifty. His suit looked expensive, as did the gold ring on his left hand. "How much?" he said.

"How much what?"

"For you to walk away."

"I'm sorry," she began, "but—"

"How about twice what's on that check you're holding?" he said, his dark eyes intense.

"It's not about money."

"What then? Can't you see I'm desperate?"

She could see that. However, so was she.

He took a deep, shaky breath. "Listen, miss. I know this is abrupt but I can explain. I'm in the middle of a business trip, right? On my way to Los Angeles, or at least I was. Then just as my plane began boarding, I got a call." He ran a hand through his dark hair. "The bottom line is my wife's been in an accident. Apparently, it's—it's bad. I live in an out-of-the-way burg of a town. It'll take two flights and a long car drive to get me home and all that takes time. This is my only chance of seeing her, of getting to her in time…"

The pilot cleared his throat. "You two could share the chopper," he said. "Miss Pierce's destination is about halfway to yours. We could combine the flights."

"But landing and taking off again takes time," the man said. "Time I may not have—"

Chelsea interrupted. "I don't need to land. All I need is for the helicopter to fly low and hover for a minute or two while I…well, I need those few minutes and a little silence. After that, I don't care where I go as long as I end up back here. As far as I'm concerned you're welcome to share the flight."

She had at first read the guy's demeanor as dismissive or even arrogant, but now that she understood what was behind his impatience her heart went out to him. Who better than she knew the ache of losing someone you love? Maybe this guy still had time to say goodbye. Tears burned behind her nose.

"You'd be willing to do that?" the man asked.

"Yes."

He took a steadying breath. "Thank you." He glanced at the money order still clutched in her hand. "You keep that. This is on me."

"I couldn't let you—"

"Please."

"You two choke me up, you really do," Bobby said with a new grin that made the first one look anemic by comparison. "You both have some papers to sign while I refile the flight plan and then we'll be off. But I have to warn you Mr.—"

"Smith. My name is Jacob Smith."

"I'm going to have to refuel at your destination before we fly back here. You'll have to pay for the extra time and miles—"

"Just tell me how much," Smith said, waving away his waiting taxi. "And hurry."

Chelsea was happy to let the two men work out the details as she did her best not to shiver in the weak spring sun. Eventually everything was settled and she was ushered into the helicopter and directed to sit in the second row of seats, closest to the door. The space behind her was piled with duffel bags and taped-up boxes of every size.

Under the pilot's direction she strapped herself in her seat and set aside the roses. As Jacob Smith stood outside talking on his cell phone, Bobby gave her instructions about what to do when the time came to throw the flowers, then closed the cargo door and ran around the aircraft to climb aboard. She expected Smith would claim the seat next to hers, but he slipped into the front with the pilot. Given his anxiety, it made sense to her that he would want to sit as far forward as possible. She was grateful for the semiprivacy of their turned heads.

Once the switches were thrown and the blades started revolving, conversation was out of the question, although Bobby had pointed out the headset they could use to communicate once she put it on. Frankly, right then she didn't want to talk to anyone. In her mind she reviewed the directions she'd given him, taken from Steven himself when she asked him to tell her about the happiest day of his life.

He'd responded, "Today. Here with you. Now."

There'd been a long pause as she lost herself in his kisses. Eventually she'd rephrased the question. "Okay then, the happiest day before we met?"

He didn't miss a beat. "That's easy. There's this little cabin not that far from here," he'd said, and then proceeded to describe a mountain getaway in such detail she could not only see it in her head, but was also pretty sure she could find it on a map. "It was one of the last places I visited with my parents. I'll never forget it."

Once she'd finally accepted his death and the repercussions that would live with her forever, the need to somehow bring peace to her life became imperative. She'd thought of visiting the lake where his plane was entombed in water.

But then she'd remembered this cabin and chosen past joy over current pain.

The helicopter rose off the ground and her stomach lurched. Ninety minutes. She retrieved the bouquet of roses, glanced at the gold foil handwritten note she'd attached to the stems and clutched them to her chest. Their perfume bathed her face as she closed her eyes.

Somehow, despite the loud and constant whirring of the blades, she managed to fall asleep, but awakened with a start. Gazing out the window, she saw little but tree-covered mountains in every direction. Where were they? She put on the headset. She could see the tops of both men's heads but there was no conversation going on between them.

"Are we getting close?" she asked.

Bobby threw her a thumbs-up. His voice crackled through the headset. "We're almost there. Look down. See the river?"

This time when she gazed out the window she glimpsed the unmistakable glitter of water winding its way through the trees.

Bobby's voice came through the comm system again. "Remember to wait until I tell you to open the window. I'll get down close, but first I'll circle the area so you can check it out."

"Sounds good."

"I told you not to do that," Jacob Smith interjected.

"We've been over this already," Bobby snapped. "Like I said, this part of the flight is Chelsea's."

"You will go nowhere near that house, is that clear?"

"Why not?" Chelsea asked.

"It'll…waste time," Smith said, his voice tight.

"No, it won't," Bobby insisted.

"It's okay, do as he says," Chelsea told Bobby. She was looking for peace and closure, not arguments. "I'm fine."

Smith's grunt sounded smug. Or maybe just relieved. But the tension between the two men was palpable. What had gone on while she slept?

Within a few minutes, the trees began to thin and a small meadow appeared, just as Steven had described, right down to the wildflowers carpeting the ground and the old rock wall bordering three sides. She sat forward as a small cabin came into focus. Bobby headed straight for it despite Smith's continued insistence that he stop. She tried to ignore their bickering. A curl of smoke drifted upward from the chimney and that surprised her for some reason. Silly that it should—Steven hadn't been here in years and hadn't known who owned it now or even if it was still here.

Broad stone decks surrounded the small residence while budding tree limbs brushed the roof. She could all but feel Steven sitting beside her, eagerly looking out the window, pointing out details, his breath warm against her cheek. Her hand pressed against the glass as her gaze swept over the meadow they once again circled. The river where Steven had caught his first rainbow trout glistened nearby.

The last time she'd seen him he'd asked her to marry him. After her enthusiastic yes, they'd made love and somehow it had been different, more profound, perhaps, more meaningful than ever before. Afterward, they'd talked for hours about the kind of house they'd build. Looking at this cabin, it was clear he'd channeled his vision from this very spot.

"Goodbye, my love," she whispered with her fingers against the glass.

"It's time, Chelsea," Bobby said. She took off the headset, craving solitude. The chopper moved away from the cabin toward the river. Was someone inside the cabin, watching their departure and wondering why they'd been subjected to this noisy intrusion? No matter, the chopper would be long gone before anyone had a chance to complain.

She unclipped the straps that held her in her seat, scooting forward a little to slide open the window as the wind immediately whipped her long dark hair across her face. The river below flowed in endless rhythm and she pictured a young Steven, fishing pole in hand, walking the grassy banks.

Was she angry with him? Yes. He'd omitted key facts about himself, been cagey, maybe even dishonest, and that went against everything she'd thought she'd known about him. But mostly, she just felt alone and cheated and sad.

Loud voices yanked her attention back to the front of the helicopter. She could only see Bobby's face and he looked livid. A sudden jerk was quickly followed by a distinct shudder, and now they made a slow turn back toward the meadow. Her stomach rolled. In her rush to find something to hold on to, the roses fell from her grasp and slid across the floor. Peering between the front seats, she saw Smith's hand close around Bobby's wrist as he clutched the control stick. The shouting between them continued while the chopper's erratic movements became even more pronounced.

She scooted back in her seat, refastening the buckles with shaking hands. The headset slid toward the door with the roses. She hooked it with her foot before raising her leg and grabbing it. She pulled it over her ears and winced as the shouts became unbearably loud and heated.

"You just had to circle the damn house, didn't you?" Smith roared. "You idiot."

"Get your hands off me. What the hell is wrong with you?"

"Land this damn thing," Smith insisted.

"Now you want to land? I thought you were so hot to trot." There was a moment of tense silence. Smith released his grip on Bobby's wrist. A second later, Bobby swore.

"Are you kidding me? Put that gun away."

A gun!

"Land the helicopter," Smith said and now Chelsea, too, saw he held a dull black revolver and it was pointed at Bobby.

"You're going to get us all killed," Bobby bellowed.

"You're overshooting the meadow," Smith growled. "Land in the meadow."

Chelsea glanced out the window. They were moving over the trees now. Green tops swayed just a few feet below but at least the chopper seemed stable. But why did Smith want to land? Wasn't his whole point speed? And why in the world did he carry a gun?

Bobby suddenly lunged toward the armed man as though trying to grab the weapon. A shot reverberated in the small cabin, deafening, terrifying. Bobby grabbed his right arm as blood oozed through his fingers. "You—you maniac!" he yelled.

"Land this damn thing," Smith repeated as he jabbed the air with the gun. As if sensing Chelsea's horrified gaze, he turned to face her, pinning her to the seat, his once mournful eyes now cold and menacing. Chills raced along her spine as he turned his attention back to Bobby.

The helicopter moved sideways like a flying crab, tilting slightly on its left side. A sudden crash came from behind them, immediately followed by a rolling shudder that vibrated through the metal hull.

"We lost the rear rotor," Bobby gasped.

"Land!" Smith demanded.

"It's too late for that. Get that gun out of my face!"

The chopper spun, the nose lower now, and plummeted

down through the greenery as Bobby obviously worked to accomplish a life-saving landing. His labored breathing played in her headset like a dirge. Seconds passed in blinding speed. Chelsea held on to the straps, her thoughts moving from the drama in the front, to the love she'd lost, to the future now slipping through her fingers.

A microsecond later, the skids hit the forest floor and all the cargo behind her shot forward like missiles, flying at her head and shoulders and at the backs of the two seats in front of her. She had a moment to assess the fact that she was still alive and then they were moving again, this time tearing through the underbrush, what remained of the blades crashing against tree trunks, skids catching on undergrowth, branches protruding through Chelsea's open window then snapping and breaking, flying into the chopper, aimed at her. Everything came to a sudden, grinding halt. The windshield shattered as the forest invaded the front with the finesse of a bulldozer, pushing the passenger and pilot seats back toward Chelsea. The baggage that had bombarded her from behind now flew into her face, burying her.

Steven! her heart shouted as she lost consciousness without forming another cognizant thought.

Chapter Two

Adam Parish took off his black-rimmed glasses and set them aside, pulled his shirt over his head and faced his image in the mirror. The bullet wound on his left shoulder looked better than it had. There would be a scar, but it wouldn't be the only one on his thirty-two-year-old body, and at this point, who cared?

That sentiment—*who cared?*—had been his calling card for so long it had become a second skin. It had turned him cynical and suspicious—not suspicious enough as it turned out, but there was no denying his mother's sweet, trusting little boy hadn't made it into adulthood.

Except for a brief moment when everything had changed.

But like most miracles, his had come and gone like the sweep of a clock's hands and he was back to square one.

He applied a clean bandage to his shoulder and taped the gash over his eye. His short beard softened his jawline while the spikey blond hair on his head always struck him as comical. He had one week to go before he cleared out of here and then he'd—

A thumping noise outside lifted every hair on his arms. Even before he separated the blinds above the bathroom sink and angled his head to peer outside he knew what he would see. A low-flying helicopter approached the cabin from over the meadow.

Oh, no…

Within seconds, he grabbed the glasses, shrugged on his shirt, rescued his gun from the top of the toilet tank and stuffed it into his waistband. He ran to the back door and snatched the loaded rifle he kept there, then let himself out and moved to the northeast corner of the deck, where he could track the helicopter.

One thought drummed in his head: *they found me.*

He expected the aircraft to land in the meadow, close to the house. He expected an army of men to disembark, guns blazing, Holton's revenge swift and lethal.

He didn't expect the helicopter to look so ancient. It wasn't his adversary's style. Was this flyby simply a matter of a stranger's harmless curiosity about the old house or was it more than that? Had Holton employed mercenaries?

The helicopter didn't land and that left Adam relieved and yet confused. It flew toward the river, gently descending above the water, where it remained for a minute or two. Then the aircraft tilted suddenly—that had to throw the passengers around a little. He stepped around the corner of the house to see better. The chopper moved away from the river, briefly hanging over the meadow, then it climbed eastward toward the forest, its movements jerky and unpredictable.

Engine trouble? Trouble of some sort, that was for sure, including trouble for him. Even if it disappeared over the far mountains, the fact that it had circled the house meant that it was time for him to clear out. It might have been reconnaissance for a ground-based unit who even now could be advancing via the only road connecting this cabin and the nearest town. He'd rigged a sensor down at the beginning of his twisting lane. Once activated, it would beep the monitor in his pocket and he would know he had about ten minutes to disappear.

A sudden noise caught his attention and he turned to see the helicopter's aft rotor tangle with the top of the tallest tree. Parts went flying. The aircraft seemed to stall. Nose down, it disappeared into the forest. He jumped off the porch, the rifle still clutched in his hand. While his brain told him to get the hell out of there while he could, his heart said he had to see this through.

Crashes and thuds echoed from the forest. A fiery explosion seemed inevitable, but none came, just the continuing cacophony of breaking trees and mangled metal. He vaulted the rock wall and sprinted across the meadow, ever wary of a sniper but growing more convinced by the moment that what had happened was an accident and that lives were in danger.

And this meant other people would be coming, as well. Friend or foe, this crash would be investigated and that would bring killers and cops right to his doorstep. *Turn around and go back—get out of here now.* He ignored his own warning.

After the full light of the meadow, the forest seemed dank, dark, secretive. He'd been away from Arizona, his home state, for more than a year now, and never more than at this moment did he miss the open desert terrain and the warm, dry air. The underbrush was difficult to traverse. His own crashing noises echoed in the dense closeness as he headed in the direction he figured the chopper had gone down. There were few other sounds.

He finally emerged into a clearing of sorts, but that quickly erupted into a battered, mowed-down trail of broken branches and flattened saplings. It had to be at least thirty feet across, lined with scarred trees and pieces of metal strewn about. The faint smell of fuel urged him forward. And sitting at the end of the trail was the downed chopper, bladeless now, the rear end still mostly intact, no signs of fire or of life.

He made his way down the newly created and narrowing path to the tail of the helicopter. As he moved forward, he saw the crumpled metal of the front of the chopper. It was about half as big as it should have been, thanks to an old growth stump that had put an end to its forward momentum.

The cargo door was the only possible way to get inside. It had jammed, though. He searched for something to use as a makeshift crowbar.

"Anyone in there?" he yelled as he picked up a branch and discarded it. Too flimsy. He continued the search. "Hello, can anyone hear me? Can you open the cargo door?"

He finally found a long piece of metal, probably a portion of one of the blades, maybe a piece of a skid. Using that, he leveraged it into the door crack and shoved. Eventually, the metal moved and he was able to slide the door half-open.

Boxes and crates filled the rear of the aircraft. The passenger and pilot seats had been pushed back. There was just room for him to step inside and almost stand. He shifted debris to clear his way to the pilot, where he paused a second before putting his fingers against the pilot's throat, but it was for confirmation only. The poor guy sat half-crushed behind the controls; broken glass had slashed his face and hands. His right shoulder sported an ugly wound that looked like a gunshot. That, however, didn't make sense.

Turning his attention to the passenger, Adam moved aside leafy branches and glass until he could check for a pulse. He detected a faint heartbeat and immediately began clearing debris, careful when he came across a two-inch pine spur lodged in the base of the man's throat. That's when he also noticed the guy had one limp hand threaded around the grip of a revolver. The safety was off. Adam gingerly reached for the weapon but as he did so, the guy's eyes opened and his grip tightened.

"Take it easy," Adam said.

The man struggled to focus as blood ran down his forehead and cheeks. He finally croaked out a single word. "You…"

"I'll get you out of here," Adam said, though he knew that was probably impossible. "Stay still."

"You're…a—a dead man," the injured man mumbled. As he spoke, he managed to raise his arm until it bumped against the spur lodged in his throat. The branch ripped free, leaving a hole big enough around to stick a thumb through. The guy's hand immediately fell back to his lap as blood spurted from his carotid artery. Adam tore off his own shirt to hold against the gushing wound but it was too late. He'd bled to death in those few short seconds. Adam shrugged his shirt back on as he studied the lifeless and unfamiliar face.

There wasn't a doubt in Adam's mind that this guy had been sent by Holton. He dug out the man's smartphone from his jacket pocket. As it required a code, he wiped the blood off the dead man's right pointer finger and held it against the fingerprint reader to get around the code, his heart sinking when he saw a call had been made to Arizona within the last thirty minutes. "Leave a number" was the only response when he hit Call. He turned it off, wiped off his own fingerprints and put the phone back where he found it. There was no reason to try to disarm the GPS system, not when the gadget was sitting in a downed aircraft with an emergency locator of its own.

He scanned the guy's wallet. It held what was probably a fake ID and a little cash. He replaced it. Straightening up, Adam glanced at the pilot, but there was no way to access the poor man's pockets. The gunshot wound in the man's arm kind of cinched his position as a hapless victim in this scenario anyway.

This had to be the work of Holton.

He dug his phone from his pocket and punched in a number.

"Yes?"

"Whip? It's me, Adam." He heard the warning buzz that announced the burner phone was running out of pre-paid time. "Holton found me again. I'm headed out of the mountains."

"Did the fake ID I sent you come?"

"I don't know. I was going to check today, but not now. I'll have to leave without it." Adam felt terrible that he'd asked Whip, a cop, to break the law to help him get false identification, and now it was pointless.

"Damn. Are you okay?"

"Yeah. There was a crash—the hit man is dead. This is important. Holton…he's still in prison, right?"

"As far as—"

It took a few seconds of silence for Adam to realize they'd been disconnected. He pocketed the phone and got to his feet. As he turned his back on the two dead men, a few scattered red petals beneath his feet caught his attention. The incongruity of their presence struck him. He kneeled to pick up one, pausing to smell it, its perfume at odds with the crashed aircraft and the encroaching odor of fuel.

"Is anyone else in here?" he called.

Was that a noise coming from behind the boxes?

He shifted a few out of the way and tossed them out

the open door, ever mindful of the seconds ticking by. The baggage and boxes felt like they were filled with rocks.

And then he heard it again, a shifting as a body tried to find comfort, but this time it was followed by a plaintive moan.

He worked faster.

HER EYES OPENED SLOWLY. She was unsure where she was or what had happened. Her body hurt in a hundred places and for some reason, she was trapped in an avalanche of heavy boxes. Admonishing herself to think despite her throbbing head, she shifted position to ease the pressure on her legs. A groan escaped her lips and faded away.

A male voice immediately responded. "Is someone back there? How many of you are there? Can you move?"

She tried to respond but could barely hear her own voice.

"I'm coming," the man called. "What's your name?"

Again she opened her mouth, but nothing came out. Where was she, what had happened to her? She closed her eyes, her head drooping.

The man kept talking. "Stay with me," he said, "I'm almost there." Crashes followed his comments as though he was throwing stuff aside. At last he cleared her face and she saw that she was all but entombed in a small airplane. She smelled gasoline and it reminded her of something— something she couldn't name, wasn't sure about.

The man continued clearing the space as she wiped her face, smearing something warm and sticky across her brow. Blood, she discovered, as she looked at her fingers.

He kneeled down to face her. His hair was bright yellow and he needed a shave. Dark gray eyes peered at her from behind black-framed glasses. As he stared at her, his expression went from concern to shock. The next thing she knew, he'd cupped her chin and kissed her, his lips undeniably soft and gentle and yet with a stirring of something else, too. Then he sat back and stroked her cheek, smoothed her hair, kissed her forehead. "Chelsea, good heavens, what are you doing here?"

"I—"

"Oh, my God," he said as though something obvious had just popped into his head. "They must have used you to— did they hurt…? Never mind, we'll talk later. We have to get out of here. Can you move? Is anything broken?"

"I don't know," she said. "I—I don't think so…"

He unbuckled her seat straps as she mumbled. He stood and extended his hands to pull her to her feet. She was able to stand but it put her and her rescuer so close their bodies touched. Super aware of her breasts pressing against his chest, she felt uncomfortable and awkward. He seemed fine with it. "Catch your breath and your balance," he said. "Where's your phone?"

She shook her head.

"May I check your pockets?"

Was he making any sense? She couldn't tell. He frisked her gently and she felt his hand hit against a small hard shape in her jeans pocket. He plucked the phone from her person, wiped it with the hem of his shirt and dropped it to the floor. "Sorry, but this has to stay here."

She nodded but her fuzzy brain immediately went back to the way his lips had felt against hers. Why had he kissed her? Why were his hands on her now?

"You were sitting alone back here, weren't you? Do you have a handbag or luggage?"

A handbag? She looked down at the cluttered floor, fighting a wave of nausea that swam up her throat. She didn't know if she had one or not. Who cared?

He pushed aside a few things and swore. "There's not

enough room in here for me to move if you're standing. Sit back down until I get outside, then walk to the door and I'll help you. Let's do it as quickly as we can, okay?"

She nodded again and sat. He climbed from the plane, reached inside and swept a bunch of crushed red flowers out of the way. "Walk over here to me," he said. "You can do it."

She stood, steadying herself by grabbing the back of the seat in front of her. Her head spun and she felt nauseous, but the sensations passed. She glanced down and to her left and found a blood-covered man belted into the pilot's seat. His sightless eyes looked blank. Her hand flew to her mouth.

"Just come to the door," her rescuer urged.

She did as he told her, mainly because she couldn't think of another plan. Gazing down at him, she paused for a second. His bloody unbuttoned shirt revealed a well-muscled chest, while the strap crossing his body was attached to a rifle held behind his left shoulder. He'd tucked a handgun into his waistband. He looked like someone you saw on a news report, a mercenary or a bandit, a man not to be taken lightly, sexy and scary at the same time.

"Are you okay?" he asked.

She nodded. He clutched her waist and effortlessly lifted her out of the aircraft. She landed right in front of him, once again standing too close.

"Steady now. Dizzy?" he asked.

"I don't think so."

"Can you walk?"

"Yes."

Unable to process the intensity of his expression, she lowered her gaze to the ground, where she found the bruised red flowers. He kneeled in front of her and plucked a small gold foil card from the ribbon that held their stems together and shoved it in his pocket. Taking her hand, he led her a few steps from the crash. She looked back once.

Not a plane, but a helicopter, or what was left of one. The image of the dead pilot's slack, bloodied face filled her head. Had she known him? Was he her boyfriend or husband or something? Then why was she sitting in the back? Why couldn't she think?

And wait, had there been someone in the passenger seat, too? She wasn't sure.

Keep moving, she willed herself as they left the path and took off into the dense forest, ripe with dark mysteries that mirrored those playing out in her brain. The only thing she was sure of was the lifeline of her rescuer's warm fingers.

Chapter Three

Okay, so where were the questions, the accusations? As Adam guided Chelsea onto the cabin's surrounding deck, he steeled himself for a barrage of all of the above, but none came. Once on the deck, he grabbed the binoculars he kept hanging from a nail under the eaves, then used them to scan the horizon and the small road that emptied into the meadow. So far, so good.

The sky had grown dark and the smell of impending rain filled his nostrils. How long did he have before more of Holton's men showed up?

He put back the binoculars and discovered Chelsea had disappeared. He found her sitting on the sofa, blood smeared across her face, hands limp in her lap. He crossed to the bathroom, where he moistened a clean washcloth and grabbed the box of bandages. As always, the glimpse of his own altered appearance in the mirror jarred him. So did the dead man's blood all over his shirt. He grabbed a clean one and changed.

Kneeling in front of her, he gently cleaned and bandaged the laceration. "You must have a million questions," he began.

She sagged against the sofa and closed her eyes. "No," she said.

"Don't you want—?"

"No," she interrupted, rubbing her temples. "All I want is to sit here."

"Does your head hurt?"

"Yes."

He got up to retrieve two aspirin and a glass of water and returned to find her staring around the room. He handed her the tablets and she swallowed them without comment. "I'd like to close my eyes for a moment," she said as she gave him back the water glass.

There wasn't time for her to nap, but how did he thrust her into action after what she'd just endured? "Go ahead. I have a few things to do." *Like pack up and get us out of here.*

He desperately wanted to know how she'd ended up on his doorstep with a hired killer along for the ride. The most likely scenario was that they'd kidnapped her and forced her into taking them to him, but that didn't wash because she hadn't known where he was. No one did. His hands itched with the desire to shake her awake and ask her what was going on, but he couldn't do that. They also itched with the desire to caress her, to tell her he loved her, that he was sorry he'd left, that finding her here was like a gift from heaven. Would she want to hear any of that? Judging from her aloofness, no, she would not. He shoved his hands in his pockets to kill the urge to shake her awake.

The fingers on his right hand brushed a hard ridge of folded stock paper. He pulled the small foil card he'd found with the flowers from his pocket and opened it, immediately recognizing Chelsea's concise handwriting.

"'My beloved Steven,'" he read. *Steven. That's the name he'd chosen when he'd relocated to California. It was the only name he'd ever given Chelsea.* He cleared his throat and continued reading. "'I think I know the location of the cabin you described the night you asked me to marry you. My plan is to drop these roses in the nearby river as a way of letting you go. I don't want to do this but the reality is you're dead. I'll never stop loving you just as I wonder if I'll ever understand what really happened to you or why that man from the government asked me a million questions, but wouldn't answer even one of mine. Sometimes it feels as though I'm grieving a shadow. Goodbye, my love. Rest in peace knowing I will move heaven and earth to make a wonderful life for our baby. Yours forever, Chelsea.'"

"Baby?" he whispered, looking from the note to Chelsea. She was pregnant?

A huge smile came and went in a flash as the enormity of this development hit him in the gut. Had the baby survived the crash? What in the world should he do?

Protect her. Protect them! That's what he should do. And right now that meant getting them out of here.

He threw his meager possessions in a box, then trotted out to the Jeep parked in the tiny shed/garage. The back was already filled with camping gear, a shovel and a chainsaw. To these he added the new box, then he went back inside to take whatever food and drink he could lay his hands on. He wiped things down and carried the perishables out to the Jeep, where he stowed them with everything else before covering the whole thing with a tarp, which he tied in place.

Small rocks separated the cabin from the riverbank. He drove across them and set the parking brake just as rain began to fall. The nonprescription glasses immediately blurred with raindrops and he pocketed them. The abandoned logging road, their only escape route, was a quarter mile downstream. The Jeep had no roof, and its engine was temperamental to say the least. It would be a miracle if it made it to the top of the ridge—if Chelsea hadn't been there, he would have left it in the shed and hiked out just the way he'd hiked in. But she wasn't up to that.

Of course, if an attack came from the air, they'd be sitting ducks, but it seemed more likely to him that ground reinforcements would show up instead. The downed helicopter had looked like someone's paycheck-to-paycheck livelihood and that probably meant there wasn't a handy fleet that Holton could summon from his jail cell at will.

"It's time to go," he said as he gently shook Chelsea's shoulder.

Her eyes blinked open. "Where am I?" she said, and for a moment, he thought the catnap had cleared her head. "Do I know you?"

There went that hope. "Kind of," he said carefully.

"I don't remember you."

"Not at all?"

Her eyes widened. "No. Should I? I mean, yes, of course I should—you called me by a name."

"Chelsea Pierce," he said.

"Then you know me?"

"Yes," he said, confused. He sat back on his heels. "Do you remember how you got in the helicopter, who the passenger was, the gunshot, the pilot? How you got here, what happened…anything?"

She shook her head and winced. "No, none of that. I don't even know who *I* am."

His throat went dry. She was talking about amnesia. He'd known she was confused but he hadn't followed that trail to this conclusion. "We have to leave," he said.

"Now?"

"Yes."

Her brow narrowed. "I don't understand. Where are we going?"

"We're both in danger. We have to get away from here right now."

She sat up slowly and his heart went out to her. He saw no blood on her tan jeans and that probably meant the pregnancy hadn't terminated. "Do you hurt anywhere besides your head?" he asked her.

"My knee hurts a little."

"How about your…tummy or abdomen? You know, where the pressure from the seat belt might have…bruised you?"

"No," she said.

He took her hands and pulled her upright, resisting the urge to hug her reassuringly, sensing it wouldn't have that effect. His gaze dropped to her midsection. She'd lost weight since he'd last seen her, but there was definitely a small swelling that hadn't existed before. He tried to figure out how far along she could be and decided on no more than four months. He handed her the rain gear he'd set aside to shelter her from the weather and helped her put it on. "Hurry," he said with a last look around.

They walked down to the river to the Jeep and he helped her climb aboard. The rain was coming down harder now. Once he'd stowed the rifle and jumped behind the wheel, she looked up at him, her face shaded by the oversized hood, blue eyes questioning. "What should I call you?"

Would the name *Steven* ring any latent bells that might help her place him? Probably not, so he gave her his real name. "Adam." He was done lying to her.

"Nice to meet you," she said with a wan smile.

The Jeep waddled into the river like an old wrestler climbing back into the ring. Thanks to the almost daily treks along this river, he knew to stay close to the western bank, where the water was relatively shallow. When he spied a small grove of red-barked madrones, it would be time to cross the river to the opposite shore, but only until a dead pine tree signaled a pool ahead, at which time he'd cross back to the west. It was slow going, the river gurgling under the vehicle, water washing under the doors and dousing their feet during the cross to the other side. A few times he turned to look behind to see if anyone was there, or to stare up into the sky. It was during one such glance that he remembered he'd left the binoculars hanging under the eaves. Lightning flashed to the south and he counted under his breath. On six, a clap of thunder sounded to the east.

At last he found the place to exit the river to access the logging road and jerked the steering wheel to the left. The Jeep grumbled its way out of the shallow water. The tires spun on the mud before finding purchase on harder ground. He drove forward a hundred feet, then ran back to scatter forest debris to cover their tracks. It wasn't perfect but it would have to do. He ran back to the Jeep and gunned the engine.

The road was eroded and heavily rutted. He dodged the worst of it while steadily climbing. Every now and again, he'd have to stop to use the front mounted winch to pull aside fallen branches, or shift rocks out of the way, then restart their journey. During those short breaks, he listened for the approach of another vehicle or aircraft. All he ever heard was the sound of thunder getting closer.

Chelsea silently allowed him to work. What did she make of this frantic dash in the rain with a man who was a stranger to her? When would she start demanding an explanation?

And what would he tell her?

Anything she wants to know, he told himself.

From the first moment he'd seen her he'd been drawn to her humor and beauty. It was like a man standing in the middle of the desert being hit by a rainsquall. All the loneliness and restlessness that had plagued him for well over a year disappeared with the genuine wattage of her smile. For someone with no past he could ever talk about, suddenly having a future had filled him with renewed energy and that bred hope. Weeks of being with her, loving her, spinning dreams, well, that had been heaven on earth, until he had to leave without telling her, knowing he'd never see her again and that she would never know he'd faked his own death.

Just as he'd faked almost everything she thought she knew about him.

If she ever got her memory back, she'd hate his guts and he wouldn't blame her.

And now, wonder of wonders, here she was, carrying his baby and not knowing who either one of them were.

"Why are you staring at me?" she asked.

"You're very pretty," he responded.

"I feel like a drowned rat and I'm the one with the rain parka. Thank you for that."

"You're welcome. How's your head feeling?"

"Probably a lot like the tires on this Jeep."

"Hopefully we can stop pretty soon and you can stretch out."

"Hmm…" she said. Her face grew serious. "Back at the cabin you asked if I remembered a gunshot. What did you mean?"

"Your pilot had a fresh gunshot wound in his arm," he said.

"Is that what caused the crash?"

"I don't know. I doubt it. I was hoping you could tell me."

"And who exactly are you?" she asked, her brow narrowing.

He felt a vibration in his pocket and took out the monitor. Back at the cabin, a vehicle had triggered the road sensor. It would take about ten minutes to get to the cabin, another five or so to tear the place apart. Maybe they'd take a look at the downed chopper. For that matter, maybe the sensor had detected a police car or emergency vehicles sent to investigate the crash site. There was no way of knowing for sure who was on their way up the road. With any luck he might be able to see when the Jeep reached the top of this blasted mountain and he could chance a scan below.

"What's that?" she asked as she stared at the little electronic device in his hand.

"Insurance."

She shook her head, then closed her eyes. "Why are we running away?"

"Someone is after me. Or us, I guess. I promise I'll tell you more but not now."

Speculation settled on her face as she peered at him. Of all her expressions he'd witnessed over the months, this one of wariness was new. He yearned for her to look at him the way she had before. Fat chance of that right now.

"Okay," she said at last. "I'll wait."

Thirty minutes later the Jeep, as victorious as a wheezing climber, crested the hill. "I'll be right back," he told Chelsea, stopping under the trees where there was still some cover from the rain.

She wrapped her arms around herself and nodded.

He fetched a smaller, less powerful set of binoculars out of the glove box and walked into the clearing. It took him a few seconds to locate the cabin. Adjusting the focus, he finally spied a dark van parked close to the cabin's deck. A man with white-blond hair stood near it, an automatic rifle in his hands. No uniform. No bells or whistles on the car. Within a few moments, two more armed men came out of the house and joined him. They moved under the protection of the eaves, apparently unaware he and Chelsea had escaped via the river. The blond guy took out his phone and made a call while the others watched.

An instant after lightning pierced the dusky skies, an explosion rent the air. Adam jerked his binoculars toward the forest on the other side of the meadow. Flames climbed the trees where the helicopter had gone down. The lightning must have made a direct hit. One man immediately jumped off the deck and took off across the meadow, while the other two held their ground. And then one of them began a slow turn toward the ridge on which he stood. It appeared he'd found Adam's good binoculars and now he held them to his eyes. Adam immediately lowered the set he held, but not before he saw the man's lips move and his arm shoot out toward the crest, seemingly right at Adam.

Adam stood without breathing, without moving, until the need to know what was happening outweighed the risk of looking. He all but oozed backward into the shadows before raising the binoculars again.

More lightning flashed, followed by thunder still startlingly close by. In that moment, Adam witnessed the man previously seen hurrying toward the explosion now running to the cabin, presumably called back by the other two. They all hopped into the van and tore off down the road.

Adam had seen enough. They might know he was up here but he knew the low clearance of their vehicle wouldn't handle eroded roads and trails. That meant they would locate the main highway and watch for him, or at least that's what he would do in their place. So, instead of finding a nice paved highway and leaving the forest, he'd stay on logging roads until he found a suitable place for them to spend the night. His first priority was to get Chelsea to a doctor and then he needed to study a map. There were decisions to be made and in her current condition, those decisions would have to come from him.

He'd envisioned his final escape many times over the past few weeks, but he'd never imagined he'd have to drag another person along with him. A month ago, when he'd asked Chelsea to be his wife, he'd thought he was safe and in the clear, never dreaming she would wind up in danger because of him. None of that mattered now because the only reality existed in this moment—not yesterday and certainly not tomorrow.

And now it wasn't just her—it was their baby, too.

Once more he got back in the Jeep.

"What did you see down there?" Chelsea asked.

"Three armed men. I think they'll try to cut us off."

Her gaze darted around the landscape. "What do we do?"

"Stay in the forest," he told her.

She nodded, but she had to be thinking the same thing he was: sooner or later they would have to leave the shelter of the trees. Then what?

Chapter Four

Determined not to pepper Adam with questions, Chelsea channeled her energy into gripping the Jeep's rusty frame with both hands. Instead of questioning her own origins and identity, she concentrated on the few facts she knew. One, she was the sole survivor of a crash and a man she knew had found her. Two, someone had shot the pilot. And three, someone was now chasing after them, causing great fear in her heart, something she mirrored in Adam's eyes. Except on him, the fear came across more as anger.

She snuck a look at him, struck by his strong profile and the aura of concentration his body language communicated. Rain had flattened his bleached blond hair close to his head while drops glistened in the short beard that darkened his jaw. His gray eyes peered into the ever-increasing twilight, apparently discerning signs of trails she could barely see. But, of course, she wasn't trying very hard to see anything. For now it was enough to trust that this man who seemed capable of anything would get them through the night in one piece. She had to face the fact that her brain wasn't up to much work right now. All she wanted was to lay her head down and sleep for a week.

It appeared they were traveling deeper and deeper into the forest. Every once in a while, Adam would slow down and check a compass, but as it got darker, even that ceased. At least the rain had quit; heavy, humid air filled her lungs.

As darkness claimed the underbelly of the woods, Adam switched on headlamps but then immediately turned them off.

"What's wrong?" she asked.

He laughed softly. "What's not wrong?"

"Why did you turn off the lights?"

"They're too bright. I'm not positive how close we are to the highway. No need to advertise our location."

"Then you think those men are still out there?" she said with a quivering voice and a strong reprimand to pull herself together.

"Yes, I do," he said. He veered off the semi-road they'd been traveling and followed a gully of relatively clear land back behind a grove of small trees. When he finally applied the brakes and turned off the key, the quiet and stillness tucked itself around them like a heavy blanket. For a few seconds, they sat very still, as though waiting.

Waiting for what, she wondered. *Waiting for whom?*

"Do you see any lights anywhere?" he asked her at last, his voice little more than a whisper.

"No. I guess we aren't that close to a highway after all."

"I guess not. Let's make camp."

Camp meant lying down and, truthfully, that's the only thing in the world she desired. Her body protested as she unwound herself from the front seat, aches and pains radiating to and fro, maybe the result of the crash she'd survived, maybe caused by the constant adjusting to the motion of the Jeep navigating roads that had seen much better days. Her left knee throbbed and she limped between the dark shadow of the Jeep and the darker shadow of a small tent. Adam had erected it with an apparent wave of his hand, and was now carrying rolled damp bedding, which he dumped inside. He soon handed her a flashlight and took one for himself but it was a few seconds before either one of them turned them on.

"It's so bright," she mumbled.

He turned his off.

"Do you have any tissues anywhere? I need to find a bush."

He snatched a small tissue package from the pocket in the Jeep door and handed it to her. "Don't go too far," he cautioned, and stared down at her with a worried expression.

"I won't."

"Are you hungry?"

"No, just tired," she replied.

"Other than that, do you feel okay?"

"Kind of."

"Where else do you hurt?"

"My knee."

"No pain, you know, like inside, like internal bleeding or a ruptured something-or-other?"

She cocked her head. "No. What exactly are you asking?"

"You were in a terrible crash," he said, studying her face. Then he shrugged as though dismissing his earlier concern. He switched his light back on as he retrieved an ice chest. "I'm just trying to make sure you're not seriously hurt," he added over his shoulder. "You'll tell me if any new pain develops or bleeding or…anything?"

"Who else am I going to tell?"

"I mean it," he said. "Tomorrow we'll find you a doctor—"

"Let's take it one day at a time," she said. With that, she walked away from him, using the flashlight in spurts to make her way until she found a big downed tree and climbed over it to the far side for privacy.

Who exactly was Adam in relation to her? How did they know one another?

Or did they? What proof did she have that they knew each other, that her name was Chelsea Pierce, that one word he told her was true?

The answer was so obvious it was like a shout in a quiet room. None. No proof at all. Zero.

Her head began throbbing anew as she tried to recall every gesture, every nuance, every word that he'd said since the moment she opened her eyes after the crash. Nothing jumped out except the kiss. That had seemed spontaneous and real, but right that moment she was no judge of character, let alone motives.

But wait, how many times had he asked her how she felt, if she was bleeding, if she was in pain. Surely that meant concern on his part.

But why?

Was she being paranoid or prudent?

Either way, she vowed to also be cautious.

THOUGH THERE WAS a definite chill in the air, Adam decided against building a fire. He retied the tarp over the back of the Jeep to guard against curious night critters and early morning dew, stowed the ice chest inside the tent and shouldered the rifle. As he stood in the dark waiting for Chelsea, he grew increasingly concerned. Had she gotten lost or fainted, or was it something even worse? Had she discovered blood, was she losing their baby?

Or had someone found her, taken her, planning to use her to get to him once again…?

"Chelsea?" he called in a soft voice that he hoped would carry.

A light momentarily blinded him and he raised the rifle.

"It's just me," Chelsea said.

He lowered the firearm immediately. "Sorry. Everything okay?"

"Fine." Her voice sounded terse and tense. Well, whose wouldn't?

Once his vision returned, he crossed the distance between them and put an arm around her shoulder. "You're trembling," he said. "Why don't you crawl into the tent and get warm." He handed her a small electric freestanding lantern, hoping that as well as a little reassuring light, it would also emit a tiny bit of heat to ward off the chill.

"Sure you aren't hungry?" he asked as he followed her inside and opened the ice chest.

"Positive."

He downed a bottle of water and a handful of nuts, then opened the flap. Picking up the revolver he'd rested beside the ice chest, he handed it to her. "Do you remember how to use this?"

"Yes," she said, "although I have no idea why."

"I taught you," he told her.

"So we know each other," she said. "Explain that to me. Tell me who I am and who you are to me."

"I will, I promise, as soon as I get back from answering nature's call. Meanwhile, keep the gun with you. When you hear someone coming, I'd appreciate you checking first to make sure who it is. If it isn't me, go ahead and shoot."

"I will," she said, her voice shaky.

Using his flashlight until he saw the trail he wanted, he moved off into the dark carrying the rifle. The forest was still and quiet and, to his relief, the dim light from inside the tent seemed to disappear behind the dense undergrowth at a surprisingly short distance. He couldn't stay up guarding the site all night—his eyes already felt grainy and fatigue had started to gnaw on the fragile edge of usefulness. At some point he was going to have to sleep.

The overriding question on his mind now was how much to tell Chelsea. How much could she bear to know, and when did the out-and-out truth of what they'd meant to each other become a burden she would have to shoulder alone once they separated? Every word of the current truth had marinated in a hot tub of lies—he wasn't even sure where to begin.

Plus, how would she handle the fact she was pregnant while running for her life? Wouldn't the best thing to do be to find her a safe spot where she could heal and he could go on alone?

He thought back to that moment on the ridge—he was positive the men at the cabin had caught a glimpse of him, but there was no way they could know Chelsea had escaped the helicopter before it blew. For that matter, there had been no sign of emergency or rescue response. That meadow was the closest staging area—if someone had arrived to search for the helicopter, there would have been visible evidence of it. That meant as far as everyone currently knew, Chelsea had disappeared or died in the chopper.

He had to make that work for her and yet in his gut, he knew she was safest if she was with him.

Oh, really, his subconscious said in a snarky voice. *Is it safer for her to be with you, a hunted man, or is it just possible you can't bear the thought of losing her again now that you've found her? Maybe the idea she'll regain memories that include the fact you allowed her to grieve for you, that you left her to fend alone, maybe that's what's really bothering you.*

But his next thoughts spoke just as clearly. *You left her once and they used her. They could easily have killed her. She's damned with or without you.*

He called out as he approached the camp to announce himself before veering to dig maps out of the Jeep's glove box. His first priority had to be to get them out of this forest and somewhere reasonably safe. Chelsea moved aside as he crawled into the tent. He set the rifle in front of the flap and turned in the tight space to sit down. She'd unrolled a couple of sleeping bags and had wrapped one around herself.

"Okay," she said. "For starters— "

"Just a second," he said as he grabbed the wilderness map. "Let me check something out." He unfolded the map and did his best to locate their position. It appeared to him that the road they'd been on had emptied into the town of Black Boulder several miles before. What if they doubled back? If he were Holton's men, he would have staked out that town yesterday afternoon and perhaps moved on to others down the line by now. Scanning the map more closely, he decided that would be their best bet. The added bonus was the place appeared big enough to support a few amenities and services. It had begun to prey on his mind that he'd lost phone connection with Whip. The old guy might have been an Arizona cop for years but he was also a consummate worrier.

Adam looked over more of the map, half plotting a route east, when he recognized the town of Spur located less than twenty miles from Black Boulder right over the state line in Nevada. With a twinge of hope, he wondered if another of his dad's longtime friends still lived there. Doc Fisher could be a lot of help if he'd maintained his Nevada address.

"Are you stalling?" Chelsea asked.

He looked up from the map to find her knees bent, arms wrapped around her legs, eyes piercing. In a few weeks, a pregnant belly would prevent that position.

"A little bit."

"Start by telling me who I am."

He folded the map and set it aside. Her dark hair glimmered in the dim light as she peered at him. Who was she? The love of his life; the mother of his baby; the woman he would take a bullet for. That's who she was, at least to him.

He started with the basics. "Your name is Chelsea Ann Pierce and you're twenty-six years old. You live in San Francisco, where you run a food truck that mostly caters to business clients. You're a fantastic chef, which makes sense since you graduated from culinary school just a couple of years ago. Your parents' names are Troy and Helen. They live north of the city in a tiny coastal town called Bodega Bay, where they run a seaside tavern. You have three sisters and two brothers. Everyone lives in Northern California except your oldest sibling, Bill, and he lives in Nevada on a few dozen acres of sand with his wife, Jan, and enough guns to overtake a third-world nation."

"Who are you and how did we meet?"

"My name is Adam Parish. I work construction." That had been true when he met her and since he was still on the fence about how much to share, he left it at that. "One day, you and your truck rolled up to the building site I was working on. You made me the best pastrami sandwich this side of New York. As you were leaving, your truck rolled over a few nails. I changed the resulting flat and our friendship was born."

"Based on deli meat and tires?" she asked.

"And pickles. We both love dill pickles."

His joke didn't even elicit a smile. Come to think of it, she'd been a little standoffish since she'd returned from the woods.

"Have you always worked construction?" she asked.

"Not always."

"What else did you do?"

"I was a cop for a while," he told her truthfully. "When that fell apart, I became a bodyguard."

"And then you decided to build things."

"Yes."

"Hmm, so to be clear—there's nothing between us except friendship?" she said.

"Well—"

"That's a pregnant 'well,'" she interrupted. "We were more?"

"In ways," he said, unwilling to trot out their romance and getting wound up in details that would no doubt make her furious.

"Then why was I flying in a helicopter to see you? I take it you were expecting me?"

"No, as a matter of fact, I wasn't, especially in that company."

"You mean with someone who wanted to hurt you."

"That's what I mean."

"Why did he want to hurt you?"

This was the tricky part. *Stick to the truth*, he admonished himself. "I testified against a guy who hurt a lot of innocent people. He's in jail but he swore revenge. Thanks to the witness protection program, I've been hiding out. Now it appears he hired the bad guys to catch up with me."

"I know about that program," she said. "How could anyone have found you?"

"Someone must have ratted me out," Adam said. Someone like Ron Ballard, his supposed liaison in the program.

"So that's why you bleached your hair?"

"How did you know—?"

"It's pretty obvious, Adam. Is that why you also keep a week-old beard on your face?"

He nodded.

"And the glasses you sometimes wear?"

"Yes."

"Hmm—" She studied him for a second, then added, "Okay, so cutting to the chase, what do I have to do with all this?"

"Well, like you said, you were traveling to the cabin to visit me. By then I'd left the Bay area. They must have gotten wind you were coming, which meant you knew where I was, and they tricked or forced you into taking them along."

"That kind of makes me an idiot, doesn't it?" she asked.

He was just about at the point of throwing his arms around her and kissing her into silence, and would have done so willingly if there was a chance in hell she'd let him. He even had a picture in his wallet, so close it burned his backside, but he couldn't show it to her—he'd ruined being able to do that the moment he told her he was Adam and not Steven.

"No, it makes you a victim of this creep and I'm really sorry about that," he said. "You didn't know about this guy because I never told you. I never warned you. I wish I had. I just thought you were safer not knowing any of the…details."

"You and I weren't really close friends, then?"

"It's kind of more complicated than that," he said.

She sighed. "Really?"

"Isn't it always?"

"I don't know, I don't remember," she said, sighing. "All this aside, it sounds as though this isn't my fight."

"You're just caught in the middle of it."

She stared at him a moment and bit her bottom lip. "Are my parents the kind of people who would take care of me while I got my memory back?"

"If they were here, sure."

"I think I should go home."

"How?"

"I'll take a bus."

"Not without first seeing a doctor," he said firmly and knew the second the words left his mouth it had been the wrong thing to say.

"Tell me you are not issuing ultimatums," she said.

"I—"

"Because that is totally unacceptable. I'm a grown woman."

"I know," he said, "but it's not that simple."

"Is everything complicated to you?"

"Living is complicated, Chelsea." He didn't want to terrify her but the thought of sending her off on a bus made his blood run cold. "Without me to protect you—"

"I'll be fine," she said.

"Someone could come after you again. They'd figure you know where I was going next."

"But I won't know."

"I don't think your word will carry a lot of weight."

"Maybe not, but that's my decision."

"That's ridiculous," he said, irritated now. "How are you and your peace-loving parents going to fight off killers like Devin Holton's merry band of misfits and thugs?"

"Who's Devin Holton?"

He clamped his mouth shut. He hadn't intended on giving her a name she could repeat at a time when it could cost her dearly. "You've been acting kind of strange since we made camp," he said gently. "What happened?"

"What do you mean 'what happened'?"

"You left here a while ago and came back minutes later kind of… I don't know, touchy."

"Touchy? Okay, maybe I am. Maybe it's because your story doesn't hold water. Maybe it's because I'm afraid.

Maybe it's because I survived a crash that killed two other people and I don't know who you are and I don't even know who I am."

"I told you who you are and who I am," he said.

"How do I know you aren't making it up? What proof do you have that I even know you, that my name is Chelsea and my parents are Troy and Susan?"

"Troy and Helen."

"Whatever."

"Why in the world would I lie about that?"

"Because," she said. "Because nothing makes sense. We're only kind of friends and yet I'm flying to see you? Why would I do that?"

"They forced you."

"Then why shoot the pilot and not me?"

"I don't know."

She shook her head and winced. "Adam, or whoever you are, all I do know is I'm confused and very tired and I wish you would go sleep outside."

"That's not going to happen," he said.

"Why?"

"Because I need to be in here with you."

"And I need you to be somewhere else."

She might not recognize that tone of voice, but he did—he'd heard it a couple of times before, never directed at him, but once with a thieving employee and again with a pushy salesman. She had drawn a line in the sand and it would take a fool to cross over it. She needed space.

"Fine," he said, getting to his knees and bunching his sleeping bag in his arms. "Have a great night."

"Leave the revolver," she said.

"Why?"

"In case the bad guys find us."

"I'll be right outside."

"Just leave the gun."

"Whatever you want," he said, sorry about the sarcasm dripping in his voice but unable to curb it. He zipped open the flap, scooted outside and pulled a sleeping bag and the rifle out with him.

"Adam," she said, and he met her gaze. Her heavily shadowed eyes and fatigue sunken cheeks touched his heart. "I'm sorry. It's not fair that I keep the tent. I'll sleep outside—"

"Not on your life," he said. "And I'm the one who's sorry. This whole thing is my fault. I'd give anything if it meant you weren't in danger."

"You've been nothing but kind to me," she said, her eyes now growing bright with tears. "You saved my life."

He reached inside and touched her face. To his relief, she didn't sweep away his hand and instead covered his fingers with hers. "Don't cry," he said softly. "It's going to be okay. I promise I won't let anything happen to you. Now get some sleep, okay?"

"Maybe tomorrow I'll wake up with all my memories intact," she whispered.

"I hope so," he said, and once again fought the urge to kiss her. As he zipped the flap closed again, the lantern light inside the tent went out.

He used the flashlight to make a bed on the ground, curled into the sleeping bag and closed his eyes. If she was determined to leave him, he'd have to let her go, but somehow he'd have to come up with a way to prepare her for the return of her memories. How would she handle the moment when she realized he was her beloved Steven, and that instead of dead and gone, he was very much alive and on the run?

And maybe not so beloved anymore...

He thought of the picture he carried. Taken in front

of the Golden Gate Bridge, where they'd gone to picnic, they'd stood arm in arm while Chelsea trusted a stranger with her phone to take their photo. She had printed it out, written their names at the bottom, drawn in a small red heart and given him a copy.

Every photo on his phone had been destroyed when his plane hit that lake. This picture was the one memory he allowed himself of the woman who had stolen his heart and now he'd gutted his opportunity to use it to reassure her by giving her his given name of Adam. Could he explain it away? Should he show her the note she'd written with the roses? Would it make things better or worse?

Maybe it would shock her memory into hyperdrive. Or maybe it would force it further underground.

I'll sleep on it, he decided. But an hour later, he was still staring into the dark.

Chapter Five

They broke camp as soon as there was enough light to travel back through the underbrush to the old road. Neither of them said much. Poor sleep, stiff joints and worrisome thoughts didn't make for sparkling conversational gambits and Chelsea was just glad to be on the move again.

"Is it my imagination or are we going back the way we came?" she asked.

"You've always had a great sense of direction," he said. "We're looping back to an outlet from this forest that we bypassed yesterday, headed to a small town called Black Boulder. My hope is that the bad guys decided we went on ahead and are miles away when we surface."

"That sounds kind of chancy."

"Chance is all we really have," he said. "We'll temper it with caution. After Black Boulder we're aiming for a town called Spur. I know a guy there. Well, I think he's still there. He's a retired doctor. He can check you out."

"Not again with the doctor thing," she said impatiently. "You're like a broken record. Anyway, don't you remember what I told you last night? I'm going home. If there's a bus station in Black Boulder, I'm getting out of here. We've been over this."

He glanced at her before looking once again at the road. "What if I take you to a bus as soon as a doctor—?"

"Stop it already," she demanded.

"Chelsea—"

"No more arguing. It's not just my doubts about our… relationship. The fact is you'll be better off without me to worry about."

"I like worrying about you," he said with another glance.

"Please," she said. "My mind, or what there is left of it, is made up. Let's just see if we can find a bus station."

Within an hour they'd turned west, and within minutes of that, the ruts and weeds in the road started to disappear. Eventually, road signs announcing a wilderness area ahead appeared. Gradually, the road became graded and the ride smoothed out. The engine had a new knocking noise, but it kind of blended in with all the others, sort of like a calypso band. Things were looking up until Adam mentioned their diminishing fuel supply and expressed hope that Black Boulder wasn't too far away.

They eventually found a bare-bones gas station, and as Chelsea warily eyed the empty road in front of it, Adam filled the tank and paid in the office. Within a few miles, a sign announced Black Boulder ahead and at this point, Adam left the main road and started traveling small arteries, always headed in the right direction. They stopped when they found a larger gas station and parked off to the side. He turned back to face her after climbing out of the Jeep. "Put the rain gear on, okay?"

"Why? It's dry and warm—"

"So no one sees your face," he said softly. "I'm going to go buy some phone minutes so we can prepare your parents for your arrival."

"Prepare them?"

"By now they either think you're missing or dead," he said gently. "It's risky to alert them of your safety—I mean, they're bound to react and if anyone is keeping an eye on them. Well, on the other hand, they'll need to meet your bus if there's one available in this little town. I'll ask at the station. Stay low, okay?"

She nodded and put on the dreaded rain gear that was still damp from the day before. He was back within a few minutes. "The bus station is down the street a few blocks," he told her as he started the engine. "I'll park in the alley on the off chance they know about the Jeep and go inside to get a schedule. If there are any buses leaving this morning, I'll buy you a ticket—"

"I can buy my own."

"With what?"

"Good point. I'll pay you back—"

"Let's worry about that later," he interrupted. "If there is a bus, we need to talk a little more before you leave. There are things you need to…well, be prepared for and maybe you'd like some breakfast to hold you, or coffee or something."

"I'm starving," she said.

"Me, too. First things first—let's see if there's a west-bound bus today."

There was the slight feeling of anonymous safety sitting in a hooded coat inside a car even if it didn't have a roof. Adam eventually pulled into an alley and parked. She could see the closed back door of the bus station across the way.

"I'll be right back," he said.

She caught his hand. "Be careful, Adam. You're the one they're after, you know."

He pulled out the eyeglasses and settled them on his nose. Reaching into the back, he produced a baseball cap and shrugged that on over his bright blond hair. With his beard growth, he looked like a lot of the guys they'd passed while driving along the streets of this tiny mountain town.

"The keys are in the ignition," he said, his voice intense. "At the first sign of trouble, get out of here. The guy at the gas station said the sheriff's office is four blocks farther down—turn left, go about a half a mile. Tell them whatever you want, just stay safe."

"Adam. Don't you want to take a gun or…?"

"Not into a bus station, no. Bad idea. You keep it, I'll be right back," he repeated and walked off as though he didn't have a care in the world.

She moved over the gearshift and sat behind the wheel, eyeing the ignition key and the empty alley in turn.

BACK IN ARIZONA, before his mother was murdered, Adam often rode out into the desert alone, but he always carried a rifle. Because his father was a cop, he was familiar with firearms. They'd seemed a part of his equipment: a saddle for the horse, a sleeping bag to protect against cold nights under the stars and a rifle in case he crossed paths with a coyote or a rattlesnake and he couldn't avoid confrontation.

So here he was in another kind of wilderness, a civilized grouping of people and buildings, knowing there was a fifty-fifty chance a killer could be lying in wait. Really, he'd rather take his chances with the coyote.

He let go of that thought and concentrated on doing what Chelsea wanted no matter how ill-advised it seemed to him. Maybe there wouldn't be a bus headed west for hours. Maybe he could get Chelsea to change her mind if she had to sit around all day or, at the very least, he'd have time to explain what he could.

No need to call her parents until they had more of a plan. That call was dangerous, he knew that, because of a wild card named Lindy, Chelsea's chatty younger sister, whose idea of a secret was something you kept to yourself until the first opportunity came to share it. He'd have to make sure Chelsea understood she had to keep his name out of it.

Running had seemed like a good idea after he'd been the star witness during Holton's trial. And running with the help of the government had been interesting as well as annoying. Getting a new identity, starting over, leaving people and places behind—it really hadn't seemed like that big a deal at first.

Eventually, however, the novelty had worn thin and he'd begun to feel like a caged bird. Ballard had been his direct link and the guy was a jerk, and that didn't help. During that time, Adam had started making plans for the day he'd either had enough or someone came after him. That's the plan he'd set in motion when he got home that night and found a gunman waiting for him.

And then he'd met Chelsea and the bars on the cage had just melted away and for a little while there, he'd been more content than he had been in years.

Having Holton's man show up at his house and having to kill him to stay alive, well, that had taken massive amounts of adrenaline and focus. Escaping without Holton's paid assassins or the government knowing where he went was something of a feat of derring-do. Leaving Chelsea without a word of goodbye or explanation had taken more guts than anything he'd ever done until now. In less than twenty-four hours and with no sense of self or a single memory of him, she'd nonetheless reawakened every powerful emotion she'd originally engendered, rebuilt the home she'd established in his heart and hand-delivered a reason to figure out how to get his life back. Thoughts of watching a bus take her off to San Francisco and away from him for the foreseeable future were depressing.

Maybe he should drive her back there himself, take what

time he could with her, take his chances that Holton's men wouldn't figure he'd return...

And keep her in the path of mortal danger? Risk his unborn baby? *Don't be such a selfish jerk*, he scolded himself.

He rounded the corner before making a U-turn to walk back up the block. The bus station turned out to be a narrow building filled with chairs and little else, including people. Obviously there weren't any imminent arrivals or departures planned. He walked to the window at the back, where a middle-aged woman with salt-and-pepper hair sat behind the glass, filing her fingernails. "I need a schedule for California routes," he said.

She tapped on her side of the glass with the file, directing his attention to a rack of brochures and he chose the right one. A bus left for San Francisco in two short hours. Fate was against him or for him—depended on your point of view.

He opened his wallet and bought a ticket, explaining it was for his sister. The woman seemed totally disinterested in his small talk so he shut up.

He left the building and started back the way he'd come, rehearsing what he was going to say to Chelsea. He'd find them some fast-food place where they could get coffee and something to eat and claim a booth at the back. He'd have to come clean, he'd have to man up and shoulder her anger and answer her questions and prepare her for the realization she was pregnant and alone. He absolutely dreaded it and for a second toyed around with tearing up the ticket and lying to her.

No more lies.

He was so caught up in thought that his usual sensors didn't warn him until two men grabbed him from either side, looping their arms through his and almost lifting him from the ground. Linked together, the three of them rounded the corner into the alley, Adam struggling to free himself while the men clamped his arms like vise grips. He tried kicking and yelling, but a punch in his gut took the wind out of his lungs.

"Thought you could ditch us, didn't you?" one of the men said and proceeded to jab a knife into his ribs. Adam sagged.

"Put that thing away before someone sees it," the other said, both men now all but supporting his weight. "You can do what you want as soon as we get him inside the van."

He had to rally. Once inside that van, he was as good as dead. And maybe then one of them would figure out he must have parked a car somewhere and maybe they'd figure out it was actually in the same alley as their van and then they'd find Chelsea—he couldn't let that happen.

The thought streaked through his mind as fast as a comet—she was right, she didn't belong in the middle of this. He couldn't protect her 24/7.

What would happen to her now? Even if these guys didn't recognize the Jeep and left her out of this, what would she do? Go to the police. What if she mentioned the witness protection program? What if the one who sold him out was on that team? Would they come after her?

He looked down the alley and saw the Jeep. Before he could see if Chelsea was still in it, he felt one of the men's grip lessen. Adam tore an arm free. The motion sent searing pain tearing through the knife wound. Using momentum, he swung the weight of his body around to ram into the other guy. That had as much effect as shaking a finger at a charging bull.

The next thing he knew, he'd been slammed against a boarded-up building. His drugstore glasses and favorite cap went flying. The man who had been pushed away came back with the knife held low and pointed up, positioned to gut him. Adam kicked the knife out of his hands. The guy switched to his fists, throwing one punch after another as Adam attempted to fend off the blows until a particularly sharp fist near his puncture site doubled him over and he fell onto his knees. The two reached down to grab Adam's arms and haul him back to his feet. Ready to use the leverage of his body to topple them over, Adam wasn't prepared for the sound of a gunned engine. A black blur brushed by the gun wielder, clipped him on the side and sent him sprawling. Gunfire thundered. The other man clutched his arm and retreated down the alley. The vehicle braked to a stop and Adam looked up to find Chelsea, all but invisible inside the oversized rain gear. "Get in—hurry," she said.

Blood seeped through his fingers as he held his hand against his bloody ribs. The man who'd been clipped struggled to his feet. Adam climbed into the passenger seat and Chelsea made a U-turn. She stepped on the gas. Adam spotted the thug who had gotten away—he was throwing open the back of a dark van last seen in front of his cabin. Exhaust from the tailpipe signaled the engine was already running. That meant there were three of them. The door slammed behind the thug just as Chelsea, one hand on the wheel, shot out a rear tire and kept driving.

Adam's jaw dropped open as he stared at her profile. "Where did you learn to shoot like that?" he croaked.

"I thought you taught me," she said. "What direction do I drive?"

"Just keep going southeast. Not that I'm complaining, but those gunshots must have drawn attention."

She handed him the gun and almost dumped him out of the Jeep as she made a tight right turn and sped up.

Chapter Six

"Now who needs a doctor?" she asked.

He groaned.

With one hand she groped around in the back until she found a pillow and handed it to him. "Hold it over that wound, keep applying pressure."

"We need to get you back to Black Boulder."

"Are you kidding?"

"Your bus leaves in a little over an hour. No one saw your face. We'll stop at the edge of town, put you in a cab to the bus station and you can get out of this mess."

"Adam—"

"I mean it." He struggled for a few moments to get his wallet out of his pocket and opened it with one hand. "Take your ticket and this cash—"

"Put that away," she said, not looking at him.

"You were right, Chelsea, I was wrong. This isn't your battle. If those two had known who you were or what we were driving, they would have snatched you to get to me. Now they know about the Jeep. I can't put you in danger like this. I've been selfish, just so blasted glad to have you back—"

"Have me back?"

"Being on the run gets…lonesome," he said quickly. "Everybody needs a friendly face."

Her gaze flicked to him, then back to the road. They drove in silence for several miles, seemingly at a stand-off that she finally broke with a protracted sigh. "See, the thing is, I've changed my mind about leaving. It's a woman's prerogative, you know. Now, where exactly is this friend you mentioned? In Spur, right? And he's a doctor? How fortuitous is that?"

"I'm not sure Doc Fisher is even in Spur anymore. I haven't communicated with him in well over a year."

"Listen to me," she said in her take-command voice. "We're getting close to Spur. Get on that phone and find out if your friend is still here. We need to ditch the Jeep. Call him—"

"Not until you're safe."

She suppressed a sigh when she saw the blood staining the pillow he gripped tightly to his side. "Any minute now a very angry man driving a van or a car full of deputies who don't appreciate wild west tactics in their town are going to roar up our tailpipe. If your goal is to keep me out of jail and the bad guys from killing us, at least find out if your friend is in town. Now."

He put away the wallet and took out a phone. As he called Information, she looked around for a side road they could use to get off the main highway. When she found one, she took it and parked behind a boarded-up building that, according to a bleached-out sign, had once been Teddy's Tavern.

"Please, connect me," Adam said into the phone. His end of the ensuing conversation was terse and short.

"We caught a break," he told her as he clicked off the call. "When I told Doc we were lurking behind this old tavern, he said we're pretty close by. He's coming here to pick us up."

"What about the police?"

"They're the least of our problems," Adam said between shallow breaths. "Holton's men won't file any complaints. By the time the cops arrive on scene those guys will be long gone. Deputies won't find anything, not even a blood splatter. But this Jeep is too noticeable. Doc is driving out here to take us back to his place. He'll get the Jeep at a later date unless someone steals it in the meantime." He paused a second. "I really wish we hadn't gone back to Black Boulder," he said as he slumped.

She smoothed his sweaty forehead. "You did what seemed right. What did you tell your friend about—" she paused to gesture at their vehicle, their wounds, their predicament "—all this?"

"I just told him we'd fired shots and I'd been knifed. Doc will be here soon. Chelsea, do you want to call your parents? Your whole family must be grief-stricken. It'll take days or even weeks for Forensics to discover your DNA isn't in the chopper."

She shook her head. She'd been thinking about what he said earlier. "After what happened in the alley…well, now I can see the scope of what you've been talking about. My parents will be safer if I don't tell them. It feels wrong, but if someone is watching them…"

"I agree," he said.

"I'll make it up to them later when I can actually recognize them."

"Your memory will come back," he said.

At that moment they heard an engine. Chelsea grabbed the gun from where Adam had stashed it under the seat and tensed herself for action. Instead of the dreaded dark van, a bright and shiny red SUV rolled around the building and came to a stop. She put the gun down and stepped out of the Jeep as a man in his seventies with a white walrus mustache got out of the SUV.

"Morning," he said, all but tipping a nonexistent hat to Chelsea. "Doc Fisher at your service." Santa Claus-blue eyes twinkled as he addressed her.

"Good morning," she said.

He looked past her, zeroing in on Adam's battered face and then his bloody shirt. "Adam, good Lord, boy, look at you!" He reached inside his vehicle, snagged a black doctor's bag and trotted around to Adam's side of the Jeep. "Looks like you've still got a talent for charming the hooligans of the world. Just like your dad, huh, boy?"

"Uncomfortably like him," Adam said through clenched teeth.

The doctor looked up from Adam's wound and met Chelsea's gaze. "Why don't you get a head start moving the stuff in the Jeep into the back of my car? We don't want to stick around here any longer than we have to."

"Not the heavy things," Adam said.

Chelsea cast Adam an exacerbated look. "Good grief," she muttered.

The doctor's mustache twitched as he smiled, but his expression changed when he stripped off Adam's shirt and examined his torso. After a few seconds of closer inspection, he seemed to relax. "You say this is a knife wound?"

"Yes."

"Well, you're lucky. It's not as deep as I feared and it's relatively clean. I'll stitch it up back at the house."

As he applied a temporary bandage, Chelsea moved the Jeep's cargo. Once in a while she caught sight of the shirtless Adam and had to force herself to look away. She recalled the strength of his powerful arms when he'd lifted her down from the chopper and the way he'd stood as close as a…as a lover.

Why was it so easy for her to imagine him holding

her against his bare chest, owning her with his kisses, his hands…

"Need some help?" Doc said.

She tore her mind away from fantasy and shook her head.

"I'll get the chainsaw and the tools," he insisted. "You help the boy into the car, get him lying down in the back. How about you? Are you hurt, too?"

"No," she said.

"Don't forget about your head and possible other injuries," Adam said.

"How can I?" she asked as she approached him. "You always seem to remind me."

DOC FISHER CLEARED off the desk in his office then helped Adam perch on top of it. "There are clean towels in the hall closet," he told Chelsea. She left the room as Doc rustled around in a wall cabinet filled with medical supplies, then spent a few minutes cleaning off the abrasions on Adam's forehead, nose and cheek.

Chelsea returned with a stack of snow-white towels. "Do you need help?" she asked.

"No, I've done this a hundred times. My wife, Val, is off playing keno but she'll be back in an hour or so. She'll call the pizza place and we can eat lunch."

"Oh, let me fix lunch," Chelsea pleaded. "Adam says I can cook. Let's see if he's right. Anything in your kitchen you don't want me to use?"

"Knock yourself out. I'll need a half hour or so to put Adam back together." He ushered her to the door and closed it softly behind her. "Are you going to tell me why she's not sure she can cook?" he asked as he turned back to face Adam.

"Long story." When Doc offered a couple of codeine

tablets and some water Adam held up a hand. "I can't take those. Someone just tried to kill us. I have to stay sharp."

Doc shook his head. "I'm going to stitch that wound of yours. That's going to hurt a bit."

"Just give me a local," Adam insisted.

"Whatever you say," Doc said as he helped Adam lie down. "What's with this scar on your shoulder?"

"Old gunshot wound."

"Not that old," Doc commented as he positioned clean towels before purging the new wound with a solution.

"Doc, let me ask you a question," Adam said as he did his best to ignore the searing pain.

"Hmm—"

"You don't seem too surprised to see me."

"Well, I'm kind of embarrassed to tell you this. See, I knew you were in the witness protection program because I hounded Whip after you disappeared. He finally admitted you were but he wouldn't tell me where you'd been sent."

"He didn't know until after I left. The man I helped put away swore revenge—that's why I was allowed into the program. A few weeks ago one of his thugs found me. I ended up killing the guy and then I staged my disappearance and death. After that I called Whip."

"I didn't know any of that."

"I 'died' under another name," Adam said. "No one from the old days knew."

"I take it you knew Chelsea by then. How did she take your 'death,' or did she know the truth?"

"I thought it would be safer if she didn't know. It was hard on her."

"But now you're back together. Did you find her or did she find you?"

"It's kind of a toss-up who found who," Adam said,

wincing as the first stitch pierced his skin. The local hadn't helped a lot.

"We've got a few minutes," Doc said. "Tell me how you reconnected."

Between gritted teeth, Adam explained about the cabin and about Chelsea coming to say goodbye and the subsequent helicopter crash. "I'm not entirely sure how one of Holton's men wound up on her chopper, but he did."

"Doesn't she know how it happened?"

"Doc, she doesn't even know who she is. She survived the crash, but she suffered a concussion of some kind. She can't remember anything."

"Including you?"

"Including everything. Including the fact she's pregnant."

Doc never missed a beat but a soft whistle escaped his lips. "Almost done here. So, that's why you didn't want her lifting heavy things?"

"I've been worried sick she would miscarry because of the crash."

"How far along is she?"

"Not more than four months," Adam said as the feeling of the surgical thread pulling through his skin sent shivers down his spine. "Yikes, that hurts."

"Tried to warn you. Well, if she'd suffered a miscarriage she would have told you. You haven't seen any blood?"

"We haven't even had a chance to change clothes. I'm beginning to bug her with all my questions. I was so worried she might have some kind of hemorrhage, either with the baby or in her brain or something."

"That would have surfaced by now. It's been about twenty-four hours, right? No, she looks a hell of a lot better off than you do. I'll give her an examination before you leave, ask a few discreet questions."

"I thought it might be better to tell her about the baby when I got her to a safe place," Adam said.

"She can stay here," Doc said.

"Thanks, Doc, but I need to take her somewhere she'll be protected if armed men show up. That's not here with you and your wife. But I think I have an idea. She has a brother about eight hours from here. I've been thinking about him since she shot that guy in the alley."

"She shot the gun? I thought you did."

"Nope, she saved my skin, not the other way around."

"You really care about her, don't you?"

Adam nodded. "We're engaged, but of course she doesn't know that, either. I haven't been sure what to tell her about herself so I haven't said a lot. I was afraid if I told her every detail she'd hate me for faking my death and leaving her and she'd be horrified she was carrying my baby. I had to get her to trust me so I could protect her. I've tried not to lie…it's just such a mess and we've been so busy running."

The doctor set aside his equipment and helped Adam into a sitting position. As he wrapped a bandage around Adam's rib cage, he sighed. "I remember young love," he said as he taped it. "It's like riding a roller coaster without a seat belt." He looked thoughtful for a second, then added, "'Course, some people keep that level of intensity their whole lives—like your parents, for instance."

"I lived in the same house," Adam said. "I had a first-row seat to their 'intensity' and to Dad's temper."

"He wouldn't have hurt her for the world," Doc said, his voice very steady.

"I hope not," Adam said.

Doc opened his mouth but closed it without speaking, then finally shook his head. "Awful business, your mother's murder. I saw her just the week before—as tied up in knots as she was with that runaway student of hers, she still had time to drop by and say hello. Wonderful woman."

"I know."

Doc grabbed a prescription pad. "Thanks to the volunteer work I do, I can write prescriptions in Nevada. Get this filled. It's for antibiotics. Take every single pill."

Adam tucked the prescription into his wallet, glad to move the conversation on. "What about Chelsea's memory? Will it come back soon?"

"I have no idea. But lacking a serious injury, I do have to wonder if she's blocking something painful."

"What do you mean?" he asked.

"I'm not sure. I just wonder if deep down, she isn't ready to remember her life, that maybe there's too much pain to face."

"Pain I caused," Adam said.

"Maybe."

"No, Doc, if she's running from something, you can bet your bottom dollar it's me."

"Listen," Doc said. "Get her to her brother's house. If he can give her some peace and quiet, she might start to relax. At the very least, she shouldn't be running. If a problem does pop up, she needs to be able to get to a doctor without being shot at."

"It would be better for our baby," Adam said quietly.

"And better for you, too," Doc added.

"Sure," Adam said. But he knew the truth. Leaving Chelsea at her brother's house would be better off for everybody *but* him.

ADAM ADJUSTED HIS body to fit into Doc's well-worn desk chair. Doc had left when he heard Val come home and Adam used the time alone to access Chelsea's brother's phone number out of the short, coded list he kept in his wallet. He punched it into his prepaid phone.

"Who is this?" Bill said by way of greeting.

Adam explained who he was, which took a second because like everyone else—except Whip and a handful of others, including Holton and his gang—Bill had thought Adam was dead.

"Escaping the Feds," he finally said when Adam finished. "Dude, that's righteous. Wait, is that the truth about what happened to Chelsea, too?"

Ignoring the misconception Bill had formed on who was chasing him, Adam went on to break the news that Chelsea wasn't as dead as reports had stated. In fact, she was in Nevada and needed refuge.

"That's a relief," Bill said. "Sure, bring Sis down here. Jan and I will take excellent care of her. I bet Mom and Dad are over-the-moon happy she's okay."

"Chelsea hasn't told them. Let's just say we've been on the run. I'll explain it all when I see you, but right now, she's in danger and I just want to get her somewhere safe. And you should know there's a couple of other issues— she's got amnesia and she's about four months pregnant."

"Whoa, that's a lot to take in," Bill said.

"She'll be safe with you as long as no one knows she's there and that includes the rest of your family for now," Adam stressed. "And because of the amnesia, we're not telling her yet about the baby. Hopefully her memory will return before that becomes an issue."

"We know how to keep a secret," Bill said, his voice serious. "We won't say a word about the baby and trust me, we won't let the Feds near her."

"Er, well, we'll talk about what's really going on when we get there, okay? Your father told me you live about fifty miles outside Las Vegas, is that right?"

"More or less," Bill said.

Adam gave him the vague directions Chelsea's parents had mentioned at a family gathering when they talked about Bill and his eccentric lifestyle.

Bill chuckled. "That's the way the old man insists on coming. You can shave off forty-five minutes of road time if you turn off the main highway when you reach a wide spot in the road named Dry Gulch. Better grab a pen and paper."

Adam did as told and jotted down half a page of colorful directions. A few minutes later, they disconnected.

His next call was to Whip and the old guy answered with a sigh of relief. "I got worried when we got disconnected last time," he admitted. "Where are you?"

"With Doc," Adam said.

"In Nevada, then. Do you have a plan?"

"Chelsea Pierce and I—"

"Chelsea Pierce—wait a second, her name was in the news. They said she'd died in a chopper crash somewhere in the mountains. Was that the same crash you mentioned?"

"Yes. I managed to get her out of there."

"Is she one of Holton's people?"

"No. She's a friend of mine. Holton's people must have used her to find me. I don't know why they didn't buy into the report that I died in the lake. Anyway, I'm going to take her to her brother's place in Nevada, where she'll be safe, and then I've got to get out of the country until things die down."

"As long as you're not coming back to Arizona," Whip said.

"I don't see what difference it makes," Adam confessed. "Holton's gotten to me twice, once in California and again in Nevada by trailing Chelsea."

"But his main power base is here. I just want you to have a life where you're not always looking over your shoulder."

"I know, Whip. But remember after the first hit man, when you asked me how they found me? I've been thinking about it. There was this one US Marshal, name of Ron Ballard, a real puffed-up jerk who threw his weight around whenever he got the chance. About a week before everything hit the fan, Ballard showed up where I worked, which was pretty odd in and of itself. He made a point of making sure I noticed his new tricked-out truck. A week later, Holton's guy tried to kill me."

"So you think this Ballard guy sold you out?"

"It sounds kind of flimsy when I say it out loud, but yeah, he might have. At least four of Holton's men have been involved in trying to get rid of me. Doesn't that sound like overkill? Maybe I know something I don't realize I know."

"Like what?"

"Like, well, I don't know."

Whip sighed. "Keep thinking. It'll come to you. Meanwhile, I'll see what I can find out about that guy you mentioned, what's his name, Ballard?"

"Yeah, but don't put yourself in jeopardy."

"I won't. You're still headed to Florida?"

"Yeah. From there I'll make arrangements to leave the country,"

"Good."

The room felt empty after he hung up. Adam pocketed the phone and got to his feet, then made himself stretch his arms over his head and then bend over and touch his toes. To his relief, the knife wound didn't restrict his movements too much. As far as the pain went, he'd just have to ignore it. Every second in this house put Doc Fisher and his wife in jeopardy and increased the possibility Holton's men were getting closer.

His growling stomach reminded him it was time to eat something and then figure out how to secure another vehicle to continue their trek. Tomorrow by this time, Chelsea would be safe. That was all that mattered.

Chapter Seven

"I can't believe you made all of this out of what was in our kitchen," Val Fisher said as she nibbled on a vinaigrette salad with pomegranate seeds and toasted cashews.

"Your fridge was full of yummy things," Chelsea said.

"You can thank our daughter, Morgan, for that. Whenever she visits, she cooks up a storm. Can you imagine preferring to cook over eating at one of the casinos?"

"Yes," Chelsea said, and Val and Doc both laughed.

Chelsea glanced over at Adam, who held himself carefully. It was going to be up to her to help him, a thought that strangely pleased her. She'd hated being wounded and afraid. For some reason, both taking control of the situation in that alley and then fooling around in a kitchen had given her a glimpse of the person she must really be.

Adam seemed to sense her scrutiny, for he looked up and smiled.

"You were deep in thought," she said.

He put down his fork. "I'm sorry to bring this delicious meal down a notch, but I need to go buy a different car so we can get out of here. If those guys find the Jeep, they'll put two and two together and concentrate on Spur." He looked at Val and said, "We really appreciate your hospitality but the sooner we leave, the better off for everyone."

"I already thought of that," Val said, "Our son is in the army. You can borrow his truck."

"No," Adam told her. "I don't want anything traceable to this family."

"Okay then," she continued, apparently undaunted. "Dorrie Simpson is selling her late uncle's truck. What about that?"

"It's kind of old," Doc Fisher said.

"Old is fine as long as it's got enough miles left in it to get to Florida," Adam said.

"Florida?" Chelsea squeaked. This was the first she'd heard of going to Florida. On the other hand, maybe Florida was a red herring, just a destination to appease curiosity. Why hadn't she stopped to wonder about where they were ultimately going before this?

"He hardly drove the thing the last five years," Val said, pushing herself away from the table. "I'll just check to make sure it's still for sale." She grabbed the cordless phone off the drain board and punched in a number.

Doc Fisher cleared his throat as he met Chelsea's gaze. "While she does that, how about you humor an old semiretired doctor and let me give you a once-over, young lady?"

"That's not necessary," she said.

"It pays to be cautious after any head injury, let alone a helicopter crash," he insisted. "And I bet both of you would like a shower and some clean clothes before you head out."

"I don't have any other clothes," Chelsea admitted.

Val hung up the phone. "The truck is still for sale. And Chelsea, you're about the same size as our Morgan and I know she left all sorts of things in her bedroom after she got her own place. There'll be something in there you can have. In fact, help yourself to anything you want. She's made it pretty clear whatever she left here isn't important to her anymore."

"Thank you," Chelsea said. "That's very generous."

"Let's go," Doc said, getting up from the table.

Chelsea met Adam's gaze. He smiled and she shrugged. He'd finally gotten his way—she was going to see a doctor.

IT WAS AFTER six o'clock by the time the truck was legally Adam's and they'd loaded it with their gear. Chelsea looked clean and refreshed in a blue T-shirt and jeans, her long hair braided down her back. They said a grateful goodbye to the Fishers, who were off to the local casino.

"What did Doc say about your head?" Adam asked as his gaze darted down every side street, eyes peeled for a glimpse of a dark blue van with three men inside.

She tore her gaze from his fishing hat and sunglasses, both donated by Doc for the purpose of disguise. The bleached hair that had been Adam's camouflage before was now hidden. "He says he sees no sign of a concussion."

"That's good news," he said.

"He sure asked a lot of questions, though," she added.

"Like what?"

"Oh, you know. Was I bleeding anywhere, cramping, in pain, did my back hurt…all sorts of stuff."

"Well, he's a doctor," Adam said.

"True." She was quiet a second, then added, "You told the Fishers you needed a vehicle that could get us to Florida. Why are we going to Florida?"

This was a conversation he'd hoped to avoid until they were at her brother's house. "I have to leave the country for a while," he finally said. "Florida's a good launching spot."

"But I don't have any ID, to say nothing of a passport," she mused. "How am I going to travel outside the country?"

"We'll talk about that later," he said.

"How about we talk about it now? I'm beginning to read

you like a book, Adam Parish. When you get all tense like this, I know you're spending more time thinking about what not to say than what *to* say."

He shot her a quick glance. "Okay then, I'll be blunt. You're not leaving the country, at least not with me. You need to get your memory back, you need to get well. I'm taking you somewhere safe. It's what you wanted this morning. Despite my misgivings, it was a good idea then and it's a good idea now."

"I thought I informed you I'd had a change of heart, that I have signed on as your designated sidekick."

He smiled. "You are that in more ways than you know, Chelsea. But today when those goons grabbed me, all I could think of was you. I'll be honest. It scared the hell out of me."

"Hmm…" she said. "So where are you going to park me?"

"Your brother's place."

"You do recall I don't remember having a brother, don't you?" she said.

"That I do. But Bill and Jan are both survivalists."

"So you figure they'll know how to protect me?"

"I know they will. As much as I want to be the one who keeps you safe, I can't right now, not when I'm on the run."

"How about your family?" she asked. "Can't they help you?"

"I'm an only kid and my folks are both dead," he said.

"Oh. I'm sorry."

He checked the rearview mirror, his nerves on edge as he watched for a dark van to pull up behind them.

"How did they die?" she asked.

"What?"

"Your folks. They can't have been that old. What happened to them?"

"My mother was killed during a break-in," he told her after a lengthy pause. "She taught high school, one of those dedicated teachers everybody loves. She'd taken a personal day off work for a meeting with my father's boss, something we found out after her murder. The car keys were in her hand when I found her—"

"*You* found her?"

He nodded. "Anyway, someone had broken the glass in the back door. I guess she surprised them by being home instead of at the school. And, well, he shot her."

"Oh, my gosh, I'm so sorry," Chelsea said softly. "How terrible for you. Was it a burglar?"

"The house was torn apart and Dad said a few minor things were missing. He figured Mom surprised the culprit when she walked into the room. A neighbor reported seeing a white male in blue jeans and a dark hoodie. That didn't narrow the field much. Despite the fact Dad was a cop, he was, of course, top suspect on the list. The department said he messed up the house to make it look like an intruder. Remember these people were Dad's colleagues. Dad felt the police department's scrutiny of him blinded them to broadening their investigation."

"The poor guy," Chelsea said.

"I know. See, the thing is that mysterious appointment with the chief of police."

"Any idea what it was about?"

"None, but the obvious conclusion everyone reached was that she was going to ask for help getting Dad's drinking under control."

"It was that bad?"

"Yeah, it was. It didn't help that Mom was involved in some situation at the school where one of her students ran off with some guy. The kid's parents had just given up ever getting through to the girl but Mom started asking questions, trying to find her and get her back in school. Dad demanded Mom stop 'poking her nose where it didn't belong.' She refused, they argued, he drank and yelled…it was pretty awful."

"Do *you* think your dad did it?"

He stared at her a second, then looked back out the window and sighed. "The drinking got worse after her death. Sometimes he'd start reliving the investigation, running through the leads that had led nowhere, the disappointments and all, then he'd segue into the good old times. Once he told me that life was just a string of choices and the trick was to be able to live with the ones you make. The comment didn't seem relevant at the time, but he died that night from a barbiturate overdose. The coroner said it was accidental, but I've always wondered if he said that to protect Dad's insurance claim—for me, you know—and if the truth was Dad just couldn't face his guilt another day."

"That's so sad, Adam. I'm sorry."

He took a deep breath. "I was about eighteen by then. It was hard…living in that house alone."

"You stayed there?"

"I had nowhere else to go. My dad's best friend and former partner, a guy named Whip Haskins, helped me out." Adam smiled at the memories. "We repainted every square inch of the place, rebuilt the attic stairs, wallpapered, installed appliances—you name it, we did it. It wasn't until later that I realized all that work kept me grounded. Anyway, long story short, I finally sold the place to a friend during the Holton trial, when I knew I was going to have to cut my losses and leave Arizona forever."

"I wish I'd known you then," she said softly.

"No, you don't. I was kind of a mess. Thought I had to make a point and become a cop, but Dad's old workplace was poisonous for me. Then I went into bodyguarding and you know how well that turned out."

"I still wish I'd known you."

He stared at her a second. No matter that her memory wasn't intact, the human being she was deep inside was exactly the same as ever: kind, loving, caring. Didn't this mean that the essence of her character was set in stone and couldn't one stretch that into believing that every feeling that had existed in her heart might still be rekindled?

Like love for him? Like forgiving him?

Adam shifted his weight in an attempt to get comfortable. His side throbbed and moving seemed to be getting harder rather than easier as he stiffened up.

"I know how to drive," Chelsea reminded him.

He glanced at her and recalled their exit from Black Boulder. "I know you do."

"Why don't you stretch out in the back and let me take over? Are we driving straight through to my brother's place?"

He'd expected more of an argument from her and in some perverted way was now disappointed she hadn't fought harder to stick by his side. Man, he was a mess, one minute wanting her safe and sound and tucked away like the jewel she was, and the next wanting her by his side, where he could talk to her, look at her, troubleshoot any problem she might have although he understood he was the root cause of every current issue that plagued her.

"There's a state park about two hours from here. It'll be getting dark by then and it would probably be better to stop there for the night rather than risk being out on the road in a vehicle we know so little about."

"Doc told me to remind you to fill the prescription he gave you," Chelsea said. "According to the road signs, there's a town up ahead. We can stop at a pharmacy."

THE PHARMACY THEY found was homey and cute. Chelsea went in alone with a wad of Adam's cash. By the time she came out twenty minutes later, she had his prescription and a Nevada Spurs sports hat.

As she walked to the car, she caught sight of him sitting with his head back and his eyes closed. He'd told her their relationship was friendly and no more, but her gut told her he wasn't being entirely honest. If he currently appealed to every female gene in her body, and under these circumstances to boot, how could he not have appealed to her before?

More likely, she thought, they'd been lovers at one time, maybe estranged now. Maybe she was more in love with him than he was with her. Maybe he'd been running away from her. Egad, was she a stalker? Is that why she'd been flying in a helicopter to see him? But wait a sec, how did she know she'd been flying to see him and not flying to flee him? How did she know he didn't somehow blow up the chopper and kill those two men?

She'd gone blindly back to accepting his version of everything and now he'd made the arbitrary decision to take her to her brother's house and she'd agreed.

"There's a puddle under the truck," she said as she slid in next to him. "I don't see a blue van, though, so I guess if they followed us they're keeping their distance."

He got out of the truck, took a look under the hood and got back in. "I think our water pump has a problem."

"That's not good, is it?"

"No. We'd better find a gas station."

"Do you think they're behind us?" she asked as they drove.

He took off Doc's fishing hat and pulled on the Spurs cap. "Nice. Thanks. As for whether or not they are following us, well, who knows? It's possible. Maybe they'll show up when we make camp."

"Something to look forward to," she muttered.

At the gas station they found out the water pump was failing and no, their mechanic wasn't working, nor did they have the part, anyway. Adam explained they would have to settle for topping up the radiator and buying a couple of gallons of water to stow in the back should it happen again. He took his first pill, then they were back on the road, hoping for the best.

Chelsea sat on her hands and stared out her window, scared about the possibility of a nighttime attack, and unsure if she wanted to stay with Adam or leave. All the strength and resolve she'd summoned to help her with the day now ebbed as the sun eked its way toward the horizon.

As the mountain terrain gave way to drier, desertlike conditions, the sky grew darker. They finally rolled into a sparsely occupied park, where they chose a spot, filled out a form, tucked a few dollars into an envelope and parked. They rolled the sleeping bags out in the back of the truck, ate without appetite, used the facilities and stopped to admire the plethora of stars in the night sky.

"Kind of nice to be out from under all those trees," Adam said after smothering a yawn.

She was quiet for a few moments and then she spoke. "Adam, this morning you said we needed to talk before I got on a bus and left. You said there were things I needed to know. What things?"

He stared at her.

"You're getting tense again," she said.

"I know I am. Okay, I have a deal to make with you. I'll tell you everything you want to know tomorrow when we're at Bill's house."

"Is my life so awful you need reinforcements? What am I, a serial killer?"

"No, no," he said, reaching up to brush a stray lock of hair from her forehead. "The truth is you're the most beautiful person I've ever met, inside and out, through and through. But you're right, I do need reinforcements. Bill grew up with you. He'll have memories of you I don't have and hopefully pictures and letters and things that will help you rediscover yourself."

She thought for a second. "Okay, I'll wait until tomorrow but there's a condition."

"And what's that?" he asked.

"Kiss me."

The silence between them stretched on as the chirping of crickets filled her ears. He finally cupped her face and kissed her forehead.

"A real kiss," she said. "I have a feeling…oh, just humor me."

His hand fell from her cheek to her shoulder then to her waist. She stepped closer and raised her face to gaze at him. She couldn't get over the feeling she'd looked at him like this a thousand times. As he lowered his head and claimed her mouth, she melted against his chest, her arms wrapping around his neck. There was a humming sexuality in him, a lustiness that shook her down to her soul. He lifted her briefly off her feet, her arms wrapped around his neck, his kiss deep and long, scorching her with its fire. When he set her down, she stepped back to collect her breath. His hands followed her retreat and she caught and clasped them in hers. If he touched her again, she wasn't sure what she would do.

"We've kissed before," she said.

"Do you remember?"

"No. But you're not denying it, either."

"No, I'm not denying it," he said.

Their heads began to drift together again. She wanted another kiss and maybe a whole lot more. Nothing else mattered. Right as his succulent lips touched hers, a car rounded the curve in the road and headlights flooded over them. Her heart went from drumming with anticipation to thundering in her ears as it kicked into stampede mode. But the car passed by them, not even slowing down, and she could see in its wake that it was a small compact, an unlikely choice for three large men.

The episode threw Chelsea back into the present. Apparently it had the same effect on Adam.

"We need to get back to camp," he said, staring into her eyes. "If Holton's guys are coming after us, we need to be ready." He kissed her forehead again and took her hand. "Come on."

Chapter Eight

"Looks like no one killed us in our sleep," Chelsea said the next morning when they both awoke to find they'd nodded off.

Adam smiled, but secretly grimaced. He'd meant to stay awake all night so Chelsea could rest… Well, as she had just pointed out, they were still alive and kicking.

As she had the night before, she insisted he lift his shirt so she could check out the wound. "It seems to be healing nicely," she announced, running her hands over his bare skin. "It doesn't feel feverish."

Maybe his skin didn't feel feverish but if she kept touching him that way, there would be blazing heat and she'd be both the cause and the solution. He found himself staring at her tempting and delicious lips, which were puffed out a little as she concentrated. Last night's kiss flared in his mind and he inched closer to her right as she lowered his shirt.

"I predict you're going to be fine in a day or two," she said.

He just stared at her. His mind was not on his wound.

"I'll be back in a few minutes," she said, and excused herself to walk to the restrooms. He took a few deep breaths and made it as far as the picnic table, where he could watch her progress and make sure no one was interested in her activities except him. The fact his attention was focused solely on the way her hips moved as she walked was just a sidetracking fact of life.

"Snap out of it," he chastised himself.

The uneasy feeling that had been eating at him since the day before returned. Where were the thugs? If he'd been determined to follow someone, he'd have waited near the on-ramp to the only highway leading out of town. Had they been lurking there and just hadn't recognized him behind the wheel of the truck? It was possible. They had changed cars and he'd been wearing Doc's old hat.

It was a chilly morning made chillier by the fact that this was the last day for an unknown length of time that he would see Chelsea. The kiss last night had opened the doorway for him to explain the true scope of their relationship. Soon. With her brother to support her, Adam would tell her about their baby. She had to know and he had to be the one to tell her. After that he'd leave to draw danger away from her and then once he had resettled, he'd get word to her and it would be up to her what she did next.

The whole thing was fraught with multiple opportunities for disaster, but at least she wouldn't be alone. Bill would know how to reconnect her to her parents and then when her memory came back—well, that's when the true decision making would start.

That was the plan, anyway.

He looked up to see her approaching and his heart did the clichéd thumping in his chest. "I'm starving," she announced as she stopped a few feet in front of him.

"Is there anything to eat in the icebox?" he asked.

"Not really. How about we go to a real live restaurant?"

"Why not?" he said.

Breaking camp consisted of putting more water in the radiator and climbing into the cab. Fifteen miles later, they came across a dusty little town named Fiddlestick with a one-stop convenience store/gas station/post office/restaurant all housed in a single rambling building.

The inside was bustling with what appeared to be regulars. No one looked suspicious, although almost all conversations paused as the two of them walked through the door.

"Looks like you order at the counter," Chelsea said. "I still have a little bit of the money that you gave me. I'll get breakfast."

"I'll have the usual," he said, and then smiled at her expression. "Yes, we've eaten together before and, yes, often enough that somewhere in your pretty head you know what I like. Order me black coffee and a bacon-and-egg breakfast sandwich. You always order an everything bagel with light cream cheese."

"Always?"

"In my experience, yes. I guess we each have our habits. I'll go scout out a table."

Breakfast was delivered fast, and was hot and tasty. As they sat at a small table, surrounded by babbling strangers and laughter, the air full of delicious smells, Adam felt whisked back to the months in Frisco. Chelsea loved eating out and with her, he'd discovered the joy of being alone, together, in a crowd to the point that this interlude struck him as not just ordinary, but extraordinary. He suddenly wanted that carefree life back with a vengeance. He cautioned himself not to get complacent. No matter how tired he was of running, he couldn't stop, because Holton wouldn't.

Filled up and ready to tackle the next several hours of driving, they got back in the truck and headed south.

After months in San Francisco's foggy, cool climate and then weeks underneath trees, the open skies of the desert aroused a host of fond memories for Adam. Even the colors were familiar: sage-green foliage, earth a dozen shades of tan, distant purplish mountains, faded blue skies.

But the driving soon became monotonous. With no air-conditioning, they rolled down their windows so air could blow through the cab, billowing their clothes, rustling their hair.

"This road just keeps going on and on and on," Chelsea eventually said. She'd propped her feet against the dashboard and extended one arm through the open window. Her head rested against the seat while windblown strands of loose dark hair flew across her cheeks. She looked absolutely wonderful. The monotony he'd been feeling fled at the sight of her blue eyes trained on his face.

Another hour passed before he finally spotted a sign that read Dry Gulch 2 Miles.

"Here's where we fill the tank and turn right," he announced as he pulled into the town's sole gas station.

After a quick stop, they drove off and it rejuvenated both of them to be off the main highway for the simple reason that this road wasn't as flat and straight. Eventually they rolled up to a stop sign, where another road crossed. This had to be four corners. He turned right and Chelsea ticked off the different steps Adam had jotted on some scrap paper. They made all of Bill's twists and turns until they found themselves approaching a barn with a giant painting of a beer bottle on the side.

"Eleven more miles," Chelsea said.

"And then what?"

"A gulch, a fence, then Bill's property. Follow the road until you hit a slight rise covered with mesquite trees. From there we can see his place." She looked up from the paper. "Or so it says here. I'll believe it when I see it."

The road, which had been steadily deteriorating, began to show signs of more frequent use as No Trespassing and

Private Property signs expressing various levels of threats and *or elses* began to show up nailed to fence posts and random trees. There was a lot of barbed wire present as well, and a gate that had been pushed aside and left open for what appeared, judging from the sandy earth currently blocking its path, to have been a season or two.

"Give me a crash course in my brother," Chelsea said as they passed a sign warning the federal government that the land was protected by patriots.

"He's a little on the aggressive side of privacy," Adam said diplomatically. "He believes in the rights of citizens to bear arms and protect themselves against any and all contingencies that threaten their sovereignty. In other words, he and his wife, Jan, take care of themselves and brook no interference. And they distrust the government."

"I see. So, how do you two get along?"

"I've never actually met him."

"What? I thought you knew him. I thought *he knew you*!"

"You and I have only known each other a few months," he explained. "We were going to go visit him...we just never got around to it."

She turned a puzzled expression in his direction. "Since when do casual friends travel hours and hours to visit each other's families?"

He started to stammer something and she waved him off. "I know, you'll tell me later."

"You and Bill," he added, hastening to move the conversation along, "have your political differences, but as far as I could tell, you adopted a live-and-let-live policy toward each other. And you should know that he didn't hesitate offering to give you sanctuary and protection."

"That's nice. How long will you stay before you leave?"

He glanced at the dashboard clock. It was early afternoon. "Until you're comfortable with your brother and his wife. Then I'd better go."

"Okay," she said, her voice noncommittal, as though she wasn't sure if she resented him leaving or couldn't wait to be out from under his wing. He guessed it was a little of both.

They finally found a scattered copse of mesquite trees topping a small hill. Adam stopped the truck and got out. His first order of business was to fill the radiator with water, then he joined Chelsea under the meager shade of the trees to peruse the compound down below.

He counted three barns, a double-wide trailer, what looked like a cinderblock outbuilding and a covered shelter surrounding a pasture that housed two goats, two cows and a horse who lurked under the shade of the only tree. Chickens roamed about in another pen and half a dozen vehicles of various configurations were scattered throughout. A small garden grew close to the house. A covered well sat next to that, complete with a hand pump and a trough. A static windmill crowned the bucolic scene.

"You're right. They are the self-sufficient type," Chelsea said.

"Well, they are out in the middle of nowhere," Adam agreed. "I bet their nearest neighbor is literally miles away."

At that moment, a man wearing dark jeans and a white shirt walked out of the double wide, looked up the hill and waved an arm, as if gesturing them to come on down.

"Is that him? Is that Bill?"

All Adam could tell from that distance was that he was blond and big, which matched the picture of Bill he'd seen in Chelsea's parents' home. "I believe so," he said.

Adam waved back at the man. As Chelsea turned to re-trace her steps to the truck, she called over her shoulder, "It's time to meet the family. You coming?"

He glanced once again at the double-wide, but Bill had apparently gone back inside, probably to alert his wife that their visitors were here. He turned to the truck to find that Chelsea already sat in the passenger seat, a smiling, hopeful expression on her face.

It hit him hard—her only reality was the loss of identity, including her family, her background and relationships. He'd done nothing but drag her miles away from a crash he'd admitted she never would have been in if it hadn't been for him. She'd be crazy to not want to reconnect with real people who could prove who they were.

That trailer and the people inside it represented the future to her and until her memory came back, he made up little more than forty-eight hours of her past. It was time to get this over with.

CHELSEA PUSHED ASIDE the sadness that the thought of Adam leaving her behind created—there was no point in dwelling on it—and instead concentrated on finally getting some answers, both from her brother and from Adam. What she might learn about herself was scary but she was ready for just about anything.

They pulled up right beside a short flight of stairs that led into the aproned trailer. It was apparently the back door to the place, but as it was open, it seemed the place to start. Adam parked alongside a truck that looked even older than theirs. It sported a gun rack in the back window, complete with two rifles. A prominent bumper sticker dominated by a pair of puckered red lips read Kiss My Arsenal.

She waited for Adam to join her and preceded him up the stairs. She kept expecting her brother and his wife to emerge from the trailer, but something must have demanded their attention. She and Adam walked inside and then paused. They were standing in the kitchen. A narrow doorway occupied the left wall. Adam called out, "Bill? Jan?"

They heard a sound coming through the doorway that led to the rest of the home, but no accompanying voices. Chelsea walked toward the inner door and moved into a darkish combined dining-living area. Closed drapes explained the gloom. The only light came from a skylight in the ceiling, and strapped into a chair situated under that beam of light sat a bound-and-gagged man. Behind him, piled high, were several cartons of weapons.

Adam immediately drew his handgun and turned on his heels. Where was the guy who'd signaled at them? Chelsea hurried to the man's side. He was a large guy with dark blond hair and a very bushy, curly beard. He wore faded denim overalls and a yellow T-shirt.

"Start with the gag," Adam urged as he joined her. "We have to know what's going on."

She loosened the man's gag and pulled it from his mouth. "They've taken Jan," he blurted out. "Did you see her outside?"

"Are you Bill?" Chelsea asked.

"Oh, gosh, yeah, sis, I'm your brother and Jan is my wife. Did you see her?"

"No," Chelsea told him. "You don't know where she is?"

"They won't tell me. They only kept me alive in case they needed bait. God knows what they've done to her."

"Who are they?" Adam demanded as he brought out a pocketknife and began slicing through knots. His voice sounded like he dreaded the reply.

"I figure they're those Feds you told me about. Man, you must have really pissed them off."

"Not Feds," Adam said. "But you don't know them at all?"

"Never seen them before."

"Did they say who they were working for?"

"No."

"How many of them are there?"

"Three. One's got a bad arm, though. Mean SOB."

Adam swore as he and Chelsea exchanged looks.

"How did they find us?" she whispered.

Adam shook his head.

Bill looked contrite as he met Adam's gaze. "I know you asked me not to tell anyone you were coming here, but I've got to admit I called Mom and Dad and I suspect they told the rest of the family. I had to let them know Chelsea was okay."

"When did these guys show up?"

"Late last night. One took Jan away while the other two tied me up and then they took turns guarding me and waiting for you two to get here. They kept talking about how to make it look like a bunch of weapons exploded, like they wanted it to look like some kind of ingrown mishap that turned into a death trap, and not cold-blooded murder. Those boxes behind me are full of weapons. No ammunition, though."

"We saw a big, blond man outside," Chelsea said. Glancing up at Adam, she added, "He must have been the driver in the alley." She untied the last knot on Bill's wrists but jerked when the sound of hammering on the kitchen door sounded through the metal structure.

Adam had now cut through the bindings on Bill's ankles and the shaken man stood up. Hours in restraints had taken their toll and he almost tumbled over. Chelsea caught him as Adam ran into the kitchen to check out the noise. Chelsea scurried to the door next to a small fireplace.

"Don't open that," Bill said.

"Why not?"

"Because they rigged it to explode if it opens from the inside."

"The kitchen door has been nailed shut from the outside," Adam said as he strode back into the dining area. He gestured at the front door. "What about that one?"

"Can't use it," Chelsea said. She looked at her brother. "Is there another one?"

"In the bedroom," Bill said, pointing behind him. "But I heard banging back there, too. There's another way—unless they found it." He took a few unsteady steps, found his legs and dashed down the short hall, with Adam and Chelsea close behind.

Adam found the door Bill mentioned and tried to open it, but Bill was tugging on the big bed that occupied the middle of the room. "You guys help me push this thing against the wall," he muttered. As Chelsea gripped a bedpost, they heard breaking glass. A second later an explosion caused the whole structure to shake and a second after that, smoke made its way to their noses.

Chelsea darted back to the living room. The opaque window set into the front door was now just shards of glass, broken by the bomb they'd thrown into the trailer. She started coughing as flames raced up the drapes. For a second, she couldn't look away from the fire.

"Chelsea!" Adam yelled.

Eyes now watering, she grabbed a throw rug and beat out the flames, then ran back down the hall to the bedroom.

"There was a fire—" she began.

"Are you all right?" he interrupted with a concerned glance.

"I put it out, but it looks as though they're trying to burn the trailer down with us inside it." Her announcement was followed by more cracking glass and another explosion.

"We have to break a window and take our chances outside," Adam told Bill. "Maybe I can pick off one or two—"

"Hang on, one more shove," Bill said. "Those goons took all my weapons, but maybe they missed the knife in the false back of the top drawer. Check for it, Chelsea."

She wedged herself between the bed and the chest and pulled out the drawer. Socks flew everywhere as she emptied the drawer to find the fake back still in place. Sheathed knife in hand, she turned into the room. Bill was now on his hands and knees where the bed had once stood. Adam had crossed to the window, which had shattered thanks to the reverberations of the other explosions. He fired into the yard, taking a second to look over his shoulder as Bill yelled.

"Give me the knife—hurry," Bill said as yet another breaking window somewhere near the kitchen signaled another bomb. By now, the trailer was filled with acrid smoke and the sound of crackling flames. They were all coughing and gasping as noxious fumes polluted the air.

Bill sliced the carpet in four quick strokes, revealing a wooden hatch built into the floor. He pulled on the attached ring and lifted a hinged lid. "If they haven't found the exit, we'll be safe," Bill said.

Adam suddenly backpedaled across the room and out into the hall as a projectile sailed through the window. It landed by his feet and he kicked it down toward the living room.

"That was a hand grenade," he said.

Bill dropped into the underground passage, pulling Chelsea after him. Adam's shoe hit her head as he followed. He pulled the trap door closed right as the grenade exploded down the hall. The cramped space became pitch-black.

A light caught Chelsea in the eyes. When she could

see again, she found Bill had donned a miner's cap with a bulb attached to the crown. "There's no headroom, you'll have to crawl. Follow me," he said. "Don't stop for anything unless you hear a rattler."

Did he mean there could be a rattlesnake in this tunnel? Chelsea swore under her breath. Apparently, she was afraid of snakes, and for a second she froze.

An explosion in the room they'd just left loosened dirt in the tunnel and suddenly, snakes seemed like the least of their worries. With gentle prodding from Adam, she scrambled to crawl after Bill.

No one spoke as they concentrated on getting as far away from the trailer as possible. Eventually Bill stopped. There was enough space above his head for him to get to his knees and push up on another hatch. Dim light flooded inside, along with straw and the smell and squawk of chickens. Bill heaved himself out, then reached down to help the other two.

They'd arrived in the enclosed portion of a large chicken coop. Chelsea saw the wire cage part through the open door, as well as smoke and flames coming from the trailer they'd just escaped, and wondered how in the world they could walk out into the open and not get blown off their feet.

Her brother was several steps ahead of her. He pulled on what at first glance appeared to be a solid piece of the nesting structure, but turned out to be a lever that opened a gap in the stone wall located at the back of the coop. Lights immediately turned on in the adjoining space. "Come with me," Bill said.

This time the door closed behind them, leaving them in jarring silence, and they were standing in what appeared to be a communication center. There was a steel door built into the far wall. Bill grabbed the controls for a radio. "I'm calling for help," he said. "And then I'm going to find Jan and then I'm going to take care of those damn Feds."

"These guys aren't with the government," Adam said. "You misunderstood me. They're hired guns. The fact they aren't very good at what they do is just plain dumb luck."

"They're still going to be dead," Bill said.

Chelsea moved to the door. "Where does this lead?"

"The back of the horse barn."

"Do you have any idea where they'd take Jan?"

He almost threw up his hands. "She could be anywhere. There are a million places to hide…somebody."

He busied himself on the radio, his words when he connected hushed and urgent. As soon as he put down the radio, he unlocked a cabinet and started selecting guns and ammo.

"The police are coming?" Chelsea asked hopefully as Bill shoved a loaded rifle in her hands.

"No cops," Bill said.

"But we need help—"

"Not the cops. I called friends."

"I hope they know what they're doing," she said.

"They know. We've prepared for this kind of situation."

Adam handed her the revolver. "Tuck this away," he said and kissed her forehead before crossing to the steel door. "How do we open this? We have to know what's going on outside."

Bill unlocked and opened the heavy door. Leaving the soundproofed communications room for the barn, they were once again bombarded by explosions. The animals in the corral bleated and whinnied as the crackling roar continued. Bill and Chelsea ran toward the front of the barn.

Out in the yard, two of the men hovered over a box of hand grenades. As Chelsea watched, one of them plucked a bomb from the box and pulled the pin. He threw it at the trailer. Seconds later another explosion sent the terrified animals racing around the corral.

"They've got to be dead by now," one of the men said. He wore a bandage around the bulging muscle in his left arm. He must be the guy Chelsea shot in the alley.

"We've got to be sure," the first one grumbled. "We'll catch hell if Parish escapes again."

"How many grenades does it take to kill two guys?" the injured one protested. "I say we go look for bodies and get out of here."

"This isn't a democracy," the first one replied. "We do what we we're told."

"If we could just shoot them—"

"No bullets, you know that. Now, clam up."

As the two men continued to argue, Bill motioned for her to stay where she was as he crept out of the barn and took up a position behind a steel water tank. She couldn't imagine his new location gave him a clear shot of anyone, but it would provide protection against an explosion. There was no sign of Bill's wife or of the blond guy, either, for that matter, and in her mind, that made shooting anyone risky.

On the other hand, the killers had talked about there being only two men in the trailer. Was it possible they didn't know she was there, too? Could she use that to their advantage?

"Look what we got here," a deep voice said as an arm the circumference of a well-fed boa constrictor circled Chelsea's neck. Every cell in her body jumped to attention as his free hand grabbed the rifle from her hands. She immediately tugged at his stranglehold but he shook her off like a gnat.

His arm still clamped in place, he propelled her ahead of him toward the other two men. Where had he come from?

Had she been so busy assessing what was going on in the yard that she hadn't heard someone roughly the size of a refrigerator approach her from behind?

She tried frantically to turn her head to scan the interior of the barn, desperate to find out what had happened to Adam.

Was he still alive? What else had she missed?

Chapter Nine

Adam threaded his way through the dark barn, searching for an alternate exit and knowing Chelsea and Bill would need back up.

He heard a creaking noise to his left and stepped behind several bales of bedding straw. He crouched down, all but holding his breath. From that position, he saw dusty loafers descend a ladder, followed by a tank of a guy wearing a white shirt and crowned with white-blond hair. The man was whistling a jaunty tune under his breath. Adam would have shot him right that moment just because he dared to whistle while attempting to obliterate innocent people if a shot wouldn't have made things worse.

The guy moved off to the front of barn. Was it possible he'd stashed Jan up in the loft? What better place? But Chelsea and her brother might be in trouble—he debated what he should do for twenty seconds, then scampered up the ladder, emerging in a small closed space filled with lockers and boxes.

He tore open the door to spaces big enough to cram a human being inside, but there was no sign of Jan having ever been up here. All he found were more munitions.

When Bill and Jan had built their homestead, they'd obviously thought in terms of defending their turf. That meant that from the vantage point of this open loft, the road leading toward the mesquite trees and the back entrance, as well as the one leading away from the yard and the front of the trailer, were highly visible so that any incoming vehicles could be dealt with. But it also meant that Bill's soon-to-arrive friends would be vulnerable.

The killers had to realize this—that must have been why the blond guy was up here. Ignoring a burning desire to check on Chelsea, Adam sidled up to the platform's bulwark and chanced a peek down to the yard. His attention was immediately drawn to the two men standing over a box of hand grenades. He was just in time to see one of the men pull a pin, wait until the count of three to lob a grenade into the trailer. Adam recalled the earlier delay that happened in Bill's bedroom, when the gap between deployment and explosion had given Adam time to kick the threat away. Apparently the man had learned to wait a few seconds before throwing.

The trailer was understandably crumbling under the onslaught and several fires had started. Black smoke circled skyward but was there anyone within miles to see and report it? Adam wasn't sure why they were still lobbing hand grenades unless it was to be certain nothing remained intact…and that the survivor rate was zero.

The man who had stood by while the grenade had been thrown now waved his arms and shouted as a heated argument erupted. The combined noise of crackling fire, panicking animals and small explosions made hearing every word impossible.

Where were Chelsea and Bill?

Adam scanned the yard and almost decided they were both still inside the barn, when he spied movement off to his left and watched as Bill slithered from behind the water tank to the cover of a small building. He was inching, it appeared, his way closer to the center of the yard and a clear shot.

Adam lifted his rifle. He was ready.

Another movement caught his attention as the blond he'd seen minutes before came from inside the barn. He pushed a raven-haired woman in front of him—Chelsea. Adam swore under his breath and lowered the rifle. A bullet through the guy's back would go right through Chelsea, too.

The guy shoved her toward his cohorts, one of whom was glued to his cell phone, then stopped several feet away and yelled at them to shut up. He trained Chelsea's rifle on her heart and bellowed toward the trailer. "Parish? Is this little gal with you? Get out here, tough guy. The party's over."

Adam's gaze darted to Bill, who now held his rifle on the blond guy. The yard seemed to attain a moment of pure silence as though a vacuum had sucked up every sound, from fire to exhaled breath. Everyone appeared caught in a moment of inertia. Even the guy with the phone fell silent.

And then Bill shattered it all with gunfire. The blond guy fell to his knees. As he shifted his rifle to return fire, Chelsea pulled the revolver from under the hem of her shirt and got off a shot. The blond's bullet went wild as he toppled over onto the sandy earth.

The other two men each grabbed a grenade and spun around, aware now that the threat came from the barn and the yard itself, not the trailer. As one of them pulled the pin, Adam saw Chelsea race for the cover of the water tank. Once she'd attained cover, he pinpointed the grenade in his sights and pulled the trigger.

The resulting explosion blew both men to smithereens. Bill staggered from his position, looking dazed but unhurt. Chelsea got to her feet, revolver still drawn. Even from that distance he could see her hand shake as she perused the devastation in front of her.

Bill ran to the blond guy, demanding to know where Jan was, but the man was motionless, staring up at the clear sky, taking Jan's whereabouts and the identity of the man behind this mayhem with him into death.

Adam made his way down the stairs and out into the yard, where Chelsea flew into his arms.

"It's over," he said, holding her as tight as he dared.

But, of course, it wasn't. Where was Jan?

BILL'S BUDDIES SHOWED up soon after. For a few minutes, everyone just stood, kind of dumbstruck, their gazes darting between one disaster to the next as though uncertain how to clean up the nastiest mess of human flesh and twisted metal any of them had ever seen.

Bill left it to Adam to explain what had happened. He decided to tell them everything he knew. The memory of one of the killers on his phone plagued Adam. Who had the man called and how much had he said? Certainly whoever was behind this knew for sure about Chelsea now, and also about this standoff. These people had to understand that they must remain vigilant.

The time for explanation was short, however, as everyone's overriding concern was what had happened to Jan. Bill quickly divided people into teams because of the number of buildings scattered across the property that would all need to be searched. He hadn't seen his wife since she'd been taken out of the trailer the previous night, and though he wouldn't say it, Adam could see as the minutes went by and people reported finding nothing, that Bill was beginning to believe they'd killed her and buried her body in a sandy grave.

It was Adam who stumbled across an old abandoned

well located out beyond the pasture. He shined his flashlight down the shaft for a cursory check and couldn't believe it when he saw a mop of red curls atop a small crumpled body at the dry bottom. He yelled Jan's name, which caught the attention of everyone nearby, and they all came running. She didn't respond—from that distance, there was no way to tell if she was dead or alive.

The rescue went surprisingly smoothly. Bill insisted on being the one lowered to his wife. A few tense moments were followed by a shout that brought tears to those waiting at the top. "She's alive," he yelled.

He was hauled up and a man Bill introduced as Tang, an aging Vietnam vet and former medic, went down with some rudimentary first-aid equipment.

"A broken ankle, dislocated shoulder and a bunch of scrapes from the fall," Tang announced once they'd rigged a harness and brought Jan to safety. "Plus she's been down there awhile so she's dehydrated."

Bill couldn't take his eyes off his wife's battered face or release his grip of her hand.

"I thought I was a dead duck," she whispered as Bill held a cup of water to her lips. She looked around at everyone, her gaze sliding past Adam and resting on Chelsea. "Some welcome we offered, huh?"

"I'm just so sorry about your home and your leg and—"

"All that can be rebuilt and fixed," Jan whispered.

"You should go to a hospital," Chelsea added.

Jan smiled. "No, honey, no institutions for me. There's work to be done here and Tang can patch me up just fine, can't you, Tang?"

"I can set the break, no problem," the former medic said as he scratched his salt-and-pepper beard. He gestured back at the gutted trailer and bombed-out yard.

"But wow, your house! Bill, what are you going to tell the authorities?"

"Nothing," Bill said.

"But—"

"But nothing. You know as well as I do that once the law gets involved, I might as well hand over my land. Those three murdering scumbags never did one ounce of good in their lives. Now they'll fertilize a few tumbleweeds."

Chelsea stood closer to Adam. "Do you think he can get away with it?"

"He might," Adam said. "Technically, I killed two of the guys."

"And I killed the other one," Chelsea said.

"I'm not anxious to try to explain any of this to anyone, are you?"

"No. But you have to wonder what the people who hired those men are going to think happened to them. Will they look for them? Don't killers have families who ask questions? I don't know, it just seems impossible that three lives can be erased without someone somewhere caring."

"Let's help clean up this mess and get out of here," Adam said.

She sighed. "So much has been destroyed. They have a lot to rebuild."

Adam nodded. He didn't add what Chelsea obviously knew. Any pictures or mementos of her that her brother once possessed were now gone. Bill might provide a story or two, but any concrete proof she had of who she was no longer existed, at least not here.

"Sorry I called the folks," Bill said while the medic worked on Jan and a contingent of others went to fire up the backhoe to dig a mass grave.

"It's not your fault," Adam said.

"Sure it is. I told them to keep it between the two of them, but Mom probably confided in Lindy."

"Who is Lindy?" Chelsea asked.

"I keep forgetting you don't remember things," Bill said. "Lindy is our gossipy twenty-one-year-old sister. Put a beer in front of her, set her on a pub stool and off she goes. If anyone wanted to know anything about you, all they'd have to do is stick close to Lindy."

Adam shook his head. "My friends knew I was coming here, too, Bill. I told both Doc and Whip."

"Would they be behind something like this?" Bill asked.

"Not consciously, not any more than Lindy would be," Adam said. "I can't guarantee one of them didn't mention our coming here to someone else, but it seems unlikely."

Bill sighed. "Either which way, this isn't a good place for Chelsea."

Where was a good place? Adam wondered. Hell if he knew. He glanced at what was left of the truck he'd bought the day before. It had suffered right along with the trailer. They were going to have to hitch a ride or hike out of here. And how long would it be before Holton thought of another attack plan from his prison cell? The only good thing Adam could think of was that no one would know where they were once they left this property. No talkative sisters or suspicious US Marshals—no one. That should provide some margin of safety.

"I have all the help I need," Bill said, and then turning to Chelsea, he added, "Will you go see how Jan is doing?"

"Of course."

As she moved away Bill dug in his pocket, withdrew a key and handed it to Adam.

"What is this for?" Adam asked.

"Jan's old van. She wants you to have it. It's got Mon-

tana plates and is registered to her under her maiden name
so no one will connect it to you."

"I can't—"

"I want you to get my sister out of here," Bill interrupted. "Take her far away. That's what Jan and I both
want, and before you get all dewy-eyed about our generous
gift, you should know the van has almost three hundred
thousand miles on it and burns oil like there's no tomorrow. Take it. Go before we dig the grave and…well, Chelsea doesn't need to see that."

"No, she doesn't," Adam agreed.

"CAR NUMBER THREE," Chelsea said as they drove away
from her brother's property.

The creaks and groans, to say nothing of the tired
shocks, gave the green van the aura of a carnival ride.

"You know what they say," Adam told her. "Third time's
the charm."

"Where are we headed?" Chelsea asked when they hit
the main highway two hours later.

"I'm not sure," Adam said. "Up until now, my priority
has been to get you someplace safe and then disappear."

"My parents—"

"Really?" he interrupted with a swift glance her way.

"No," she said. "There's no point in going there."

"Bill called your folks before we left his place," Adam
told her. "He wanted to check about Lindy. They admitted they got the family together and shared Bill's news
about your safety and that you were going to be at your
brother's house. They were all getting ready to drive to
Nevada to collect you."

"They'll kill me with love," Chelsea said.

"And not know they were doing it," Adam added.

"What about Florida?" she asked.

"You'd be willing to run away with me? You'd be breaking several laws, you know. False ID, no passport."

"I shot a man yesterday and killed one today," she said quietly. The reality of killing a man had been settling over her heart like a shroud, growing heavier as the hours passed.

Adam covered her hand with his and squeezed it. "You didn't have a choice," he said.

She nodded. As bad as killing someone felt, sitting there lamenting a necessary act seemed self-indulgent, even selfish, especially as Adam had fired the shot that ended the siege and ultimately saved them all.

He pulled into a gas station a few minutes later and they topped off the tank, added two quarts of oil to the gluttonous engine and bought sandwiches in the attached deli. They mutually decided to eat while they kept driving.

The hours piled up as they headed south, skirting Vegas, the world reduced to a million stars and broad stretches of empty land where the moonlight illuminated it. Sometime later, Adam's voice shook Chelsea from a half-dreamlike state, where she'd been lazing on a rope swing located inside her brother's chicken coop. She blinked a few times to reenter reality.

"We're both exhausted," he said.

She couldn't argue that.

"There's a motel up ahead. Let's get a room—two if you want—and try to get some sleep."

"One room," she said emphatically. She was not going to sit alone in a dark locked room, not tonight.

"Sounds good."

The motel was one of those long chains of connected rooms fronted with a swimming pool. A few motley-looking palms rustled in the slight breeze. Truthfully, Chelsea didn't care what kind of motel it was as long as it wasn't green, had beds and didn't move.

They checked in, paid cash, parked in front of unit 101 and took their meager possessions inside the room. Chelsea slumped onto a chair, and Adam sprawled across the bed.

After a while, they took turns showering. Dressed in clean clothes, they crawled beneath blessedly white sheets. For a few minutes, images of the day flashed in Chelsea's head like photographs. When Adam cleared his throat, she turned in his direction.

"You didn't get the answers to any of your questions today like we planned," he said.

"I met my brother and his wife," she said. Speaking into the dark room without the benefit of seeing his expression actually made talking easier. "He didn't really know you, though."

"I warned you about that," Adam said. "So, ask me anything you want or I can just start at the beginning and tell you the absolute factual truth of everything I know about you and everything you know—*knew*—about me."

She considered his question for several seconds. "You're willing to be honest and forthright without fear of how it may make me or yourself look?"

"Yes."

"Why now?"

"Because it's time. And because it looks as though you're stuck with me. I can't protect you if you're not close and yet when you're close, I almost get you killed. Seems to me like you deserve to know whatever you want. But on the other hand, I have to warn you there's enough… information for you to absorb that it might hit you like an overload. Doc told me that one reason you might have this amnesia is because there's a part of you that doesn't want to remember everything, that you may be protecting yourself from …pain."

"From what you know of my life, is that a possibility?" she asked after a moment spent thinking about this comment.

"Yes," he said softly. "And that's why I'm giving you the option of asking questions and learning what you want at whatever pace you're comfortable with."

She thought for a second. "We were lovers," she stated baldly.

"Yes."

"I knew it," she whispered. "I've always known it."

"You see—" he began, but she reached over and pressed her fingers against his lips.

"Not tonight," she said. "I want every detail, all at once. I want to know exactly who and what I am and what my past and future look like. But I killed a guy today and I almost died and that's a lot to assimilate. If we're driving to Florida, we're going to have a lot of time in that green van. Time to talk and think. I'd like to wait until tomorrow, Adam."

"Are you sure? I've been dragging my feet. Today underlined the stupidity of that. You can handle anything."

"Do you think so?" she asked softly.

The bed creaked as he turned on his side. She felt his face move close to hers. "I know so," he whispered. "You're an amazing woman, Chelsea Ann Pierce, whether you know it or not…you're special, unique."

"Those sound like words spoken by a man who cares about a woman," she whispered.

His lips brushed her forehead. "That's because they are," he said.

She willed him to find her mouth with his, and as his warm breath caressed her skin, her heartbeat tripled.

"Prove it," she said, unable to resist the temptation that seethed between them like molten lava. Something had changed that day, some mountain had been topped, a river forded—something had given way under the pressure of their experiences and left them in this bed, facing each other on a more level playing field than ever.

His lips finally touched hers, his perpetually short beard pleasantly brisk against her skin. The kiss lit a firecracker, sparked an explosion that cascaded into more as his hands slipped up under her T-shirt to caress her breasts. Another firecracker heralded the removal of her T-shirt and then the pink thong, and as she freed him of his boxers, they were at last naked together, alone, vulnerable and suddenly so in tune with each other they began to merge into one being.

His erection was hot and throbbing in her hand. He gently pushed her onto her back and started kissing and sucking every square inch of her from her mouth to her throat, down to her breasts, to her belly, where his hands stroked her skin. He kissed her a hundred times between navel and pelvic bone as though treasuring that most female part of her body. When he found the center of her desire, she all but jumped out of her skin. He slid inside of her with gentle urgency as they easily fell into an ageless rolling rhythm, mouths locked together, breathing labored, her hands digging into the wonderful flesh of his butt, wanting him closer, wanting to absorb him. The thought of him ever leaving her created a second of anxiety, but that disappeared as he worked his magic. When they climbed to a crescendo it felt as if the motel must have surely rocked on its foundation.

When it was over, it still wasn't over. Within a few moments, he'd started kissing her again, slowly this time, thoroughly, discovering places that sent her soaring just as she investigated the miracle of his body with her hands

and mouth. His muscles delighted her fingertips, his ear-
lobes were delectable. She felt she could kiss his eyelids
and cheekbones forever, smooth his fine hair away from
his forehead until time stopped, luxuriate in the delight of
his head buried in her throat, his heartbeat so strong it traveled right through his skin into her body. She knew they
had done all this before, she could tell—they weren't carnal
strangers. In fact, Adam Parish was the only real person
in the world to Chelsea—everyone else from Doc Fisher
to the bad guys to her brother seemed to be actors who
took their few moments on the stage and then shuffled off.

Adam was real. Adam was permanent.

Eventually, spent and replete, they fell asleep in each
other's arms.

Chelsea awoke around midnight. Adam's breathing
was deep and even, his relaxed, heavy arm warm across
her stomach. She laid there awhile, content in a way she
hadn't been in her short memory, unafraid, ready to face
the truths tomorrow would bring.

The minutes on the illuminated bedside table continued
to pass and instead of growing sleepier, she grew more and
more awake. Finally, she carefully moved his arm aside
and slid to the edge of the bed. The springs creaked as she
got to her feet but Adam's breathing didn't change. She
smiled as she crossed the room to the bathroom, flicked on
the light, closed the door behind her and washed her face.

Leaving the door ajar so a little light would spill into
the bedroom, she found her discarded underwear and put it
back on. Next she searched the bag that functioned as her
suitcase and the brush she'd bought at the pharmacy. She
went back into the bathroom to work the tangles from her
hair. When she grabbed a towel, she accidentally knocked
the clothes Adam had left draped over the towel rack to
the ground.

Leaning over to retrieve things, her attention was caught by a small gold foil card wrapped inside a wrinkled receipt. The receipt was from the last gas station they'd visited. The card was a little battered, as though it had been stuffed somewhere and folded more times than intended. Without pausing to consider whether or not she should read it, she did just that.

"'My beloved Steven,'" she whispered. "'I think I know the location of the cabin you described the night you asked me to marry you. My plan is to drop these roses in the nearby river as a way of letting you go. I don't want to do this but the reality is you're dead. I'll never stop loving you just as I wonder if I'll ever understand what really happened to you or why that man from the government asked me a million questions but wouldn't answer even one of mine. Sometimes it feels as though I'm grieving a shadow. Goodbye, my love. Rest in peace knowing I will move heaven and earth to make a wonderful life for our baby. Yours forever, Chelsea.'"

It was dated the day of the crash. On numb feet, she left the bathroom and moved like a wraith to the small desk. She picked up the courtesy pen and found the small notepad. She wrote "Goodbye, my love." Before she'd finished the sentence, she knew she'd written the note.

Of course she'd written the note. She'd been the woman on the chopper. She tore the paper from the pad and tore it into pieces.

Wait, where was this baby she mentioned? And who was Steven?

She walked back into the bathroom, flushed the shredded paper and turned sideways to run her hand over the small swelling in her belly that she had attributed to her body type. The baby was inside of her, growing.

That realization left her dizzy and she sat down on the

edge of the tub. Adam had asked her over and over again if she was bleeding anywhere, if she hurt. He'd cautioned her about lifting heavy things and tonight, when they made love, he'd caressed her abdomen with such tenderness she'd noticed it despite the burning passion racing through her veins.

He knew. He knew she was pregnant and he hadn't told her. That meant Doc probably knew, too, and that's why he'd asked those questions when he examined her. Maybe even her brother knew—everyone knew about her baby but her!

What had happened to Steven, the man she'd apparently adored? Was his death the reason she couldn't remember anything? Was she scared to face the pain that painted every word in the note she'd written?

And when had Adam really come into the picture? Had he and Steven both loved her, both wanted her? Was it possible Adam killed Steven to achieve his goal? Would a man really go that far to win an ordinary woman like her?

She picked the foil card from the floor and read it again.

Maybe he would. She'd imagined herself capable of stalking Adam—was it so far-fetched to think *he* might have been stalking *her*? Could he have killed Steven to get what he wanted? Was he some kind of psychopath? Was the baby she carried Steven's or had Adam and she—?

How could she know? Adam would tell her what he wanted her to believe. He'd been doing that from the start—he'd as much as admitted it.

She recoiled at the thought of thinking these things about him, unwilling to believe the man she'd just given heart and soul to an hour before, the man she'd felt she instinctively knew down to his core could actually be her nemesis instead of her savior.

And yet all along, she'd known she'd too readily accepted the world as he presented it. She'd attempted to fight the temptation to fit into the niche he created, but she hadn't fought hard enough.

She stood abruptly and grabbed his jeans, looking for his wallet and identification, suddenly wondering if his name was even Adam Parish. The wallet wasn't there and she recalled the way he tucked it away every night. She'd thought he was protecting it from invaders of some kind— was he really just protecting it from her?

Sneaking back into the room, she pulled on shoes, jeans and a sweater and visually gave the room a quick search. She didn't see the wallet but what did it matter? He'd bought a car using that ID, Doc Fisher had called him by that name—what would seeing it on a license mean at this point?

She closed her hand around the van keys on the desk and opened the outside door. For a second she stared back at the bed, at the slumbering man. A huge part of her wanted to wake him up and demand explanations.

But she knew he would tell her whatever he believed she wanted to hear and she also suspected she would convince herself to be satisfied with that—for a while at least. The only way this would ever be resolved was to regain her memory of Steven, the helicopter, the roses, the baby... Adam. This was something she was going to have to do herself.

Closing the motel room door was like stepping on her own heart. She wasn't sure where she was going, just that she had to get away.

Chapter Ten

For one blissful moment Adam felt totally at peace. He opened his eyes with anticipation, anxious to see Chelsea. It was a small room and she wasn't in it. Getting up, he pulled on the boxers that had wound up on the floor and walked to the bathroom, where he could now see the door was ajar.

Tapping on it, he called her name. "Chelsea? Are you all right? May I come in?"

There was no answer. Alarmed now that she might be sick or have fainted, he opened the door wide and stood there for a second looking at the empty room, taking in the fact his jeans and shirt had fallen from the towel rack, but nothing else seemed amiss.

He draped his clothes back on the towel rack, wondering why the fact they'd fallen alarmed him. He always took his wallet out of his pants at night, was determined to guard that damning picture of him and Chelsea in San Francisco. He trotted back into the room, opened the closet and took his wallet from the highest shelf, where he'd shoved it under a stack of extra bedding.

The wallet held the photo, just as it always did. Today he would use that picture and the foil card she'd included with her flowers to help explain to her his true identity and what they had meant to each other—

The thought sent a shiver through his heart. Where was the card?

It wasn't in his wallet. He must have taken it out when he bought oil for the van—it was bulky and a pain in the neck to shove into the wallet's limited space. He would have stuffed it in his jeans pocket.

He almost ran back to the bathroom, but he knew with every step that the card wasn't there. Chelsea must have found it.

What would she think?

He pulled on his clothes then scanned the table for the van keys. When he didn't see them, he opened the motel door.

The parking spot in front of their room was empty.

Within minutes, he'd put on his shoes and jogged over to the tiny motel office. It was still too early for a long check-out line, though one couple, who were apparently settling their bill, took up most of the available interior floor space. As he waited outside for them to finish, his mind raced with questions—how was he ever going to find Chelsea? Without the van, he was stranded here and even if he had wheels, what direction would she have gone?

How had he managed to handle this so poorly? Dumb question—he knew how. He'd put her off and put her off, trusting that some inner well of latent feelings for him would keep her by his side until he could face telling her the truth.

She now knew she was pregnant and no doubt believed the father of her baby and the love of her life was dead. She knew that she'd been traveling to drop flowers in an act of farewell. How would she interpret Adam's presence in the scenario?

Bottom line, she was alone out there somewhere. Holton knew about her, knew she made the perfect bait.

The couple came out of the office and Adam went inside. A young man who hadn't been at the counter the day before greeted him. "Checking out?" he asked. He looked to be in his late teens, with a gold stud in his left nostril and a half-shaved head.

"Probably," Adam said. "Have you been in the office long?"

"A couple of hours," he said. "I'm covering for my mom. What room are you in?"

"One-oh-one. Listen, did you happen to see the van parked in front of the room take off a while ago?"

"Nope."

"Do you remember if it was there when you got here this morning?"

"Nope." He narrowed his eyes. "Why? What's wrong?"

"My girl and I...had a fight," Adam said after a pause.

"She took off?"

"Yeah."

"Bummer."

"Yeah. But the thing is the van is old and unreliable and I'm worried about her. Is there a place to rent a car around here?"

"Man, you'd have to go back to Vegas for that."

Adam shook his head. This was getting worse by the moment.

"Or I could sell you my bike," the kid said.

"Your bike? What bike?"

"That Honda out there," he said, gesturing to the right of the office. Adam followed his lead and saw a beat-up old red motorcycle chained to the Coke machine.

"Does it run?"

"Like a bat out of hell," the kid said. "It's loud and I won't kid you, it's got...issues, but it's a real ass-burner. It'll take you where you want to go."

"And you're willing to sell it?"

"Mom kind of gave me an ultimatum," he said. "You know how it is."

"How much?" Adam asked.

"Eight hundred."

"Assuming it runs, I'll give you five and you throw in a helmet," Adam countered.

"Six," the kid said, then reached behind him and produced a black helmet that he set in front of Adam.

Adam considered his options, then picked up the helmet. "Get my bill ready, I'll be right back."

ADAM STRAPPED ALL his gear on the back and took off. The kid hadn't been bluffing—the bike could move. As he neared the outskirts of the tiny hamlet, he found a set of highway mileage signs pointing in three directions. Right to Los Angeles, straight ahead to Phoenix and left to Santa Fe.

Phoenix was near his home, but why would Chelsea choose to go to Arizona? Santa Fe was in the direction they would have taken had they been together, traveling toward Florida, but again, would Chelsea charge off into the unknown under the circumstances? He doubted it. With her memory compromised, there were already too many unknowns in her life. That left Los Angeles, which, of course, also meant a highway that would eventually lead to the Bay Area and her parents and family.

He turned right.

The bike was as loud as advertised, too. Between the sun beating down, the vibration of the cycle and the unrelenting screech of the engine, all his senses were on overload. The wound in his side protested every bump. He kept his eyes peeled for an old green van either traveling on the road, broken down beside it or pulled into a car rest or parking lot. The miles droned on, the trip made longer by his determination to stop at every establishment he passed to ask the proprietors if they'd sold oil to anyone with a green van or seen anyone in trouble. He was flying blind and he knew it.

It would have helped to have some idea when she took off. The earliest it could have been was after they made love. That meant she could have up to a four-hour lead. Four hours at even fifty miles an hour gave her two hundred miles. She could be approaching Los Angeles by now if the car had held up. How in the world would he ever find her there? He'd have to head to the small town of Bodega Bay and her parents and hope to intercept her but that could be days from now. Judging by what had happened at Chelsea's brother's place, Holton must have placed someone in Bodega Bay to watch her family and listen to her talkative sister. Was that someone still there?

The debacle at Bill's place also brought out the undeniable fact that the three men sent there to fake an accidental bombing had failed in their attempt and subsequently disappeared off the face of the earth. Whoever had sent them had to have figured this out by now.

And what about Ron Ballard? If a US marshal was involved in this, how much did he know and what kind of advantages did he have when it came to ferreting out information? Adam had bought two vehicles now using his real ID. Did someone have a flag out for that contingency? Adam didn't know, but he wouldn't be surprised to find that Ballard had a way of keeping abreast of Adam's location.

No matter. There was nothing to be done but continue trying. This was his lover and his baby—his family, his life and all of it was in danger because of him. There was no quitting.

AFTER FIFTY MILES, Adam admitted to himself that he needed a break of more than a couple of minutes. Coffee, maybe something to eat, a respite from constant vibrations and the pain to the knife gash that flared as he leaned forward to grasp the handlebars. He pulled up in front of a small gas station advertising cold drinks and snacks.

Inside, he found an older man behind the counter. He ordered coffee and snatched a prepackaged pastry off the shelf then downed one of his antibiotics and a couple of aspirin. A few other travelers meandered around. Probably, like Adam, they loitered as much for the air conditioning as they did the merchandise.

Adam spied a produce section in the cooler and chose an apple to take along for a future snack. As he approached the counter to pay for everything, a tinkling bell announced another man coming into the store through a small back door. He nodded at Adam as he walked behind the counter. "I finally got it out of her, Sam," he said to the guy ringing up Adam's purchases.

"Yeah? What's her problem, then?"

"She's broke. We're going to have to help her out."

Sam shook his head. "We can't just give her money," he said.

"The kid doesn't have a penny. Don't be so damn cheap."

"I'm frugal, not cheap," Sam said with a sigh as he handed Adam his change. He shook his gray head. "On the other hand, I guess we can't have her parked out back forever. What does she need exactly?"

"A couple of quarts of oil, that's all."

Adam looked up quickly.

"That's not too bad," said Sam. "Okay, just give it to her and get her out of here."

"Someone needs oil for their vehicle?" Adam said.

The second man nodded. "Some little gal. Needs a couple of quarts."

"Where is she?"

Sam's eyes narrowed. "Why do you want to know?"

Adam smiled. "I had some bad luck lately. Someone helped me get back on my feet on the condition I pay it forward. This sounds like an opportunity to do just that. Plus I'm a mechanic. If there's something else wrong with her car, maybe I can help."

Sam nodded, obviously delighted to get off the hook. "She's parked out back under the only tree around. Been sitting out there all morning."

"She was too shy to ask for a handout," the second guy added. "I had to worm what was wrong out of her. It doesn't seem she knows anything about cars and that old van she's driving is on its last legs."

"Point the way," Adam said, "but first sell me a half-dozen bottles of motor oil. Might as well get her a few spares. Oh, and add in one of those breakfast burritos you have back there, a cup of coffee and a bottle of orange juice."

"That's mighty decent of you," the second man said as he filled a box with the right number of oil bottles from a display. Sam gathered the food and rang everything up, a big smile on his wrinkled face as he presented the total to Adam.

CHELSEA, SITTING INSIDE the sliding side door of the wretched van and fanning herself with a folded road map of Montana, heard approaching footsteps and held her breath. It was no doubt Thomas, the nice older guy who worked at the store. He'd been out to talk to her three different times until she'd finally admitted she didn't have the money to pour more oil into this blasted engine.

If she hadn't bought that breakfast yesterday, she'd have had enough to pour oil into this thing at least until California. But she knew that would have only been a stop-gap measure. The Bay Area was a long way from Los Angeles. Gas, oil, food—all of it took money. She'd set off ill-prepared, fleeing on emotional energy alone, not factoring in logic.

Hopefully, Thomas had taken pity on her and was bringing the oil, as he'd hinted he might. It was either accept a handout or sit out here until she keeled over from heat exhaustion or, worse, Adam found her. Not good, not when she had a baby to consider.

The footsteps grew closer and she stood up, a smile in place for Thomas, a smile that slid from her lips when she saw Adam instead. She sat back down on the floor of the van and covered her eyes with her hands.

He sat down beside her. A moment later, she smelled the aroma of hot coffee. "You found me," she whispered through her fingers.

"Dumb luck," he said. "Here, I thought you might need this."

She dropped her hands. Ignoring the proffered coffee, she met his gaze. "I had to leave," she said.

"I know. You saw the card, didn't you? The one you wrote."

"Yes. I know about my baby, I know about Steven. Adam, who was he? Did you—did you kill him?"

He set aside the coffee and dug his wallet out of his pocket as he answered. "In a way, but not how you think," he said. He opened the wallet, took out a photograph and handed it to her.

She faced both of their images, standing side by side, smiling, Adam's arm around her shoulder. They both looked relaxed and happy. It was dated two months earlier. And there was her handwriting again. It identified Adam as Steven. "I don't understand—"

"You will in a while," he said. "I wish you'd woken me up and asked me about this," he added.

"I was scared and angry and didn't trust my feelings. After what we shared last night—"

"Wasn't that a pretty good reason to give me a chance to explain?" he interrupted.

"You've had days to explain," she said softly as she gave in to the aroma of fresh, hot coffee and picked up the paper cup.

"True. Okay, here we go. My name really is Adam Parish. I really did turn state's evidence against a snake of a man accused of human trafficking. I got him convicted. Because of his threats and connections, the US Marshals offered me a new identity in a new state and I took it. I moved to San Francisco, where I got a job working construction. I met you just as I said I did. I didn't tell you about my past because it wasn't allowed and because I knew it might put you in danger if you knew the truth. I fell in love with you and you with me. All that is true."

"And you're my baby's father?"

"Absolutely."

"How did you 'die?'"

"One of the snake's men found out where I was. I'm not sure how. He came after me, right on the night I asked you to be my wife. I managed to subdue him."

"You mean you killed him," she said.

"Yes. I had worked out my own escape route if this event should ever come to pass. I'd purchased a plane and stored it out of town, kept my own identity… Anyway, there was this marshal who more or less 'handled' me and I didn't trust him. I knew if my cover was blown I'd have to disappear for good, so I staged my death by putting the plane on autopilot and parachuting to safety. The plane went down into a glacier lake. I knew they couldn't dredge it. The only body aboard the plane was that of the would-be killer."

"And you didn't tell me."

"I didn't know you were pregnant, Chelsea."

"But you knew I would mourn you, didn't you?"

"Yes."

"And you left me behind, anyway, ignorant and grieving. I can't imagine how devastated I was." He said nothing. "So the police questioned me. I gathered that much from the note."

"Yes, they apparently did."

"Who knows what I told them?"

"You didn't really know anything except what I told you," he said.

"The story of our relationship. You in control of all of the information, calling the shots. It seems the only independent thing I did was my ill-fated grand gesture to leave you at the motel."

"Chelsea—"

"One of the bad guys somehow got on that helicopter with me," she continued. "And he died when the chopper crashed and you were there on the scene because you weren't dead, you were hiding."

"Yes," he said, his body tense.

"So why didn't you explain all of this when you found me on the chopper?"

"I planned to, but then I discovered your memory was gone. I decided to wait until it…came back."

"You could have shown me that picture."

"By then I'd given you my real name instead of the Steven that's written on the photo."

"So in other words, you would have had to tell me you left me."

He nodded.

She stared into his eyes. "I can tell from that note that you broke my heart," she said, "and I have to assume since you didn't know I was coming to drop those flowers that you didn't even try to contact me. You just…left."

He winced but met her gaze. "That's pretty much it," he said. "I wasn't sure the hit man had come alone. I couldn't chance anyone following me to you, which they did, anyway. These people are dangerous. I loved you—love you—too much—"

She held up her hand to silence him. "Your decision caused an innocent pilot—at least he might have been innocent—to die, and you've lied or omitted things since the moment you laid eyes on me again. And now we're running for our lives and more people have been hurt or killed. So tell me this, Adam. When does it stop?"

"When we get to Florida."

"No. That won't stop it. They'll still look for you. And why? Revenge? In the face of all the mayhem and death, doesn't that reason seem kind of implausible? What else aren't you telling me?"

"I don't know," he said. "That's the truth. I've thought the same thing about the degree of vengeance but I have no idea why it's so intense."

"But you've kept with one plan. Escape. Run."

He looked stricken and any pleasure she might have found in challenging him to assuage her own hurt fled. She yearned to cup his face and kiss his lips, ached to hold him. She could tell he loved her, or at least thought he did, and she knew she had deep feelings for him, but those feelings were confused. The ultimate conclusion was that the reality he had created and was continuing to create had no future, especially in light of the fact there was an innocent new life to consider.

"From the beginning, my plan was to get out of the country and let all this animosity wear down. I've been a loner since my dad died. It's my default nature to take care of unpleasant things on my own and not involve anyone else."

"But you asked me to marry you. And whether you knew it or not, you helped create another life."

"I know. And since you came back into the picture, my focus has been to make sure you're safe. I haven't been very successful at that."

"Maybe it's time for a new plan," she said.

"Like what?"

"I don't know, like being part of a team that gets to the bottom of what's really going on, by letting me help you. By thinking of me as an adult to be leaned on and not a child to be protected. I would like my baby to have a father."

"You're willing to stick with me?"

"I don't know, Adam. Long-term, I can't promise anything. I don't know for sure how deep my resentment toward you runs and I might not know that until my memory returns. If Doc Fisher was right about my amnesia being caused by fear of pain, it's pretty obvious to me that you're the cause."

"I know," he said.

"However, I will stay with you as long as it takes for you to get your life back and assure a future, to make sure our baby won't fall victim to this same danger. That I'll stick around for."

"That's a beginning," he said.

She nodded.

They sat in silence for several minutes until he finally

got to his feet. "I'll get the van running again and we'll take off."

"If you change your mind and run again, you're doing it alone," she warned him.

He touched the top of her shoulder and stared down at her. "You're right, it's time to get to the bottom of this."

"How?"

"By using my head instead of my feet. All I ask is that you trust me."

"I'll try," she said as she stood. "It's up to you."

He reached into the box containing several quarts of oil and took out a bottle of juice and a wrapped burrito, which he offered to her. "This will give you something to do while I get this heap running."

"Thanks."

He leaned toward her and she moved toward him. The kiss felt like a lover's version of a handshake at first, but then Adam gripped the back of her head and touched her lips with his tongue, and the kiss blossomed into more.

She pulled away. He stared into her eyes and she could see that he understood. They could not go back to where they'd been just hours before. She would stick by him for their baby's sake.

That's all she could guarantee.

Chapter Eleven

"We're going to Hard Rock, Arizona," Adam announced after he'd rigged a ramp to roll the motorcycle into the back of the van. He tied the bike upright and slammed the door. "We're going to need to change our appearances."

She climbed into the passenger seat as he got behind the wheel. "Is Hard Rock a big place?" she asked. "Do you know a lot of people?"

"It's pretty small, actually, and I hardly know anyone. I moved there from Tucson to take the job as bodyguard for Devin Holton and his wife, Aimee. Which brings up the matter that we have to assume Holton's men have reported my current bleached hair and your description must have been circulated. Have you ever wanted to be a redhead?"

"How do I know? But what the heck, why not? What do we do when we get to Hard Rock?" she asked.

"For starters, I want to get some idea what Holton's wife did after he went to prison."

"Wouldn't she just stay at their house?"

"It's a big estate. The government must have seized it upon conviction. But there may still be someone I know hanging around up there, so I can't poke around as Adam Parish. I think I'll use my dad's name, Frank, and my mother's surname, Mason. As for what comes after that, it depends on what I find. Holton had a few cronies—maybe I can infiltrate them and get wind of what's going on."

"Sooner or later, won't they recognize you?"

"Maybe not. A good bodyguard's face is almost invisible. You're more a walking muscle with a gun than you are a human being."

"But they must have seen you at the trial."

"Most of them stayed away from that trial unless they were subpoenaed. It had been moved to Tucson so it wasn't in their backyard. Plus I grew a big old beard and wore a ponytail."

"I'll need a new name, too," she said. "I think I'll call myself Daisy Hanks."

"Cute," he said. "Let's get another room and change our appearance."

Two hours later, Chelsea had short red hair and bright red lips. Adam's hair was the same length as his beard, less than half an inch. When he donned the reflective glasses Chelsea had chosen, he hardly recognized himself.

Adam admitted that he dreaded the moment Whip learned he was back in Arizona. The man had made it pretty clear that he was in favor of Adam getting out of the country—this change of plans would no doubt alarm him.

On the other hand, maybe he'd heard something about US Marshal Ron Ballard or discovered whoever was acting as liaison between Holton and the outside. Or even better, maybe he'd gleaned some clue as to why Holton seemed to be moving heaven and earth to hunt down and eliminate Adam.

IT TOOK UNTIL the next afternoon to get to Hard Rock and by the time they drove into the small hamlet, they were tired, hot and hungry. They stopped to eat tacos from a food truck doing brisk business and settled at one of several picnic tables, commenting on how good the food was with every other bite. Chelsea wasn't fooled by Adam's idle chatter. His obvious case of nerves set her on edge.

The feeling was enhanced when he suddenly shaded his face with one hand and looked down at the table. "What's wrong?" she asked.

"Dennis is over there."

"Who's Dennis?"

"Dennis Woods, a very old friend. He's the one who bought my parents' house when I went into the program."

She looked toward the food truck. Two women ordered lunch at the window, while one man stood behind them, hands shoved in his pockets. He caught Chelsea staring at him and flashed her a brilliant smile. She looked away at once.

"Did he see you?"

"Yes. But remember, he doesn't know me from a hole in the wall. He probably thinks I'm flirting with him."

"We'd better get out of here," he said.

But Dennis turned as Adam stood. His eyes narrowed and then he grinned. "Adam?" he called. "Adam Parish, is that you? Man, I haven't seen you in forever. Where the hell have you been?"

He said all this as he strode across the grass, headed for Adam, who was powerless to quiet him without creating more of a scene.

"Dennis," Adam said, extending his hand.

Dennis shook it vigorously, then turned his attention to Chelsea. "Do we have you to blame for Adam's mysterious disappearance? Not that I would blame him."

Adam performed the introductions. "What are you doing all the way up here in Hard Rock?" he asked.

Dennis laughed. "It's only an hour or so from Tucson, you idiot. Anyway, I'm doing a job, what else? My company is replumbing the old Stop and Shop. They're making it into a tropical fish store." He paused for a second. "Tell me what you've been up to. I called around trying to find you—"

"Why? Is anything wrong?"

Dennis laughed. "Man, you're jumpy, aren't you?" He looked at Chelsea and shook his head. "Our boy is wound a little tight."

"Tell me about it," she said with a smile for Adam.

Dennis slapped Adam on the shoulder. "Well, the main reason was to tell you that Stacy is pregnant again. As a matter of fact, the baby is due in three weeks. We're growing right out of your old house."

"Congratulations," Adam said after a swift glance at Chelsea's stomach.

"The other reason is the exterminators found something that must belong to you when they were crawling around the basement looking for termites."

"What do you mean?"

"A sealed box, pushed way up in the crawl space under the smallest bedroom there in the front. Someone wrote Do Not Open on it. Ring any bells?"

"None."

"Didn't your dad build that house when you were a baby?"

"Yeah."

"So the box has to have belonged to someone in your family, ergo, as the last surviving member, it's yours."

"So what's in it? Discarded toys, old dishes?" Adam asked.

"I asked around but no one knew where you'd gone, so I opened it to make sure it wasn't trash or something. It looked like a lot of papers so I taped it back up. It's heavy, I will say that."

"Interesting," Adam said in an offhand manner. But Chelsea heard the curiosity in his voice and she suspected Dennis did, too. "Where is it now?" he added.

"We were getting ready to paint the inside of the house so I took it and a lot of other things to our storage garage," Dennis said. "Good thing I did, too, because the house was broken into a few days later."

"Oh, no, did you lose a lot?"

"Just some electronics, stuff like that, but they tore the place up pretty good. Thankfully no one was home, no one got hurt." He paused and shook his head. "Sorry, bro, I forgot for a moment about your mom and…everything."

"It's okay."

Dennis looked at Chelsea. "His mom was the greatest. Always went to bat for 'her kids.' Remember, Adam, re-member that girl who ran away from home?"

"I remember," Adam said, his voice subdued.

"Your mom was determined to find her and get her back in school. Ms. Parish was just outright amazing."

"I wish I could have known her," Chelsea said.

"Yeah." He looked back at Adam. "I'm real glad you're back. I hope you can stick around."

"Me, too," Adam said.

"I know Stacy will want to see you. And you, too," he added with a glance at Chelsea. "Maybe you guys could come for dinner."

"Let's talk about it in a few days," Adam said. "Right now would it be too much trouble for you to get the box out of storage?"

"No trouble at all. The place is on the way home. I'll be back in Hard Rock tomorrow so I could give it to you then. Will you still be here?"

"I'll be here."

"Say four or so, right where we're standing?"

"Sounds good. And until we can talk some more, mind not saying anything to anybody about my being here?"

"Always the man of mystery," Dennis said. "Sure, why not?" He glanced back at the taco truck. "I'd better go order something. See you tomorrow." He looked at Chelsea and added, "Great meeting you."

As Dennis returned to the truck, Adam and Chelsea walked across the street to the van.

"You okay?" she asked him as he unlocked and opened the back door. He sat on the floor of the van and pulled her to stand between his legs before wrapping his arms around her waist and resting his head against her breasts.

"Adam?" she prodded. "Are you okay? Do you have any idea what's inside that box?"

"No," he said, lifting his head to look at her. "It's hard to picture my mother crawling around under the house with all the spiders and bugs, so that leaves Dad. I can't stop thinking about that appointment my mom had with the police chief. Dad could have cleaned out any evidence she'd intended to give the chief to prove he was running wild. Maybe he had a diary or something, maybe he crossed a legal or ethical line—maybe he hid what he found under the house after he—"

"Killed her? Oh, Adam, honey, you're borrowing trouble," Chelsea cautioned. "Wait and see what's in the box."

"I've never told anyone this," he whispered without looking at her. "I heard the fight they had the night before she was killed. She was begging him to tell the chief something and he kept saying he couldn't. He was drinking, she was crying. The last thing I heard was her saying she'd do it herself and then it sounded like he slapped her. I left the house when he started apologizing."

"Adam, listen to me," Chelsea said, lifting his chin to stare into his deep gray eyes. "You were a kid interpreting what you heard. Who knows what was really going on or who slapped who?"

He rested his head against her again, hugging her tight as though grounding himself. "It killed me not to tell Dennis you're having our baby."

"Why didn't you?"

"That's what normal people do. They hold normal conversations. I don't feel very normal right now, do you?"

"No."

He was quiet. She'd been trying to stay at least a little aloof, but his vulnerability shook her. She smoothed the back of his head and ran her hands down his neck to his broad shoulders. "Being here is hard for you, isn't it?"

"I just hadn't counted on running into Dennis and all these old feelings… He lived three doors down from me when we were in school. I've known him forever, but so much has happened in the last year or so that today he seemed like a stranger." He looked up at her, the expression in his gray eyes unfathomable.

"When this is over, we'll go have dinner with him and Stacy, who I assume is his wife. You'll have a couple of beers and talk about old times—it will all come back." She leaned down and brushed his lips with hers.

"How do you know?" he murmured.

"Isn't this what you keep telling me? My memory will return and presto, I'll have a family I remember, friends, a career…our past?"

"For better or worse," he said.

"Exactly."

He stood up. "Then it's time to make it happen. I'm going to take the motorcycle up to the Holton place."

"Okay. I'll take the van into the city center. I need some

walking-around money." He gave her his wallet. "Whoa," she said as she glimpsed a row of large-denomination bills.

"You're looking at the bank of Adam," he said.

"What about later, when this is over?"

"I'll have to make more," he said. "But right now, my main goal is to keep both of us alive." As she stared at the money and absorbed his words, he took out a fifty and handed it to her. "Is that enough?"

"Plenty. Adam, did you ever tell me what kind of human trafficker Holton was?" she asked as he opened the back of the van and climbed inside. Kneeling by the bike, he started untying the knots he'd created to keep it upright.

"The worst kind. Young girls used as sex slaves. While hiding behind a more or less legitimate commodities business, he coerced, corrupted, bought and sold teenagers."

Chelsea shuddered. "That's just awful."

"Yes. And now he's sitting in a nice clean jail cell getting three meals a day and orchestrating this assault on you and me and heaven knows who else, while many of the girls whose childhoods he stole still struggle to survive drug addictions and sex slavery. Doesn't seem very fair, does it?"

Chelsea helped him get the bike out of the van. "That's an understatement but at least you helped put an end to it. That's got to make you feel good."

He grabbed the helmet. "It does. I couldn't save those who were lost into the ether but at least it's not still continuing, at least not with Holton."

She stared into his eyes, caught up in a wellspring of emotion. Chills ran up her spine and arms, radiating across her shoulders, and in a complete turnaround, she suddenly wished they were on their way to Florida, still running, still hiding.

Instead they stood in what felt like the lion's den.

THIRTY-EIGHT MILES of more or less straight highway bordered by fields, cactus, rocks and tired old buildings connected Hard Rock and the Holton property. Hazy mountains in the distance glimmered in the afternoon heat. Many of the small farms and ranches along the way could only be reached via long, dusty driveways, leaving acreage close to the highway. One farm appeared to have tried raising a grain crop. Whatever it had been, it was now a few acres of what looked like shriveling yellow weeds. In another month, even those would dry up and disappear.

Adam wasn't sure the mesa that Holton had owned was really a mesa. It did have three sheer, vertical sides, but one sloped enough for some enterprising soul in the past to have created an access road. This road was usually traffic-free, so Adam was surprised to pass a couple of trucks. He wondered if there were new owners now.

The small guard shack at the top of the road stood empty and he drove onto the property unchallenged. He knew from experience that the main house was at the far northern edge. Other than the main house and the staff quarters, the only other major structures on the property were a new storage shed and an old house and goat barn that had been occupied years before by homesteaders, who'd tried to raise goats but gave up after several disasters wiped out the herd.

He slowed down the bike when he caught sight of a building under construction. He came across what appeared to be a road leading in that direction and, out of curiosity, he turned.

Judging from the boxlike contours, it was going to be a modern-looking structure. Had the acreage been divided into lots and sold? Would the mesa someday resemble a subdivision? That would really set Holton off. He'd liked being the king of his mesa.

Half a dozen vehicles cluttered the work site, along with more than a dozen workmen. Adam stopped the motorcycle next to a white trailer marked with a sign that identified it as the project office for Diaz Construction. The familiar noises of saws, hammers, drills and men shouting to be heard over the din filled his ears and reminded him of San Francisco.

This was as good a place as any to start asking questions and narrowing down possibilities. No doubt these people would also know what had become of Aimee Holton. He took off his helmet but kept the sunglasses in place. Who knew whom he might run in to around here? He wasn't taking any chances of being recognized.

CHELSEA FOUND A parking spot and took off on foot. Her plan was to strike up a conversation with someone willing to talk about Aimee Holton. In a small town, Devin Holton's arrest, trial and conviction had to have fueled the rumor mill for months. Surely someone would know where his wife went after she lost her home.

Occasionally Chelsea caught an unexpected glimpse of the small bump in her abdomen in a shop window. Until today, she'd not yet started to think of herself as a mother-to-be and that realization now filled her with a mix of joy and trepidation. What if her memory never came back? Sure, she could get reacquainted with her old life, with family and friends, but would she ever regain the connection to them she must have once felt? On top of that, the possibility of losing Adam terrified her, but that created another conundrum. Did she feel so close to him because he was the only familiar person on earth? She'd accused him of fear—was she just as guilty?

Well, at least she and her baby would start out on the same playing field.

The first business she reached was a furniture store. The sole saleswoman was so focused on selling the brocaded chair Chelsea had feigned an interest in that all her leading questions and comments fizzled out and died.

Next she found a clothing store, and for a moment, she stood outside the window admiring the pink, form-fitting dress on the mannequin, as it was so unlike the jeans and T-shirts she currently lived in. She wondered for a second what her closet at home looked like, then stepped inside. The dress from the window seemed to call to her from the back of the store, where one just like it shone as a glittery beacon of femininity. She wove her way through the circular racks and this time was able to touch the silky fabric and admire the daring plunge of the neckline. She could almost imagine Adam's expression if she showed up wearing this dress...

"Beautiful, isn't it?" a saleswoman said, startling Chelsea out of her daydream.

"Very."

"It would be lovely on you." She looked Chelsea up and down, and took another off the rack. "I bet this is your size."

"I couldn't," Chelsea said.

The saleswoman smiled. "It's a slow day and I would love to see this dress on a grown woman who can pull it off. Please?"

Her comment seemed strange to Chelsea. She shrugged. "Why not?"

After putting it on, she stared at her red-headed bedazzled reflection in the mirror. She had a gut feeling she'd never dressed like this in her life, but she had to admit the garment made her breasts look bountiful and her hips enticing. She opened the curtain and faced the saleswoman, a striking brunette, who smiled.

"That dress was made for you."

"I'm pregnant," Chelsea said. It was the first time she'd said it to anyone but Adam.

"That's wonderful. I guess you won't need a tight-fitting slinky dress, will you?"

"Not really," Chelsea agreed. "But it was fun to try it on. I wondered, though, why you said what you did, you know, about seeing the dress on a grown woman?"

The saleswoman straightened the skirt. "Someone else bought this same dress this morning. Actually, it was an older guy buying it for his granddaughter. She couldn't have been over fifteen and she appeared mortified by the way she looked in it. I tried to talk the man out of buying it but he said she'd like it when she got used to it."

"It really bothered you," Chelsea commented.

The woman nodded. "The look on the kid's face got to me. Grandfathers shouldn't shop for young girls."

"Isn't it hard on guys of all ages to figure out women's attire?" Chelsea asked softly.

The woman shook her head. "Maybe, but anyone could see the child was way too self-conscious to wear something so revealing. It'll make her want to hide in a corner." She caught herself and sighed. "I have a thirteen-year-old daughter at home. I guess I'm kind of sensitive to things like this. Now, what are you looking for?"

Chelsea started to make up a story about needing a yellow blouse and then decided against inventing a story. "Do you know Aimee Holton?"

"Kind of," the woman said. "She came in here once, scoffed at our selection and left." Her expressive eyebrows furrowed. "Why do you ask?"

"I was wondering what she's like," Chelsea said, and suddenly did a one-eighty and invented a tale to explain her curiosity. "I'm a chef and I'm thinking of working for her."

"Yeah, I heard her cook quit again."

"Really?"

The chime on the door rang as a woman entered the store. *"Buenas tardes,"* the saleswoman called. *"Ahora vuelvo."*

The customer waved a hand. *"Bien."*

And Chelsea almost gaped. She'd understood every word! Who knew?

"Ms. Holton has an ad up at the culinary store across the street and the girls over there like to…chat," the saleswoman said, turning her attention back to Chelsea. "They told me she wanted them to cater a party she has planned for two days from now but they declined." She arched her eyebrows. "You can extrapolate from that what you like."

Chelsea nodded. Once outside she spied the culinary store across the street and crossed the road. If anyone knew about Aimee Holton, it sounded like it would be the people who ran this store.

Chapter Twelve

Adam hadn't taken three steps before the trailer door opened and a slender middle-aged guy carrying a set of blueprints emerged. He descended the two stairs before addressing Adam. "You must be here about the electrician job," he said. "You have to talk to that man walking up the path."

Adam turned toward the path leading up from the new construction site. He found a man with piercing black eyes and colorful tattoos running up his tanned arms. The hard hat perched on his black hair was emblazoned with Diaz Construction on its brim. "I'm not here about a job," Adam said. "I used to know a family who lived up here."

The man with the blueprints shook his head. "I'm a recent transplant from New Mexico," he said. "The only name I know is Holton."

The other man approached and introduced himself. "Diego Diaz," he said. "The people who originally built the little farm on the other side of this property were named Mendoza."

Adam introduced himself as Frank Mason. "I must have the wrong place." He raised his gaze to peer over the few trees and contour of the land. "Looks like the house you're building is a big one."

"Sixty-five hundred square feet," Diaz said. He looked at the man with the blueprints. "You headed back to town?"

"Yeah. I'll work on the modifications and get back to you by Monday."

"Thanks."

"Owners change their mind?" Adam asked Diaz.

"Don't they always?"

"Every job I've ever worked on, yeah, they sure do."

"You've worked construction? Are you here about the electrician job?"

"When I got tired of being a cop I worked for a crew up north. But, you know, electricity is a different matter than pounding nails or putting up drywall."

"That it is. You from around here?"

"Just traveling through. On vacation, kind of."

"That must be nice."

Adam laughed. "I'm on a shoestring so that means not quite as nice as you might think. I stop here and there and work for a few days, then move on."

Diaz groaned. "Sounds kind of cool. At home I've got a pregnant wife and two little kids and out here I have a finicky owner who changes her mind every other day. Now she wants a designer refrigerator that's going to take up two thirds of the wall which means the stove has to be moved and rewired. Last week it was a skylight in the entry. — It's one thing after another with Aimee. Anyway, what you're doing right now sounds pretty good sometimes."

Aimee still lived here? How could that be? As Adam commiserated with Diaz, he noticed Diaz studying him. "So, tell me, Frank," he said at last. "How would you feel about a short-term job? I'm asking because you said you used to be a cop and this might be right up your alley."

"What do you have in mind?" Adam asked.

"A sort of watchman thing."

"Are you losing supplies or something?"

"We take our tools with us every night or lock them up in the trailer, but someone is messing with stuff and now it's escalated to vandalism. They've been spray-painting some pretty nasty words, too. I mean, given the nature of what landed Mr. Holton in prison, it isn't too surprising, but that's not his wife's fault. We clean it up when we find it so she won't see it. That takes time and as they say, time is money. I think it's a few teens from town, but I need to know for sure before I go accusing them. They're well-off kids, the sheriff would laugh at me if I came to him with nothing but suspicions."

"Why not just put someone at the guard shack?"

"The owner nixed a guard on the road. I'd stay out here myself, but the wife needs me at home and my guys won't do any overtime until the boss catches up on their wages. Anyway, there's a room off the workshop you could bunk in. It's not fancy—"

"Neither are the motels I frequent," Adam interjected.

"You'd make my life easier, earn a little cash, then ride off into the sunset just like the Lone Ranger."

Adam laughed, but then grew serious. "I'm not interested in getting involved with the law," he said. "If your proof requires eyewitness testimony, I'll have to pass."

"Then get some kind of proof that doesn't depend on your input."

"Like what?"

"Listen, you're a big guy with a certain…air about you. I have faith you'll figure something out."

Adam stuck out his hand. "I'll give it a shot. If I think it's impossible, I'll let you know so you can hire someone else."

"Deal. Come on down to the house and I'll fill you in."

After an enlightening hour, Adam pulled on his helmet and mounted his bike. He had a job, but he also had misgivings. In his desire to look different to Holton's henchmen, he'd actually gone back to looking more like himself, as proven by Dennis's easy recognition of him. Aimee might do the same—they had lived on top of each other for the six months he worked for and spied on her husband. His hope was that from the outside like this, on her land but not in her space, he could watch who came and went.

There was only one hitch. Nights spent here meant nights alone for Chelsea. How would that work? If the danger was here, how could he leave her?

The road curved to the right and straightened out as it approached the exit. His mouth all but dropped open when he saw an unmistakable green van drive through the gate. What was Chelsea doing here? Had something gone wrong in town? He automatically slowed down and pulled to the side of the road, assuming she would do the same, but she drove right past him, a slight nod of her head the only clue she'd registered his presence. He turned and watched her continue up the hill, fighting the urge to follow her.

Back in town, he parked on the street near the taco truck, found a palm tree casting a bit of shade and sat on the ground to wait.

CHELSEA FOUND A spot across the street from Adam's motorcycle. He sat on the ground several yards away but as he saw her park, he got to his feet and jogged across the street.

"What were you doing up on the mesa?" he asked before the door had even closed. "Why didn't you pull over and talk to me?"

She shook her head. He looked hot and stressed. "Man, your friend Dennis is right, you are wired. Remember the whole treat-me-like-an-adult speech I gave you yesterday?"

He sat very still for a moment and then took a deep breath. "I remember it. I'm sorry."

She smiled. "Thank you. I didn't stop because who knows who was watching that road and why advertise we know each other?" She shifted her body position so she could face him and added, "I went for a job interview."

"A job interview for what?"

"I'm the new cook. And the first thing Aimee Holton confided was that she is off to visit her husband a week from now."

"Looks like she's sticking by her man," Adam said. "Did she mention any reason she was off to see Devin?"

"She said she was 'reporting in.' She didn't explain what that meant."

"Interesting," Adam said. "Why exactly do you want a job working for her?"

"Isn't it obvious?" Chelsea asked. "I'll be inside the house. I can find out if she's bitter against you. I can see what makes her tick."

"Honey," he said, "I was her bodyguard for six months. Money makes her tick. Period."

"But you haven't seen her recently," Chelsea pointed out.

"True. The last time I saw her was when she sashayed into her husband's trial wearing several thousands of dollars' worth of designer clothes and claimed her husband was as innocent as the day was long. She called him a pillar of the community and a loving spouse while she dabbed at crocodile tears with a tissue. The jury saw right through her. It only took them two hours to reach a guilty verdict.

Chelsea smiled. "She may have changed. For instance, I have a feeling she has a new boyfriend."

"What gave you that impression?"

"She took a call while I was whipping her up a sandwich. It was clear she was talking to a man. She got all flirty. I think she mentioned the name Tom."

"Tom Nolan?"

"I didn't hear a last name. Who is Tom Nolan?"

"One of her hubby's cohorts. The prosecutor thought he might be involved in some of Holton's other criminal activities, but there wasn't enough evidence to indict him. The dude is married, though. Tell me how this job for Aimee Holton came about."

She explained about the women at the kitchen store not wanting to cater her party.

"I wonder if we could get a guest list," Adam mused.

"I could try," she said.

"Okay. Wait a second. Didn't Aimee ask to see some sort of identification?

"Nope. I mentioned my purse had been stolen and she shrugged. Said she paid the help in cash, so what did it matter? I don't think she's too worried about breaking little laws."

"Or maybe big ones, either," he said.

"Okay," Chelsea announced. "It's your turn. Tell me about your afternoon."

"Well, believe it or not, I got a job up there, too, kind of undercover work for the foreman building the new house. The job does come with a condition, however."

Chelsea raised her eyebrows. "You have to sleep with the boss? She's really quite attractive, but—"

"*My* boss is a forty-year-old dude with two kids and another on the way," he interrupted.

She grinned. "Good luck with that."

"The thing is I'm going to have to spend nights on the estate. Since I have to be away, maybe you could stay with Whip."

"I don't even know him! Besides, when Ms. Holton

found out I was just traveling through town she got worried I wouldn't have a kitchen to practice making goodies. She offered me a room for a couple of days and I, of course, accepted."

"That means our deadline is Friday night. If we can't figure out if anyone attached to the estate is involved in Holton's vendetta by then it's time to look elsewhere."

"Like where?"

"One problem at a time, okay?" He touched her face, ran a finger over her mouth. "You know, we'll both be up on that mesa tonight. Maybe we should arrange a midnight tryst."

She looked down at her hands.

He tilted her chin up and kissed her. She made sure to stay present in her head and not yield to his lips, but not because of him—her own motives and emotions were the ones she didn't trust.

"My love," he said against her cheek, his fingers brushing her ear before he lowered his head to kiss her again. It was clear he didn't have the same reservations about embracing intimacy that she did. However, he wasn't the one who'd been abandoned, the one subsequently misled. She didn't need her memory back to know how all of this had hurt.

He held her for a minute or more, his arms strong, his embrace sure, and despite her resolve, she was whisked back to the night they'd made love and how right it had felt, how familiar and exciting.

"This place is turning out to be Hard Rock's damn watering hole," he said into her ear.

The comment jarred her and she straightened up. "What?"

"The taco truck. That's Whip walking across the grass. What in the world is he doing here?"

"Let's go find out," Chelsea said as she turned to get a look at Adam's mentor. She saw a man in his fifties with gleaming gray hair, a tanned face and a beige suit.

She turned back to Adam. "I want to meet him."

"Might as well get it over with," Adam said and they both scooted out the passenger door and crossed the street. "He doesn't know I'm in Arizona," Adam explained as they stepped up on the opposite curb. "He's likely to be a little short with me."

"Why?"

"He thinks it's dangerous for me to be here."

Chelsea cast him a wry smile. "Well, isn't it?"

Adam smiled. "Yeah, I guess so. Especially if everyone I know shows up at this taco truck."

As if his policeman's instincts warned him of their approach, Whip turned. His expression went from curiosity to surprise as he saw them. He immediately broke away from the line and approached Adam, hand outstretched.

"Adam?" he said, as though not believing his eyes. "What are you doing here? I figure you had to get to Bill Pierce's place the day before yesterday. Good grief, do you have any idea how worried I've been?"

Adam performed introductions before responding to Whip's concerns. "We were ambushed," he said in a low voice. "The killers seemed determined to try to make it look like some giant survivalist explosive mishap or something. It wasn't well thought out and it didn't work."

"Was anybody hurt?" Whip asked.

"Bill's wife was injured but only the killers suffered casualties."

"Stupid bastards," he said. "But I haven't read or heard a thing about it."

"And you won't," Adam said, his voice ominous. He

looked Whip over and added, "How are you? Why aren't you in uniform?"

"I have an interview this afternoon over in one of those buildings," Whip said, gesturing behind them. He dropped his voice again. "I thought you'd be in Florida by now. The thought of you just disappearing into thin air bothered me, but I have to admit not as much as seeing you standing out here in the open after what's gone down. What are you thinking?"

"We're on our way to Florida," Adam said. "I just wanted to show Chelsea Arizona before we left."

This was news to Chelsea.

Whip shook his head. "You're as reckless as your father was."

Adam seemed to ignore the remark. "Did you learn anything about Ron Ballard?"

"The marshal? A little. Rumor has it he's not a happy camper at his job. One of those disgruntled types, you know. In my book, that makes him dangerous. But worse, my contact said the man disappeared from California a week ago."

"Damn."

"Since you mentioned him, I've been thinking. Ballard has access to where you came from, who your friends are, everything. If he's the one after you, he'll look here next. He also has to know of any number of hired killers willing to make a few bucks by eliminating you—and yours. You opened a can of worms when you left the program."

"They failed to protect me," Adam insisted, his voice wary. "So I protected myself."

"At great cost," Whip said with a sidelong glance at Chelsea.

Adam looked down at the ground then into Chelsea's eyes. "You think I don't know that?" he muttered. She caught his hand and squeezed it tight. "Anyway, Ballard has no personal vendetta against me. The most he did was finger me and fail to warn me when trouble came. I can't see why he would come after me."

"You're being shortsighted. If he's guilty of fingering you and it comes out he's in danger of losing his job, you, son, constitute a loose end and men like Ballard don't like loose ends."

The silence stretched on and Whip shook his head. "Look, I know I'm being blunt. I'm just worried."

"Yeah," Adam said.

Chelsea attempted to break the tension with an off-topic remark. "We heard Aimee Holton is still living on the mesa."

Whip's eyebrows furrowed. "Aimee Holton? Why are you asking about her?"

"Everything Holton is on our radar right now," Adam said. "I thought the government confiscated his possessions after his conviction."

"All I know," Whip said, "is that Aimee's father is some wheeler-dealer back east. Tons of money. Bought the place through a holding company or something. The mesa didn't belong to Holton so the Feds couldn't touch it. For all intents and purposes, it's Aimee's. You did her a favor by helping to cut her loose from her husband." He clasped Adam's shoulder and softened his voice. "It's time to cut your losses. Does anybody else know you're here?"

"Just an old friend," Adam said.

"Old friends mention things to people and then they mention it to other people—"

"One way or another," Adam interrupted, "I've got to put an end to this."

Whip finally looked resigned to Adam's will. "Okay, if you won't listen to me, then at least let me help."

"I think it's better if you don't," Adam said. "Frankly, Whip, I want you out of this mess."

"I'm not the kind of guy to back down, you know that," Whip grumbled.

"Please."

He glanced at Chelsea again. "I really wish you two had stayed away from this place. I have a bad feeling—okay, but remember I'll be here if you need backup. You can always depend on me. All I want is your safety."

"I know. Thanks," Adam said. He took Chelsea's hand. "We'd better get going."

They took a few steps toward the van before Chelsea asked a question. "Why did you tell him you were here to show me Arizona? Don't you trust him?"

"With my life. But as you can see, he's overprotective at times. I gave in and owned up to my real reasons because he saw through me. He always does." He peered down into her eyes. "I'm banking the answers we need are up on that mesa."

She sighed. "Well, there's only one way to find out."

Chapter Thirteen

A youngish woman with a black ponytail opened the Holton door. With a sweep of her arm, she ushered Chelsea into the house.

"I'm Daisy Hanks, the new cook," Chelsea explained. "Ms. Holton is expecting me."

"Maria," the woman said, tapping her chest. *"Sigueme,"* she added as she gestured for Chelsea to follow her. Instead of going down the hall that appeared to lead to the bedroom wing of the spacious house, they went in the other direction, through the kitchen, where a teenage girl stood at the sink with her back to the room. Her jeans and T-shirt were good quality but hung on her small frame.

"Aqui," Maria coached, and led Chelsea past the laundry room and a small bath, ending in a square room with one window set high in the wall. "You sleep," the woman said in broken English. She pointed at the bed.

Chelsea assumed she didn't mean they had an early curfew but that this was Chelsea's room.

"It's very nice," Chelsea said.

A honking car startled both women. It sounded like it came from right outside the window.

"Mi amiga," Maria said with a smile. She nodded at Chelsea and hurried from the room.

"It was very nice to meet you," Chelsea called after her

as Maria disappeared toward the kitchen. A minute later, Chelsea heard a nearby door close. She moved to the window and stood on tiptoe to look outside in time to witness Maria getting into a sedan driven by a friendly-looking woman. The car drove away almost at once.

It took Chelsea less than five minutes to unpack her bag and stow her toiletries in the bathroom. She returned to her room, sat on the edge of the bed and found herself missing Adam.

Time to put her mind elsewhere. Time to spy.

She returned to the kitchen, hoping she might run into Aimee. Snooping might be the reason she'd taken the job, but cooking was what was going to keep her around long enough to ferret something out.

The dark-haired teen still stood at the sink washing what Chelsea now saw was a cupboard's worth of stemmed glasses. "Hi," Chelsea said.

The girl turned anxious brown eyes in her direction. Only the bruise on her cheek distracted from the beauty of her heavily lashed eyes and smooth olive skin.

"How about I dry these for you?" Chelsea asked.

The teenager's expression remained blank. Chelsea opened a drawer and pulled out a clean cloth. She dangled it from her fingers in what had to be the universal language for "I can dry." Eyes now wide, the girl turned back to the sink.

Chelsea looked around to make sure they were alone. Touching the girl's shoulder to get her attention again, she parroted Maria's gesture and touched her own chest. "*Yo me llamo* Daisy," she whispered in her newfound second language. It was the first Spanish she'd spoken in the house and the reason was probably silly. Aimee had made a point of asking Chelsea if she spoke Spanish. Something about the way she asked the question caused Chelsea to shake her head.

Was that James Bond-like or what?

For several seconds the girl said nothing but finally her lips parted. "Mariana."

"Mariana," Chelsea repeated. She touched her own cheek and added in Spanish, "Did someone hit you, Mariana?"

The girl's sudsy hand flew to her face. They stared at each other for a long moment, and then Mariana nodded.

"Who?" Chelsea asked in English. *"Quien?"*

Mariana's lips parted, then she quickly turned her head and went back to work right as Aimee Holton wafted into the room.

"You'd be wasting your time with that one even if she did speak English," Aimee said. "The girl has a foul temper."

"Don't you find it hard to communicate your wishes?" Chelsea asked. There was no way she was going to address the temper remark. For one thing, did that mean Aimee had inflicted that bruise on Mariana's cheek? And for another, the kid looked scared, not angry.

Aimee responded to that question by firing off a flood of Spanish directed at Mariana. It was like her words were battering rams, each one striking the girl until her eyes clouded over and she shook her head. She rinsed the glass she was washing, set it too hard on a folded towel, where it bumped against another, which toppled over and created a domino effect. Chelsea dived to save glasses from crashing against the floor. Mariana's hands flew up to her face as she watched in horror.

Chelsea expected Aimee to scream or gasp, but what she did was worse. *"Fuera de aqui,"* she said in a deadly quiet voice, firing the girl on the spot.

Holding her jeans up around her waist with one hand while dabbing at her eyes with the other, Mariana fled the room.

"Daisy, don't just stand there, clean up that mess!" Aimee demanded as she stormed after Mariana. "I have a call to make!"

By the time Chelsea had disposed of the debris and Aimee returned, the dishes were all washed and put away.

"Can you believe that brat?" Aimee said as she sat down.

"I think someone hit her earlier. She seemed kind of afraid or nervous—"

"Give me a break," Aimee said. "Someone got exasperated with her and I don't blame them."

"But hitting—"

"I can't abide busybodies," Aimee interrupted with a warning scowl. "I sure hope you aren't one. Now, how about some iced tea?"

"No thank you," Chelsea said.

"Tea for me, Daisy, not for you," Aimee said.

"Oh." Chelsea found a pitcher of tea in the fridge and poured a glass. Aiming to get the conversation back on track, she delivered the iced glass with a question. "I see another house is being built up the road. Are you going to have neighbors?"

"That's my new place," Aimee said. "This house is so dated and small. And it reminds me of Devin. That's my husband."

"Oh. I take it you're divorced or—"

"No," she interrupted. "He was framed and sent to jail. I'm going to tear this place down and build an indoor tennis court. I love it up here. Oh, everyone thought Devin was the driving force behind buying this land, but it was really me."

"You must be livid at the people who put your husband in prison," Chelsea said.

"Do you know what he did?"

"No," Chelsea lied.

"You'll hear soon enough. People love to talk."

"Don't you resent the people who, um, accused him or testified against him?" Chelsea said, still trying to get a response to her question.

"The main rat behind it was my sexy bodyguard," Aimee said in a confidential tone. "What a hunk, but Devin should have known better than to hire someone as straight-arrow as him. I can't tell you how often I pranced around in next to nothing and he never made a move." She thrust out a lower lip. "Don't you have something you need to do?"

Everything about this woman grated on Chelsea's nerves. She wore entitlement like a badge of honor, as though it was something she'd earned. The sneer beneath her smile and smirk lingering in her eyes bore this out. And if there was an ounce of compassion or humanity in her, it was well-hidden. "Yes, ma'am," Chelsea murmured as she began wiping down a counter.

Aimee gave no sign that she'd noticed Chelsea's sarcasm. She tapped her fingernails against the windowsill as she sipped the tea. In contrast to her afternoon ensemble of shorts and a cotton blouse, she currently wore a plunging white jumpsuit. High-heeled sandals gave her a two-inch lift, aided by mounds of reddish brown hair piled atop her head. She was a pretty thirty-something-year-old woman living all alone on a mesa.

"On a different subject," Chelsea began, "since I really only have tomorrow to plan and shop for Friday night, I need a few details about your soiree."

"My what?"

"Soiree. Party."

"What details?"

"Like who's invited."

"My guests enjoy their privacy."

"Well, that's great but I need some idea of quantity and allergies…"

She waved her hand. "We can discuss all that tomorrow when you whip a few things up. Actually, I'm glad I ran into you. I'm having a breakfast meeting in the morning. Maria can't cook worth a lick so I'll have to depend on you to have a carafe of hot coffee in the garden room at six thirty, followed by breakfast at seven."

"Okay," Chelsea said. "What are your menu preferences?"

"Oh, anything. Eggs benedict with smoked salmon, biscuits, pancakes, sliced fruit—you know, the usual."

As Chelsea's idea of the usual was apparently a bagel, she only nodded. Aimee's cell phone rang and she slipped it from an invisible pocket, checked the screen and swiped it on. "About time you called," she said, as she walked out of the room. "Where are you?"

Chelsea thought about eavesdropping on Aimee's side of the conversation but abandoned the idea. Instead she let herself outside onto a narrow porch. A closed gate on her left invited investigation and she opened it cautiously. It was dark by now, but as she moved inside the gate, sensors activated low-wattage lights that illuminated a footpath that led to a spacious patio.

Several rooms of the house bordered the patio. One was brightly lit and drew her attention. She saw Aimee perched on the corner of a desk in a room that was decidedly masculine. Her husband's old den or office? Maybe. She was still on her phone.

The path curved around a built-in grill and toward a lovely pool. Native rock and clever use of the land's natural contours made what had to be an aboveground pool appear like a sunken one. It would be heaven to jump in and paddle around but she knew without asking that was a no-no for the hired help. She walked around the pool and let herself out through another gate.

All pretense of prettiness disappeared. This was the utility part of the property, the place where garbage was collected and yard tools were scattered. Its dominant feature was a small building from which the tantalizing aroma of chili wafted on a welcome breeze. A clothesline with various female garments hung on it ran between the structure and a fence. Since the front door was ajar, Chelsea craned her neck to see if this was where Mariana had disappeared to, but the only person she saw was a woman fanning herself with a magazine.

She continued walking until the trail split, the left leading to some weathered-looking buildings a good distance away, and the right toward the bluff.

The wind grew stronger as she reached the guardrail that kept unwary pedestrians from walking too close to the edge. She perched atop it and rested one hand on her abdomen. Her new short hair blew around her face in a pleasant way.

She counted back in her head, wondering how "old" she was in this rendition of her life without a past. Day one would be the crash. Day two would be Doc Fisher. Day three, her brother, day four, the day she bolted and that made today day five. In those five days she'd traveled from California to Nevada to Arizona, shot two men, killing one, been cold, hot, terrified and lost in rapture. Not bad for the first five days of "life."

She turned her attention to the valley below. From this vantage point, she could see the town in the distance and the more or less straight road that led between it and the mesa, obvious because of the moving headlights of vehicles traveling north and south. Many other lights twinkled, indicating occupied homes, but the brightest glow came from Hard Rock.

"I thought I might find you out here," a man said, Recognizing the voice, she smiled as she turned. Adam settled his hands on her shoulders, leaned down and kissed the top of her head. It felt so right to have him near. Safer, too, though that was an odd thought as nothing remotely dangerous had happened since they'd gotten to Arizona.

Which must mean they'd fallen off their nemesis' radar.

"Aren't you supposed to be rousting rowdy teenagers?" she asked.

"Not until later," he said, sitting on the fence beside her. "Aren't you supposed to be cooking something?"

"Not until later," she mimicked with a smile. "Tonight all I accomplished was getting a girl fired."

"Why do you say that?"

She told him about Mariana's upsetting departure from the kitchen. "She has a bruised cheek. Do you think Aimee's capable of hitting her?"

"Aimee is impetuous, self-centered and impatient, so, yes, it's possible she lost her temper," he said. "How about this party? Who's coming?"

"She isn't saying. Claims people want their privacy. And why can't anybody who works in her house speak much English?"

Adam considered her question. "It might be a holdover from her husband wanting everything he said and did to be a secret. It came out in the trial that he was also importing drugs. Maybe she got used to his ways. She's very fluent in Spanish. Have you discovered yet that you know some of the language, too?"

"I overheard two women talking to each other and actually knew what they were saying. But Aimee talks too fast for me."

"Where is she now?" Adam asked.

"Aimee? Inside. She's all dressed up like she's going out, but the last I saw she was talking with someone on the phone."

"A broken date?"

"I have no idea."

"Man, we have nothing."

"Well, she did mention a six thirty a.m. meeting tomorrow."

He perked up. "Did she say with whom?"

"A business associate."

"What kind of business associate?"

"She didn't say."

He swore under his breath. "Diego told me Aimee is behind in paying his crew's wages. I wonder why."

"Knowing Aimee for all of two hours, I can say with some authority that if she thought yanking their chains would amuse her, she would do just that. She likes power."

He stared at her. "You think so?"

"Oh, yeah."

"I wish I knew if the boyfriend is Tom Nolan," Adam said. "I never noticed the two of them cozying up to each other while Holton was around, but then again, she had a husband and he had a wife to consider. Still, he's the kind of older, suave guy that Aimee might be drawn to."

"What does he look like?"

"About fifty, a silver ponytail and a diamond stud in his left ear. You'll know him if you see him."

"You said he was a crony of Holton's," Chelsea said. "Are you thinking he might still be doing Holton's bidding?"

"In other words, orchestrating these attacks on me?

Yeah, that's what I'm thinking. Maybe he lost a bundle when Holton was arrested so he has a stake in retribution. This is all guesswork, of course. Everything seems to be." He pulled Chelsea to her feet but didn't release her hands. "Almost everything, that is. Right now, you're the one sure thing in my life."

And he was the only reality in hers. It had been a long, long day. Chelsea allowed herself to be coaxed into his arms. It felt wonderful to be pressed against his chest and when he kissed her, she didn't pull away. His hands slid down her back, where his caresses awakened the lust that was never buried very deep when he was near. "How about a moonlight tour of my new home away from home?" he whispered.

She'd be a hypocrite to deny she wanted him, but wanting and taking were two different things. If she gave in now, she would weaken her resolve to stay at arm's length until this situation was resolved and her memory returned. She knew she should push his hands away, but he'd reached under her blouse and his fingers stroking her bare skin seared her with pleasure.

As the tip of his tongue teased apart her lips, he cupped her breast. She ran her hands beneath his shirt, passing over the small bandage that protected the knife wound, before gliding over the smooth ridges of his defined abs. She longed to feel his bare skin press down on hers…

"We need to take this someplace private," he said, his lips moving against hers, his breathing heavy.

She summoned willpower. It took a second, but finally she placed her hands on either side of his head and looked up at him.

"We have to stop," she whispered.

"Chelsea, I love you, you know that."

She nodded. But she knew he must have said those

same words when he asked her to marry him. The next day he'd disappeared without a word to her. So, really, what did love mean?

"There isn't anything I wouldn't do."

"I know. But I need space, I told you that."

He dropped his arms and turned toward the bluff. After a second, he turned back to her as he plucked his phone from his pocket. "I have to make a call. Why don't you go inside? I'll see you tomorrow."

She looked past him toward the valley. "What's that orange glow near the highway? Is that a fire?"

He nodded as he spoke into the phone.

"Look at the speed it's spreading," she said, almost mesmerized, but also suddenly anxious, as though fire licked at her feet. The breeze drove the flames that now seemed to race exponentially faster as they headed from the road back up the land toward an illuminated building.

She touched Adam's arm. "I hear sirens," she said.

"So do I." He clicked off his phone. "They put me on hold. Half the valley is probably reporting this."

"Do you know what's burning?"

"I passed a parched field this afternoon when I drove up here," he told her. "If it's the same place, I think there's an old abandoned barn up where it's headed. But there are houses and other buildings near that one as well as bushes and trees."

They fell silent as the sirens grew louder and flashing lights appeared on the highway.

Chelsea heard a sound behind them and turned around to face the house. Even from this distance, she was able to discern Aimee's lithe figure, illuminated under the outdoor lights, hurrying from the front of the house to the nearby garage, where she disappeared inside. A moment later, an engine roared to life and she drove off down the road. "Aimee just left," she said softly.

Adam turned. "I wonder where she's going?"

"Maybe to make up with the boyfriend."

"Driving alone? She usually has Miguel drive her."

"Who's Miguel?"

"He works here, or at least he used to. Aimee is going to get caught in traffic if she heads toward Hard Rock." He swore, then added, "I should have been ready to trail her and see where she's headed and who she meets." He looked down at Chelsea, his eyes little more than glistening pools. "I got distracted."

"Don't blame your inattention on me," she said with a smile. "You started it."

He kissed her forehead. "Don't worry, I know who's at fault. But trust me, the next time that woman leaves this place by herself, I'm going to be right behind her."

As the sirens grew louder they turned back to gaze at the fire, which had doubled in size and now seemed to light up the night. Traffic had all but stopped as cars pulled off the highway to watch. A few human figures, illuminated by the flames, appeared on the burned-out edges of the field. The fire trucks finally pulled onto the property while the fire kept spreading. Police cars now raced down the highway, blue lights pulsing like an anxious heart. Chelsea shivered. She could almost feel heat in the smoke.

Adam wrapped his arm around her shoulders. "Are you afraid?" he asked softly.

"Not for myself, no, but the people down there are so vulnerable…"

"I know."

THEY WATCHED THE fire burn until the last flame died away. Before that happened, the fire had jumped into a few trees and from there to rooftops. They'd witnessed two ambulances arrive and eventually depart. Chelsea had been crying for the past ten minutes. Not sobbing, just tears rolling down her cheeks.

He knew a very dark memory caused her tears even though she didn't. He'd tried to protect her by getting her to leave the bluff when he first spotted the fire, but that hadn't worked. Was it possible the fire affected her so deeply because it stirred one of her darkest memories? Might that be a sign other memories, hopefully more pleasant ones, would start returning?

"We've escaped death at least three times in the last five days," she said as she leaned in against him. They watched as the ambulances' taillights raced back to town, their sirens heralding the journey. "I hope those people are half as lucky as we've been."

"I do, too," he said and wished with all his heart that he could spend the night comforting her. He wanted to fall asleep with her in his arms and wake up with her in the morning. He wanted to be there if the fire brought nightmares and she needed him.

But that was not to be. She was dazed and worn by smoke and events, and he had vandals to go find.

"Aimee still hasn't come home," she commented.

He settled his arm around her shoulders. "She could be caught in that mess down below. Come on, I'll escort you back to the house. It's time for me to go watch for some stupid kids."

Eventually, after a quick shower to wash off the stench of smoke, he found himself a concealed spot created by the turn of the deck and a cantilevered window. The night had finally cooled off and he knew that it would be downright cold before long. Tonight he'd observe. Tomorrow he would borrow Diaz's phone and tomorrow night, he would capture them in the act, whatever that turned out to be.

Maybe viewing a good incriminating photograph with their parents looking over their shoulders might be all the dissuasion the kids needed.

The most noteworthy thing that happened was that Aimee's car—at least he assumed it was hers—arrived back on the mesa at one thirty. By three o'clock, shivering in his T-shirt and literally unable to keep his eyes open another moment, he gave up on the vandals. Maybe they'd gotten caught up in the traffic out on the highway. He needed to get some sleep if he was going to function tomorrow. He walked back to his modest trio of rooms and let himself in. He was asleep two minutes after his head hit the pillow.

Chapter Fourteen

Chelsea dared only glance at Aimee's early morning visitor, a well-built guy packed into a blue T-shirt decorated with a setting sun. His back was to the room and he didn't turn as she settled the heavy tray on a round table by the window.

He did not have silver hair in a ponytail, nor could she see a diamond stud. The guy was not Tom Nolan.

It wasn't until he grumbled something, paused, then spoke again that Chelsea realized he was on the phone.

"Where are the pancakes?" Aimee demanded right as the man on the phone finally started speaking.

Chelsea jerked to attention. She gestured at one of the plates. "Right here."

"They look funny."

"They're johnnycakes."

"That's cornmeal, right? Did I ask for cornmeal? I hate the stuff."

Chelsea had had a miserable night and Aimee's complaints irritated the heck out of her. "I'll just pour the juice," she said.

"I can pour my own damn juice." Aimee turned to the man who had just ended his call. "Davy? Breakfast."

He pocketed his phone and turned to face them. His friendly, tanned face, blue eyes and straight teeth seemed to indicate he was a guy who would stay young-looking into middle age. "It smells great," he said as he brushed long hair off his forehead. "I'm starving."

Aimee was obviously still distressed about something. "Maybe I should cancel the party," she told him.

Davy poured a glass of juice and handed it to her. "Calm down, everything is going to work out. We need the party, the noise, the distraction. Now drink this, you'll feel better." He wrapped his arm around her. "Besides, I have a plan."

"Like what?" she asked then seemed to remember Chelsea. "Are you actually eavesdropping on us?" she snapped.

"No… I—"

"Close the door on your way out."

Chelsea fought the urge to curtsy and headed for the door.

"Thanks for the food," Davy called as she left the room.

This was the boyfriend? Well, maybe it took someone as laid-back as him to cope with Aimee's mercurial moods. More importantly, Chelsea still had no idea what the meeting had been about. The only two words she'd managed to glean from Davy's phone conversation were *trouble* and *adjustments* and they seemed appropriate for any business situation.

When Chelsea started to pack up the leftovers she suspected Aimee would never eat, she had a better idea. She filled another tray and took it out to the small house she'd seen the night before. Surely someone out there could eat this food. She was also hoping for a chance to talk to Mariana.

Her brisk knock was answered by the woman whom she'd seen fanning herself the night before. Her lovely eyes widened as she scanned the huge tray of goodies Chelsea held in front of her.

"I'm the new cook. I brought, well, food." This was said in English with a few words of Spanish thrown in, but the woman, who shared that her name was Sofia, apparently understood. Although she looked wary about accepting the tray, she unburdened Chelsea. *"Gracias,"* she murmured.

"Is Mariana here?" Chelsea added.

Sofia frowned. "Mariana?"

"About fifteen, maybe sixteen. Long hair."

Sofia shook her head. "I don't know…"

"You mean she never stayed here?"

"No."

"Maybe another building—"

"There is only the men's building," Sofia insisted. "That's where my husband, Miguel, lives. I would know if there was a girl there." This last comment was accompanied by a shy smile.

"I see. Well, okay then. I—I hope you enjoy the food."

"I'll share it with Miguel," she said.

A young married couple living apart? Could she stand being that close to Adam and not in the same bed? Judging by the bad dreams that had plagued her last night, the answer was no.

Instead of heading back to the house, Chelsea turned toward the bluff. As she walked, she thought about Mariana. If the girl had been working for Aimee for any length of time, wouldn't Sofia have heard of her? Even if she'd never stayed overnight on the mesa, Chelsea thought Sofia would have seen her. Where was Mariana?

The view from the bluff stunned Chelsea. Acres of blackened land, burned-out buildings and ravaged trees covered a large swath. How had the people the ambulances evacuated fared? Tears once again burned her eyes. The fire had haunted her sleep, had filled her dreams. She had no idea why it bothered her so much. There'd been flames during the attack at Bill's place and they'd frozen her for a heartbeat, but they hadn't tortured her this way.

She returned to the house to find Maria hard at work. As Chelsea joined in to clean the kitchen, she wondered if she should drop the pretense of not understanding or speaking much Spanish so she could ask a few pertinent questions. Tomorrow, she decided, unless Aimee fired her first. Maria left the kitchen when the work was done.

With tomorrow's party in mind, Chelsea grabbed a pencil and paper and started making a list. Pool parties equaled buffet in her mind. The grocery list of appetizers, vegetarian shish kebabs and seafood skewers grew as the menu came together.

With the vision of the scorched valley still on her mind, Chelsea switched on the small television built into the cabinetry, hoping to get news about the fire. She flipped through several channels before catching the tail end of an interview obviously filmed at a hospital.

"All we can do for my dad now is pray," a distraught-looking man said right into the camera.

The camera switched to a woman reporter standing in front of a burned-out building. "Again, to recap," she said, "Wednesday night at nine thirty-five, Hard Rock Fire Department responded to a grass fire on Hanson Road. One man is dead, another hospitalized for third-degree burns. Both men are thought to have been trapped in their respective homes. The fire burned about twenty acres of grassland along with several buildings. Though still under investigation, sources report it's suspected a burning cigarette thrown from a car is the cause. Stay tuned to Channel—"

Chelsea turned off the TV. The expression in the man's eyes as he talked about his father filled her head and she suddenly understood what it was that struck a chord in her heart with him and with Mariana. She'd lived with the same thing day and night since Adam had pulled her from the helicopter, and last night when the fire in the valley looked like a flowing river of lava, she'd felt it cut to her very quick.

Fear. They were both very, very afraid.

ADAM AWOKE TO a knock on his door. He pulled on his jeans and answered it to find Diego Diaz standing on the threshold with a cinnamon roll wrapped in a napkin and a mug of coffee grasped in his other hand.

"Hey, Frank, thought you might need something to eat," he said as he handed Adam breakfast.

"Thanks," Adam said, taking a grateful sip of coffee. "I'm afraid the kids didn't show up last night."

"Yeah, nothing's missing, no new insults. The fire must have kept them away."

"The fire was terrible. Do you know if anyone was hurt?"

"One man dead," Diaz said, "and one in the hospital. I live about a quarter mile from him. Jim's an okay guy, I hope he makes it."

"Did your house—?"

"Some smoke, nothing else."

"I need a favor," Adam said before Diaz left. "This is none of my business, I know that, but yesterday you mentioned the boss is holding the crew's wages back."

Diego shook his head. "I'm paying you myself, you don't need to worry about that, Frank. Ms. Holton has some cash-flow issue or something. She'll come through and I'll get my money back. Anything else?"

"Yeah, I need to borrow your camera tonight. I want to catch those kids in the act."

"Won't they see your flash or hear the noise it makes?"

"I'm betting on it. They'll run like scared dogs."

"What if they turn on you?"

Adam smiled. "Don't worry about it."

"Dude…don't hurt them," Diego said, eyes narrowed.

"Please, I'm an ex-cop. Maybe you can share the photo with their folks and avoid the police altogether."

"Good idea. I have an extra phone in the glove box. I'll leave it before I go home. Don't worry if you're busy, I have a key."

"Thanks."

After Diaz left, Adam ate the cinnamon roll and drank the coffee. He quickly dressed and walked toward the Holton house. In a garden shed, he found an unattended straw hat and some clippers. Thus camouflaged, he staked out a rambling bush next to the house. A big SUV was parked close to Aimee's front door and he quickly memorized the plate, though he'd have to get Whip to check it out as he had no pull with the police. After pretending to be a gardener for over an hour, the door opened and a man about his own age exited the house.

To Adam, the emerging man didn't look like Aimee's type in that he didn't look wealthy or connected. Just a guy who hung out at the beach, but hell, maybe she was tired of movers and shakers and felons and villains.

The car pulled away and Adam remained at his post, trying to figure out a way to get in the house to see Chelsea. He told himself it was to find out if she'd overheard anything, but the truth was he just wanted to see her.

Toward that goal, he walked quickly along the drive that jutted off behind the house, where he could see in the kitchen window. Chelsea's red hair announced her back was to the sink. It appeared she was talking to somebody he couldn't see. He waited until she faced the sink, then waved a hand until the motion caught her attention. She shook her head and turned back into the room, but a moment later, she left the sink and a moment after that, she came through the back door.

"Did you hear that someone died in the fire and another person ended up in the hospital?" she said softly as she reached his side.

He took her hand and led her to a spot where they wouldn't be visible through a window. "Yes, I did."

"I had nightmares about that fire last night," she said with a shudder. "I don't know why it got to me on such a deep level. I kept seeing an old woman in the flames. Today when I heard it was a man who died, I was actually surprised. It was so real."

He looked into her eyes. "I should have told you last night," he said. "I didn't want to upset you, but I can see now my silence didn't help. Chelsea, your grandmother died in a fire when you were twelve. You adored her, she was a constant in your life because your mom was at the tavern working so much—anyway, her death devastated you."

"My grandmother." She swallowed hard. "I don't remember her. What was her name?"

"Ann, same as your middle name."

"I want so much to remember her. Well, at least it explains the tears and the dreams—oh, my gosh, Adam. Does this mean my subconscious memory is returning?"

"I don't know. The fire at Bill's didn't get to you like this, but on the other hand, you were fighting for your life."

"It was different this time, more profound. I must be getting better. I hope so."

"So do I." He hugged her close, relishing the smell of her hair and the feel of her body next to his. But he could also feel the restraint in her embrace.

"Where are you staying in the house?" he asked. "Which room is yours?"

She pointed to the windows a little distance from the kitchen. "My room is right there. Why?"

"I don't know for sure. I just want to know where you are. Did you get a guest list for tomorrow's party? What did you learn about the business meeting this morning? Did—?"

"You want a rundown?" she interrupted as she held up a closed fist. "Okay, here goes," She raised a finger. "One, Aimee almost canceled her party but don't ask me why. Two, she is in a foul mood. I don't think she got much sleep last night. Three, Miguel is going to man the grill."

"Then he's still here. Good."

"I met his wife earlier. Her name is Sofia."

"They got married? How about that! Okay, continue."

"Four, no guest list, just forty or so unidentified people who are on their own when it comes to any allergies because Aimee can't be bothered to ask them. Let's see, her visitor this morning used the words *trouble* and *adjustments* while on the phone. I don't know if he's just a business associate or a boyfriend."

"Did he look like a surfer dude?"

She nodded.

"I saw him leave. Did you get a name?"

"Davy."

"Not much help there. Anything else?"

She thought for a second. "Let's see. The party people called to say that they couldn't get here to decorate the patio until tomorrow, which set Aimee off big-time." She held up the other hand. "A refrigerator for the new house is being delivered this afternoon and that has Aimee spitting nails because it's not supposed to come for another two months and now it's got to be stored in the shop or shed or something way off down that way."

"The new shed."

"Yeah. Lastly, Aimee is headed off to the spa pretty soon. That's all I've got." She smiled and added, "It's getting late and I have a ton of shopping to do for the party. Want to drive into Hard Rock with me? I could use the company."

"Sounds good, but I think I should follow Aimee. I'm also going to meet Dennis later on today. Take the teenager you told me about last night. Maybe you can ferret out how she got the bruise."

"Mariana's whereabouts are currently a mystery. I'll manage."

He grasped her shoulders and gently kissed her lips. "I'll check the oil in the van, then I'd better get ready to trail Aimee. Love you," he added, noting the anxious look in her eyes as he uttered the words. Well, she could hem and haw all she wanted, his feelings were crystal clear.

He waited for Aimee to leave the property from behind the cover of the guard shack. When she finally drove by in her white convertible, he gave her a few minutes to get ahead so the sound of his motorcycle wouldn't draw her attention. Once she hit Hard Rock city limits, she slowed down and turned off Main Street, traversing small roads to the seedier side of the city. It surprised the hell out of him when she pulled into a motel parking lot. The place was definitely not her style, but she got out of her car, quickly approached one of the outside doors, knocked, scanned the area around her as though looking to see if anyone was watching, and scurried inside when the door opened.

Interesting.

Two hours later, Tom Nolan walked out of the room with a smug grin on his tanned face. He ambled out of the parking lot and down a side street, where he got behind the wheel of a black Mercedes and drove off. Aimee didn't appear for another thirty minutes. No sauntering for her. Huge sunglasses partially concealed her face as she scanned her surroundings and practically ran to her car. He followed her to the ritzy part of town. She handed her keys to a valet and entered her favorite spa, where he knew from experience she would linger for hours.

So Tom Nolan was the boyfriend and the guy from the morning, Davy something, was just a business associate? What business, and did either man have anything to do with the attacks on him and Chelsea?

Why had the attacks stopped? The reasonable explanation was that no one knew where they were. While it was nice not to be shot at or to have Chelsea threatened, it seemed the momentum of their situation had ground to a halt.

And that meant that now was the time to keep alert and not become complacent. Whip was right, sooner or later, Dennis would tell someone he'd seen Adam or Adam would be spotted again—it was inevitable that something would tip someone off. Sooner or later the "bad guys" would be back on their trail. This was his opportunity to get to them before they got to him.

Maybe he'd have to depend on Whip after all.

He drove to the taco truck to meet Dennis, his thoughts now centered on the mysterious box. He found the place more crowded than usual and alive with music thanks to the efforts of a three-man band set up on a makeshift stage. People swayed to their country beat, occasionally dropping a dollar or two into the band's open guitar case as the taco truck did a booming business.

Good grief. Could he have chosen a more public spot to center his activities in Hard Rock? This was the absolute last time he was coming near this place. He took off his helmet but kept his cap pulled low on his face and his sunglasses in place.

A man walking across the grass caught his attention. There was something about the way he moved—a little stutter in his gait. He wore slacks and a sports shirt. A baseball cap covered most of his head, but a few strands of auburn hair showed down by his neck. The guy looked over his shoulder as he approached the alley that ran behind the taco truck and Adam glimpsed his profile. In that instant, he knew who he was looking at.

US Marshal Ron Ballard, here in Arizona, just like Whip had predicted.

Adam waited until Ballard focused his attention back on the alley and then he began threading his way through the jostling crowd, the confusion created by the loud music masking his movement. He caught one last glimpse of Ballard before he turned a corner and disappeared into the alley. Adam broke into a trot until he stopped near the corner. He checked to make sure no one was watching him, then retrieved his gun and turned the corner carefully in case he was being set up for an ambush.

The alley was heavily shadowed. Adam tore off the sunglasses and spotted Ballard fifty feet ahead of him walking toward the light at the far end. He picked up his pace as he followed the man, reviewing his options as he moved between shadows. Without a vehicle at hand, he couldn't trail Ballard. He needed to confront him. Why was the guy here? Was it like Whip had said, that Adam was a loose end? And most important, who was Ballard working for?

Adam left the shadows to stand in the center of the alley, gun still at his side. "Ballard!" he yelled.

The marshal turned but with his back to the light, Adam couldn't read his expression. A sudden laugh jarred Adam.

"Is that you, Parish?" Ballard called, sounding anything but happy. "I knew you weren't really dead, you jerk. Do you know what trouble you've caused me? I wish you had gone down with your plane, at least then I wouldn't have to—"

Ballard's hand suddenly rocketed up from his side. A single shot erupted from behind Adam, so he threw himself to the ground, aware as he did so that Ballard had crumpled to the pavement where he stood. Adam turned his head to find Whip standing several yards behind him, his arm still held out in front, his gun gripped in his hand.

Lowering his weapon, the older man immediately walked up to Adam and extended a hand to help him to his feet. "Are you okay?"

"I'm—I'm fine," Adam stuttered. "I'm…wait. Why did you shoot—?"

"He drew on you," Whip interrupted. "I aimed to wound him so he could tell us who's behind all this… I don't know, though, I was kind of rushed." Whip strode toward the fallen man, Adam right on his heels.

Ballard was lying on the pavement, a Glock 23-caliber pistol clutched in his right hand. "See?" Whip said, gesturing at the Glock. His voice sounded a little relieved. No cop liked shooting an unarmed man.

Adam kneeled to check for a pulse. "He's gone."

"Damn. I'm sorry, son."

Adam kept his gaze on Ballard's body as he stood. "I saw him raise his hand but I didn't see the gun," he said as he met Whip's gaze. "If you hadn't been here… How *did* you happen to be in this alley?"

"Ballard was waiting for me after my interview," Whip said. "He started asking me a lot of questions about you. There was something off about him. I got the feeling he knew you were in Hard Rock so I decided to find out where he went next. My heart almost stopped when I saw you follow him into this alley."

Adam shook his head, still dumbfounded by Ballard's presence in Arizona and by the finality of the man's death. "You better call this in," he said.

"I'm not calling in anything until you get out of town," Whip said.

Adam shook his head. "I'm not leaving—"

"This isn't your decision. This is self-defense with or without your involvement. What with him being a Marshal and me being a cop, none of this will hit the news until the facts are known. Once Ballard's activities are exposed, there won't be a problem for me, trust me. Now go so I can start the ball rolling."

"But—"

"No, Adam, now listen to me. Think about Chelsea. You don't know that Ballard didn't already tell Devin Holton's goons he found you, there could be a new attack coming any minute. She'll be a sitting duck if you get caught up in this, too. There are so few ways I can help you but this I can do. Go. Get Chelsea, get out of Hard Rock for good."

Adam nodded as he tucked away his gun. It went against the grain to walk away but Whip was right. As soon as Adam got involved with the police, Chelsea would be left high and dry. He looked Whip in the eyes. "I don't know when I'll see you again—"

"Don't get all touchy-feely on me," the older man said, then gave him a spontaneous hug.

Adam walked away. As he crossed the park, he tried calling Dennis but the call went immediately to voice mail. He rode out of town but not before making one fast stop at a small store, where he bought Chelsea a prepaid phone of her own. She needed a way to call for help should the occasion arise.

By the time he got back to the mesa, the sun was well on its way down and the construction crew was long gone. He stopped off at his place to leave the bike so he could hike up the road.

When he got close to the house, he heard music coming from the patio. Past experience at this house told him Aimee was out by the pool and that meant he could chance going around back to see Chelsea. Her welcoming smile went a long way toward easing his anxiety and she pulled him inside without hesitation.

"I take it Aimee is on the patio?"

"For the time being," Chelsea said. The kitchen smelled wonderful. Trays of pretty little food lined the drain boards while the sink was filled with piles of dirty dishes. She was in her element and it brightened her eyes and flushed her cheeks a beguiling pink.

"We have to talk," he said as he snatched a shrimp and popped it in his mouth.

"These are the test hors d'oeuvres. Aimee is coming in soon to choose what she likes."

He swiped another shrimp, and then told her about Ballard.

"Dead?" she whispered. "Thank God Whip was there."

"I know. He'll still have to go through an investigation, though. Without a witness and with the other gun unfired—"

"He told you he'd take care of it," Chelsea said. "Let him. If you have to come in later to make things right, you can."

"We have to leave tonight—"

"No," she said immediately. "Not tonight. Not until after the party."

"But—"

"Just because the guy who fingered you is dead doesn't

mean you're out of danger. The deal was to find out the truth. I know it sounds silly, but I have a feeling about tomorrow night, Adam. Something is going to happen at that party, I know it in my bones. Something that tells you exactly who is behind what."

He had the same feeling and it probably was silly. But neither Whip nor the police knew he was on this mesa—if he stayed out of sight until Saturday morning, they should both be fine. "Okay," he said.

She handed him a little biscuit with flecks of prosciutto baked in the dough. Heaven. "Did you see Dennis?" she asked. "I've been dying to know what's in the box."

"I missed Dennis."

"Shoot. Well, how about Aimee. Who did she meet?"

"Tom Nolan and at a motel no less. Probably because of his wife."

"I overheard her on the phone a little while ago. It sounded like she was talking to her father and she was asking for money. I think Aimee may have stretched herself too thin."

"That explains the paycheck thing," Adam said.

"And judging from the way she threw her phone after she disconnected, I don't think Daddy said yes."

"Speaking of phones," Adam said and produced the new one he'd bought her. When they heard a door close somewhere in the house, it was time for him to go.

She pressed a napkin filled with appetizers into his hands. "Hurry," she said, "I hear footsteps."

"Call me later, okay?"

"I don't know your number."

"I programmed it into the phone. Call me. I miss you."

"I miss you, too," she whispered and sounded as though she meant it.

HIS PHONE RANG as Adam patrolled the deck. Half expecting a call from Whip, he was pleased to hear Chelsea's voice.

What she didn't know, couldn't remember, were the hundreds of calls they'd made to one another. Some people fell in love over endless texts and emails but he and Chelsea had used the phone, craving the sound of one another's voices, discussing their days and dreaming about what was to come. Sometimes they'd spend the whole day and evening together and still find things to talk about in midnight calls.

And so it was tonight. Was it a pipe dream to think she might fall in love with him again even if her memory never returned? As for him, the sound of her voice transported him to her side. But eventually, he had to remind her to stay around other people the next day, that he was going to find Dennis and retrieve the box. He made her promise to call him if anything alarmed her. When he heard an approaching vehicle, he ended the call. He stood up and dug Diego's camera out of his pocket.

What if it wasn't the vandals? What if this was the beginning of another attack on him and Chelsea?

He moved down the path toward the clearing, careful to stay out of the moonlight, gun drawn.

It sounded like the vehicle stopped out by the construction office, out of view of where he lurked. He heard doors open and close, then male voices, adult voices, and he tensed. "Where is it?" someone said.

"I think we turned too early. Didn't they say the second right? It's up the road."

"Man, we're so late."

"That engine trouble wasn't our fault. At least we can still make today's deadline if we deliver before twelve. Don't forget the bonus."

"But we still have to unload—"

"Stop whining. It's up the road, I'm sure of it. Look, you can see lights."

"I can't believe we have to drive back to Phoenix tonight," the complainer grumbled as the sound of opening and closing doors reached Adam's ears. The vehicle soon continued up the mesa toward the main house. By the position of the headlamps, it appeared to be a truck.

That had to be the refrigerator people and the delivery bonus had to be huge to justify these hours. He walked back to the house and leaned against an outside wall, where he could look down at the valley below. Thirty minutes later the delivery truck bounced and squeaked its way back down the hill, refrigerator apparently signed, sealed and delivered.

He walked around the house a few times, something made possible because of the 360 degree deck. Were those kids ever going to show? This was the last night he planned on waiting out here—a lot of good he'd done Diaz construction.

Forty minutes passed before the bass beat of a rap song and skidding brakes announced more visitors. Adam was once again alert for someone with worse intent than vandalism. Doors slammed, high-pitched giggles erupted. A thud announced someone had fallen and the subsequent slurred warning to be quiet made Adam certain he was listening to three or four drunk kids.

Was the driver sober?

Pounding footsteps ran toward the house, slowing down when the vandals reached the front deck and entered the semi-skeletal structure. Judging from discernable shapes, there were three of them and they could barely stand up straight. One held a can above his head and shook it, the sound of the marble rattling inside the can disturbing the still night air. The kid staggered around a bit before he randomly sprayed. The other two followed suit, weaving their way around the structure, pausing to spray when the mood hit them.

Adam took a few pictures of them through the window opening and caught the open beer bottles each was holding. They were so preoccupied they didn't even notice the flash. Tiptoeing off his perch on the deck, he made his way up the trail, using the flashlight on the phone to check out the truck while keeping his senses alert for any trouble that might come from Holton's direction.

He found no additional teens, drunk or sober. He opened the hood and took the distributor cap, then closed it. He strode off the road to another concealed spot behind a couple of tall bushes and called Diego. It was answered on the second ring.

"What?" Diego responded abruptly, though his voice was fuzzy because he'd been woken up.

"This is Adam. Get on up here ASAP."

"Now?"

"Yep. The kids are here and they're too drunk to drive. I disabled their truck, but you need to be the one to call the police."

"I'll be there in fifteen minutes," Diego said.

"Make it ten. And don't forget the cops."

Adam waited around until Diego showed up in his dark truck, lights and engine off, momentum carrying the heavy vehicle to a rolling stop. A shadowy Diego exited like a sooty ghost. Adam disengaged himself from the bushes and approached Diego.

"I called the police on the way up the hill," Diego whispered.

"They took a six-pack down there with them," Adam said. "Every once in a while I hear glass breaking." He gave Diego the distributor cap and the phone. "It's up to you now."

"Thanks. You'd better go."

Adam clapped the other man on the back and took off at a trot. He'd taken care of Diego's problem.

Would that his own could be so easily resolved.

Chapter Fifteen

Chelsea was up bright and early. She'd done some of the prep work for the party yesterday, but there was still a ton to do. Maria was there to help and that was nice, but as Maria's English seemed nonexistent, Chelsea found herself missing the back-and-forth banter so common in this kind of work.

Wait? How did she know what was common behavior in a commercial-like kitchen? But she did: she could remember jokes and laughing, but not faces. First the reaction to the fire, now this—was it a start? *Oh, please let it be so and let it progress quickly into memories of Adam and her family.*

Aimee showed up around ten and Maria immediately stopped helping Chelsea and served Aimee coffee and a toasted muffin. "Take it out to the patio," Aimee said as Maria approached the table with the tray. "Wait. Where's the juice and a bowl of fruit? Honestly, Maria."

"Perdón," Maria whispered.

Aimee rolled her eyes. "Daisy, have those damn party people shown up yet?"

Chelsea piled strawberries in a bowl and then froze. She shouldn't have been able to understand Aimee's request for fruit as it was delivered in her quicksilver Spanish. But Aimee was still complaining and not paying any attention. Maria took the bowl and placed it on the tray.

"Daisy?" Aimee repeated. "The decorators? Am I alone here? What am I paying you for?"

"Catering your party," Chelsea answered as she handed a glass of juice to Maria. "And no, as far as I'm aware, the decorators haven't come yet."

Aimee got to her feet and swept out of the room. Maria followed behind her with the tray, but she glanced over at Chelsea before leaving.

When she got back, Chelsea, in Spanish, apologized for disguising the fact she understood a little Spanish.

"Don't worry about it," Maria said in perfect English.

"You lied, too?" Chelsea asked her.

Maria nodded. "Sofia worked up here before me. She's the one who told me about the job, but she said Ms. Holton wouldn't hire anyone who speaks or understands much English so I just pretended to be fresh off the boat instead of born and raised in Portland, Oregon. My family knows me as Mary Louise, but in this house, I'm Maria. Man, I about split a gut when you told the boss lady exactly what she'd hired you to do. She presumes too much."

"No kidding."

"I'm glad we can talk openly to each other," Maria said. "Sofia's husband is sick of them living apart. He wants to take off. I bunk out there during the week and if she leaves, I'll be here all alone. Maybe you could move out there with me."

"I'm not staying past tonight," Chelsea admitted. "I'm just here for this party."

"Shoot," Maria said.

"Who's coming, do you know?"

"She threw the last one for some would-be politician. I

heard via Miguel that this time she's invited a TV star I've never heard of. She likes to rub shoulders."

"Were you here when Mr. Holton—?"

"No! I wouldn't work for a man like him. It's hard enough working for his wife."

"Maria, I have a question. I met a teenager here named Mariana."

"I didn't know her name," Maria said.

"Then you met her?"

"I saw her when Ms. Holton paraded her in to wash some crystal glasses. I admit it, I can be clumsy, but honestly, three glasses in nine months service? Anyway, when I spoke briefly to the girl, Ms. Holton told me to leave her be. Kind of timid, right?"

"I thought she seemed frightened and with good cause. I believe she may be a battered kid, but I'm not sure. I'd like to talk to her. Do you know where she went after Aimee sent her away?"

"Not a clue. I can ask Sofia—"

"I already asked her."

"Hopefully she went home."

Would that be any better? Not if it was her family who was abusing her. "Why do you work here if you hate it so much?" she asked Maria.

Maria shrugged. "I'm thirty-three years old. My two kids currently live with my late husband's parents in Phoenix. I'm going to college online and I'm just about done. Then I can get a job as a court reporter and get my kids back. I miss the little monsters like crazy. Aimee Holton is the means to my end."

Chelsea smiled. "I hope she's the means to my end, too," she mumbled, thinking of what Adam had said last night on the phone, that his plan was to spend the party in disguise, getting a good look at each and every guest, looking for connections to his past and to Holton. It sounded a lot easier said than done.

ADAM TRIED DENNIS'S phone first thing in the morning but there was still no answer. Since he hadn't fallen asleep until almost 4:00 a.m., it was now well after ten. That meant Dennis was undoubtedly already at work, where he wouldn't answer a personal call. Knowing Chelsea was elbow-deep in food prep and surrounded by people, he decided to drive to the old Stop and Shop in Hard Rock and see if he could catch Dennis during his lunch break.

That meant showing up in the town he'd sworn to avoid, but he had to get his hands on that box and he was wearing his trusty helmet so he was more or less invisible, right?

He found the renovation of the small grocery into a fish pet store in full swing. Several contractor vehicles were parked along the sidewalk in front while men toted supplies and tools in and out of the building. Adam pulled to the curb and waited.

At noon, the site began to clear but there was no sign of Dennis. Adam got off his bike when a burly guy with unruly eyebrows left the building and crossed the street.

"Excuse me," Adam called out, taking off his hood. "I'm looking for Dennis Woods."

"You a friend of his?"

"Yes. I've been trying to get ahold of him."

"He called in earlier. Stacy gave birth about two o'clock this morning. I guess she and the baby are both okay, but the hospital's keeping them a few days on account of it's a couple of weeks early."

"Where are the other kids?"

"Up with Stacy's sister in Phoenix."

"Thanks," Adam said as the guy moved along. What was it going to be like when Chelsea gave birth and he saw his son or daughter for the first time? Amazing, yes, but would the world suddenly look different? In a few short months, he was going to be a father and he'd find out.

God willing…

Frustration just about choked him. What would they do tomorrow morning if nothing had changed?

Suddenly Adam knew. If Chelsea agreed, he'd send her somewhere no one would ever think of looking for her and set himself up here as a target with Whip to watch his back. No more waiting around. He thought back to everything he knew about Chelsea and remembered her talking about a woman she'd met at the culinary school she'd attended in Los Angeles. They'd become friends. Sarah Miller, that was her name, and she'd taken an executive chef's position somewhere in the greater L.A. area. Chelsea wouldn't remember Sarah, but Sarah would certainly remember Chelsea, and she would also have pictures and stories.

But first there was that box Dennis had found under Adam's childhood home. He had to know what was inside. The possibility it could condemn—or clear—his father was too strong to ignore. He had to know.

The motorcycle got him to Tucson in good time and by two thirty, he'd found the hospital birthing center. He took the elevator to the second floor and walked down a nondescript hall toward the nurses' station. Before he reached it, he happened to glance through an open door into a square room and found Dennis sprawled in one of many chairs, his head flung forward, chin touching his chest, eyes closed.

Dennis looked up as Adam sat on the chair beside him. "Hey," he said in a gravelly voice.

Adam studied his friend. "You look terrible."

Dennis's smile was fleeting. "It was a long night."

"Boy or girl?"

"Boy."

"That's great, man. Congratulations."

"Thanks. He's small but perfect. The doctors say he can go home in a couple of days.

"And Stacy is okay?"

"Fine. She's asleep with the baby right now. I came down here for coffee and kind of collapsed."

Adam got up and poured his friend a cup from the carafe on the counter then sat back down.

Dennis took a long swallow. "That's good," he said, and stared at Adam a moment. "Remember our old plan?"

"You mean the tavern?"

"Yeah. You and I were going to open a place, remember? Artisanal beer, music, hire a chef and serve really excellent bar food—"

"Chelsea's a chef," Adam said. "A good one."

"Really? Well, I know all about beer and the plumbing it takes to brew it and you, my friend, can build anything."

"It would be fun. Maybe someday, who knows?" He paused for a second, then added, "I have something to tell you."

Dennis almost spit out his latest mouthful of coffee. "The box! I forgot about it. Oh, Adam, I'm sorry. I haven't even been answering the phone. You must have waited—"

"No, no, don't worry about that. My news is that I'm going to be a dad in several months. Chelsea is pregnant."

Dennis's grin was wonderful. "That's great." He slugged Adam in the arm. "Then you and her are serious?"

"Very. We're already engaged—well, it's a long story and we're doing our best to make sure it has a happy ending. I'll keep you posted."

"Fatherhood's the greatest," Dennis said. "My kids and Stacy mean the world to me."

"I can see that," Adam said. "You're an inspiration."

Dennis laughed. "I bet Whip is thrilled."

"I haven't told him," Adam said. "But you're right, he'll be excited. Anyway, about the box. If I can borrow your key I'll go get it myself."

"No need. I had already stopped at the storage garage when Stacy called and said her water broke. The box is in my car and my car is out in the parking lot."

"That's great. I'll go get it and bring your keys back."

"Maybe a walk and a breath of fresh air will revive me," Dennis said as he got to his feet and stretched. "I'll go with you."

The parking lot was out in the open and Dennis took a deep breath as they walked to his car. Their friendly catch-up chatter stopped when they found the back window of Dennis's vintage Chevy smashed. Dennis quickly stepped through the broken safety glass and unlocked the front door. He swore. "They ripped the CD player right out of the dash," he said, "Damn, that thing was brand-new!" He peered into the back seat. "Oh, Adam, shoot, your box is gone, too."

Adam stared into the empty backseat. "Maybe you put it in the trunk?" he asked hopefully.

"No, man, the trunk is full of birthday presents for our oldest." He unlocked the trunk, anyway, to reveal bags and boxes of toys.

"I'm sorry," Dennis said.

"It's not your fault."

"Yeah. First my house and now my car. What's next?"

Adam stared at the broken window and wondered the same thing.

"GONE? THE BOX IS really gone? Just like that?" Chelsea said as she juggled two trays of appetizers. The party was in full swing and Adam had just returned from Tucson. He'd spent the afternoon having Dennis's window fixed and a new CD player installed so Dennis could stay at the hospital with his wife and baby.

"Just like that," he said, relieving her of one of the trays.

"I'm sorry. You must be so disappointed."

"Yeah. He's had a couple of break-ins recently That seems really suspicious to me. Tomorrow you and I have some decisions to make and then I want to take you to the hospital to meet Stacy while I ask Dennis a little more about that box."

She agreed, pleased he was including her in his life. If they were to be married and create a family, he had to get over living like a lone wolf. But visiting friends was also such a contrast to outrunning killers that she had a hard time wrapping her head around it. Holton seemed to have a dozen henchmen willing to do his bidding. Would she and Adam live through another Nevada-scale attack?

"Anyway, that's why I'm late. What have I missed?"

Maria and Sofia came to the door. Sofia stared at Adam for a moment, then broke into a smile. "Adam? Does Miguel know you're here?"

"No, I'm kind of undercover. I haven't been around long."

"Don't let Ms. Holton see you," Sofia said, her eyes wide.

"Not on your life," he said, handing her a tray.

She nodded and hurried after Maria.

"Your Spanish is excellent," Chelsea said, proud she'd understood every word of their conversation.

"My grandmother was born and raised in Mexico City."

"I was going to say I didn't know that, but hey, that's the story of my life, right?"

He suddenly leaned over and kissed her forehead. "Okay, what did I miss today? Give me one of your famous lists."

"Let's see. According to Aimee, the contractor—your boss, right?—looked at the fancy refrigerator they delivered last night and declared it was the wrong model, so she called the store and read them the riot act. They're re-ordering and meanwhile, those poor delivery guys have to drive up here after work this evening and take this one back because she can't stand to have it on her property another night.

"The afternoon drama continued when the decorators didn't show up until almost four. They strung sparkle lights, strategically placed a few potted palm trees and paper lanterns, scattered flowers and presto, the patio now resembles a tropical paradise. The liquor is flowing, the television actor brought groupies and last but not least, Tom Nolan arrived."

"He's out there?"

"In the flesh. He and a jumpy Aimee exchanged a few kisses and then she reverted to a hot mess. Oh, and Nolan brought a big hulking guy instead of a wife."

"Is Davy here, too?"

"Not yet. He was here earlier when the debacle about the refrigerator was going down. I guess he had to check the numbers on the box and make sure it was indeed the wrong one. Took him forever, too. Maybe he can't read." She furrowed her brow and looked up at Adam. "I'm still expecting something to happen, something that finally helps us understand who Devin Holton designated to orchestrate your murder."

"I am, too," Adam said. "Maybe we're desperate."

"I think it's Aimee, at least for me. The first day I was here she was conceited and mean, the next day she was angry and nervous, and now she's jumping out of her skin. Something is up. What about Whip? Did you hear from him today?"

"As far as Whip knows, we're halfway to Florida so I don't expect to hear from him. There wasn't anything about it on the radio, though," he said. "Whip said they'd keep it hushed up because the guy was a US marshal." He looked longingly toward the patio, "I need to go out there and look around."

Chelsea frowned. "Maybe you could hide out in the den. It fronts the patio."

"I'll try it," he said to appease her.

"I should take more of this food out to Miguel."

"Go ahead. I know my way around this place."

ADAM FOUND THAT the den, by virtue of being the thoroughfare to the bathroom, had been decorated just like the patio, with paper lanterns strung overhead and straw hats, grass skirts and silk leis tacked to the walls. He made his way to the open glass doors and peered outside. The music was too loud to hear conversation, but Aimee and Tom Nolan had chosen to stand directly under a string of paper lanterns and so were clearly visible. He glimpsed a burly figure behind Nolan and immediately fingered him as Nolan's bodyguard.

His attention was diverted for a moment as Chelsea walked across the patio carrying a couple of trays she deposited in an icebox next to the grill. She wore a red apron that hugged her body and he fancied the slight bulge that was his baby that had grown a little in the past week, a fact that made him grin. She stopped to chat for a moment with Miguel and then left the patio.

Adam shifted positions in order to change his angle of observation, but it was no use. He would never find out why Nolan brought along a bodyguard unless he got out there and mingled.

Studying the patio for possible hiding places solved

nothing, but he did make an observation that gave him an idea. Some of the guests had dressed in bright Hawaiian wear, some of them even to the point of costumes. He studied the walls around him and considered options, then snatched a grass skirt, straw hat and several leis. In a flash he went from the guy-on-the-street to the whacko-at-the-party, but the leis and hat covered most of his face and the skirt confused the issue. He walked outside and grabbed a cocktail glass someone had abandoned on a table. The trick would be to stay off the bodyguard's radar.

The safest place to get the lay of the land was near Miguel so he walked that way. "Need some help?" he asked when he reached the grill.

Miguel looked up from turning chicken kebabs. "No thanks," he said, then a flicker of recognition lit his eyes. That was quickly followed by a disbelieving glance at Adam's clothes.

"I'm incognito," Adam said softly.

Miguel smiled, his teeth very white against his brown face. "You look like a cheesy ad for a tiki bar. I wouldn't have known who you were if I hadn't heard your voice. What are you doing here, of all places? You have to know there's more than one gun on this patio that would shoot you dead in an instant. You should go."

"I can't. I'm snooping on Tom Nolan."

"At least tell me you're armed."

"Yeah, I'm armed."

"Brilliant."

"What do you know about Tom Nolan and Aimee?"

"They're tight. I call Nolan 'Little Devin,'" Miguel said.

"Why do you call him that?"

"Well, he took over Holton's wife and his business."

"What about his own wife?"

"She left him a couple of months ago." He handed Adam

a pair of tongs. "Make yourself busy. Take the skewers off the grill and put them on that platter." He raised his voice and called his wife, who showed up seconds later. Adam handed Sofia the tray and she winked at him.

After she'd left to distribute the chicken, Adam lowered his voice. "What do you mean he took over Holton's business?"

"Not the human-trafficking thing, that's too much for a lightweight like Nolan. I'm talking about the drug smuggling Holton ran on the side. Small-time, perhaps, but lucrative. Word is Nolan has rubbed a few people the wrong way, though. Ms. Holton better watch it or she'll get caught in the crossfire."

"That explains the bodyguard." Did it also explain the violence against Adam? Why would Tom Nolan care what happened to Adam Parish? As long as he stayed away, so what?

Unless Holton was paying Nolan, but was Nolan connected enough to come up with all these hit people?

Miguel looked around, then lowered his head and spoke. "Don't just stand there thinking like that. There's an icebox by your feet. Hand me something."

Adam did as asked, lifting from the chilled box a tray covered with raw seafood. He glanced over at Nolan as he handed the tray to Miguel. The bodyguard was scanning the crowd and Adam looked away before they made eye contact.

"How about Ms. Holton? Does she know Nolan took over for her husband?"

"Probably. Maybe they're in it together."

Well, he knew she needed money and that her father had turned into a dry well. Maybe she was a partner in this.

"I heard about your marriage," Adam said. "Congratulations."

"Thanks. Ms. Holton said she'd pay us our back wages

next week along with a bonus. Once she pays up, I'm taking Sofia away from here. I'm sick of sleeping apart from my bride and I don't want her up here when things go sour."

"I don't blame you," Adam said. He felt the same way about Chelsea. That's what love was—the desire to protect at any cost.

But, as he was learning, love was also sharing good and bad, danger and peace, everything. In a way, love was allowing yourself to let go of the illusion of control.

What if he'd approached Miguel two days ago? Instead of slinking around learning next to nothing, he could have gotten all this information on Tom Nolan and made inroads into understanding what Aimee was up to. Lesson learned.

He was about to risk moving closer to Aimee and Tom when his phone vibrated in his pocket. "Keep an eye on those two," he said. "Watch for some kind of drug exchange or money or… I don't know, something."

Miguel laughed. Adam picked up a couple of dirty trays and made his way toward the gate that led to the kitchen. Outside the gate, he put the trays down on the table placed there for that purpose and dug his phone out of his pocket.

"Hello?"

"Hey, hombre, this is Diego. I didn't see you today."

"I was on an errand," Adam said. "Listen, can I call you later? I'm in the middle of something—"

"No bother. I just wanted you to know that I heard from every one of those kids and their parents this evening. It was like a parade at my house. Two written apologies and one kid is going to weed the yard every week this summer. Who says there aren't still some responsible parents out there? I'm grateful for what you did. And ultimately, those kids will be grateful, too."

"Thanks," Adam said. "Sounds like you had quite the

day what with the refrigerator thing up here and all that down there."

"Yeah. Wait. What refrigerator thing?"

"Aimee Holton's refrigerator."

"What refrigerator?"

"I heard you discovered the special-order fridge that was delivered last night is the wrong model."

"A refrigerator was delivered last night?" Diego said. "Why wasn't I informed? And it's the wrong one? Wait, we only ordered it a few days ago and it was on back order… it can't be here already."

"I'll ask around and let you know," Adam said. "There's a party here tonight, maybe I misunderstood in all the confusion."

"Man, it's always something with that woman. Okay, I'll check in the morning."

Adam knew he hadn't misunderstood anything. The refrigerator had to be some kind of diversion for a drug drop or something. He needed to talk to Chelsea. He entered the kitchen, where he found both Maria and Sofia fussing with food. "Where's Daisy?" he asked.

"She left with Mariana," Maria said.

"Mariana? The kid with the bruise? What's she doing here at this time of night?"

"I don't know. She was all dressed up but really upset. She and Daisy talked a minute, then Daisy went off with her."

"How long ago?"

"Fifteen minutes or so."

"Where did they go?"

"No idea. She told us to tell you she went to see the goats, whatever that means."

The old goat barn was next door to the shed, where the phony refrigerator had supposedly been delivered. He threw aside his costume and took off through the house, exiting out the front door. The slight breeze whispered an omen through the dead grass as he veered off on the path to the left.

Had someone forced or coerced Mariana into laying a trap for Chelsea?

Had Devin Holton finally organized his next attack?

Chapter Sixteen

Chelsea pulled on Mariana's bloody hand to halt their dash down the hill. In the distance, thanks to the moonlight, she could see what appeared to be the outdoor light for a large new building and the darker shapes beyond it. That must be the old goat farm. The girl stopped abruptly and the two of them almost collided.

"Mariana, tell me what's wrong," Chelsea urged.

The dark shadow of Mariana's head turned to look toward the buildings. "Shhh," she whispered as she turned back. "He'll hear."

"Who'll hear?"

"The guard."

A guard? On a refrigerator?

"What's going on? Where did you get that dress?"

"That man bought it," she said. The girl was attired in the pink dress Chelsea had tried on. The saleswoman's comments played themselves out in Chelsea's mind. "Who is 'that man'?" she demanded.

"It doesn't matter," Mariana said, "Please—"

"First tell me where you went after you broke the glasses and where we're going now and why," Chelsea insisted.

"I was sent to the barn in the valley," she said so quickly and through so many tears that Chelsea had to concentrate on each uttered word. "Then the fire came and burned some of it and I was brought up here. Last night a truck delivered a whole bunch more girls. Lucia, she's one of them, she was pregnant. One of the men hit her and hit her. Now she's moaning and bleeding—I think she's dying. Please help her."

"How do we get past the guard?" Chelsea asked.

"The way I got out," Mariana said, and took off. Chelsea followed. Once near the building, Mariana slowed way down and the two of them crept past the well-lit front door of the shed and the man sitting on a chair outside of it. They continued their careful trek around the side of the structure until they turned a corner. They were now standing outside the back of the building.

It was very dark. Mariana reached above her head, apparently searching for something on the side of the building. Chelsea suddenly recalled the phone Adam had given her and dug it from her jeans pocket. She turned it on. The light from the screen was enough to reveal that Mariana was attempting to grab a windowsill eight or nine feet off the ground. Chelsea leaned over and cupped her hands, her phone clutched in her teeth. She hefted Mariana up farther against the wall until she could pull herself into the window, where she scuttled about a few seconds, then disappeared inside. That left Chelsea stranded on the ground.

A noise to her left sent her heartbeat racing. She used her phone with the intent to blind whoever was approaching, but the light wasn't bright enough. She directed it to her feet. Shards of broken glass littered the rocky earth and she quickly used the hem of her apron to pick one up to defend herself.

"It's me," a man whispered as he came to a stop a foot or two away. She dropped the shard as his hands grasped her arms. "Chelsea, are you all right?"

"Oh, Adam," she said. "Thank goodness you're here."

She pointed up to the window and stuffed the phone in her pocket. "I need a lift up."

"It might be a trap," Adam said. "I'll go first."

"No, you'll terrify Mariana. It's not a trap. Someone is in trouble. Just help me."

He cupped her face and kissed her lips, then pressed his gun into her hands.

"Adam—"

"Please," he said.

She tucked the gun in her waistband as he leaned over. She stepped into his folded hands. As he pushed, she caught the windowsill, cutting her palms on the broken glass caught in the frame. No wonder Mariana's hands had been slippery with blood. She paused in the shallow window, looking down at the dimly lit room below, preparing herself for the jump to the cement floor almost eight feet below. Her body and the baby it nurtured had already been through so much—could she withstand this punishment, too?

Then she finally saw the teetering stack of boxes and old appliances piled up against the wall to her right. Turning to look down at Adam, she gave him a thumbs-up. The very fact he was here, close by, gave her courage she didn't know she possessed. She turned back to the interior. Mariana appeared below, motioning with one hand for Chelsea to hurry down. Chelsea tore off her apron and laid it over the sill to protect Adam's hands when he followed, then found the top step with the toe of her shoe and climbed down to the floor.

BECAUSE HE HAD approached the building from the bluff side, Adam now took the time to reconnoiter the building's perimeter to find out exactly how well it was guarded. He was relieved when he ascertained there was only one man and he appeared half-asleep.

Then he attacked the window. His first jump fell short. In the near dark, he backed up and then ran forward, jumping at the last minute, catching a cloth of some kind and slipping back to earth with it grasped in his hand. He shook out what he now realized was Chelsea's apron.

Ever aware of the guard, he stuffed part of the apron in his back pocket so as not to leave a red flag behind. He backed up again. This time he caught the sill with one hand, grabbed with the other and, using his feet, managed to attain the opening. Scrunched in the window frame, he peered into the room. There had to be twenty or so teenage girls standing in a semicircle and, as a unit, they turned and stared up at him.

He spied Chelsea on her knees in the middle of the group and scrambled down the makeshift ladder into the hot, humid gloom. The girls parted for him to pass. He'd never seen so many terrified faces in one place in his life. Chelsea was attending to a young girl lying prone on her back, dried tears on her battered, swollen cheeks, her clothes bloody.

"What's wrong with her?" he asked as he kneeled down.

Chelsea cast him a swift glance. "Her name is Lucia. As far as I can tell, Davy knocked her around this morning. I think she's miscarrying her baby or maybe he ruptured something inside her."

"He did that here?"

"Yes. She was part of the 'shipment' that came in last night in that phony refrigerator delivery. They're waiting now for someone to come load them up and take them to Denver."

He stared at her, too angry for a moment to make a sound.

"Aimee knows what's going on," Chelsea added. "She's been lying about it all day."

"That's why she's so jumpy. She's waiting for the truck to take these kids away."

"That witch," Chelsea muttered. "Lucia's been bleeding for a long time. Her skin is hot and dry. She needs a doctor, Adam. But right now, I need some water to cool her down and something absorbent for the blood."

A young girl wearing a very fancy pink dress and with a bruise on her cheek stepped forward. "I'll take care of it," she said.

"This is Mariana," Chelsea said, smiling at the girl. "Mariana, this is Adam."

"Nice to meet you," Adam said. He turned back to Chelsea and handed her the red apron. "Have you called the police?"

"I tried but the battery is gone thanks to the fact I used it as a flashlight for too long."

"I'll call." As he pressed the numbers, he asked another question. "Why didn't the other girls escape out the window after Mariana left?"

Chelsea shook her head. "I don't know. I think they're too frightened to move or speak. Most of them are spaced out on drugs. Maybe they didn't want to leave Lucia. Or maybe they don't know where else to go."

The call went through. Adam explained what was going on and added they needed an ambulance as well as police.

"How did Mariana get in the middle of this?" he asked. "You met her before these other kids got here."

"She was a runaway, 'found' by an older man with white hair. Tom Nolan, maybe? I'm not sure. She fought him when he forced her to put on that dress and tried to sell her to his friends. He pawned her off on Aimee, who decided to use her as kitchen help until it was time to ship her off with the others. When Mariana broke the dishes, Aimee dumped her in a barn down in the valley, which I gather is their usual place to stage these transactions, but the fire damaged that place so Mariana was brought up here to wait for the other girls to arrive."

"But how did Mariana get back in that dress? She wasn't wearing it when you saw her the first time, was she?"

"No. I noticed her clothes were too big. Aimee had given them to her when she got to the house, but once everything went wrong, she made Mariana put the dress back on. That woman is a bitch with a capital *B*."

"She's more than that. All this means she took over Holton's human-trafficking deal," Adam said.

"Along with her 'business associate,' Davy."

"He must be a designated 'recruiter,'" Adam said.

"What's a recruiter?"

"The guy who finds lost, hapless girls, befriends them, gets them dependent on him for drugs, turns them into prostitutes and then sells them. There are too many here for one guy, though. They must have gathered kids from the whole state. There's an underground network in this country to move children sold into sex slavery. Denver is one of the hubs."

Mariana showed up with two bottles of water, a roll of paper towels and a few old rags and items of clothing that Adam passed along to Chelsea.

He had a decision to make. Should he get Mariana to help him move the girls' outside via the broken window and into the old goat barn so they weren't trapped in this building? Or did he go outside and take care of the situation from there until the police showed up? They were still almost thirty minutes away…

Once again, he scanned the faces around him and decided on the latter. The girls were frightened, impaired and cowed by abuse. He wasn't even sure the goat barn would hold all of them or what shelter it would provide.

"It's going on midnight," he told Chelsea. "I don't think we have much time before that truck gets here. I hate to leave you alone with Lucia, but I need to go subdue the guard."

"Take the gun," she said as she reached for it.

"No," he said, catching her hands. "You keep it. Anyone comes through that door, use it."

"But Adam—"

"I can't leave you and the kids here unprotected. I'll 'borrow' the guard's gun, don't worry. Caution the kids to stay away from the door and try to stay out of sight. I love you, Chelsea."

She looked up at him as he stood. "I love you, too," she said.

ADAM RAN UP the dark hill, then circled back and approached the building from the road. He walked toward the pool of light by the main door, where the guard sat in a chair. The man stood as he caught sight of Adam.

"Who are you?" he asked.

Adam kept advancing. He fiddled with his pocket as though to show identification at the same time he spoke. "Davy said the truck will be here any second."

"I know. I just got word they're five minutes out."

Adam stopped a foot or so in front of the man, made as if to show him identity and instead delivered a very fast blow to the man's jaw. He went down in a flash. Adam dragged him to the side of the barn and quickly relieved him of his weapon. He checked it to make sure it was loaded. He also took his keys, flashlight, hat and jacket. He used the guard's handcuffs to attach him to a drainage pipe and gagged him with his own necktie.

Satisfied, Adam shrugged on the jacket. It was tight

but manageable. Now to unlock the shed. The noise of an engine and the creak of old springs alerted him that a vehicle was approaching, sans headlights. He saw its dark shape stop, turn and back toward the shed door.

Adam walked quickly back to the guard's post, arriving in the pool of outdoor light right as the driver jumped out of the truck, a shotgun gripped in his hand. The passenger was half his size. He darted to the back of the truck, where he rolled open the back gate.

"Who the hell are you?" the driver asked as Adam approached.

"The other guy got sick. Davy sent me down here to relieve him," Adam said as he glanced into the now open back of the truck. Lines of wooden benches ran along either side. No windows, nothing to hold on to. His stomach turned as he thought of those poor scared kids riding in the sinister enclave of this joyless truck.

"Open the shed," the driver said. "We haven't got all night.

"It's hot out here, Lou," the passenger complained as he mopped his forehead with his sleeve. "I haven't eaten anything since noon. I don't know why—"

"Stop complaining," Lou said. "Cripes, Bennie, you drive me nuts." He pointed the shotgun at Adam as if to motivate him. "Open the shed."

These were the same two guys from the night before, Adam was sure of it. He found the right key. "One of the girls isn't well," he said as he swung open the door. "She needs a doctor."

"That's Denver's problem."

"She might be dead by Denver."

Lou shrugged. "Hurry it up. We've got a long way to go tonight."

Lou and Bennie both strolled into the dimly lit shed with authority, shining powerful flashlights, highlighting a bevy of frightened faces, including Mariana's but not Chelsea's. Adam's gaze went immediately to the open window in the back—he half expected to find her hiding up there. Nothing. Mariana met his gaze and looked away.

The driver strode right over to Lucia, then called over his shoulder, "Bennie, get the girls into the truck."

Bennie started yelling in very bad Spanish interspersed with equally poor English. The girls began moving outside. Adam glanced at Lou to find that he'd kneeled down to study Lucia's condition more closely. As soon as Bennie looked away to reprimand one of the kids, Adam drew his stolen gun and slammed the grip hard against the guy's round head, catching him as he slumped to the floor. He pocketed the man's gun, worried for a moment the commotion would catch Lou's attention, but the guy remained on his knees.

Adam crept forward until he was close enough to shove the barrel against the base of Lou's skull. "Drop your weapon," he said.

Lou didn't move.

"A shot will paralyze you if it doesn't kill you first," Adam added. "Now, put the shotgun on the floor and push it away."

The weapon clattered against the cement floor. The man shoved it off with his right hand.

"Stand up."

"Who *are* you?" Lou snarled as he heaved himself upright.

"No friend of yours," Adam said. He carefully retrieved the shotgun, then dragged a dazed-looking Bennie to his feet and prodded both men toward the door. The girls parted to let them pass.

They had just cleared the shed when another man approached from around the truck, his arm around Chelsea's neck, a revolver pushed against her temple. Davy had finally made an appearance.

"Stop right there," he called.

Adam looked right into Chelsea's eyes. "Don't do anything he says," she said and paid for the remark as Davy tightened the arm around her neck.

"Stay where you are or I shoot her," he growled. "Lou, take the shotgun and frisk him." Lou paused. "It's okay," Davy prompted. "He's not going to fire at you because he knows if he does I'll kill this pretty little cook and then I'll kill him and then I'll still do anything I want with the girls."

"You won't risk a house full of Aimee's guests hearing gunshots," Adam said.

"Are you kidding? Why do you think the music is so loud?"

"The police are coming," Chelsea added, her voice hoarse.

"Let 'em come. Go on, Lou. Do what I told you."

Lou took all three weapons from Adam, then smashed his fist into Adam's jaw. He would have kept it up if Davy hadn't yelled at him to stop.

"Get the girls into the truck," Davy ordered, "and then get the hell out of here."

Bennie kind of staggered away but Lou took out his aggression by shoving the nearest teens past Adam. Mariana was one of them. As she passed Adam she whispered, *"Mira en el delantal."*

He frowned as he tried to make sense of what she said but his thoughts quickly moved on as Davy pushed Chelsea toward him. He caught her before she fell. "You two, back inside."

The trunk gate clanked closed behind the last girl and Lou secured it with a big padlock. Adam wrapped his arm around Chelsea's waist and did as directed. It felt like a death march.

"I'm sorry," she whispered as they walked. "I thought I could help if I was outside but Davy found me hiding over by the guard you must have knocked out."

"Don't worry, it's okay," he told her and kissed her hair.

"By the way," she added, "I think we should get married right this moment. Here and now. Forever. I love you, Adam."

He kissed her again.

"Okay lovebirds, that's far enough," Davy said, but his attention was immediately diverted as he caught sight of Lucia tossing and turning on the bed of castoffs Chelsea and Mariana had created for her. Something red draped her body.

"Who the hell is that?" he demanded.

"She's the girl you all but killed today," Chelsea said.

"Oh, the knocked-up one. She's not your main problem right now."

Adam realized the red cloth was Chelsea's apron. Mariana had whispered something about an apron—what other one but this? She'd said to look at it but all he saw was an apron.

"You two have really screwed this up for me," Davy said. "What am I going to do with your dead bodies?"

"Here's an idea," Adam said, his mind working on how to examine that apron. "Don't kill us."

"It's too late for that." Davy studied Chelsea. "Such a shame because you, babe, are a beaut. All that red hair. I bet you're hot, aren't you?"

"Hot enough to burn you to a cinder," Chelsea said defiantly. He grabbed her and roughly kissed her. Adam rushed him, but Davy once again used Chelsea as a shield and fired a bullet. It grazed Adam's left arm. Chelsea screamed. Davy slapped her with the gun so hard she fell to the floor. Adam heard her head hit the cement and in a flash, he kneeled beside her. That put him close to the red apron. It was turned so the pocket was hidden next to Lucia.

Davy paced nearby, the gun trained on them, but his brow furrowed. It looked like he wasn't used to doing his own dirty work, as though intimidating little girls was more his style. Chelsea moaned and Davy stopped pacing, his gaze riveted to her pale face, the gun clutched in a white-knuckled fist. It was like he longed to squish a bug but was too squeamish. Adam knew Davy would get over that as he considered his options.

He used the man's distraction to drag the apron from Lucia and was immediately aware of the heavy shape inside the long pocket. When the garment bumped against his thigh, he knew. The object in the pocket was a gun and odds were good it was the one he'd left with Chelsea. She must have given it to Mariana when she left the shed and Mariana had then hidden it in the apron. He slid his hand in the pocket. His fingers closed around the grip. Without a second's hesitation, he raised the weapon. Davy, sensing movement, turned. Adam fired—the bullet hit Davy right between the eyes and he went down like a ton of broken bricks.

Ignoring the fallen man, Adam rushed to gather Chelsea in his arms right as headlights shone into the shed. Thank goodness, help had arrived! As he gently lay her head back down, it finally registered on him there were no flashing lights, no sirens.

What now, or better yet, who now? He moved cautiously to the front of the shed, gun drawn.

A familiar shape emerged from a police vehicle with a darkened rack on top of the car.

"Whip?" Adam said.

"Good God almighty!" Whip said, his gun drawn. "Adam? Lord, boy, have you been shot?"

"It's nothing," Adam said for the first time recognizing the searing pain in his left upper arm. "I'm just so glad to see you. Get on the radio, get ambulances. There's a van full of kidnapped minors on their way to Denver." He stepped closer and handed Whip his gun. "This is the weapon used to kill the guy inside. It belongs to the guard, but I did the shooting." His voice petered out as he noticed Whip didn't lower his weapon.

"Whip?"

"Where's Chelsea?" he asked.

"She's unconscious back in the shed. We need an ambulance—"

"Is this where you've been holed up? Man, I'd laugh if I didn't want to cry. Why didn't you leave?"

"We had something to finish—"

"Finish? Is that what you call this?" Whip swore under his breath. "I begged you not to come to Arizona but I always knew you would."

"I had to find out who was trying to kill me and why," Adam said, stepping back. What was going on?

"When your friend Dennis told me about finding that box I knew eventually you'd come for it. I tried to steal it but he'd locked it away by then. Then you said something yesterday about a friend and I knew it was Dennis, I knew."

"Whip, what's in that box?" Adam said, an ominous feeling growing in his gut.

"I wanted you stopped but not here, not by me," Whip continued.

"Listen," Adam said, "first things first. We need to get help for Chelsea and the girl—"

"What girl?"

"The man I just killed, his name is Davy, he beat up a fourteen-year-old. She's burning up and—"

"Is she wearing a pink dress?"

"No, she's one of the new kids—wait. How do you know Mariana?" Adam asked as shivers ran up his spine. Was it possible Mariana's tormentor wasn't Tom Nolan, but…

"Damn Davy," Whip grumbled. "Thinks he knows everything. I've been in this business for more than a decade, taking partners when I had to. Holton was a screwup, but I swear, Aimee is worse. When she brought in Davy things went from manageable to chaos."

Adam stared at Whip. His head told him things his heart didn't want to hear and for several seconds, the ensuing battle of truth vs. wishful thinking deafened him. Whip's mouth moved but Adam couldn't decipher a single word until all of a sudden, sound returned like a sonic boom. "I had everything under control," Whip said.

"You're in on this," Adam said woodenly. "My God, you're not only in on it, you started it. You and Ballard—"

"Ballard?" Whip scoffed. "No, I found someone else in the system who needed cash. When Ballard found out this guy sold you out, he came looking for me."

"He drew the gun because he saw you coming up behind me," Adam said.

"Yep, but he wasn't fast enough. Now he's under five feet of desert sand. It pains me, it truly does, that you and your girl will soon be lying right alongside him."

Adam stared at a man he once thought he knew inside and out. "Has everything about you been a lie?"

"Just about," Whip admitted.

"For how long?"

"Forever."

"You were searching for the box after my father died. That's why you wanted to renovate the house, so you could look for it. What in the world is inside it?"

He shook his head. "I'm not sure," he said finally. "Okay, go back inside. I'll make it quick."

"The police, ambulances—"

"All canceled. No one's going to ride to your rescue. Go hold Chelsea's hand. Tell her you love her. It's your last chance."

Adam stood his ground. His head throbbed with disbelief and yet discrepancies in Whip's behavior began to eat through his denial. Ballard's shooting, sure, but even before that.

"I'll shoot you right here if I have to," Whip said.

"No, you won't," Chelsea said from behind Adam.

Adam turned and there she was, framed in the doorway, Davy's gun clutched in her hands. She might be deathly pale but she was also strong and beautiful and when she smiled at him, her whole face looked…different.

"Give the gun to Adam, Whip. I used Davy's phone, the police are on their way."

Whip made no effort to do as she said.

"You're the man Mariana told me about," Chelsea continued. "You're a depraved and evil soul. No more killing. It's over. Give Adam your gun."

The silence was deafening.

"Move out of the way, Adam," she said.

The truth was he couldn't move. His feet just wouldn't budge.

The silence stretched on until Whip shook his head. "She's right," he said, his voice incredulous, his gun hand sinking to his side. "It is over."

Adam reached for the weapon.

Whip met his gaze. "It's over," he repeated and in a flash, he'd pointed the gun at his own temple. "Over." Adam closed his eyes as Whip pulled the trigger.

Epilogue

One week later

"I'm ready to open it," Adam said and, taking a knife, slit through the tape.

Chelsea had wondered when he would be able to face the box. Unwilling for anyone to see what was inside it until he did, Adam had taken the cardboard container from Whip's car and hidden it in their van before the cops got there, before Lucia had been whisked to safety by an ambulance or Aimee Holton had been led away in handcuffs or Tom Nolan had been caught red-handed in a high-stakes drug deal with who else but the television actor.

Truth be told, the last few days had been wonderful. Without a vendetta against them, they'd had time to enjoy each other, enhanced by the miraculous fact Chelsea's memory was back. She credited Davy's push and the subsequent bash of her head against the cement. Adam was prone to saying his guardian angel had woken her just in time. Whatever, the fact was she now had a past. Her mom and dad, her sisters, her brother Bill, her grandmother's face, her cute little food truck, her cat, her apartment, her overdue book—she had all that. And thanks to the baby growing in her body and the man sitting six inches to her right, she had a future.

All the pain and anger she'd assumed would engulf her once her memory returned had not happened. She'd already worked through all those feelings because while Steven had morphed into Adam, she had morphed, as well. She knew what it was like to be almost two different people, but not quite, not really.

And Chelsea's next goal was to help Mariana discover the same thing about herself. The police had stopped the truck before it crossed the state line and the girls had been delivered into child protective services. Mariana couldn't go home to her abusive parents so Chelsea had arranged to take her in. That meant relocating to Arizona, but Adam and his pal Dennis had big plans to build a tavern and she was open to anything as long as they were together. The important thing was that Mariana understood she had survived largely due to her own wits, that she was strong and unique and the future need not be a reflection of the past. Adam was as anxious to help Mariana as she was, so it looked as though before she gave birth to their own child, they would have Mariana to parent.

Adam, whose injured arm had healed as fast as all his other wounds seemed to, spread open the box flaps and removed a piece of dusty plastic revealing a diary with his mother's name written on the cover. Tucked inside were a couple of pieces of paper clipped together.

"This is Dad's writing," he said as he looked at the papers. "I'm starting with them."

She sat back as he read to himself, content to be here if he needed her, anticipating what he would really need was time to assimilate what he learned.

She'd almost dozed off when he put down the papers and looked at her. "I guess I should be flabbergasted, but after everything that's happened…at least now I know the truth."

She waited as he gathered his thoughts.

His voice was soft when he finally spoke. "I'll paraphrase what I've learned, okay? Unbeknownst to me, it seems my mother suspected that Whip was the guy who seduced her student into running away. He was a young cop then, as fit and strong as his nickname implied. When she confronted him he told her she was mistaken. She talked to Dad but he didn't believe her. He argued that poking around would only jeopardize their friendship. In other words, he stood by Whip instead of her. And apparently, he told Whip that Mom kept a diary."

Chelsea didn't say a word. What could she say?

"So, my mom made an appointment to talk to the chief," Adam continued. "You know, to elicit his help. Whip got wind of this and decided to steal her diary while she was at the appointment, but she was running late and surprised him by being home. Panicked, he killed her and searched for the diary, but couldn't find where she'd hidden it. Dad learned all this later."

"Good grief. Whip killed your mother."

Adam nodded. "Yeah, and then hinted to me that Dad had done it."

"Oh, Adam."

"Dad felt guilty about not supporting Mom, by letting her down before her death…about everything. Then he found her diary and read it. Apparently, after she talked to Whip about her student, he started showing up the same places she was. She felt threatened. If she told Dad this part, he was too drunk to remember it and that just fed his guilt. He talked to Whip, hoping he was wrong, but Whip admitted everything I told you before. He said the chief would never believe a drunk, not when Whip had a different story. That's when my father put all their old love letters and the diary and these two little pieces of paper into a box and hid it under the house. I don't think I'll ever know if he killed himself or just died from guilt."

"Maybe it doesn't matter," Chelsea said gently.

"He could have shown the chief the diary. He could have fought Whip and ultimately saved who knows how many other kids. But he didn't. He was a coward."

"But you're not," Chelsea said. "And maybe now you can find some peace with the past. You're going to need it with Mariana and your own child to raise."

"I know." He stared at the box and then looked down at her, melting her with his gray gaze. "I'll look at the rest later, then I'll figure out what to do with it."

She nestled against him. "That sounds like a good idea."

"I have an even better idea," he told her as he tipped her chin and claimed her lips.

* * * * *

THE GIRL WHO COULDN'T FORGET

CASSIE MILES

To all the girls who survive and thrive
in spite of tragedy.

And, as always, to Rick.

Chapter One

The petunias were dead. That was the first thing Brooke Josephson noticed when she parked at the curb. Two months ago when she'd planted the flowers, her intention was to brighten up this dull brick building and make it into a more welcoming place for Franny. Instead, the yard had become a petunia graveyard with the tortured faces of faded purple, yellow and pink blooms staring helplessly. Withered leaves reached out in silent entreaty. All they'd needed was a splash of water. August in Denver could be hot and dry, but this wasn't the blazing Sahara.

Brooke leaped from her SUV and hurried along the sidewalk. The dead petunias were a bad omen—not enough to push her into a panic attack, but close. She had the symptoms: labored breathing, tremors, accelerated pulse and more. She paused. *Slow down. Shake it off.* At a more controlled pace, she proceeded toward the front door of her friend's one-bedroom at the end of a one-story, L-shaped apartment complex.

She never should have expected Franny to take care of the plants. Her friend's life was a wild, erratic whirl, and she'd never change. Why should she? If she was happy with chaos, so be it. Brooke loved her crazy friend like the little sister she'd never had. They even resembled each other. *Of course we look alike. He chose us for our black hair and blue eyes.*

It had been twelve years, but she remembered every detail. Her past was inescapable.

As she stepped onto the concrete stoop, she checked her precision quartz wristwatch. Twenty-seven minutes ago, she'd gotten Franny's call and had responded ASAP. She'd logged off her computer, dashed to her car, checked her GPS and adjusted her route to avoid the traffic slowdown for repairs on Alameda.

And here she stood, worried and scared. But ready to save the day if need be.

She punched the doorbell and called out, "Franny, it's me. Open up."

Most likely, this was a lot of fuss about nothing. If so, she'd bite her tongue and wouldn't scold. Extra caution was better than ignoring potential signs of danger, even though Brooke hated to waste time with unnecessary disruptions. Sometimes she could go a full week without leaving her house. Some people—including FBI Agent George Gimbel and her therapist—thought her behavior was borderline agoraphobic, but they didn't understand the importance of organization. There was no such thing as being too efficient.

From inside the apartment, she heard her friend chattering in a high-pitched jumble of words. She was answered by a man's rumbling voice. That wasn't right! Franny didn't date. She had no male relatives.

Brooke whipped her phone from the pocket of her khaki shorts and hit the emergency call button. *Better safe than sorry.* She unzipped her fanny pack and wrapped her fingers around the palm-size canister of pepper spray. "Franny, are you okay?"

She heard someone moving across the hardwood floor

inside the apartment with a heavy tread; it must be the man. He was coming toward her. The pepper spray trembled in her hand. *I can handle this.* She had to. Nobody else would protect her and the people she loved. With the screen door open, she balanced on the balls of her feet—ready for action and glad that she'd worn sneakers instead of sandals. She braced herself. The first move would be hers.

The green-painted door was opened by a tall, dark-haired man in a suit.

Her phone squawked as the 911 operator answered, "Hello, what is your emergency?"

"You called the police," the man said.

Though law enforcement had failed her many times, Brooke needed backup. She shouted Franny's address at the phone and added, "We need help. Hurry."

"That's not necessary," he said.

"Where's my friend? What have you done to Franny?"

"Take it easy." He slid his hand inside his jacket. "Everything is fine."

Really? Then why are you reaching for a gun? She sprayed a blast of pepper spray. He dodged and threw up his arm for protection, but she knew that she'd scored a partial hit. While he winced and squinted, she darted into the apartment and positioned herself for another, more devastating blow.

"Brooke, stop!" Franny rushed from the back of the apartment. "What are you doing?"

"Taking care of this creep," she said.

She fired a karate kick at his knee and missed. Her next attempt aimed at his groin.

Her foot shot toward him. Before it connected, he grabbed her ankle and held on. It was all she could do not to lose her balance.

He held a wallet with his credentials toward her. "FBI."

"Let go of my leg!"

"Are you going to kick at me again?"

"Not if I don't need to." She brandished her pepper spray. "Don't try anything."

He dropped her ankle. "I ought to arrest you for assaulting a federal officer."

"Everybody please settle down," Franny said as she stepped between them. "Agent Sloan, you're not going to arrest anybody. Brooke, don't be a brat."

Oh, this was rich. The wildly irresponsible Franny Hennessey was telling her not to misbehave. As far as Brooke knew, that badge was a fake. If he was really a fed, he should have showed his credentials the minute he opened the door. Okay, maybe that was what he tried to do. Maybe this was as much her fault as his. Still, she said, "I'm not going to apologize."

"Don't care."

He glared at her through his right eye. The left squeezed shut, though the redness that came in reaction to the spray spread across his throat and stopped at his cheekbone. The blotch looked painful. "If you please," she said, "I'd like a closer look at that badge."

Without relinquishing his grasp on his wallet, he held his ID inches away from her nose. The documents appeared to be official. She read his name: Special Agent Justin Sloan.

She didn't usually make mistakes like this. Assaulting a fed? She placed her hand on her chest and felt the drumming of her heartbeat. Her adrenaline was running high, which wasn't a bad feeling, but not a good one, either. If she'd been home right now, she'd be opening mail and eating her midafternoon snack of fruit and crackers. Instead, everything was up in the air.

She turned to her friend. "Why is he here?"

"I contacted him."

"Why?"

She shrugged. "I was trying to get ahold of Agent Gimbel. Remember him? The guy who handled our case?"

"Of course I remember." He was a kind man who had taken a genuine interest. She hoped nothing bad had happened to him. "Why couldn't he come?"

"Gimbel retired. The FBI office sent Sloan instead."

He pointed to Brooke's phone, which was still connected to an emergency operator asking questions. "Are you going to talk to her?"

This situation just got worse and worse. She'd requested emergency assistance, and she knew from past experience that nothing would divert the officers from coming to her aid. Rather than wasting time with long explanations to the dispatcher, she disconnected the call. Another rule broken.

Sloan asked, "Franny, do you have milk?"

Her ingenuous blue eyes opened wide. "Are you thirsty?"

"He wants milk to counteract the sting of the capsaicin in the pepper spray," Brooke explained as she snapped the cover onto the small canister and returned it to her fanny pack, where she also kept a supply of medicated wipes to use in case the pepper spray got onto her fingers. She opened the package, took out a wipe and handed it to Sloan before using one on her own hands. "Water is ineffective in washing off the oil-based propylene glycol."

"About that milk," Sloan repeated.

"Come with me," Franny said as she scampered barefoot toward the arched doorway leading to the kitchen. "I always have milk for the cats. Don't worry, I don't give them much. It's not healthy, you know. But they do love it."

Brooke trailed behind Special Agent Sloan and Franny, whose curly black hair bounced around her elfin face. For

some unfathomable reason, she was wearing a purple se-
quin tiara. In her paisley-patterned yoga shorts and pink
T-shirt with a sparkly unicorn on the front, she looked
childlike and vulnerable. Actually, she was only four years
younger than Brooke, who was twenty-six but felt like
she'd already lived three lifetimes. No tiaras for her. She
kept her long hair slicked back in a no-nonsense ponytail,
which she twisted into a bun.

Her attention shifted to Sloan. He was tall, approxi-
mately seven inches over her five and a half feet, and he
appeared to be in good physical condition. His gray suit
jacket fit neatly across the wide expanse of his shoulders.
There was something disturbing about the way he moved.
Athletic and masculine, he seemed to exude confidence.
Or was it arrogance? Either way, his presence unnerved
her.

When she looked away from him, her gaze ricocheted
around Franny's small apartment, where the decor was
based on clutter, half-finished projects and more clutter.
Brooke counted no fewer than four cats. The table in the
dining area was covered with stacks of unopened mail,
multicolored scraps of fabric and a sparkling array of
beaded jewelry. Beside the table was a wicker basket of
unfolded laundry that a fat gray-and-white cat was using
as a bed. A teetering tower of books lurked in the corner.
Instead of a curtain, Tibetan prayer flags draped across the
dining room window, offering an alarmingly clear view
of the sidewalk outside. Any passerby could easily see
into the house. The security here was even worse than
her last place.

In the kitchen, dirty dishes filled one side of the double
sink. Half-eaten meals were scattered across the counter. Brooke couldn't help herself. She started washing
the dishes.

"What are you doing?" Franny asked.

They'd had this conversation a hundred times before. "Left-out food attracts mice. I'll have this cleaned up in a sec."

"Don't bother." Franny laughed and pointed to a black cat and a calico. "My mousers will protect me from varmints."

"Do any of these cats actually belong to you?"

"I don't own them, if that's what you mean."

As soon as Franny moved into a neighborhood, she made a point of befriending the local feline population. Brooke never knew from whence the cats came or where they went or why they liked to hang out with her friend. Maybe they recognized a kindred spirit.

"If you're looking for something to do, take care of him." Franny pointed to Agent Sloan, who had found a carton of milk in the fridge. "You broke him. You should fix him."

There was a certain amount of logic in what she said. *If Franny is making sense, I must be losing my mind.* Brooke directed Agent Sloan toward a straight-back chair beside a table where pots, pans and a basket full of green glass baubles took up most of the space. She took the carton from him, searched the cabinets for a clean bowl and poured the milk. While trying to find a fresh dish towel in the drawers, she said, "Take off your jacket, and be careful where you touch. The left sleeve probably has pepper spray on it."

He removed the holster clipped to his belt and placed his gun on the table next to the baubles. Then he peeled off his jacket and folded it into a neat package, which he stuck into a paper grocery bag that Franny handed him. The striptease didn't end there. He loosened his necktie. "I should probably take off my shirt, too."

Her already-speeding pulse jolted into high gear. "By all means, take off the shirt. Your collar might be…compromised."

Being careful to avoid handling the collar, he removed the short-sleeved cotton shirt. He wasn't wearing anything underneath. His nicely muscled chest showed off his tan.

Her fingers itched with an unexpected urge to rake though his black chest hair and slide over those taut pecs. *Snap out of it!* True, it had been a long time since she'd been this close to a half-naked man, but she wasn't the type to get all hot and bothered. Self-control was her middle name. With the bowl of milk and dish towel in hand, she approached the chair where he had taken a seat.

"Tilt your head up and to the right," she said.

His gaze connected with hers and…her heart stopped. Held in suspended animation, she couldn't breathe, couldn't move. Her ears were ringing. This wasn't a panic attack; it was something different, something she'd never experienced before. She blinked until her vision was clear and she found herself staring into the most fascinating eyes. They were deep set and gray with glittering facets of silver and green. His angular cheekbones matched a square jaw. His face was saved from severity by an ironic twist of his mouth. He had the kind of lips that were meant for kissing. Not that she was an expert. Her social life was only slightly more interesting than Franny's.

Her friend spoke up. "I'll see if I can find something for Sloan to wear."

"Excellent idea," Brooke said.

In an uncharacteristically clumsy manner, she swabbed the milk on the red blotches near his left ear. Excess from the dish towel dripped down his chest. She reached out with her bare hand to wipe it away. As soon as her fingers touched his flesh, a jolt of electricity traveled up her hand to her arm, then across her shoulder and down her chest, where it zapped her heart like a cardiovascular defibrillator. She jumped back. The milk spilled.

Breathlessly, she said, "No use crying over that."

He took the bowl from her. "Maybe I should do this myself."

"Yes, that would be easier." Aware that they were alone in the kitchen, she stepped back. This federal agent was a clear and present danger to her mental stability. "Have you spoken to Franny about why she called the FBI?"

"I have."

"Would you care to share that information?"

"She was trying to contact your mutual friend Layla and couldn't reach her." He dabbed at his cheek with the milk. "The text messages to her weren't answered. The phone calls went straight to voice mail."

"It's not unusual for Layla to go off the grid, and it's hardly a reason to call in the FBI." Brooke eyed him suspiciously. "You're not telling me everything, are you?"

"Franny's fears appear to be connected to what happened twelve years ago."

She didn't want to hear about this but had to know. "Tell me."

"Wait!" Franny dashed into the room with a crocheted poncho that she threw toward Sloan. She turned to Brooke. "Maybe we should forget about this. I'm feeling lots better, and I don't want you to get all freaked out."

Too late. Brooke was verging on a full-blown panic attack. She had to get this over with and go home. "You've got to tell me."

"Are you okay? You look kind of feverish."

"She's right," Sloan said. "Maybe you should sit."

As if she needed advice from a half-naked fed? "Will you excuse us, please?"

Without waiting for an answer, she dragged her friend through the messy front room into the equally cluttered bedroom, where she closed the door. Fearing she might pass out, Brooke lowered herself onto the edge of the unmade bed, trying not to think of this mattress as a breeding ground for bacteria and dust mites. She concentrated on breathing slowly, struggling not to drown in the fierce torrents that churned inside her.

Franny sat beside her. "I was scared about how you might react. That's why I didn't call you first. I figured Gimbel could look into stuff and make it all better."

But Gimbel had retired. Brooke asked, "What kind of stuff?"

"For the past couple of days, maybe a week, I've been getting phone calls from a number I didn't recognize."

"And?"

"They were weird."

Extracting information from her was like peeling an artichoke one leaf at a time. Brooke turned her head and focused on the blue of Franny's eyes—a color that was almost identical to her own. "Why did you think the calls were weird?"

"My voice mail picked up a couple of them. I can play them back."

"Maybe later." She didn't want to spend any more time here than absolutely necessary. Either there was reason for concern or not. "For now, just tell me."

"His voice was whispery." Her eyes lowered, and she sucked on her lower lip. "He said that little ladies who didn't do as they were told would be punished."

The terrible warning—one she'd heard before—set off a screeching alarm in Brooke's brain. *No, no, no, no, I don't want to remember.* "What else?"

"My finger." She held up her left hand. The little finger had been severed at the second joint. "He asked if I missed my finger."

"It wasn't him," Brooke said firmly. "Martin Hardy is locked away in prison for life. He can never touch you again."

"That's what Sloan said. And he promised to check on the other girls, to make sure they were safe. That's why I wanted you to come over to meet him." Though tears swamped her eyes, she forced a wobbly smile. "He's kind of gorgeous, huh?"

"I hadn't noticed."

"Yeah, you did. You were blushing."

Brooke scowled as she rose from the bed and paced on the small portion of floor that wasn't covered by a jumble of discarded clothing. Recently, she'd experienced a few odd incidents herself. Twice during the past week her car alarm had gone off, even though it was parked in the attached garage. She'd never found an explanation, but it hadn't seemed particularly threatening until now. "Was there anything other than phone calls?"

"Should I be scared?"

"I don't know."

"Do you think it's a copycat?" Her voice went high and nervous. "Our case was written up in the newspapers and online. And there's that movie guy who wants all six of us to get together for a follow-up story."

"His documentary is never going to happen." She'd vowed to sue the pants off anybody who tried to take advantage of them. "Until we have some answers, you should stay at my house."

"Why?"

Not wanting to get Franny riled up with more criticism, Brooke didn't mention the lack of security in her apartment or the uncurtained windows that were open to public view or the fact that cats could dart in and out at will. This place was unsafe. "If something is truly wrong, we need to stick together."

The doorbell rang, and she heard Agent Sloan cross the front room. He called out, "I'll answer it."

The fact that there was an armed federal agent in the other room reassured her. She pulled Franny to her feet. "Where's your suitcase?"

"I don't want to pack. Do I have to?"

"Not a problem. I've got everything at my house that you might need." With a renewed sense of purpose and a laser focus on home, she propelled her friend through the bedroom door. "Grab your keys and let's get out of here."

In the front room, Brooke would have preferred to make a beeline for the exit, but Sloan and two uniformed officers blocked the way. With his holster clipped to his belt and Franny's too-small poncho covering his shoulders, Sloan looked like a deranged outlaw. She wondered how he had explained his outfit to the cops who had arrived in response to her 911 call.

She checked her watch. Thirty-three minutes had elapsed since she'd spoken to the emergency operator. If this had been an attack by a homicidal maniac, they'd all be dead by now. Nonetheless, she thanked the officers for coming and apologized for the false alarm.

To Sloan, she said, "I'm taking Franny to my house. She'll be safe with me. Do you plan to investigate the phone calls she received?"

"Yes," he said curtly.

"Please keep me informed."

Franny popped up beside them holding a black plastic garbage bag filled with the scraps and glitter from the table. Her fears seemed to have disappeared. She was beaming. Brooke envied her friend's resilience, even though she didn't completely believe that bubbly smile.

Before they could escape out the door, one of the uniformed officers stepped forward. "I know you," he said. "Matter of fact, I recognize both of you with the black hair and blue eyes. You're two of the Hardy Dolls."

The emotions Brooke had been holding back erupted. Every muscle in her body tensed. Twelve years ago, six girls—all with black hair and sad blue eyes—had been abducted from their foster homes by a psychopath named Martin Hardy. He had held them captive in an isolated house in the mountains where they'd been shackled, drugged, starved and brutalized. He'd done unspeakable things.

"Hardy Dolls," the cop repeated. "I'm right, aren't I?"

She despised the demeaning nickname the press had labeled them with. *Hardy Dolls* sounded like the six of them were a soccer team or a rock group, instead of the cruel truth that nobody wanted to face—they were throwaway foster kids who nobody missed and nobody searched for. They'd had to save themselves.

"We're not dolls. Not now. Not ever."

Without another word, she turned on her heel and stormed out the front door. *I never should have left my house.*

Chapter Two

Yesterday, when Brooke dashed out the door from Franny's apartment, Sloan hadn't made the mistake of thinking that she was running away. Fear hadn't been her motivation. Anger had driven her. She'd left to avoid a fight, and he'd been grateful. Unless he missed his guess, Brooke Josephson was a formidable adversary who might have eviscerated that cop with the big mouth.

In order to verify that opinion and learn more about the victimology of the young women who had been kidnapped, he paid a midmorning visit to George Gimbel. At the retired agent's home in the foothills west of town, the two men sat on rocking chairs on the front porch, drinking black coffee and watching the pecking chickens outside their coop. A dappled, swayback mare with a big belly that mimicked the girth of her owner grazed in the corral attached to the small barn. Though Sloan could make out the downtown Denver skyline in the faraway distance, the peaceful setting made him feel like he'd gone back in time to the Old West.

Gimbel took off his cowboy hat and dragged his fingers through his unruly gray hair. "There hasn't been a day in the past twelve years that I haven't thought about those women. Never felt like we did right by them."

Sloan had read the files on the case. "From the record, it looks like you were thorough."

"Oh, yeah, the proper forms were filed. But when it came to an investigation? *Nada.*" His thumb and forefinger formed a zero. "They were abducted over a period of four or five months. Six girls went missing, one after another. Where were the cops? Where was the FBI? We dropped the ball. And why? Well, these were all foster kids—teenagers or younger. Everybody assumed they were runaways."

All too often, victims fell between the cracks. These women had been taken from different homes that were as far apart as Colorado Springs to the south and Cheyenne, Wyoming, to the north. They hadn't known each other, and there hadn't seemed to be a connection...except for one. Sloan pointed it out. "If someone in law enforcement had lined up their photos and noticed the similarities in appearance, they would have paid more attention."

"That's exactly what happened when the public learned about the kidnappings—intense publicity. Some of the victims were traumatized by the spotlight."

"Like Brooke."

"I'm not so sure about that," Gimbel said. "She's hard to read."

Sloan remembered her trembling hands, rapid breathing and darting gaze. "From the minute we met, it seemed like she was about to have a panic attack."

"But she didn't."

"Oh. Hell. No. She blasted me with pepper spray and tried to kick me in the groin."

Gimbel chuckled. "Brooke avoids confrontation, but she never backs down."

"How did the FBI get involved in the case?"

"When the women escaped, they went to the Jefferson County police, who realized that they were dealing with

kidnapping. Since two states—Colorado and Wyoming—
were involved, JeffCo was only too happy to pass this big,
fat, complicated case to us, where it landed in my lap." He
leaned back and folded his hands across his gut. "I'll never
forget the first time I saw all six of them together. Skinny
little things with black hair and blue eyes, they looked so
much alike that they could have been sisters. Actually, two
of them are identical twins."

"Hardy Dolls," Sloan said.

"Brooke hated when the media started using that moni-
ker, and I don't blame her. If that girl is a doll, she's sure
as hell an action figure. To survive in captivity, she had
to be tough. To engineer an escape with five other girls,
she had to be smart."

Sloan agreed. In the testimony given by the others, it
was obvious how much they respected Brooke. Their de-
scriptions of the escape showed an extreme degree of planning from the fourteen-year-old. Oddly, Brooke had said
very little. Her statement was limited to short answers and
claims that she didn't remember. A complex woman, there
was something about her that fascinated him. "She took
charge, but she wasn't the oldest."

"Layla was sixteen."

"And Layla Tierney is the reason I'm following up.
When Franny started getting threatening phone calls, she
contacted the others to find out if they'd received similar
anonymous contacts. She never reached Layla."

"She disappears from time to time," Gimbel said.
"Brooke will know how to find her."

He was glad for another reason to be in touch with her.
"I appreciate any advice. Victimology is new to me. My
training put more emphasis on the criminals and psycho-
paths."

"Three months ago, when you got assigned to the Denver office, they said we were lucky to have you." There was a hint of bitterness in his tone. "You're only a few credits short of a PhD in psychology. Is that right?"

Sloan nodded. "I'm working on my dissertation."

"To tell you the truth, I'm more impressed with the fact that you served in the navy."

"Which is how I paid for college." He hadn't joined the navy out of a sense of duty or patriotism, but he'd gotten more from his service than he ever expected. His dad had told him that the US Navy would teach him to be a man. In this case, Dad might have been right.

"I never enlisted," Gimbel said, "but I figure I paid my dues with a twenty-seven-year career in the FBI."

Sloan rose from his chair and went to the banister, where he watched the hens and avoided making direct eye contact with Gimbel. He didn't want their meeting to turn into a confrontation between the grizzled old veteran and the smart-ass college boy. Not that he was a kid at thirty-two.

"I've only got a couple years' experience in the field," he said. "Dealing with six different victims who have each developed their own coping behaviors is complicated to say the least. Your insights would really help."

"Let's get to it," he said.

"From your notes, it's clear they're all experiencing a degree of post-traumatic stress."

"You don't need a PhD to figure that out." Gimbel was kind enough not to scoff. Instead, he took a sip of his coffee. "Give me your profile of Franny."

He didn't like making a snap diagnosis but didn't have time to analyze his subject. Unlike therapy, profiling drew broad conclusions. "The clutter in her house and immature behavior points to ADD. She hides her feelings behind a bright, happy exterior—shiny enough to deflect close examination. Inside, she's a drama queen."

The older man nodded. "You got that right."

"Not being able to contact Layla for a few days shouldn't have been a big deal, but Franny was extremely agitated. The anonymous phone calls triggered her fears."

"Tell me about the calls."

"There were references to her time in captivity." Sloan repeated the words verbatim. "Everything the caller said was public knowledge."

"Did you check out the number?"

"It traced to a burner phone. Even the dumbest perverts use throwaways."

"But you investigated. Good."

Sloan was glad he hadn't immediately dismissed Franny's complaint. As Gimbel had pointed out, the law enforcement system hadn't paid enough attention when these women disappeared the first time. He refused to be the guy who failed them again. "I see two possibilities. The first is that Franny is getting targeted by a prison groupie who idolizes Martin Hardy. He's a copycat and bears watching but probably won't go further than crank calls. The other, more disturbing scenario suggests unresolved issues from the original crime. In your reports, you listed other men who knew Hardy and might have assisted in the abductions."

"There's no shortage of creeps out there," Gimbel said. "I hope Franny's fears are nothing but a feather on the wind, but you can't take that chance. It's your job to protect them."

"That's what you did."

"Damn right," Gimbel said. "I had to be sure they weren't just dumped back into the foster care system.

And I got a lawyer to manage their interests. I'll give you his name."

Gimbel was turning out to be a valuable resource. Sloan folded his arms across his chest and leaned against the banister. "Tell me about Brooke."

AFTER A LATE LUNCH, Sloan parked his SUV outside Brooke's gleaming white stucco house with a red tile roof. Hers was one of several Spanish Mission-style homes in this architecturally diverse urban neighborhood. The two-story house was surrounded by a tidy lawn, perfectly trimmed shrubs and colorful flower beds. And the place was well protected. He spotted two security cameras. One was mounted over the front door. Another peered down from the attached garage. Wrought iron latticework—in a decorative pattern—shielded the door and the arched windows on the first floor.

As soon as he exited his vehicle, the August heat hit him like a blast furnace. He straightened his striped necktie, smoothed the wrinkles from his linen suit jacket and tried not to sweat. He was eager to see Brooke again. Her personality—an impossible combination of fire and ice—fascinated him.

Not that their relationship could be anything but professional. She was a witness, possibly a victim, and he had to keep his distance. His reason for being here and talking to her was to determine his starting point in this widely disparate investigation. In addition to the anonymous phone calls to Franny, threats had been made to the other women. He needed Brooke's sensible approach to sort the real from the unreal, ultimately making sense of the situation. And, first and foremost, he needed to locate Layla.

As soon as he rang the bell, Franny yanked the door open and dived into his arms. After a giant hug—so much for professional distance—she bounced away from him. This young woman was as energetic and enthusiastic as a puppy looking for a pat on the head.

"Hey there," she said brightly. "You did a pretty great job of contacting everybody. They all called me, except for Layla."

"You said Brooke would know how to find her."

Franny grabbed his hand and pulled him into a two-story foyer with a terra-cotta floor and a curved staircase on the right. Compared to the hot weather outside, the house was cool and serene. He felt like he'd walked into a shaded glen in a perfectly organized forest.

"Those two, Brooke and Layla, are birdies of a feather," Franny said. "Both really smart and focused and, you know, tidy."

He grinned. Franny's casual description matched Gimbel's more technical analysis of OCD tendencies brought on by post-traumatic stress. "They like to keep things orderly."

"And I make them crazy," she confided.

An alarm shrieked, and Franny ran to a keypad near the door, where she punched random numbers. "I forgot to turn it off. Oh my God, that's loud. Can you help me?"

Brooke charged into the foyer. "Step away from the keypad."

Franny leaped backward as Brooke plugged in the numbers to turn off the alarm. She placed a cell phone in Franny's hand. "The security people are going to call and ask if we need help. Do you remember what you're supposed to tell them?"

"The code words," she said. "Happy trails to you."

"And then?"

"They'll tell me to repeat, but this time I'll say, 'Hi-ho, Silver, and away.'"

When Franny left to handle the call from the security service, Brooke turned toward him. "Good afternoon, Special Agent Sloan. You didn't mention that you were coming over when you called earlier."

"I was afraid you'd bar the door."

A hint of a smile twitched the corner of her rosebud mouth. If she ever actually laughed, he suspected she'd have dimples. "Given our previous encounter," she said, "I understand."

This was the cool version of Brooke Josephson. Her raging tension was gone, and she appeared to be completely in control, probably because she was at home. Safely tucked away in her lair, Brooke could relax and be comfortable. She was shoeless and bare-legged, wearing an untucked dark blue shirt and knee-length white shorts. Her black hair tumbled loosely to her shoulders.

Though he could have spent an enjoyable few moments studying her features—the classic nose, sculpted brow, wide forehead and pointed chin—Sloan went straight to business. He reached into the inner pocket of his navy blue blazer and extracted a small spiral notebook. "I know you don't like to waste time, so I made a list."

"Efficient." She gave a small nod of approval. "Would you like something to drink? Water? Juice?"

"A glass of water would be fine."

Franny bounded back into the foyer and returned the phone to Brooke. "I handled the security call. This is the third time, so I think I'm getting the hang of it."

He gave her a smile. "Mind if I ask you a question?"

"Shoot." She mimicked a gunslinger doing a fast draw—an image this little pixie couldn't really pull off.

"You answered the doorbell as soon as it rang. Were you watching from a window?"

"We're way more techie than that." With a giggle, she

picked up a computer tablet that was sitting on a rectangular wooden side table below the staircase. Franny tapped in a code and showed him a screen divided into four separate video feeds. "These are live pictures from the three cameras outside the house and the one in the office. I saw you park and watched you walk to the door."

"Impressive," he murmured.

"The cameras might seem excessive," Brooke said, "but I work from home, and I have a lot of very expensive electronic equipment to protect."

"No need to explain. I like all this tech stuff."

"And yet you carry a spiral notebook."

Not exactly a subtle put-down. His attempt to bond with her by pretending they shared an interest in electronics had fallen flat. She wasn't buying it. He stifled an urge to explain his lousy relationship with computers. Giving her too much information gave her an edge, and he needed to stay in charge. An uncomfortable silence filled the entryway.

"Wow," Franny said. "There's some real chemistry between you two. I mean, it's combustible. And that's my cue to leave you alone. Don't do anything I wouldn't."

He watched her scamper up the stairs to the second floor. "I understand that she's marching to her own drummer, but I don't know this tune."

"Franny has decided that you and I are some kind of match, and we should start dating. I told her it wasn't acceptable, not according to the rules."

"And I'll bet she doesn't care."

"Not a whit."

He followed Brooke as she bypassed the pristine living room, decorated in earthy Southwestern colors, and went down a corridor to the kitchen. The sleek black cabinets and polished marble countertops were clean and organized. Brooke had her life choreographed down to the smallest detail. "I have a question that isn't written down in my spiral notebook," he said. "You and Franny are very different in habit and temperament. How do you put up with her when she stays with you?"

"We have an agreement," she said. "No cats are allowed in the house. And her clutter is confined to the upstairs guest bedroom and attached bathroom."

"Does she follow those rules?"

"Not always, but I can't blame her for living her life the way she wants. Like the clown at the end of the circus procession, it's my job to follow the Franny parade and sweep up the mess after she rides past on a bejeweled elephant."

Her comparison surprised him. In no way did he think of Brooke as a clown. Playing the fool might hint at low self-esteem issues, but he was more interested in her willingness to set aside her own requirements for neatness when it came to someone she loved. She liked order but wasn't rigid about it.

She took two blue glasses from the shelf above the sink and filled them with purified water from a pitcher in the fridge. "What's first on your list?"

He made a point of consulting his notebook. "When we talked on the phone, you mentioned that your car alarm went off while it was parked in the garage. Now that I've seen your security precautions, I'm even more curious about how that could happen."

"I don't know." She stood behind the center island and slid the glass toward him. "I checked at the time. Nothing had fallen and bumped the SUV. All locks were secure."

"Did your cameras pick up any sign of an intruder?"

She shook her head. "The only explanation I've been able to come up with is a glitch of some sort. I'm not an expert in car mechanics."

When he'd talked to the other women, they had all reported similar issues that amounted to minor annoyances. One of them thought a man had been following her. Another reported personal items that had gone missing from her house, but she wasn't sure if she'd just misplaced them. The one who had left Denver and moved to Las Vegas mentioned that she was contacted three times by a documentary filmmaker.

He glanced at his list. "Have you had other threats?"

"Not recently. People have always wanted to get close to us, and they act like we're some kind of notorious celebrities." Anger wove through her voice. "In the early days after we escaped, there was a great deal of unwanted attention. For some reason, folks thought it was all right to call or write letters or walk up to us on the street as though we were old friends. Not exactly threatening, but I considered their behavior to be intrusive. I hated it."

"Gimbel said he put you in touch with a lawyer."

"Tom Lancaster," she said. "It was handy to have his card to warn people away. And he was useful in other practical ways. He set up a fund for us to handle various donations. There was enough money to fund private school for Franny and the twins."

"What about you? You didn't return to high school."

"There was no way I'd go back and be gawked at. I got my GED and enrolled in community college. Layla did the same, and she continued to law school. She recently graduated and has been studying for the bar exam."

According to Gimbel, Brooke breezed through college, earning scholarships and completing her course work for a business degree before she was twenty. After an internship with an IT firm, she set up a home-based business doing medical and legal transcriptions. "You and Layla have much in common. Both intelligent. Both ambitious and successful."

She pushed a wing of black hair away from her face and gave him a smile. "You're a profiler, aren't you?"

"Not yet. But I've had psychological training."

"Well, you hit the jackpot with this case. Me and my friends are every shade of crazy."

Though he didn't approve of labels, he appreciated her relaxed attitude. Yesterday she'd been as prickly as a cactus. "Do you know how to reach Layla?"

"I tried. Yesterday Franny and I stopped by her apartment, and I tried to contact her on a computer link. I tried the link again, about three hours ago. No Layla."

"Would you give it another try?"

"Sure, come with me to my office." She gave him a more genuine smile, and her dimples appeared. "I'll send out the bat signal."

Sloan followed her down a corridor into a large room with a wall of file cabinets and three distinct workstations, each equipped with computers and ergonomic chairs. A wide window, covered with wrought iron grillwork, showed a shaded, verdant backyard with two peach trees and a vegetable garden.

He went to the window. "You grow your own food."

"Gimbel accused me of planting a garden so I wouldn't ever have to leave my house." She slid into place behind a computer. "He might be right. I love being able to step outside and pick a salad. My tomatoes this year have been brilliant."

He stood behind her so he could see the screen as her slender fingers danced across the keyboard, clicking icons and tapping in passcodes. "I'm not very computer savvy," he said.

"I guessed."

"Tell me what you're doing."

"This program activates a camera that provides a live

feed from a one-room mountain cabin that Layla and I share. We're both reclusive. Sometimes we need a hideout where we can be completely alone." She glanced over her shoulder at him. "Layla uses the cabin when she's studying. After a big work project, I like to go there to decompress."

"But you don't want to be completely out of touch," he said. "That's why you set up this system. What did you call it? The bat signal?"

"It's a safety concern," she said, "only to be used in urgent circumstances. Though I'm not sure this investigation rises to the level of emergency, I'll feel better after we've checked in with her."

When she tapped the final key, a picture appeared on the screen. He saw a wood-paneled room with a desk, a fireplace and a bed. The only light came from a window.

"There she is," Brooke said as she pointed to the bed.

He needed confirmation on where Layla had been and if she'd been threatened. "Can you talk to her through the live feed?"

"Sure." Loudly, she said, "Layla, it's me. Get up."

"Zoom in closer?"

"Come on, sleepyhead." Brooke tapped a few keys.

The screen filled with a close-up of Layla's image. Though her nightgown reached up to her chin, Sloan noticed the discoloration at her throat. Layla's face was drained of color. Her cheeks were hollow. She lay unnaturally still.

He'd witnessed enough autopsies to know that this woman would never respond to Brooke's calls for her to wake up.

Chapter Three

Riveted, Brooke stared at the screen, unwilling to believe what she was seeing. Layla, beautiful Layla, was carefully posed on the bed in the one-room cabin. Her head tilted to the right, toward the door and the kitchenette. Her shiny black hair fanned out on the pillowcase. Her pink gown was buttoned all the way up to her chin. The flowered peach comforter tucked under her arms had been smoothed to perfection, and her long fingers laced together below her breasts. Brooke stared at the plain gold band that gleamed from Layla's left hand—stared so hard that her eyes strained and began to water. *Not again.*

Twelve years ago, Layla was forced to be Hardy's bride. That had been her role in the sick little family he had created. Night after night, he'd come to her, demanding his rights as her husband. At first, Layla had screamed. And she must have struggled, because Brooke had heard the crashing around and had treated Layla's wounds the following day. Her blood had been literally on Brooke's hands.

After a while, Layla had given up and quit fighting. Her desperate cries had faded into quiet sobs. At the end of the seven months they were held captive, Layla's voice had been silent in the night.

Brooke buried her face in her hands. Layla didn't de-

serve an early death, not after what she'd survived. She'd
worked so hard to get through law school. Her dream had
been to defend other victims who had given up hope and
had nowhere else to turn. Why had she been taken? Why?
Brooke dropped her hands. There was no answer. Sometimes, life didn't make sense.

In a flat voice, she said, "Layla's dead."

"We don't know for sure."

Sloan didn't make the mistake of trying to comfort her
with a touch or a pat on the shoulder or a hug. He kept
his distance. *Smart man.* She could already feel her grief
transforming into anger, and she might lash out at whatever or whoever was in her path. "I should call the sheriff."

"I'll handle it," he said. "Give me directions to the cabin
or an address so I can contact the authorities and the ambulance."

She wrote the information on a sticky note. Her fingers
trembled, but she took care to make her penmanship leg-
ible. "We don't have a spare key hidden at the cabin, and
the windows are secure. Still, I'd appreciate if they don't
break down the door."

"I'll pass that along."

He stepped away from the desk but didn't leave the
office. Hovering in the doorway, he kept an eye on her.
His voice was a smooth murmur as he made phone calls.
She overheard him tell someone to treat the cabin like a
crime scene.

The image on the computer screen wavered before her
eyes, and she forced herself to inhale a steadying breath
before she made a promise to Layla Tierney. "You will
have justice, my sister. I will find the bastard who did this
to you, and I will make him pay."

Adrenaline surged through her veins. *A wake-up call.*
This sensation was unlike her panic attacks or the nervous

tension that sapped her energy and left her paralyzed. She felt powerful, strong and filled with purpose. There was nothing more she could do for Layla, but she'd make sure the killer was caught and no one else came to harm.

With a few keystrokes, she exited the computer connection to the cabin. If Franny came in here and stumbled across the image of their dead friend, she'd be devastated. Brooke rose from behind her desk and confronted Sloan when he ended his call.

"I'm coming with you," she said.

"Please sit, Brooke. I need to ask you a few questions."

Still standing, she said, "We should get going."

"You tried to reach Layla at the cabin yesterday. What time?"

"It was after Franny and I left her apartment—between four thirty and four forty-five. The cabin was empty."

"And today?"

"It was three hours ago, before I made lunch. One of the twins contacted me, and I told her I'd check again." At the time, she hadn't been worried. Over the years, she'd grown complacent, believing all of them were safe and could lead relatively normal lives. *Clearly, a mistake.* "This was my fault. If I'd gone to the cabin this morning, I could have prevented Layla's murder."

"You don't know that."

"Based on the time I contacted her, she must have been killed during the three-hour window between eleven thirty and right now."

"I advise against making assumptions," he said in a firm voice that was both aggravating and authoritative. "Until we investigate and have evidence, we can't draw conclusions."

"But it's obvious."

"Think about it, Brooke." Rather than handling her with

kid gloves, he seemed to be using a direct approach. "Did you see signs of violence in the cabin?"

She appreciated his candor. "There wouldn't be blood spatters if she was strangled."

"But she would have struggled," he said. "I see no defensive wounds on her hands or arms. No bruises or scratches. We don't know what happened. Or when. To determine the time of death, we need a coroner's report."

"You're right."

"She might have died elsewhere and been transported to the cabin."

Brooke was ashamed that she hadn't considered all those possibilities. Where was her brain? Her intelligence seemed to have deserted her at a moment when she needed to calm down and concentrate. Sloan was right when he told her not to base her thinking on unfounded suppositions, which was precisely why she needed to go to the crime scene and gather information. "Shouldn't we be going?"

"When was the last time you spoke to Layla?"

"I can check my phone records, but I think it was four days ago, on Monday. She'd made an appointment to look at a property she might lease as an office and wanted me to come." Brooke sat behind her desk, brought up her digital calendar and pointed to the notation. "See, right there. It was supposed to be tomorrow at ten in the morning. I should call and cancel."

Verifying a meeting with a property manager seemed trivial, but Brooke knew she'd make that call before the day was over. She was compelled to take care of details. Life went on even when Layla was dead. Oh, God, this was so unfair. Tears threatened, and she tossed her head, shaking them away. "I'm ready. We should go now."

"I can't take you with me, Brooke. Bringing a witness to a crime scene is against the rules."

The clever man already knew her well enough to present the argument that would be most persuasive. He was aware that she hated to disobey normal conventions. But her need to avenge her friend surpassed her habit of coloring inside the lines. She had to convince him.

"Lipstick," she said.

"What about lipstick?"

"Layla is wearing a particular color—Rosy Posey—that Hardy liked. She'd never choose that disgusting pinkness for herself. And the shiny, narrow wedding band is almost a perfect match for the one that Hardy forced her to wear." She could be straightforward, too. "I know more about Layla and the things that happened to us than anyone else. You need me. I can be a valuable asset in your investigation."

"And I'll review my findings with you. But you should stay here, where you're safe. It might be best for you and Franny and the others to go into protective custody."

"I won't object if you arrange for a patrol car to park outside and keep an eye on Franny."

"Consider it done."

"I'm going to the cabin. Either I can ride with you or I'll drive myself." She took a small key from the rectangular wooden pencil box on her desktop, unlocked the lower right drawer and took out her Glock 42 handgun in its holster. "Your choice, Sloan."

He approached her desk and stopped when he was close enough to reach out and snatch the weapon from her hand. "Do you have the necessary registration and permits?"

"I take the ownership of a weapon seriously," she said. "Not only have I gone through the certification and qualified as expert in marksmanship, but I have a shooting range in the basement for target practice."

His eyebrows lifted, and his gray eyes widened. "In the basement?"

"Soundproofed, of course." She'd managed to surprise him, and that pleased her.

"You don't need a gun," he said. "When we get to the cabin, there'll be several armed officers."

"When we get there…" She parroted his words, underlining his implied acceptance. He had almost agreed to bring her along. "I promise that I won't get in the way."

"Why does it feel like you tricked me?"

Before he changed his mind, she wanted to get him out the door and into the car. Quickly, she slipped into her espadrilles under the desk. "I'm ready. Let's go."

"Leave the weapon here."

She weighed the alternatives. The gun made her feel safer, but she wanted Sloan on her side. Pushing him too hard might be a mistake. She returned the Glock to her desk drawer, locked it and grabbed her handy-dandy, all-purpose black fanny pack. "Do you have a problem with this?"

"Not if you keep your pepper spray in the holster."

After he called in a police car to guard the front door and she dashed upstairs to tell Franny to stay put, they were on their way.

FROM THE STREET in front of Brooke's house to the cabin was a drive that took seventy minutes, more or less. This afternoon would be more. Traffic snarls, detours and bumper-to-bumper jam-ups slowed their progress. Though impatient, Brooke was grateful for the extra time to figure out exactly what she was doing.

Her first instinct had been to launch herself into the investigation, even though she knew for a fact that impulsive actions were often regrettable. She'd be wise to trust the police and the FBI. After all, it was their job to nab murderers. Sloan would probably be the officer in charge, and he seemed competent.

She studied his profile as he drove. His firm jaw hinted at a determined attitude, and she hoped that trait held true, that he was unstoppable and wouldn't rest until he caught his man. But she knew better than to count on his physiognomy to understand his character. Hadn't the notorious serial killer Ted Bundy been an attractive man? She didn't know Sloan well enough to trust him.

He seemed to be a careful driver but had been talking on his hands-free phone the whole time they were in his SUV. He'd plugged the address for the cabin into his GPS and was relying on the dashboard information for directions rather than asking her. He probably thought he was being efficient. But he wasn't. If asked, she could have directed him to a shortcut that would have avoided the usual slowdown on Sixth.

Sloan ended his call and looked toward her. "I've asked Agent Gimbel to meet us at the cabin."

"Smart move." Not only had Agent Gimbel studied their case, but she'd be glad to see him. The older man was a reassuring presence.

"I have one more call."

"Take your time."

Brooke would have preferred being in charge. She never enjoyed riding in the passenger seat, but she forced herself to lean back and let the air-conditioning wash over her while she kept her mouth shut. When Sloan took a sharp left turn, she pinched her lips together to keep from blurting out her criticism of his momentarily inattentive driving. She closed her eyes.

Relaxation was impossible. The inside of her head filled with the image of Layla from the computer. Brooke popped her eyes open and blinked hard, hating that high-definition memory. *Why can't I just forget?*

Being too smart was a curse. She'd rather be blissfully dumb. *But not really.* She appreciated her intelligence. The secret was how to use it. Recalling what Sloan had said about details that might be clues, Brooke purposely brought back the vision.

Except for the garish pink lipstick, Layla hadn't seemed to be wearing much makeup, which was her preference. She seldom bothered with mascara and foundation, preferring a clean face and frequently washed hands. Her personal hygiene habits were even more compulsive than Brooke's. Had the person who murdered Layla known about that trait? Had he made sure that her hair was freshly washed? Her hands clean? Was he someone who knew her well? Or was he a stalker who had watched her for a long time?

She needed a profile of the killer. Supposedly, that branch of psychology was within the realm of Sloan's expertise. "We need to get started," she said, interrupting his phone call.

He excused himself to the person on the phone and looked at her. "Started with what?"

"The profile," she said. "I want a basis to work from."

Finally, the SUV hit a path of smooth, unobstructed highway as they approached the foothills. At the end of an arid summer, the vegetation was dull as dirt. He ended his phone call and said, "A profile isn't guaranteed to be accurate. It provides broad parameters of personality type and behavior."

"A parameter is just fine. Like I said, I want the profile as a basis—a starting point for the investigation."

"You can help me." He shot her a quick glance. "I can't pull a detailed profile out of my back pocket. I can start with gathering more information about Layla."

"Like what?" She gestured for him to speed it up. "Ask me questions."

"From reading Gimbel's files, I know that she was an orphan with no family ties."

"Like me." The demographic was the same. They were both orphans, but Layla's life was far more complicated. Her parents were both addicts who died together in a car accident when Layla was five or six years old. Brooke had been abandoned at birth—wrapped in a cheap blanket and left outside a fire station. "We both had lousy upbringings but were doing okay until we got kidnapped by a psycho. Move along."

"I'm sorry," he said.

The gentleness of his voice surprised her. She hadn't expected sympathy or empathy or whatever this was. Her shields went up. "We're going to be at the cabin in twenty-five minutes or less. What else do you need to know?"

"Tell me about Layla's social life. Was she a party girl? Did she have a lot of boyfriends or only one special guy?"

"Parties and clubs weren't her thing. She didn't drink or do drugs. Two years ago, there was a guy in law school that she got serious about, but nobody recently."

"Online dating?"

"Never." Like her, Layla was protective of her privacy. "I don't understand all these questions about her. Shouldn't your profile focus on the murderer?"

"The victim comes first. Understanding why the killer attacked her can help in building a profile." Following the GPS directions, he made a right turn onto a secondary road that went deeper into the pine forests. "It might seem obvious to you that Layla's murder is tied to the abductions twelve years ago, but the scope of an investigation is widespread. She might have been targeted by someone she knew at school."

"Then why would they put on that lipstick or the wedding ring?"

"The quick answer is that they were interested in her history and looked up the details on the computer, but there are many other possibilities."

"You're being thorough."

"That's right."

She nodded in approval. "I'll make a list of the men Layla dated in the past couple of years. And another list of professional contacts—people she's worked for, schoolmates, professors and mentors."

"Also doctors, therapists and your attorney," he said. "It'd help if you put it on a thumb drive so we can build a database."

"All those guys are suspects?"

"Most will be quickly eliminated, but it helps to cover all bases."

"You can turn off the GPS," she said. "We're here."

The cabin that she and Layla had purchased for their private hideaway perched among the trees on the side of a steep hill. The main road ascended the incline, and her driveway peeled off, cutting straight across the hill, forty-seven yards to her cabin. Several official-looking vehicles, including an ambulance, had gathered at the start of the asphalt driveway but hadn't driven up to the house.

She looked toward the house, where she counted two men in sheriff's uniforms and one in a suit like Sloan. "Why didn't they drive closer?"

"They didn't want to disturb possible tire tracks or footprints."

The driveway was mostly asphalt, but there was dirt on

either side. Again, she was impressed by the methodical approach used by law enforcement. She unfastened her seat belt and inhaled what she hoped would be a calming breath. In moments, the image on the computer screen would become real. She would see Layla's motionless form. The only other dead bodies she'd seen had been neatly tucked away in coffins at funerals or displayed scientifically as cadavers when she took an anatomy course.

"You need to stay in the car," Sloan said.

She felt a glimmer of relief. She wasn't squeamish— far from it—but she would rather picture her friend laughing or picking flowers or reading a book. It had taken a long time to partially bury her memories of Layla after her nights as Hardy's "bride." The thought of her death was worse.

Still, Brooke couldn't back down. "If you didn't want my help in your investigation, why did you bring me along?"

"I didn't want you to race up here, half-cocked and looking for trouble."

An unfair characterization if she'd ever heard one. "I'm never half-cocked."

From her fanny pack, she heard the buzz of her cell phone indicating a text message. While engaged in conversation with another person, she usually ignored texts. But she was worried about Franny.

She checked the message and read it twice: Settle down, Brooke, or you'll be next.

Chapter Four

Sloan took the cell phone from her hand and read the message. The "you'll be next" part seemed like a generic threat, but the effect of the text on Brooke indicated something more significant. Her lower lip quivered. Her blue eyes wavered as though frantically seeking an escape route. For the first time since they'd met, he caught a glimpse of raw vulnerability.

Watching her reaction, he said, "'Settle down,' it says. What's behind those words?"

"Hardy always said that to me. 'Settle down, Brooke.'" Her fingers knotted in her lap, and she stared down at them. "Is the murderer watching us? Is he close enough to see what's going on?"

He couldn't guarantee that she was safe from an observer with binoculars or a rifle scope. This area was too heavily forested, and the hills were dotted with boulders that a sniper could hide behind. "I can arrange for you to be taken home."

"I want to be here. I owe it to Layla." She hunched her shoulders, fighting her fear. "I can't let a stupid text message throw me."

"A reminder of the past," he suggested.

"I'm fine."

When she looked up, her defenses slammed back into

place. She was twice as prickly as before. Her blue eyes were as hard as tempered steel. Her chin jutted at a stubborn angle, and her spine was ramrod stiff. His natural instinct was to be gentle, to reassure her and hold her close, but that wasn't going to happen. If he reached toward her, she might rip his arm off.

The main reason he'd brought her along was to gather information, and he needed to penetrate her shell to find the insights he needed. Keeping his tone conversational, he asked, "When Hardy told you to settle down, what did you do?"

"I settled."

"Did he use that phrase with all of you? Franny mentioned that her mystery caller said something about little ladies who don't behave."

"His commands were different," she said, "depending on our role in the sick, disgusting family he put together."

Sloan waited for her to continue. He'd read about their captivity in Gimbel's reports and knew that Hardy had kidnapped the six young women for different reasons. Only two had been sexually molested: Layla and Sophia. All had been restrained, chained, starved and brutalized.

"His family, ha!" Her rage and loathing erupted. "We weren't allowed to have feelings or opinions. Everything revolved around him. Layla was his bride. Sophia was his girlfriend. The younger girls—Franny and the twins—were his playmates, his little ladies. And if they didn't do as he said, he'd take great pleasure in disciplining them."

Hardy had punished Franny by cutting off the tip of her finger. To make it worse, he'd forced Brooke to hold Franny's wrist and had told her that if she refused, he would lop off the whole hand. Calling them *family* was one of the cruelest things he could do to these foster kids who either had come from dysfunctional families or had been abandoned—or both.

She continued, "I was the mother. My job was to keep the house clean and do the cooking with whatever scraps he brought home. If I dared to ask for more or burned the food or left a speck of dust on the table, he'd tell me to settle down. And there would be a punishment so I wouldn't forget what I'd done wrong."

Her early life had been a horror show, and Sloan was impressed with her fortitude and her ability to handle her post-traumatic stress. Again, he wished he could embrace her. Quietly, he said, "I'm sorry for what you went through."

"Enough about the past," she said abruptly. "We should get on with the investigation."

He'd already decided against bringing her into the cabin crime scene. There was no need to retraumatize her with the sight of her murdered friend. But how was he going to convince her to stay in the car? Handcuff her to the steering wheel?

"A few more questions," he said. "Tell me about your security at the cabin. Is it like your house? Do you have cameras?"

"Not anymore. I had a couple of motion-sensitive cameras, but they were difficult to maintain. When they got stolen by vandals a few months ago, I never bothered replacing them."

"You had a robbery?"

"An attempted robbery," she said. "There was a screaming loud alarm that went off when someone tried to break in the door. There was nobody close enough to hear it so I got rid of it. All the windows are triple-pane glass, which is really hard to shatter. And there's a dead bolt on the door."

He appreciated her efforts to protect herself and the people she loved. "How often do you come here?"

"At least once a month. Layla is a more frequent visitor." She exhaled an impatient sigh. "Why are you wasting time with these questions?"

"To help me build a profile." He doubted she'd argue with that logic, but she scoffed. Brooke had never met a nit she didn't pick.

"I don't get it," she muttered. "What do my security precautions tell you about the murderer?"

"The fact that you and Layla kept your cabin locked up tells me that the killer needed to exercise care and intelligence when he chose to use this place. The murder wasn't a random attack. He planned his actions." For the moment, she seemed satisfied. "Now, let's go back to those special phrases, like *settle down*. How many people would know them?"

"Only a few hundred thousand." She gave a cold, ironic laugh. "We were written up in the newspapers and online and in all kinds of journals, plus there was the television documentary by Nick Brancusi."

"He's the same guy who's talking to Sophia in Las Vegas, right?"

"A scum bucket." Anger threaded her voice. "I told Sophia that I'd never agree to another project like the last one, but she was free to do whatever she wanted."

"Sophia is the only one who moved away from the Denver area."

Brooke shrugged. "She always held herself kind of separate, as though she was better than the rest of us, and I'd have to admit that she was definitely the prettiest. After her attempt at a career in Hollywood fizzled, she ended up in Vegas. She thinks another documentary would be good publicity."

"And you don't."

"Oh, hell no."

He looked through the windshield toward her cabin and saw Gimbel coming down the driveway. The old man gave a cheerful wave. With plastic booties on his feet, his plaid shirt and red suspenders, he looked like a cowboy clown. As soon as Brooke spotted him, she beamed a smile, flung open her car door and dashed toward him. Had she already forgotten the potential watcher in the woods? It didn't seem like her to ignore a threat.

Though she was obviously fond of the retired agent she'd known for twelve years, she was still skittish. First, she shook Gimbel's hand and exchanged hellos, then Gimbel touched her arm and spoke quietly to her, and finally she collapsed against him. It wasn't a real embrace, because Brooke held her stiff arms close to her body, but she allowed the older man to hold her. For a brief moment, her shoulders shuddered, and Sloan thought she might cry. Instead, she tossed her head and stepped back two paces.

"Glad to see you," Sloan said to the former agent. "Would you stay here with Brooke while I take a look inside the cabin?"

"I'm coming with you," Brooke said.

This was where he had to draw the line. "No civilians at crime scenes. Not until the forensic team is done gathering evidence."

"But it's my house."

"Those are the rules," he said. "But I'm willing to offer a compromise. While I'm inside, I'll take photos. Then I'll bring them out here and show you. If there's anything you have a question about, I can go back in and get an answer. Deal?"

Through clenched teeth, she said, "I don't like it, but okay."

"I've got a problem," Gimbel said. "I'm happy to spend

time with Brooke, who's one of my favorite people in the world, but this heat is kicking my tired old butt. Give me your car keys, Sloan. Your FBI-issued SUV has a better cooling system than my truck."

And it provided better protection against watchers. He dropped the keys into Gimbel's waiting hand. "Do you miss the perks of the job?"

"I do, but not the responsibilities."

"Don't worry about us," Brooke said. "We'll stay cool… in your air-conditioning."

A joke? As if she was lighthearted? He did not understand this woman.

Leaving them behind, he strode up the inclined driveway toward the cabin. He hoped to kick-start his profiling before the news of Layla's murder leaked to the media, and he needed to clarify his responsibilities with the other agents involved.

Investigating had already begun. At the edges of the asphalt driveway, he noticed a few numbered placards indicating footprints and tire tracks. The one-room log cabin perched on the side of a steep, forested cliff with the front porch facing a retaining wall and a direct view of the opposite side of the canyon. The setting was isolated. He doubted there would be witnesses who might have noticed the arrival of the murderer.

At the side door to the cabin, he approached Special Agent Sam Keller, who—like Gimbel—had beaten him to the scene. Disposable booties covered Keller's shoes, indicating that he'd been inside and had chosen to leave. Sloan understood. He hated death scenes. His expertise was discovering motive, not dealing with the physical, forensic evidence.

"Hey, Sloan, why did you bring the girl along?" In spite of the circumstances, Keller's greeting was cheerful. "Are you keeping your enemies close? Scared she'll attack you again?"

He never should have mentioned the pepper spray to the other guys in the FBI office. "Have you been inside the cabin?"

"Yeah, and we caught a break. I've arranged for the body to be delivered to our morgue and ME in Denver for autopsy, but the local coroner is a retired MD. He's got preliminary results. According to him, she's been dead for over forty-eight hours."

Brooke would be relieved to know that Layla had been killed before yesterday when she checked the camera in the cabin. Nothing could have been done to prevent her friend's murder. "Cause of death?"

"Ligature strangulation. No defensive wounds." Keller lowered his sunglasses and glared over the rims. "Assistant Director Martinez put me in charge of this investigation. Everything coordinates through me."

His alpha-male stance was unnecessary, because Sloan didn't want to be the boss. "It makes sense for you to take the lead. I haven't been here long and don't have your connections with the locals. There could be jurisdictional problems."

"Count on it." He pushed his glasses back onto the bridge of his nose and leaned back on his heels to make himself look taller. "Anything that involves the Hardy Dolls is high profile."

He had the distinct feeling that Keller enjoyed the attention. "I suppose you'll be talking to the media."

"I've got no choice. They're going to want a statement." He preened. "I'll keep the murder quiet for as long as possible, but things are going to get crazy. I wasn't at the Denver office twelve years ago, but I saw the segments on national TV news shows."

Sloan remembered the sad photos of six little girls. "It was a lot of coverage."

"Have you ever been part of a big story like that?"

During his years in Texas, he'd participated in several serial killer investigations but had never been the agent in charge. "Here's what I'm thinking, Keller. I'd like to spend most of my time with Brooke and the other women, setting up profiles and following leads. I'll report directly to you."

"Fair enough."

In the interest of full cooperation, he told Keller about the text Brooke had received and suggested they might want to search the hillsides. Quick and efficient, Keller dispatched a couple of the local law enforcement officers who were hanging around outside the cabin, waiting for the FBI forensic people.

He glanced over at Sloan. "The coroner's still inside, if you want to talk to him."

Before entering through the side door, Sloan put on booties and latex gloves. "Were there signs of a break-in?"

"No scratches on the wood frame. No pry marks. Both doors—the one in front and this one—were unlocked when the locals arrived."

"What about a vehicle? Was her car here?"

"No car," Keller said. "The killer must have transported her to the cabin in his vehicle and then left."

A preliminary picture formed in Sloan's mind. Two days ago, Layla had been murdered somewhere else. Today, between eleven thirty and two, when Brooke checked the camera, the killer brought her here. Why did he wait two days? Why here? Why go to the trouble of bringing her to the mountains?

Bracing himself for what he'd see inside, he entered through the side door. The interior of the one-room cabin was paneled in warm, knotty pine. Waist-high shelving units separated the kitchen and dining table from the bedroom and desk area. The A-frame ceiling and open beams made the area seem larger than the actual square footage.

Sloan didn't need to look at the bed to know that death was close. Some people claimed that the smell of death was sweet. Sloan had never thought so. The stink tainted the air and welcomed the ubiquitous buzzing flies.

A spry gray-haired gentleman came toward him, introduced himself as the coroner and shook hands. "The name is Edwards, but everybody calls me Dr. Ted."

"I'm SA Justin Sloan, FBI. Did you know the deceased?"

"I only met her and her friend one time at a community meeting to discuss the beaver problem. With their matching black hair and blue eyes, they were striking women. I recalled the story of their kidnapping but didn't mention it to anyone else. I don't much care for gossip." His frown emphasized his long, horsey-looking face. "It was a real shame what happened to those young girls. And now this?"

Sloan saw a flicker of empathy in Dr. Ted's eyes, but he didn't fit the stereotype of a kindly small-town doctor. He was cool and methodical. Murder didn't shock him. "How long have you been in practice in the mountains?"

"After I retired from the VA hospital, I moved up here and started a small general practice. That was about eight years ago. I still see a couple of patients now and then."

"And you're also the coroner," Sloan said. "What can you tell me in addition to time of death and probable cause?"

"I'm guessing that when your ME does an autopsy and runs a tox screen, he'll find trace amounts of sedative or narcotic in her system. She must have been drugged. Otherwise she would have put up some kind of fight."

There were other explanations for the lack of defensive

wounds. "She might have been purposely nonresistant in an attempt to outsmart her killer."

"Not likely," the doctor said. "Even if she was trying to be cagey, her instinct would be to struggle."

Thinking of what Brooke had told him about their captivity and Layla's role as Hardy's "wife," he asked, "Was she raped?"

"No external trauma to the genitals, but you'll need a rape kit to know for sure."

"Can you tell if she was tied up or restrained?"

"I didn't find marks on her wrists or ankles." He went to the bedside and stood looking down thoughtfully at the dead woman, who was covered to her chin by a flowered peach comforter. "No unusual bruising."

"You rearranged the body."

"How did you know that?"

Sloan thought twice before speaking. He never liked to give out more information than necessary. "Before we drove up here, Brooke and I saw her on a computer feed."

"Agent Keller took photos of the way we found her. He asked me not to take off her nightgown, but I pulled back the covers to get a better look."

Gazing down at Layla's face differed from viewing her image on a computer screen. Her cheeks and eye sockets were hollow, and her skin had taken on a grayish pallor. The only color came from the Rosy Posey lipstick. Sloan was glad he could spare Brooke from seeing this tragic end to her friend's life.

"There isn't any blood," he said.

"I didn't notice any external lacerations, but there might have been superficial scratches. She was carefully scrubbed, probably postmortem." The doctor leaned over the body and took a whiff. "You can smell bleach. Her hair was washed and combed out, nice and pretty."

With his gloved hand, Sloan adjusted the position of the body. "The side of her left arm is discolored."

"Also her left shoulder and the left side of her back. I figure that shortly after she was murdered, she was positioned in such a way that she was lying on her side, maybe curled up in the trunk of a car. The blood drained to the lowest point."

Wishing he could be more detached, Sloan avoided thinking of this husk as a vibrant young woman with her future ahead of her. Instead, he stuck to direct observations. "She couldn't have been in the trunk of a car for long, not in this heat."

"You're right about that. Her body was kept in a cool place, like a cellar or somewhere air-conditioned. Otherwise, decomp would be further along, and we'd have maggots."

Not something he wanted to think about. "Any jewelry other than the wedding band?"

"Not a thing," the doctor said. "She didn't dress herself. Panties were on backward."

From a profiling standpoint, the act of redressing her was significant. The killer had also washed and combed her hair. Her body had been arranged in an almost respectful pose—fully dressed with her hands folded below her breasts. Her killer cared about her and didn't want to humiliate her. The wedding ring and the lipstick indicated a familiarity with Layla's past.

"Thanks, Dr. Ted. I appreciate your expert help."

"I hope you catch the son of a bitch who did this."

"So do I."

In the kitchen, Sloan recognized Brooke's touch in the neatly arranged shelves and drawers. Other than canned goods, there wasn't much in the way of food. The fridge held a jar of pickles along with mustard and other condiments. The contents were unremarkable, but he took several photos for Brooke.

Likewise, he snapped pictures of the shelves. A bridal magazine on the desk seemed out of place. The forensic team would take fingerprints, but he doubted they'd be lucky enough to find anything useful. He checked out the tiny lens tucked away in a crystal vase on a shelf opposite the bed. Too bad the camera hadn't been set up for constant surveillance.

Outside, he inhaled a deep breath. He stretched and shook himself, knowing that the smell of death would cling to him for hours.

Keller approached. "It makes sense for you to contact the other women."

"Got it," Sloan said. "When Brooke and I get back to town, I want to check out Layla's apartment."

"With Brooke tagging along?"

"She could be helpful. She knows every detail of their time in captivity, and she was particularly close to Layla. Brooke might come up with insights that I wouldn't notice."

"Is that so?" Keller was openly skeptical.

"You bet." *Profiler, heal thyself.* His rationale for taking her along wasn't great. Sloan acknowledged to himself that he wanted to spend more time with Brooke because he liked being with her. For Keller's benefit, he gave other excuses. "She's smart. For example, she's been checking the camera in the cabin and discovered a window of time—between eleven thirty this morning and two this afternoon—when the killer must have brought Layla's body here."

"Okay," Keller said. "I'll keep the timing in mind when we interview witnesses and check surveillance cameras on the highway."

"I'll be in touch," Sloan said.

He saw Brooke storming up the driveway with Agent Gimbel in her wake. Her former vulnerability was gone. Her eyes flashed blue flames. She looked like Joan of Arc, ready for battle as she stomped toward him, holding her cell phone aloft.

Oh, yeah, she was going to be a great help.

Chapter Five

Never a patient woman, Brooke held herself to a high standard and expected the same from everybody else. Sloan had taken too long to explore a one-room cabin, and she'd just received a text message from Tom Lancaster, the attorney who handled her and the other five. Mentally she corrected herself—there were only four. Layla was gone.

Her absence echoed in Brooke's mind, distracting her and pulling her toward sadness. She would miss her friend. They'd been as close as sisters, maybe even closer. The time for mourning would come later. Right now she needed to find the killer and end this threat before anyone else was hurt.

She came to a halt in front of Sloan. "Is it safe for me to be out here?"

"I can't guarantee anything," he said, "but several deputies and cops are scouring the hillsides, looking for the person who sent the threatening text."

She scanned the forested hills and spotted a uniformed officer. "It doesn't seem likely that this murderer is a sniper."

"You're right. Killing from afar doesn't fit the profile."

"Does that mean you have a profile?"

"The start of one," he said.

She needed to know more about the current status of

the investigation and what she should tell Lancaster, but she held herself in check and lowered her phone. He introduced her to Agent Keller, a deputy and the local doctor she'd met before and refused to call "Dr. Ted" because it made her think of the long-ago television show about Mr. Ed, the talking horse.

Forcing herself to stay calm, she pulled Sloan to one side. "We need to hurry. I just got a text from our attorney."

"Is that why you were frantically waving that phone at me?"

She didn't acknowledge his implication that she was overly excited. "Lancaster has been trying to reach Layla. Should I tell him about the murder or not? Should I lie to him? What do I say?"

"Don't call him back."

His simple solution didn't cover all the bases. "If Lancaster is looking for her, there might be other people she has appointments with. How do I handle them?"

"That's not really what's bothering you, is it?"

He was too perceptive. *Annoying.* "It's the media," she said darkly.

"You don't want reporters to ask questions before you're prepared."

"I don't want them anywhere near me or my friends."

"I understand," he said. "It's important for us to get ahead of the media. Franny shouldn't have to hear about her friend's death on the five o'clock news."

"She'd be heartbroken." To be honest, Brooke was close to having her own panic attack, and she had a hundred times more self-control than Franny and the twins. She unzipped her fanny pack and tucked the phone inside. "Let's get this over with. I need to go inside the cabin."

"I can't let you do that. Not until after the forensic crew is done."

"But this is my property." Her well-practiced assertive voice masked her sense of relief. She ought to be able to investigate like a pro, but she dreaded what she would see. The image of Layla on the computer had been horrible. Still, she said, "If I want to go inside, I can."

"I advise against it."

"But you can't stop me," she said.

"Actually, I can. This is a crime scene."

They were at a standoff. She didn't want to argue with him…or maybe she did. Maybe she needed to fight, to be angry and build a barrier between them so she wouldn't collapse against his shoulder and weep.

"Excuse me." Agent Gimbel hitched up his baggy jeans and inserted himself into their conversation. "Here's a thought, Brooke. Why don't you stay here with Sloan, and I'll go to your house in Denver and keep an eye on Franny?"

"I should be the one who tells her about Layla," she said.

"Agreed," Gimbel said. "And I won't tell her. I'll stay at her side and keep her away from the news. Won't say a word until you're there."

"She shouldn't be alone."

"I can handle this," Gimbel said. "Trust me."

She turned her back on Gimbel and Sloan. *How can I trust them?* They couldn't possibly understand what her life was like. They hadn't walked a mile in her shoes. They didn't see Franny the way she did—as a ten-year-old child, broken and tortured. How could anyone else be trusted to do the right thing? "I'm not sure."

Gimbel said, "Trust is one of the issues you've worked on with your therapist."

"It is," she admitted. And she was overdue for an appointment with Dr. Joan. Until yesterday, her life had seemed to be on track. "Give me a minute to think."

Her options were simple: hitch a ride back to town with Agent Gimbel, talk to Franny and contact the twins, or stay here with Sloan and dig into the investigation. She remembered the text message warning that she would be the next to go. Her priority should be to discover the identity of the killer so they'd all be safe.

She whipped around to face the two men. "Thank you, Agent Gimbel. I appreciate your offer to take care of Franny. If you need me, you have my cell number."

After he smiled and patted her on the shoulder, he ambled down the driveway to where his truck was parked. When she turned and met Sloan's gaze, she noticed an assessing look in his eye that made her feel like a bug under a microscope, waiting to be dissected. She didn't want to be analyzed.

"If you won't let me go through the cabin," she said, "why am I here?"

"Good question, and I'll try to give you a reasonable answer. You're not a trained investigator, but you're smart and I trust your insights. If Layla's murder is related to the threats you've all been receiving, I think you'll be able to make those connections a lot quicker than I could."

"Even though you're an ace profiler."

"Even though," he said. "First, I want to be sure the murder is related to what happened twelve years ago."

She threw her hands in the air. "What else could it be?"

"Layla had a life that was unconnected to her early trauma."

Not really. How could she explain to him? A life-shattering experience touched every part of you and never faded. Like a broken vase that had been superglued back together, the trauma was always evident. The victim was always fragile, easily broken. "You mentioned that you took pictures inside the cabin?"

Taking his phone from his pocket, he scrolled through the photos. "I'm guessing that you aren't impressed with my psychological skills. You probably don't think I can understand you."

"Maybe."

"Give me a chance," he said. "I want to know what's going on inside you."

When she thought of tall, gorgeous Agent Sloan being inside her, Brooke tried not to take him literally. A giggle escaped her lips. *Hysterical laughter?* She was tempted to make a very silly and inappropriate joke about how she might be open to his probing analysis.

Glancing over her shoulder, she saw a van park at the end of the driveway. A four-man crew climbed out. Two of them wore FBI T-shirts and caps. "The forensic guys?"

"They got here quicker than I expected. Still, it'll take a couple of hours for them to process the evidence."

And she'd have to wait, to sit idly by while her anxiety built to an unbearable level. "I can't stand it. Let's take a look at those photos."

She led him down the driveway to a picnic table that had been positioned to catch the afternoon sunlight slicing through the trees. Side by side, they sat on the attached bench and watched the forensic team approach her cabin, pausing at the side door to put on booties and gloves. "What are they going to do? Take fingerprints and look for fibers and stuff?"

"Something like that," he said. "This is a nice little cabin. Tell me about how you and Layla decided to buy it."

"The property belonged to one of the doctors I do transcriptions for, and he sold it for a great price. We were both feeling stressed—Layla and me—and we thought it might be good to have a place where we could escape and unwind."

Growing up as a foster kid, she'd never had a family home, and she'd thoroughly enjoyed the process of furnishing and redesigning her house in Denver to suit her needs. When she heard about the deal she could get on this cabin, Brooke saw another opportunity to create a special sanctuary. She and Layla had talked about adding another room or building a garage. She used to feel safe here.

She gazed past the yellow crime-scene tape to the window beside the door, where sunlight glinted on the triple-pane glass they'd had installed for insulation and protection. They'd done most of the work on the cabin themselves. On a long weekend, they'd painted the window frames green to match the door and the railing on the front porch. "I always wished we had a fireplace. We were planning to install a potbelly stove."

"Have you done a lot of work here?"

"I like do-it-yourself projects. They're a hobby." She smiled at the thought of Layla installing the bathroom faucets backward with the hot on the cold water and vice versa. "I have good memories."

"That's what you want to hang on to."

He was right. She didn't want to go inside and face the horrible reality of death. Instead, Brooke would remember Layla trying to paint the window frames without getting a single smear on her shirt. "We used to come out to this picnic table in the afternoon and drink lemonade."

He held up a photo of the nearly empty fridge. "I'm guessing that you didn't keep the refrigerator stocked."

"Not unless we knew we were going to be here for more than a day or two." She scowled at the photo. "Layla didn't bring any food. She didn't intend to stay."

"It's doubtful that she planned to come here at all," he said. "According to Dr. Ted, she's been dead for over forty-eight hours."

The time of death information hit her like a bolt of electricity. "Since Wednesday?"

"More or less. The autopsy will give us more accurate information."

She was relieved. There was nothing she could have done to keep Layla safe. The murderer had struck before Brooke was aware of the threat. "That means she probably wasn't killed here at the cabin."

"I doubt that this is the primary crime scene. I expect the forensic team to confirm that."

She looked at the cabin with fresh eyes. If she could insulate herself with good memories, she might be able to reclaim this sanctuary, to live here and make the improvements that she and Layla had talked about. She wouldn't be haunted by the ghost of a murderer. "How was she killed?"

To her surprise, Sloan set down his phone on the picnic table and grasped her hand. His touch warmed her. When his gaze linked with hers, the official FBI agent morphed into a different person. In his multifaceted gray eyes, she saw sympathy, kindness and a sharp edge of curiosity that kept him from being a sentimental goop. The bustle and activity around them faded to background noise as he asked, "How much do you want to know?"

"All of it. If I'm going to be any help to you, I need details."

"We'll have to wait for the official autopsy for complete information, but I trust Dr. Ted's findings. He believes she died from ligature asphyxiation. That means—"

"I know what it means." She yanked her hand away from him. "You don't need to be condescending with me. My job is to input transcriptions for doctors, and I understand the terminology. You're saying that Layla was strangled with a cord or a chain."

"There were no bruises or lacerations that showed she'd

been restrained," he said. "The lack of defensive wounds indicates that she didn't struggle."

"Was she drugged?"

"That would be my guess, but we won't know for sure until after the autopsy and tox screen."

She hoped Layla had been unconscious and hadn't felt any pain when the ligature tightened around her throat and cut off her air. Through pinched lips, she forced out the single word that encapsulated Layla's worst fear. "Raped?"

"We won't know until there's a rape kit." He leaned forward on the bench so he could see her face. "Do you want to hear more?"

Not really. Her heart was beating too fast, and her lungs constricted. But she couldn't stop now. She had to get past her fears if she meant to find the killer. When she stood, her balance shifted. The afternoon heat hammered down upon her. Her face flushed. A rivulet of sweat trickled between her breasts. "What did she look like, in person?"

He stood beside her, a steadying presence. "She was posed under the covers with her hands folded."

"When you say 'posed,' what does that mean?"

"Neatly dressed in a nightgown, she'd been scrubbed clean. Her hair was washed. Her features were calm."

Brooke wanted to believe that death had come gently to Layla, and she was finally at peace. *It still wasn't right.* "Can you arrange protection for the twins and for Sophia in Vegas?"

"I'll talk to Agent Keller."

She knew better than to expect guarantees of safety from the local police and the FBI. They didn't have the manpower to act as bodyguards. The only way she could keep all of them safe was to hire a private security firm. "Let me see more of those pictures."

He scrolled through the photos he'd taken of the wall

opposite the bed. In the bathroom, he'd opened the medicine cabinet. When he returned to pictures of the kitchen, she finally noticed something significant. She pointed to the screen. "There it is."

"Could you be more specific?"

"You wanted proof that Layla's murder was connected to Martin Hardy? It's right there." She shuddered. "Do you see the apron hanging on a hook in the kitchen?"

"What about it?"

"Blue gingham," she said. "It's a message for me."

"Why?"

Every day of her captivity, she'd worn an apron that looked exactly like the one in the photo. When she spilled on it or when it had been stained with blood, she'd scrubbed and scrubbed it in the sink until the gingham was spotless and bright. Hardy wouldn't stand for her to be messy. His little mama had to be perfectly clean.

"I don't think the pattern of the apron was mentioned in the reports," she said.

Never would she forget that pale shade of blue and the innocent checkerboard pattern. Her nightmares were filled with images of being strangled by that apron. The ties took on a life of their own as they tightened around her throat and cut off her air. Ligature asphyxiation, just like Layla.

Chapter Six

During the drive into town, Brooke buried her fears and sorrow while she figured out what to do next. In the driver's seat beside her, Sloan talked to his colleagues on his hands-free phone. His conversations were quick and cryptic. No more Mr. Nice Guy Profiler, he was all business, all cop. She found his lawman persona sexy—a distraction she didn't want right now.

Looking down into her lap, she considered her first order of business: Make sure everyone had adequate protection. Franny would continue to stay with her. The twins were more problematic. One of them, Megan, had managed to create a normal life with a husband and child in the suburbs. Somehow, she had to convince the whole family to accept protection. The other twin, Moira, was an artist and more footloose. Then there was Sophia in Las Vegas, who would need her own bodyguard.

Next on her list of things to do was making contact with Tom Lancaster. Not only would he be useful in handling the arrangements associated with Layla's murder, but he could also administer her will. If they needed to hire bodyguards for an extended period of time, Tom had access to their joint funds and investments.

With the sun setting behind them, the SUV crested a hill, and she looked down on the silhouette of downtown

Denver. The red glow from the skies reflected off distant skyscrapers while a stream of taillights marked the route into the city.

"This view makes me think of Oz," Sloan said. "I like the way the tall buildings rise from the plains."

"After you've been here for a while, you won't think it's such a magical place."

"Why not?"

"For one thing, magic doesn't exist. Life isn't a fairy tale." At least, not *her* life. She couldn't waste time believing in ogres, witches and ghouls when a real-life monster had murdered her best friend. "Also, the traffic is awful and the whole city is under construction with new apartments springing up like mushrooms. It's getting crowded here. Don't get me wrong, Denver is a great place to live. The weather is sunny. It's relatively clean with plenty of parks, museums and galleries."

"And weed," he said.

"Not my thing, but I appreciate the systematic approach the state has taken to the implementation of the marijuana trade."

"Ditto."

She checked her precision wristwatch. It had been twenty-seven minutes since they left the cabin, longer than that since Gimbel joined Franny at her house. He'd called her once with an update. "As soon as we're done at Layla's apartment, we need to get back to my house. Gimbel has things under control. The twins are coming over to my house, and Franny is getting suspicious, especially since there's a protective police car parked in front of the house—which, by the way, I appreciate."

"You're welcome."

She was duly impressed that law enforcement was operating efficiently. From what she'd overheard of his conversations on the phone, she could tell that the pieces were shifting into place. "How can I help move the investigation forward?"

"It's hard to believe that Martin Hardy had friends, but there were a few. Also, there were witnesses and relatives—people who knew enough about what happened to threaten you."

"With things like the wedding band, the lipstick and that horrible gingham apron."

"What can you tell me about those people? Do you remember them?"

"I remember everything."

Even though she hated her dark thoughts of the past, she recalled a face at the window in the moonlight. Black hair, full beard, sunken cheeks and a nose as thin as a knife blade, he had watched her as she slept with her right wrist and ankle cuffed to the bedframe. With her free hand, she had signaled to him and she had whispered, "Help me." Hoping that she'd finally found someone who would set them free, she twisted around and repeated, "Help me, help me, help me." His deep-set eyes had been invisible in their dark sockets, but she could tell that he was grinning.

He had returned several times to torment her. "Zachary Doyle, the bastard."

"A peeping Tom," Sloan said. "He lived less than a mile away from the cabin where you were held. You identified him from mug shots."

"At the time I knew his face but not his name." She'd never confronted him. None of Martin Hardy's possible accomplices had been allowed in the courtroom during the trial. Her testimony had been taped in the judge's chambers.

"You never forgot him."

"He's kind of a recurring nightmare," she said. "Are we going to question him?"

"Maybe. I'll arrange for an officer to stop by his house and check his alibi. Is there anybody else you remember?"

"There was a brother-in-law. I never actually saw him, but his son came to the cabin to play with the younger girls. The kid claimed to be eleven but looked younger." He must be twenty-three or twenty-four by now, a grown man. "His name was Peter Channing. Martin enjoyed when the boy was there. Peter completed his fantasy of creating a family."

"Any others?"

"Not that I knew. Six or seven times, Martin brought friends to the cabin. They had sex with Layla and Sophia while the girls were blindfolded. None of those scumbags were identified." She could only hope there was a special place in hell reserved for them. She shuddered. "Do you think those guys worried that Layla might see them on the street and recognize them?"

"It's a motive for murder."

"True, but I don't believe it." She unzipped her fanny pack and took out a packet of tissues that she used to blow her nose. The conversation was making her fidget. "If Layla had seen them, she would have told me. She's a lawyer now. She'd find a legal way to make them pay."

They rode in silence while dusk spread across the mountains and plains. The shadowy landscape seemed appropriate for the haze of memory that lurked at the edge of her conscious thoughts. If she closed her eyes, she could see Doyle. Never would she forget the whimpers from the bedroom when Hardy brought his so-called friends to the cabin.

"At the start of an investigation," he said, "there's one question that needs an answer. Why now? What triggered the attack on Layla? This wasn't an impulsive murder. The killer planned ahead to drug her."

Picking apart the pieces of the crime didn't disturb her. In fact, it was the opposite, somewhat soothing. She liked to apply logic to what was intrinsically a senseless act. "Layla must have become a threat to the killer, but I don't know why. She was graduating from law school and preparing to set up a practice."

"Did she mention anything about Peter Channing, Doyle or anyone else connected with Hardy?"

"She didn't say anything to me." Brooke made a mental note. "I'll talk to the others."

"It's possible that the murderer wasn't directly a part of the long-ago crime. He could be part of that vast, faceless mass of lawbreakers and perverts who were aroused by the highly publicized stories of your captivity."

"Copycats," she said with disgust, "creeps who want to be like Hardy."

"With one big difference," he said. "Hardy never killed anyone. Layla's murder means this copycat has taken his obsession to a different level."

"How will you narrow the crowd?" she asked.

"A combination of police work and profiling. When I interview each of you, certain names will rise to the surface. I'll check the names against criminal records, and the threat will become clearer."

Her contacts with the outside world were few and far between. Most of her transcription work was done online with no physical meetings. "I won't have much to tell you."

"Don't be so sure," he said. "Over the course of the past month, you might have had workers to the house. And you go out into the world to shop, to get gas for your SUV, to pick up dinner. Maybe you go to church."

"Not lately, but I get your point. No man—or woman—is an island."

Following the GPS directions, he exited the highway and drove north on Lincoln toward downtown. Layla's apartment was located in the Capitol Hill area amid a cluster of other high-rise buildings. The front entry required a key, but they wouldn't need to bother the concierge. Brooke had both of her friend's keys for use in emergencies.

Outside Layla's apartment building, Sloan parked the SUV at the curb. "As of right now, I'm your bodyguard. I exit the car before you, scan the area and open your door."

His authoritative tone made her blink. "Okay, if you say so."

"You sound surprised."

"Usually, I'm the one giving orders. I take care of everybody else."

"It's my turn now."

He escorted her to the entry, where she used her key to open the door. The open counter in front of the office was vacant, and she led the way across the furnished lobby to the elevators. Layla's apartment was on the seventh floor.

"Before we leave, I'll talk to the concierge," he said as he stepped onto the elevator. "I should let her know that the forensic team will be dropping by. And I want to take a look at the tapes from their surveillance cameras."

She'd checked out the security with Layla before she moved here. There were cameras at every entrance and in the underground parking garage. Each apartment had a dead-bolt lock. Brooke hoped it had been enough. A shudder trickled down her spine. She didn't want to walk into the apartment and find a pool of blood staining the beige carpet. "Do you think she was killed here?"

"If we see any signs of violence, we'll leave and let the CSIs do their work."

Mentally preparing herself for the worst, she turned the key in the lock and stepped aside to let him go first. She followed him into a small, square entryway that led to a hallway. Something was wrong! Carefully, she went down the hall to the front room with the forest green sectional and the glass-topped coffee table.

"Oh, no, this is horrible."

The killer had been here. He had violated Layla's home.

SLOAN HAD NO idea why Brooke was so upset. She gasped and came to an abrupt halt in the front room. Her entire body went tense, and she looked like she was in shock.

He saw nothing disturbing. Layla's apartment was tidy and pleasant with modern furniture and a balcony view of the mountains. To the right was a long trestle dining table with a couple of stinky candles and a cactus garden as a centerpiece.

Brooke jolted into action. She unzipped her fanny pack and took out a pair of purple latex gloves. She passed another pair to him. "We should wear these. I'm sure there are prints all over the apartment."

He wasn't sure what bothered him the most: the fact that she carried latex gloves in her fanny pack or his negligence. He hadn't expected her apartment to be a potential crime scene. "If there's really a problem, we need to step aside and let forensics come through here first."

"I'll be careful." In a nervous frenzy, she darted from the coffee table to the dining room table. "I mean, the place is trashed."

Giving her plenty of room, he stepped back and observed. Brooke's intimate knowledge of Layla might uncover more evidence than an expert FBI team of CSI investigators. She pointed to a stack of books beside an overstuffed chair. "Look at this Leaning Tower of Pisa. Layla would never put hardbacks on top of paperbacks. And the trash can is half-filled with envelopes and receipts."

"Why is that unusual?" he asked.

"She shreds the paperwork to guard against identity theft."

Okay, that wasn't so weird. Lots of people were careful with their trash. "What else?"

"You can tell by the marks on the carpet that this standing lamp has been moved. And the sliding door on the credenza is open."

He squinted at the credenza. "That gap can't be more than two inches wide."

"Layla would never leave it like that. It's obvious that somebody went through her things, searching for something." She bent double to study the gap. "Is it all right if I pull this door open, or should I wait for the forensic people?"

"Let me take a picture." He aimed the camera in his phone. "You can open it but don't go through the stuff inside."

"The books on the lower shelf are out of order," she said.

How the hell could she tell? "What makes you think so?"

"The spines are out of alignment. I'm guessing that an intruder took them out one by one and searched through the pages."

If so, the so-called intruder had to be the most OCD searcher in the history of modern crime. "Can you tell if anything is missing?"

"I don't know." She straightened and braced her fists on her hips above the strap for the fanny pack. She looked youthful with her black hair pulled up in a loose ponytail and her casual blouse and shorts. But her determination gave her a sense of gravity. Slowly, she shook her head. "I can't be sure if the intruder found what he was looking for."

In the bedroom, she noticed that the lid on the jewelry box was up, organization in the closet was disturbed and the drawers in the dresser weren't closed all the way. These tiny details might be clues, but they could just as likely be coincidence. Though Layla was as compulsively neat as Brooke, an open lid on a jewelry box didn't prove anything.

The second bedroom was a home office, where—once again—Brooke found several bits of disorder. She sat at the light green acrylic desk with drawers on each side. "Is it all right if I check out her computer?"

He snapped a couple of photos of the desk. In his capacity as a federal agent, Sloan knew that he should back off and save the computer research for the FBI cybercrime investigators. But the main reason he'd brought Brooke along was for her unique insights into Layla and the murder. "Do you know her password?"

"It's OCD321, a combination of her diagnosis and her birthday—March 21." She opened the lid on the laptop. "Can I?"

"Don't delete or change anything." He doubted they'd find much. If there had been evidence, the intruder would simply have stolen the computer. "What about a thumb drive or some other kind of data storage?"

"Right here." She opened the top right drawer and pointed to a padded case the size of a deck of cards. Inside were slots for thumb drives. He couldn't tell at a glance if anything had been removed. Again, if the intruder wanted to hide evidence, he would have grabbed the case.

He watched as Brooke brought up the geometric-patterned screen saver and checked out the files and apps. Without asking his permission, she opened the email and started scrolling down the list of messages and ads. Her speed and quick comprehension impressed him, but he wasn't surprised. Her job required excellent computer skills.

Prowling through the office, he began to develop a sense of Layla's identity. Like Brooke, she kept her world under control with strict efficiency, but she didn't seem to be cold or unfeeling. The photographs and keepsakes in her office were polished and dusted, lovingly tended. He circled the desk to the left side, where the drawers appeared to be locked. As he reached down to try the bottom drawer, Brooke spoke up.

"Look at this file. The label says 'PChanning.'"

"Peter Channing."

The first email in the file was dated two weeks ago. It said, Been thinking of you, Layla. I'd like to meet.

Though Layla hadn't responded, Peter had sent four messages. The final one was dated a week ago and was longer than the others.

"I don't believe it," Brooke said. "He says he's getting married."

The impending wedding might be the trigger for Channing to confront his past. "What's the date for the wedding?"

"He doesn't say. I need to make a note of this and of his email." She pulled open the left-side drawer of Layla's desk, looking for a scrap of paper. "Oh my God!"

Inside, he saw a tangle of wires. A bomb. The digital countdown showed less than four minutes.

Chapter Seven

The red digital numbers on the device tucked inside the desk drawer silently counted down. Brooke stared as the clock went from 3:48 to 3:47 and then 3:46. In three minutes and forty-six seconds, the bomb would explode.

Sloan grabbed her arm and yanked her out of the desk chair with such force that her knees buckled. Roughly, he dragged her upright and shoved her toward the door leading from Layla's home office. "Go," he commanded. "Go. Now."

"Can you make it stop?"

Instead of answering, he propelled her toward the exit. This wasn't right. *A bomb?* Layla's possessions would be destroyed. Brooke dashed from the office, past the trestle table, the credenza, the sofa and tasteful chairs. All this would be gone. The evidence would be wiped out.

In the corridor outside the apartment, Sloan hit the fire alarm. A siren wailed through the hallway. Lights above the alarm flashed, strobe-like. He pushed her toward one of the apartments next to Layla's. "Knock on the door. Get everybody out."

He went to the neighboring apartment on the other side. With a heavy fist, he hammered on the door and shouted, "Emergency. There's a bomb."

A young woman holding a yappy little dog peeked into the hallway.

"Get out," Sloan yelled over the screeching fire alarm. "Take the staircase. Go."

Brooke relayed the same message to the young couple in the apartment where she was knocking. The man gave her a curious look and said, "Layla, is that you?"

People often confused them because of their matching black hair and blue eyes. His mistake touched a nerve. Losing Layla was like losing her sister, her twin, a piece of herself that meant she'd never be whole again. Layla was gone. Evidence of her killer would soon be destroyed. She couldn't think about that now. "Just go. Save yourself."

Other doors on the seventh floor swung open. Sloan waved the residents toward the stairwell. *Don't use the elevator in case of fire or electrical emergency.* She clearly remembered the safety precaution rules. Though scared, this fear was different from when she was a helpless child. A bomb threat was more like combat. She wasn't out of control. Neither was Sloan. He directed the evacuation with one hand and made phone calls with the other. He never lost his cool. Was he contacting the fire department, or did the FBI have a special team for dealing with explosive devices?

The apartment corridor was almost empty. It was time for her and Sloan to follow the others. The red digital numbers on the clock must be close to zero.

He held her arm as he opened the door to the concrete stairwell. Other residents from other floors of the high-rise were already on the stairs. It was crowded, but everyone moved in an orderly fashion while grumbling and complaining about the inconvenience. They didn't yet know that the bomb was real.

"Stay close," Sloan whispered in her ear. "The stair-well is dangerous."

"Why?"

"The person who killed Layla is still at large."

She hadn't forgotten.

The metal door from the seventh floor was almost closed when she caught a glimpse of raging orange flames and heard the explosion, crashing and echoing. Loud. Violent. Terrible. The floor shuddered beneath her feet. The building seemed to sway.

Voices in the stairwell changed from conversation to sobs and screams. They were yelling. Chaos rippled through the crowd. If Sloan hadn't been at her side with his arm around her waist, she might have lost it.

He was good in a crisis. He instructed people to move carefully and get out onto the street. He assured them that the fire department was on the way.

The lights in the stairwell blinked out. A smothering blackness enveloped them. In the dark, every voice sounded like a threat. Every accidental nudge felt like someone grabbing at her, slipping a knife between her ribs, poking the barrel of a gun against her skull. Disoriented, she forced herself to move forward, clinging to the railing. Sloan and others held up their cell phones, providing light.

Only seven stories, but she felt like she'd been trapped in the stairwell for hours. When she burst into the lobby with the others, Brooke almost wept with relief. Still staying close to Sloan, she allowed herself to be herded out the front door.

A fire truck roared up to the entrance of the building. Two police cars were already parked at the curb, and she could hear the siren from an ambulance. As soon as the emergency people emerged from their vehicles, they stared up at the seventh floor. She looked over her shoulder and saw flames and gushing black smoke.

"Keep moving," Sloan said. He guided her along the sidewalk with an iron grip on her arm. "I need to get you away from here."

"It's okay. I'll be fine."

"I've done a crap job of protecting you, Brooke. Let me make it right."

Her instinct was to assert herself, but she wasn't a fool. If a trained agent like Sloan thought she needed protecting, she should pay attention and follow his instructions. She noticed that he'd drawn his gun and wished that she'd insisted on bringing her own weapon. The pepper spray in her fanny pack felt woefully inadequate.

While Sloan identified himself to a uniformed officer and asked for assistance, she unzipped her fanny pack and reached inside. Sloan might feel better about the supposedly "crap job" he'd done if he knew that she'd slipped the storage case with Layla's thumb drives into her pack. At the time she took the data, she'd thought she might be tampering with evidence. Now, she congratulated herself on her foresight. The bomb hadn't destroyed everything.

A FEW HOURS AFTER he sent Brooke home with a police officer, Sloan returned to her house. He parked his SUV at the curb opposite her tidy, well-protected abode. The two-story white stucco glistened in the moonlight like a fairy-tale castle. Instead of a dragon and a moat, a cop car with an officer behind the wheel was parked in front. There were other vehicles on the street, and George Gimbel's truck was in the driveway outside the attached garage.

The old man had agreed to stay with Franny until Sloan came back from FBI headquarters. Gimbel hadn't taken much convincing. Sloan had the impression that the retired agent enjoyed his advisory role in the investigation. He obviously liked these six women and felt protective toward them. Twelve years ago, their abduction had been his case. Partly due to his efforts, their captor had been tried, convicted and sentenced to life in prison. Right now, when danger had resurfaced, Gimbel didn't want them to be hurt again.

Sloan exited his air-conditioned car, straightened his necktie and fastened one button on his navy blue blazer. If he'd still been in Texas, the August temperatures would have been uncomfortable. But this was Colorado, where the nights were cooler. During the three months he'd lived in Denver, people had told him repeatedly that it was a dry heat.

Nonetheless, he was sweating. The bomb at Layla's apartment had shaken his confidence and made him plenty angry. On the plus side, the fire department had extinguished the blaze quickly, and nobody had been seriously injured. But those two details did *not* mitigate his sheer stupidity. What the hell had he been thinking? Taking Brooke to the apartment before the area had been cleared by the FBI forensic experts almost got her killed. Evidence had been destroyed. Any hope of keeping the investigation quiet had vanished in a puff of ugly black smoke. He'd half expected to see news trucks encamped outside Brooke's house, but there was nothing yet. For now, the media was focused on the bomb and the fire, but it was only a matter of time before they made the connection with Layla and the so-called Hardy Dolls. As the assistant director had reminded him and Keller, this was a high-profile case.

After identifying himself to the cop parked at the curb, Sloan marched up the sidewalk to the front door. All things considered, his meetings at headquarters had gone well. SAC Keller had cut him some slack, allowing him to stay on the case—strictly in a profiling capacity—instead of recommending disciplinary action. To be realistic, Keller's decision wasn't all luck. He was also protecting his own ass. Sloan had advised him that he intended to go to Layla's apartment, and Keller hadn't raised an objection.

Neither of them had expected a goddamned bomb.

The explosive device didn't fit the profile for a killer who had transported Layla to the cabin and carefully, almost lovingly, arranged her body. Brooke's observations about a nearly unnoticeable search stood in direct contrast to the explosion. A bomb was the opposite of subtle. If the killer meant to blow everything up, why was he so careful not to trash the apartment?

As soon as Sloan pressed the doorbell, Gimbel answered. Though still grinning, the old man looked ragged around the edges. "Get in here," he growled. "It's after my ten o'clock bedtime, and somebody who is more awake needs to handle these women."

"Franny and Brooke?"

"And the twins, Moira and Megan. And Megan's four-year-old daughter, Emily, who finally went to sleep." He hooked his thumbs in his red suspenders and rocked back on his heels. "If their chatter isn't enough to drive you straight up the wall, Tom Lancaster just got here."

"From what I recall, you recommended him."

"Tom's a decent guy, not contentious. He's not a trial lawyer—more of a paper pusher who does estate planning and property law."

"Why is he here?"

"Brooke called him. She wants to hire a security firm, which means she needs to access funds from their joint account."

Sloan had a few questions about how that account worked. Brooke seemed to think that their funds were unlimited. "Earlier today, Brooke mentioned that Lancaster called her. Did he say anything about business he had with Layla?"

"I haven't interviewed him," Gimbel said. "That's your job. But I can give you a heads-up. The lawyer might have been the last person to speak to Layla a couple of days ago. One of the twins had a message from Layla and tried to call back, but they didn't connect."

Sloan had spoken on the phone to both twins but hadn't met them in person. He heard voices from the kitchen. Somebody sounded angry, but he couldn't identify the voice. "What can you tell me about Megan and Moira?"

"You first," Gimbel said. "I want to hear about the bomb."

"We won't know details until the ATFE experts are done investigating, but the preliminary report says that the device was triggered when we opened the door. A fairly sophisticated mechanism but not brilliant, it was set to detonate fifteen minutes after somebody turned the key in the lock."

"A booby trap," Gimbel said. "You can't blame yourself for what happened. Anybody could have set off the bomb."

"But it wasn't just anybody. It was me."

And he should have known better. Sloan had come to Denver with a reputation for being an effective agent with training as a profiler, but he'd pulled an epic fail on his first investigation. He'd missed the signs that this guy was a bomber. According to the four women in the other room, he was also a prank caller and possibly a stalker.

The conversation in the kitchen got louder as the women argued. When Sloan glanced longingly toward the exit, Gimbel chuckled. "I feel like a grandpa," he said. "These ladies are interesting but a little crazy. I'm glad they're not my problem."

"They're my problem?"

"You're their designated handler." He gestured down the hall toward the kitchen. "Nothing to worry about—it's just four deeply traumatized women who are scared out of their minds and in mourning for their dead friend."

"Piece of cake," he muttered.

In the kitchen, Franny and a woman with a long black braid sat on high stools on one side of the polished marble-topped island. Lancaster left an open stool between himself and Franny. Brooke stood opposite them, nearest the sink. The fourth woman paced at the far end of the island, speaking nonstop about how she refused, absolutely refused to have a bodyguard interfere in her busy life.

Noticing him, she stopped midsentence. All four women stared with their identical blue eyes. Though their features were unique, except for the twins, they resembled each other enough that he was both fascinated and unsettled. Twelve years ago, when Martin Hardy assembled his family of dolls, he'd chosen carefully to make a matched set. They all had black hair, but the styles were different.

Brooke introduced him and welcomed him into their circle. Tom Lancaster—a skinny, nervous-looking guy with a shaven head and heavy glasses—rose from his stool and shook hands. None of the women made a similar offer. He understood why they might distrust him. He'd failed to save Layla and had put Brooke in danger.

"I want to speak with each of you separately," he said. "Your experiences and observations are integral to developing a profile of the killer."

"There's only one thing I need to know." Megan ceased her pacing, braced her palms on the marble countertop and glared at him. "Is there a danger to me and my daughter?"

"Duh!" Her twin, Moira, flipped her long braid. "Layla's dead, murdered. And a bomb nearly killed Brooke. If that isn't danger, what is?"

"You're no expert." Megan's smooth, precision-cut bob and bangs shone in the glow from the overhead track lighting. "Special Agent Sloan has been trained to deal with violent danger and death, right?"

He'd never heard his job described that way. "If you're wondering about the need for full-time protection, I believe you'd be well advised to hire a bodyguard."

"Thank you," Brooke said emphatically. "I've arranged for us to meet with two different security firms tonight."

She went on to describe how the bodyguard duties would be arranged with one guard at her house, where she and Franny would be staying, another for Moira, and another for Megan and her daughter. Megan was quick to point out that if her husband were in town instead of on a tour of duty in the Middle East, he could protect them.

"Yeah, yeah, yeah," Moira droned. "We all know that your Special Forces stud could dominate any psycho killer. Lucky you, Megan."

"I don't tempt fate," she snapped at her twin. "Not like you. I don't go floating around to Wiccan events or dance naked in the full moon."

"You have your kind of protection and I have mine."

Throughout the sisterly exchange, Franny was uncharacteristically quiet, with her eyes averted, looking down. Sloan appreciated when Gimbel circled the island and stood beside the curly-haired pixie who wore a crown of silk flowers—red roses and rosemary for remembrance. She slid from her stool, wrapped her arms around Gimbel and buried her face against his barrel chest.

With her ADD and bipolar tendencies, Franny tended to be demonstrative, vividly expressing her emotions. At any given moment, she might burst into tears or launch a medley of show tunes. The tricky part to understanding her would be reading the subtext.

Sloan didn't know what to expect from the twins. According to Gimbel, they both suffered from depression. Megan—with her husband and daughter—appeared to be a typical soccer mom but she had an edge and it didn't take much to ignite her rage. The main thing she had in common with her twin was involvement in charity work. Megan volunteered at various veterans' groups and homeless shelters, while Moira focused on the arts, raising money for a dance troupe and being a docent at the art museum. She also did some oil painting and was known for disappearing from sight for weeks at a time.

"Agent Sloan," Megan snapped, "you don't need a private interview with me. We can talk right now. Let's get it over with."

"I don't work that way." After his negligence at Layla's apartment, he meant to play his role as an investigator by the book. Turning to Brooke, he asked, "Can I use your office?"

"Wasting time," Megan said. "I'll tell you what happened. The last time I had contact with Layla was two and a half weeks ago. She came to my daughter's soccer game and brought oranges for treats. It would have been nice if she'd cut the fruit into smaller pieces, but she knew nothing about raising children."

"How would she? Layla didn't have kids." Moira scowled. "And she didn't have much of a childhood. None of us did."

"Layla was sixteen when Hardy took her. We were eleven."

Franny pulled away from Gimbel. "You two were the last taken. You don't know what it was like before you got there."

"Stop bickering," Brooke said. "This is why Sloan

wanted to talk to us alone. If we're in a group, we interrupt each other."

He took his spiral notebook from his inner jacket pocket. "Come with me, Brooke. We'll go to your office."

With a brisk nod, she came out from behind the island. "If any of you want more to drink or eat, help yourselves. Franny knows where everything is kept."

Brushing past him, she went down the hall to the office, where, he noticed, she'd been smart enough to lower the blinds, hiding the interior of her house from outside threats. She'd changed into a white button-down shirt and khaki shorts—a plain, practical outfit that she somehow made sexy. Her long black hair hung loosely to her shoulders, and she was barefoot. For some reason, she was still wearing her fanny pack.

"Have you left the house?" he asked.

"Not since the officer brought me home from Layla's apartment." She closed the door and leaned against it, not retreating behind her desk. "I've had my hands full with Franny and the others. Why do you ask?"

"You're wearing your fanny pack."

Her eyebrows lifted, and her lips spread in a cool, clever smile. "There's a reason."

He should have been asking questions, digging for the truth, but she disarmed his professional intentions. In spite of his bad judgment at Layla's apartment and his inability to get a grip on a profile for the killer, he experienced a profound sense of happiness when he looked at her and heard her voice. "I'm glad you're okay."

"Back at you." She unzipped the fanny pack, reached inside and pulled out a small padded container. "Surprise!"

She'd grabbed the case of thumb drives from inside Layla's desk. Because of her quick thinking, that evidence survived the blast. "Brooke, you're a genius."

"I know."

Chapter Eight

Brooke kept her smile small and restrained. In the midst of tragedy, an excessive display of joy would be gross and inappropriate. But she couldn't help beaming inside. She liked when he'd called her a genius. Having Sloan acknowledge her intelligence was an even better compliment than if he'd raved about her body or her hair or the blue of her eyes. Her eye color seemed especially unimportant—nothing more than a genetic trait she'd inherited from parents who hadn't cared enough about her to stick around.

"I should tell you," she said, "that I grabbed the case with the thumb drives before you found the bomb. My plan was to take it whether or not you approved. It's a keepsake. The data will remind me of Layla."

"And it's evidence," he said.

"That, too."

"Is it possible that you swiped evidence because you don't trust the FBI to do a good job of investigating?"

More than possible! The way she figured, Layla's murderer was someone who slipped through the net on the first FBI investigation. She blamed the institution and the bureaucracy. But not him. "All due respect, Sloan, I'm sure you're competent."

He looked down at the padded case in his hand with

the sort of reverence that was usually given to a precious artifact. His gaze lifted, and he connected with her. "I'm not proud of the way I've handled the investigation. Never should have taken you to Layla's apartment. Never should have gone inside until the forensic experts gave the all clear. If you'd been injured in the blast, it would have been my fault."

"But I wasn't. Not hurt. I'm perfectly fine." After her years of therapy, Brooke recognized his guilt-ridden mea culpa as a sign of an overprotective nature. She shared those control issues. "Besides, if we hadn't gone to the apartment, we would have had to wait a long time for the forensic people to tell us about Channing, the little twerp."

"Give the CSIs some credit," he said. "They would have discovered Peter's emails pretty quickly."

"Would they have shared that information with you? Would you have told me?"

"Yes and yes. I'm not taking part in the active investigation, but it's understood that I need access to all the evidence to create a profile."

"Speaking of which, when can we see Peter Channing?"

He didn't flinch at her demand, but he didn't applaud, either. "I'll have to check with SAC Keller. He's running the show."

Not good enough. She was impatient to move forward. The longer the investigation dragged on, the longer she and her friends were in danger. Channing was the most obvious suspect. His childhood connection to all of them was creepy to say the least, and he'd been reaching out to Layla, trying to establish a line of communication.

"I need to talk to him face-to-face."

If he'd murdered her friend, she wanted revenge. Nothing would make her happier than to see Channing locked in the prison cell next door to his uncle. A sick, disgusting family reunion was exactly what they deserved.

Martin Hardy's trial had taken place when she was only fifteen, and she'd never had the chance to appear in open court. Testifying in judge's chambers wasn't as satisfying as taking the witness stand and pointing at the monster who had ruined her life. *J'accuse, you bastard.*

"When we have him in custody, I'll do what I can to set up an interview," Sloan said. "But we need to follow the rules."

"I agree."

"That means I have to turn these thumb drives over to Keller."

"Wait!" She went toward him. Her hand rested on the sleeve of his blazer as if she could stop him with a touch. "Shouldn't I have a say in what happens? I had the foresight to take the thumb drives. At the very least, I should have a chance to look at the contents."

"You're a witness, not a detective."

"But I can help."

"Rules," he said.

"What could it hurt for me to take a look?"

His jaw tensed. She figured that he'd refuse to share the evidence. The cops and the feds—even Gimbel—were oh-so-secretive about their investigation. She shouldn't expect Sloan to be different from the others.

He surprised her by handing the case back to her. "As long as I'm not putting you in danger, there's no harm done. I won't tell Keller about the thumb drives until after I interview Franny, Megan and Moira. That gives you enough time to make copies."

Standing close to him, she glanced up and whispered a thank-you. After all they'd been through today, he should have been frazzled, but he still appeared calm and collected. The only sign of disarray was a shadow of stubble on his jaw. "Do you always wear a suit?"

"Not always. When I get shot with pepper spray, I strip down."

If that was all it took to get him undressed, she could snatch the pepper spray out of her fanny pack right now. "There must be a less painful way to make you relax."

"We could experiment."

The husky note in his voice alerted her to what was really happening between them. They were flirting. Not an unusual occurrence for a typical twenty-six-year-old woman. But she never made suggestive remarks or batted her eyelashes or flashed her cleavage. Flirting with a fed? Unheard of! And yet, with her free hand, she reached for his striped necktie and gave a tug.

"Maybe you could loosen this knot," she said.

Without breaking eye contact, he reached up and wrenched the knot lower. He unfastened the first button on his light blue shirt. "This feels better."

Her lips parted, and her pulse accelerated. She found it hard to swallow. Her reaction wasn't due to a panic attack. She was aroused, sensually aroused. Her tummy churned. A heated flush crept up her throat, and she knew she must be blushing.

Brooke had experienced fully consummated sex with penetration exactly three times in her life. The first time was out of curiosity—a desire to find out what all the hype was about. She'd researched, selected a suitable partner and propositioned him. The results disappointed her. She was *not* overwhelmed by ecstasy, the earth did *not* move and she didn't hear a symphonic crescendo. The second time—with the same guy—had been undertaken in an attempt to improve. It wasn't a zero but certainly not a ten.

After her third try with a different mate, she decided that she just wasn't someone who enjoyed sex.

Standing close to Sloan and watching him loosen his necktie caused a more thrilling response, a trembling from deep inside. Maybe the danger had cranked her endorphins into high gear. Maybe his protective nature turned her on. Or maybe the timing was right. Whatever the reason, she wanted him.

With a gentle caress, he brushed a wisp of hair off her cheek and tucked it behind her ear. The silver facets in his gray eyes sparkled and shimmered. Whether this was sexual magic or some kind of delusion, she liked it and leaned even closer to him, close enough that she could smell the smoke from the explosion that still clung to his clothes. The danger was real. She shouldn't allow herself to be distracted. But their bodies were almost touching.

There was a tap on the door. She heard Lancaster call her name. "What is it?"

"A representative from the security firm is here."

Though irritated by the interruption, she was also a little bit relieved. To Sloan, she said, "I have to deal with this. The rep from this company agreed to come over tonight, even though it's after ten."

"Bodyguards are used to working odd hours."

Her eyelids squeezed shut, and her lips pinched. The moment with Sloan had passed. Now it was time for her to get back to the business of managing everybody else. She responded to Lancaster, "I'll be right there."

The attorney pushed open the door and poked his head inside. "If you want, I can handle the hiring. That's why you wanted me to come over, isn't it?"

"Not really." Though she viewed him through the sensual haze of her attraction to Sloan, Tom Lancaster had less appeal than a long-tailed gecko. His shaved head sloped down to thick glasses that magnified his eyes. He was skinny and fidgety. How dare he suppose that she couldn't take care of hiring the security firm? "I know what I want."

"I'm just saying." He shrugged his narrow shoulders. "I've worked with this company before. They're the ones I recommended to install your security cameras and locks."

She'd been satisfied with their work but had gone with a more experienced team to design and build her panic room in the basement. "I'll talk to the rep."

"Just trying to help," he said. "Tell me what to do, and I'm on it."

"Come over early tomorrow. I need your help to put Layla's affairs in order. For now, you might as well go home."

Sloan stepped forward. "Before you go, I have a few questions for you."

She shooed both men toward the door. "If you don't mind, I'd like to use my office for the interview with the security rep. Agent Sloan, I'd advise you to talk to Franny first. When we were growing up, she had the most contact with Peter."

Before he exited, Sloan gave her a wink so quick and unexpected that she almost missed it. If he was flirting again, she had to admit—grudgingly—that she approved.

As Sloan accompanied the lawyer to the front foyer, he took the spiral notebook from his pocket to record Lancaster's answers. He didn't expect this to be a deep discussion, but Lancaster might have been the last person to have contact with Layla. Sloan wanted that information to construct a timeline. "You had an appointment with Layla. When was the last time you talked to her?"

Lancaster pushed his glasses up on his nose and shot an angry glance over his shoulder toward the kitchen, where they could hear the women introducing themselves to the rep from the security firm. "This is typical of Brooke. She refuses to ask anybody else for help, thinks she can do it all herself. She should have let me handle the business with the rep."

"There are specific issues she wants covered." Without thinking twice, Sloan defended Brooke. "She can take care of the hiring."

"Can she?"

The glow from the chandelier in the entryway reflected off his shaved dome, making his head seem too big for the rest of his body. Sloan smiled to himself, wondering if the oversize noggin was a literal manifestation of an ego-driven personality. "Brooke seems like a competent businesswoman."

"Oh, sure, she likes to think she's in control, but I can tell she's upset. Didn't you see how her fingers were trembling? She was breathing hard and blushing—all signs that she's scared to death."

Sloan had a fair idea of what was going on inside Brooke, and it wasn't fear. After their intimate moment in her office, his heart thumped in double time. He was turned on, and he guessed that she felt much the same. "There are many possible reasons she could be agitated."

"You barely know her. I've spent time with these girls, watched them grow into women, and I don't mind telling you that I'm worried. Layla's murder is going to have an effect." He jabbed a long, skinny finger at the center of Sloan's chest. "You need to catch the killer, and you need to do it fast."

As if he had intended to drag his feet? Sloan had already gotten himself into trouble once by rushing into Layla's apartment instead of waiting for the forensic people. Speed wasn't as important as doing the investigation right.

A lawyer ought to understand, but not this guy. Sloan was beginning to take a serious dislike to Lancaster. "Rest assured that the FBI will handle the investigation with all due haste."

"I should hope so."

"Again, I'm asking you. When was the last time you had contact with Layla?"

"I spoke to her on the phone three days ago, on Tuesday. Hang on and I'll tell you exactly what time."

Lancaster opened an app on his phone and scrolled down the screen. Waiting in silence, Sloan could hear the conversation from the kitchen but didn't recognize the tone of Brooke's voice. She'd probably taken the rep into her office.

He stared at the lawyer, who continued to play with his phone. Keeping Sloan waiting was a power play, a way to show that his time was more important. "Never mind, I'll contact your office."

"Here it is. My phone consultation with Layla lasted from 1:16 to 1:33 on Tuesday, and it fell into the category of billable hours."

His statement fit with what Brooke had told him. "What did you talk about?"

"Not so fast, Agent Sloan. Let's not forget attorney-client privilege."

The pretentious lawyer enjoyed thwarting the FBI investigation while simultaneously demanding immediate answers. Sloan's dislike for Lancaster was rapidly turning into hostility. "If you don't cooperate, I'll take you into custody for questioning."

"You wouldn't dare."

Sloan drew himself up to his full height, a good five inches taller than bigheaded Lancaster. "According to Brooke, Layla was looking for an office to lease. My assumption was that she contacted you, her lawyer and the administrator of the group funds, to make sure she had the financial wherewithal."

"I'm not saying." Lancaster gave a smug little smirk.

"It's been one hell of a day. I'm in no mood to dance."

"Too bad."

As a general rule, Sloan tried to avoid exerting his authority, but Lancaster and his phony attitude made him want to hammer the lawyer, watch him crumple to the ground and drag his limp remains to jail. "Last chance to cooperate."

"I've got to respect the rule of law."

"Turn around, put your hands behind your back."

He yelped, "What?"

"Your reluctance to discuss such a banal matter makes me think you have something to hide." Sloan wasn't carrying handcuffs, but he had a couple of zip ties in the pocket of his blazer. He took them out and dangled them from his forefinger. "Your refusal to answer my questions amounts to obstruction of justice on a time-sensitive case where the safety of other people is threatened."

"It's my right."

"And I'm within my jurisdiction to arrest you."

Sloan heard a gasp. He turned and saw Franny, Moira and Megan standing in the doorway, watching the argument. Their blue eyes were wide, curious. He gave the ladies a nod. "Sorry you had to see this."

"Tell him." Lancaster stamped his foot on the tiled floor. "You ladies need to tell him how much I've helped you and taken care of you. I'm like a father."

Franny shook her head. "Not that I have experience with fathers, but I don't think so."

Lancaster continued, "I managed your funds brilliantly.

Whenever you needed money, it was there for school fees and down payments. Never once have I turned you down."

"That's not true," Moira said. "You refused to make a ten-thousand-dollar donation to my friends who needed to rent space for a dance concert."

"I borrowed from our joint account for the down payment on my house," Megan said, "but I paid the money back."

Sloan found it interesting that the women weren't defending the attorney who had handled their affairs for twelve years. Lancaster wasn't winning any popularity contests with this group. Had Layla argued with him?

He intended to take a closer look at Lancaster, possibly to subpoena the records for the fund he managed. He clamped his hand around the lawyer's scrawny arm. "You need to come with me."

"You don't have to do this. I'll cooperate." Behind his glasses, his eyes flickered from the left to the right. "When Layla called, she wanted to know if funds were available to lease an office. She gave me a ballpark figure, and I gave her my approval."

"Why did she need your approval?" Moira demanded. "It's our money."

Anger tinged her voice. When he'd turned her down for the dance company donation, he'd made an enemy. Sloan focused on Lancaster. "According to what you told me, the phone call was over fifteen minutes long. What else did you talk about?"

"She wanted my advice as a lawyer on whether she should join a group or go into private practice. I gave her my opinion and a few referrals to other young lawyers. Anything else I can tell you?"

"I advise you not to leave town until this investigation is over."

"Fine."

As soon as Sloan released him, the lawyer stomped to the front door and waited for Franny to enter the code to deactivate the alarm. Lancaster left without saying good-bye to his clients. Before she could scamper back to the others, Sloan spoke to her. "I have a few questions for you."

"Nothing to say." She covered her mouth with both fists.

"Please, Franny. We can go someplace quiet."

"Fine, we'll go to the basement." She gestured, and he followed. Halfway down the staircase, she turned and said, "You need to catch him."

"Who?"

"Peter Channing."

Chapter Nine

If Sloan had been more alert, he would have remembered that the shooting range was in the basement. Before he could suggest a quieter place, Franny had skipped down the hallway and used a code to unlock the door to the soundproofed range. Inside the well-lit but sparsely furnished room, there was another code to access a locked case holding an array of handguns.

He wanted to question Franny about her direct accusation of Channing, but she had dropped that topic and moved on. Humming to herself, she reached into the case and selected a Walther P22 with a pink handle and frame.

"This will help me relax," she said with a cheery grin. "Shooting gives me focus. When I take aim, I have to clear my brain and concentrate. Moira says it's like meditation."

He'd never heard of Zen target practice before, but it made sense for someone like Franny, whose bipolar tendencies could send her mind scampering in many directions. While she aimed and fired at a target, her field of interest was limited.

"I understand," he said. "Before we start talking, I want to tell you that I'm sorry about what happened to Layla. It's hard to lose such a close friend."

"I haven't cried yet. The tears are right there, but they

won't come out." Her smile wavered. "Brooke told us she was already dead before I tried to reach her on the phone."

"I haven't developed a timeline yet, but you can be sure that there was nothing you could have done to stop the murder."

"Maybe or maybe not." She pivoted and went to a counter where two shooting areas were separated by a partition. As she loaded a clip into her automatic, she said, "If you want, you can fire your own weapon. I bet you're pretty good."

This was a competition he didn't want to start. "I'd rather watch."

She squinted down the lane at a paper target of a human silhouette with a bull's-eye superimposed on the torso. The distance from the counter looked to be twenty-five or thirty yards. Sloan had no doubt that Brooke had been responsible for this setup, from selection of a target that mimicked the human form to the distance. Fifty yards would be a more challenging shot, and if Franny was training to be a sniper, the greater distance would be important. Mastering twenty-five yards was better for self-defense.

Franny removed her crown of roses and rosemary to put on noise-canceling headphones. She pointed to a second pair. "Those are for you. It gets loud in here."

In her paisley blouse, cutoff jean shorts and red cowboy boots, she looked perky and carefree, but her stance when she aimed her weapon was all business. In less than two minutes, she'd emptied the magazine and reloaded. After another ten shots, she turned away from the target.

Her cheeks were flushed, and she was gasping for air. Many gun novices held their breath while they fired. Her eyes were bright as she pulled off the headphones.

"Peter Channing," she said. "Three months ago, I thought I saw him in a grocery store."

"You were kids when you knew him." Sloan adapted to her change in topic. "He was only eleven years old. He must have changed."

"This guy wore his hair short, just like Peter when he was a kid. And he had the same lopsided grin with a dimple on one side." The words gushed from her. "He was skinny—Peter was always skinny. When we were kids, I could wrap my arms all the way around him. He didn't see me in the grocery store."

"Did you approach him?"

"The opposite. I wanted to run away and hide, but then I wondered if I had the right guy. It's happened to me before. I'll catch a glimpse from the corner of my eye, and I'll be sure—I mean, totally sure—that it's Hardy coming after me with his big, jagged hunting knife. Even though I know he's locked up in jail, I think he's there until I get closer and see that I'm wrong. So I decided to follow the guy in the grocery store."

"If you ever feel threatened again, you can call me or emergency services."

"You sound like Brooke. She has nine-one-one on speed dial."

As he well remembered, Brooke hadn't hesitated to hit that call button and lash out with her canister of pepper spray. He was curious about how she'd convinced unicorn-loving Franny to pick up a handgun and shoot. Later he might ask. Right now, he refused to be sidetracked. The focus was on Peter Channing. "Tell me about how you trailed him."

"I ducked behind the cantaloupe," she said, "went past the dairy and the meat. In the frozen food aisle, he picked out three pizzas. That made me think he was a bachelor."

"Good reasoning."

"It was springtime, and he was wearing baggy shorts. I

tried to get close enough to see if he had a scar on his calf. That would have been positive identification. One time when we were playing, he got tangled in the long chain that tethered my ankle to the bedframe. Peter fell against the fireplace. He had a terrible gash. It was bleeding and bleeding and I couldn't make it stop. If Mr. Hardy came in and saw what happened to his nephew, I'd be punished. He'd already cut off the top of my finger, and I didn't know what would come next. Peter saved me."

"How?"

"He ran out the door into the forest and pretended that he got hurt out there. His uncle believed him, and I didn't get blamed." Her forehead twisted into a frown. "Peter was my hero, but he was also my captor. At any given time, he could have talked to the police and rescued me and the others."

Her story reminded him of Stockholm syndrome, when hostages became deeply attached to their kidnappers. Her insight added a layer of complexity to an emerging profile of Peter Channing. "Did he want to be your hero?"

"Oh, yeah. We played lots of games where I was a princess and he had to fight a dragon to save me."

"Was he in love with you?"

"We were ten and eleven years old. Too young to be in love." A tremor in her voice hinted at an emotional connection, and he wondered how many times she'd been in love. The intense childhood trauma had to affect her relationships with men. "We were just friends."

Sloan shifted the topic. "Did you see the scar on his leg?"

"I never got close enough. When he went into the parking lot, I lost track of him." She quickly reloaded her pink pistol and fired one shot without the headphones. "I don't know if I really saw him, but I couldn't stay in my apartment near the grocery store. I moved before the end of the month."

"Why didn't you call the FBI?"

"I wasn't sure, and I didn't want to be the girl who cried wolf."

"When you started getting the crank phone calls, did you recognize the voice?"

"I don't know if it was Peter." Though she wasn't crying, she dabbed at the corner of her eye. "His voice would have changed a lot, so I can't tell. The person who called repeated things Mr. Hardy said to me about how little ladies had to behave or else they'd be punished. I could lose another finger or a toe or an arm."

Her self-control was slipping. He needed to rein her in. "Before we came down to the basement, you said I needed to catch Channing. Why were you so sure?"

"The killer is from our past." Her conviction was strong, and she sounded angry. "You need to arrest Peter. Who else could it be?"

He remembered Brooke's story about the face at the window. "Do you remember Zachary Doyle?"

"The creepy neighbor," she said. "I didn't know his name until the trial, and I only saw him peeping in the window once. He was more interested in Brooke and Layla and Sophia."

Though Sloan didn't have a psychological workup on Doyle or any of the other men who had visited Hardy's cabin, they seemed to be a better fit for the profile of a killer who had terrorized the other girls and killed Layla. Their sexual experience, twelve years ago, would have made an indelible impression.

The little boy who'd played with Franny didn't seem to have a clear motivation, but the fact that Layla hadn't been sexually molested pointed to Channing. He might think his relationships with the women were pure. He considered himself to be their hero. If he had engaged in crank calls and weird stalking, he meant to frighten them so that he could, when the time was right, come to their rescue.

A buzzer sounded, indicating that someone was at the door to the shooting gallery. When he opened the door, Moira immediately grasped his hand and pulled him along with her. "You've got to come quickly. Brooke is going to kill him."

He knew better than to ask what was going on. If Brooke believed that the only way to protect her friends was murder, he had no doubt that she was capable.

SITTING BEHIND HER DESK, Brooke aimed her Glock at the bearded middle-aged man who looked like he was trying to be a young hipster in his skinny jeans, combat boots and fedora. Nick Brancusi, documentary filmmaker, had bluffed his way into her house by pretending to be a rep from one of the security firms she had contacted.

At first, the manicured beard and mustache had thrown her off, and he'd talked a good game in describing bodyguard services. But his presentation had sounded too slick, and she'd smelled a phony. As soon as she recognized him, Brooke invited him into her office, told him to sit, took out her gun and aimed. Icky Nicky probably wasn't feeling so glib right now.

"Let me explain," he said.

"No talking." She sighted down the barrel of her gun. This should have been a nerve-racking confrontation, but she was experiencing a profound sense of inner peace. She hated the threat and the danger it posed, but she loved being in control.

"Come on, Brooke, just listen to me."

She bounded to her feet and stood behind the desk.

Glaring down at him, she struck a two-handed shooter's pose. Her fingers didn't tremble. The adrenaline pumping through her veins elevated her pulse, but she was breathing easily. *No panic attack here!* "I don't want to hear anything you have to say. Don't beg."

"This is a legit business opportunity."

"Save it, Nicky. There's an FBI agent in the basement. He'll be here any minute, and he will take you into custody."

"Protective custody," Brancusi muttered. "I hope he can keep me safe from you."

It would serve him right if she shot the fedora off his head, but that would ruin the wall and she didn't want to spackle. "Not another word."

When Sloan entered the office with Moira and Franny following close behind, he quickly assessed what was going on, and he grinned. "I appreciate your alert action, Brooke. I'll take it from here."

She slipped her Glock into the desk drawer and locked it. "The creep is all yours, Special Agent Sloan."

His expression darkened as he confronted Nick Brancusi. "Show me your ID."

"I never meant any harm." He slouched lower in the chair as though trying to make himself disappear. "I'm a documentarian."

When Brancusi reached into his vest pocket, Sloan drew his weapon. Towering and threatening, the nose of his gun was less than a foot from Brancusi's forehead. "What do you think you're doing?"

"Reaching for my passport." He held up both hands. "It's in my pocket."

"On your feet," Sloan growled. "Now."

Brancusi stood, but his nerves wouldn't let him keep still. He shifted back and forth from one foot to the other in a cowardly dance that pleased Brooke no end. She truly disliked this man who had exploited their childhood trauma.

"I haven't done anything wrong," Brancusi protested. "I'm here with a business deal."

"Were you invited?"

"Not exactly."

"How did you get into the house?" Sloan demanded.

"I pretended to be from a security firm."

"You entered under false pretenses."

"Well, yes." Brancusi's hands were still raised. "I wanted a chance to make my pitch. I have a pretty good offer for a follow-up documentary on the Hardy Dolls, especially since Layla is, you know..."

Franny squeezed her eyelids shut and threw her head back. A high-pitched keening noise squeezed past her clenched teeth. A violent tremor shook her shoulders and went all the way down to her feet. *Poor Franny!* This was tearing her apart. She felt everything so deeply.

Brooke rushed around the desk and gathered her friend in her arms. Together, she and Moira guided her to the sofa by the window, where she collapsed in a boneless heap.

Her wailing continued. "She's dead. Layla's dead."

Her outburst was disturbing, but Brooke understood what was happening, and she actually approved. Holding too much grief inside was difficult and painful, especially for a gentle soul like Franny, who desperately needed to vent.

Embracing her friend, Brooke patted Franny on the back while her cries subsided and she wept. This was a difficult balancing act. Brooke needed to take care of Franny. At the same time, she had to follow the investigation and help Sloan. Finding Layla's murderer took precedence over everything else...if there truly was anything she could do.

She watched Sloan intently.

"You make me sick," he said to the filmmaker. "You planned to use Layla's death for publicity."

"Hey, it's not my choice. I'm just giving people what they want. The media is going to be looking for answers, and I happen to be an expert on what happened to these ladies."

"I'm taking you in for questioning."

"I don't see why."

"You've got a motive. You might have killed Layla for the great publicity."

"You've got to believe me when I say I haven't done anything wrong." His cynicism vanished. His voice sounded meek and complaisant, but she remembered that he had been an actor before becoming a filmmaker. Nothing he said could be trusted. "Am I under arrest?"

"Not yet."

"I'll come quietly. You don't need cuffs."

"Technically, I don't," Sloan said, "but I want to use them."

It was obvious that Sloan wasn't buying Brancusi's phony innocent act. He continued, "I want you restrained so you can know what it's like to be caught, trapped with no hope of escape. If the FBI wants you in jail overnight, that's where you'll be. And your confinement is nothing compared to the trauma suffered by these women. Their abuse wasn't a movie, a game or a stunt. And I won't let you treat them like victims. They're survivors, and I never want to hear you call them 'dolls' again."

Brooke mentally applauded every word he said. Sloan came close to understanding the damage that had been done to them. The ordeal started with Martin Hardy and continued after they had escaped. Every time they were recognized or their names came up in the media, they were thrown into the inescapable past and weren't allowed to forget. Sloan's empathy came from a deeper source than psychological training. She wondered if he had undergone a similar trauma.

Leaving Franny with Moira, she crossed the room toward Sloan as he tightened the zip ties on Brancusi's wrists and escorted him out of the office. Standing in the front entryway under the chandelier, Sloan made a phone call. There was no need for him to hold on to Brancusi's arm. Those tiny zip ties were enough to restrain the documentarian, who stood silently with his head drooping forward and his gaze focused on his combat boots.

When Sloan finished his call, she asked, "Where are you taking him?"

"Headquarters," he said. "Will you input the code to turn off the door alarms?"

"I should be with you for the questioning." In her heart, she didn't really believe that Icky Nicky was capable of murder, but he might know something vital. "I don't want to be cut out of the investigation."

"I'll stay in touch," he said.

Brooke knew when she was being blown off. Sloan was trying to dump her. She didn't intend to sit quietly and let that happen. "I'll meet you at headquarters."

"It's late, after midnight. Might be best if you stay here and take care of Franny."

He made a good point. Brooke had always tended the pains and sorrows of her friends. As foster kids, they'd all been abandoned by their families, which gave her strong motivation to be steadfast and loyal. She couldn't leave Franny when she was so upset. With a frustrated sigh, she tapped the keypad to disengage the alarm and held the door for Sloan to make his exit.

Standing on the front stoop, she watched as he approached the police car parked at the curb and handed Brancusi over to the cop on duty. The soles of her feet itched to race down the sidewalk and jump into the passenger side of his SUV before he pulled away. She and her friends had been threatened, and she needed to know everything—every tiny detail—about what had happened.

Franny stepped onto the stoop beside her. Her eyes were red and puffy, but the tears had stopped. She held Brooke's fanny pack. "Your keys are inside. Go."

"Are you okay?"

"I'll manage."

"But I need to talk to the security firms."

"Tomorrow is soon enough."

That was true. With a couple of phone calls, Brooke could postpone the meetings. "Are you sure you're all right?"

"There's nothing you can do to change my grief. Go," Franny said. "Find the monster who killed Layla."

That was precisely what she intended to do.

Chapter Ten

After a conversation with SAC Keller at FBI headquarters, Sloan returned to the fourth-floor conference room where he'd left Brooke. At one end of the room was a conversation area with a long rectangular brown sofa, chairs and a coffee table. The other end was set up for demonstrations with whiteboards, easels and a pull-down screen for PowerPoint presentations. The long table in the middle was used for briefings and meetings. Through the windows that lined the west wall, he could see the distant lights of downtown Denver.

During his absence, she'd made herself comfortable, curling up on the sofa and kicking off her shoes. Her head rested on the arm of the sofa, which she'd cushioned with her ubiquitous fanny pack. Her eyes were closed. He lowered himself into the chair beside the sofa and exhaled a heavy breath. Today had been intense, and the pressure didn't show any sign of easing. He was exhausted, running on fumes.

Special Agent in Charge Keller and his boss, Martinez, weren't real happy with Sloan's decision to share information with Brooke and use her as a resource. He had to admit that their doubts were reasonable, because he couldn't be certain that he was doing the right thing for her. Even though she insisted on taking part, an investigation could be traumatic and dangerous—as evidenced by the bomb in Layla's apartment.

He watched her as she slept. Her white shirt had come untucked, and he caught a glimpse of her smooth skin above her waist. Her expression was untroubled, peaceful. Black lashes formed crescents on her cheeks. Her full, pink lips parted slightly.

Rousing her from a sound sleep could be a problem. Some people who had been hostages reacted badly if jolted awake. Their barely conscious minds flashed back to the trauma, and they lashed out. He had no desire to be on the receiving end of another Brooke attack. And so he sat quietly, waiting and watching until her eyelids fluttered and opened.

Immediately alert, she bolted upright. "How long have you been sitting there?"

"A couple of minutes."

"Watching me while I sleep? Kind of creepy, Sloan."

Or prudent. It was entirely possible that she'd wake with a start and blast him with pepper spray. "Can I get you something to drink?"

She shook her head. "When do we start questioning Brancusi?"

"As soon as we figure out a timeline we can use to check his alibi."

"Let's get to it." She jumped off the sofa, slipped her feet into her espadrilles and charged toward the opposite end of the room with the whiteboards. She picked up a marker and wrote the word *Monday* on the board. "We'll start here. Layla called me in the morning. She was planning to rent office space and wanted me to come with her to an appointment on Friday."

He sauntered toward the whiteboard, impressed by her

vigorous show of energy. "Organization comes naturally to you."

"Too much?"

"It's a good quality," he said. "I like that you set up our timeline on a whiteboard. And I'm in awe of the way you've got everything you need in that fanny pack."

"Good." She grinned as she smoothed a wisp of her hair back into her ponytail. "I've always been like this and don't think I can change. *Organized* sounds much nicer than *displaying OCD tendencies*."

"You're not crazy," he said. "Maybe a little bit annoying, but not psychotic."

"Professional opinion?"

Actually, it was. He had the necessary qualifications and training to be a therapist. "In your Monday phone call with Layla, what else did you talk about?"

"She had concerns about starting a solo career but didn't want to join a group of other lawyers until she knew them better. And she meant to ask Tom Lancaster about the money needed for rent." She shrugged. "That's all I can think of."

"Tuesday," he said, "was when she talked to Lancaster for fifteen minutes at a quarter past one in the afternoon."

She made a note on the board. "Tuesday night was the first time my car started honking in the garage for no apparent reason."

"Did the other women talk to you about when the harassing phone calls and stalking started?"

"I'm not exactly sure about the timing. I'll have to check with Franny and the twins. And Sophia—especially Sophia. She's the only one who had contact with Brancusi in Las Vegas."

The first time he met with Franny, she'd stated that she'd been receiving weird phone calls since Wednesday.

Moira thought she'd noticed someone following her car on Tuesday night or maybe Wednesday. And Megan clearly remembered a suspicious-looking man watching her and her daughter at the playground on Wednesday.

Accurate reports from the witnesses were important. If Brancusi had been in Las Vegas on Tuesday and Wednesday, he had an alibi.

"Wednesday," he said.

"That's the day Layla was murdered." After she wrote on the whiteboard, she turned to face him. "Has the autopsy been done? Do we have a precise time of death?"

Her question was direct and concise, not emotional. Brooke was managing her sadness without weeping or wailing, but her blue eyes reflected a depth of sorrow, and her voice quavered. Her posture was stiff but not frozen.

When they met for the first time at Franny's house, she'd been on the verge of a panic attack—gasping for breath, twitching, trembling and blushing. As they'd gone deeper and dealt with more horrific aspects of the investigation, she rose to each occasion. Her self-control got stronger and stronger.

"Sometime on Wednesday," he said, "Layla was murdered. Prior to that, we can assume that she was drugged. We don't know exactly where or when this happened or how long she was unconscious. After the murder, lividity showed that her body was on its side, maybe in the trunk of a car."

Brooke swallowed hard. With her left hand, she dashed away a drop of moisture below her eyelid. Had his description been too graphic? She turned away from him, stared at the whiteboard and then pivoted and spun around so quickly that her ponytail bounced. Her actions spoke for themselves: she intended to face the facts. "Her murder and the harassment of the others took place in the same time frame. What does that say about the killer's profile?"

Though she was clearly under stress, her question was smart and appropriate. He'd been debating with himself about how much he should tell her. Carefully watching her blue eyes for signs of panic or any other intense emotion, he talked to her the way he'd speak to any of his colleagues.

"The evidence thus far doesn't point to a sex crime. And the killer wasn't excessively violent." He wasn't saying anything that she didn't already know. "He took care to dress his victim, and her body showed few signs of bruising. He didn't beat or torture her."

"I'm glad for that." Her increased tension was evident but minimal. Her lips thinned. Her left eye blinked and twitched.

"It's possible," he said, "that Layla's murder was an accident."

"Are you saying that he accidentally drugged her? That doesn't make sense."

"He meant to drug her but maybe not to kill her. While she was unconscious, she was under his control. That's part of his motivation. Self-aggrandizement and control."

"Which means he gets a thrill out of frightening somebody like Franny."

"He's aroused, but not necessarily in a sexual way. He might not be important in his everyday life. By taking charge, he has power. Hoping to win your trust, he might offer to help you or to take care of you."

"That sounds like Brancusi," she said. "He kept blabbing about a lucrative business deal."

"Did his documentary actually make much money?"

"I can't give you exact figures, but it was a lot. He sold the piece to a cable network, and there was a book deal. A percentage of his profit went into our joint fund, and we made even more from donations. Lancaster has the figures."

"And you're sure the numbers are accurate."

"Layla reviewed the audits and kept him honest." She frowned. "I guess that will be my job now."

He pointed to the whiteboard. "On Thursday, I responded to Franny's phone call."

"Duly noted." She filled in that blank. "And today is Friday."

Today, the most significant thing they'd discovered, timing-wise, was that Layla's body had been delivered to the cabin between eleven thirty and two—a fact that had not escaped Brooke's notice. As she wrote on the board, she said, "Brancusi drives a van. Transporting Layla to the mountains would have been easy. And he's a filmmaker. If he grabbed her from her apartment, he would have known how to disable the cameras in the parking lot."

He moved toward the whiteboard and held it on both sides. "I'll take this to Keller and we can get started with the questions."

"Leave it where it is," she said as she took her phone from her fanny pack. "I'll take a picture and we can transfer it to Keller's phone."

"Good plan."

"I could teach you the basics of using your electronics," she said. "It's crazy for an investigator like you to be wandering around with a spiral notebook in your pocket. Well, maybe not crazy/psychotic, but definitely annoying."

"Professional opinion?"

"As a certified techie nerd, you bet it is."

BROOKE WALKED BESIDE him through the mostly empty FBI building, an impressive structure that had been completed in 2010 and handled FBI business for Colorado and Wyoming. Past hallways with offices, down a short staircase and through a bullpen area, they took the elevator. When they emerged, he led her into an open area with a fridge and vending machines. On the counter was a microwave, a toaster oven and a coffeemaker.

"Can I get you something to drink?" he asked.

As a rule, she never drank caffeinated beverages after six o'clock. "Herbal tea?"

He fed coins into a machine that offered coffee, decaf and hot water while pointing her toward the selection of tea bags in a case on the counter. Leaving the brewing to her, he made himself a coffee with a pod that brewed one cup at a time.

After her tea had steeped, he asked, "Are you ready?"

"I can handle Icky Nicky Brancusi."

"You and I won't be conducting the interrogation. We'll observe from an adjoining room as Keller asks the questions."

"We'll be behind a two-way mirror." She'd watched enough cop shows on television to know how this worked. "Cool."

"Don't get too excited. These interviews can also be very boring."

Feeling like a superspy, she allowed him to escort her into an office where they met SAC Keller, who, unlike Sloan, was still wearing his necktie. Even at this hour, after midnight, Keller maintained his men-in-black, FBI grooming with a clean-shaven jaw and neatly combed hair. His impeccable white shirt told her that he must have changed when he came back to headquarters.

Though she'd already met him at the cabin, Keller was quick to shake her hand. "Thank you for observing, Ms. Josephson. I appreciate your insights."

"I'll bet you appreciate this timeline even more." She

held up her phone to show him. "If you want, I can transfer this image to your phone."

"That would be useful." Instead of giving her his phone, he took hers to perform the transfer of information. Obviously, Keller was more computer-savvy than Sloan. He studied their timeline with interest. "Very useful."

"Will you be interrogating all the suspects at this location?"

"Possibly."

She didn't want to miss her chance to hear what Channing, the nasty little twerp, had to say for himself. "Have you brought in anybody else for questioning?"

Keller glanced past her shoulder to make eye contact with Sloan. "We'll keep you informed."

After providing the very useful timeline, she didn't deserve to be brushed aside. "What about Channing?"

"He's on our radar."

"But you haven't taken him into custody," she said.

"We're doing our job."

When SAC Keller pivoted on his heel and exited the room, she turned to Sloan. "What's his problem? The person who killed Layla set a bomb that could have harmed a lot of other people. It's important to move fast."

"It's not in Keller's nature to share information. I hate to say 'trust me' because of what happened to you when you were a kid, but we're pretty good at what we do. If somebody needs to be in custody, it'll happen."

Was he trying to tell her that Channing was already here, hiding behind one of the many closed doors in the long, empty hallways? Was the peeper, Zachary Doyle, being held in another place? "I want to know everything."

"You've got to be patient. This is one place where you're not the boss, Brooke. We're in charge. That's the FBI culture. I've got to tell you that Keller didn't much care for the idea of allowing you to observe, and it took a firm suggestion from Assistant Director Martinez to make him change his mind."

"I get it. You FBI guys are secretive."

"I could tell you it's for your own protection." He held the door open for her. "But that's not always true."

In a narrow room with dim lights, they met three other agents. Silently, they lined up behind the two-way mirror to watch Keller and Nick Brancusi, who sat at a table facing the mirror. After the basic name, address and time of interview, Keller started at the beginning of their timeline.

"Where were you on Tuesday?"

"Vegas." Brancusi fidgeted in his chair. On the table in front of him was a half-empty water bottle. He'd peeled off the label. "I can't provide witnesses for every minute of the day, but I played poker from five o'clock in the afternoon to after midnight."

"Wednesday?"

She leaned closer to the glass. Wednesday was the day Layla was murdered. The drive from Denver to Vegas took about twelve hours straight through, but a plane ride was only a couple of hours.

"Still in Vegas," Brancusi said. "I talked to Sophia Rossi in the morning."

"In person or on the phone?" Keller asked. "Keep in mind that we can subpoena your phone records."

Brooke whispered, "That's good. His phone records will show if he called Franny."

Sloan responded, "Unless he used a burner phone."

"In person," Brancusi said. "We met for coffee. By the way, she's in favor of having me do a follow-up documentary on the Hardy Dolls. She's the only one who really appreciated what I did for those girls twelve years ago. She thanked me."

A memory rose from deep inside her. Sometimes the pieces from the past were sounds or music. Other times, a taste would waken a hidden thought. This time, the remembrance was visual. She saw them all as they were twelve years ago. Skinny and scared, they did their best to keep from crying or complaining as they were filmed on a soundstage or a theater—a place where the lighting could be adjusted.

After the trauma they'd already endured, the court-appointed guardians for the younger girls didn't want them to participate in the film. But they agreed when Lancaster told them about the money that could be made, enough cold hard cash to finance college and set them up for life. To his credit, Lancaster watched over the production like a hawk. There were interviews but no re-enactments.

Brancusi had run a small crew. At that time, the director hadn't bothered with the hipster pose. He typically dressed in a Hawaiian shirt, and his hair was a mass of wild curls already turning gray though he couldn't have been more than forty.

He'd taken a special interest in Sophia. What man wouldn't? She was gorgeous. None of them were ugly, but Sophia was breathtaking. Though barely sixteen, she'd looked like a woman. Of course, Brancusi noticed.

Brooke remembered watching while the filmmaker leaned close to whisper in Sophia's ear. She seemed to be enjoying the conversation, giggling and making teasing little flicks of her wrists and wiggles of her hips. She moved like a dancer. Brancusi cupped her breast in his big, ugly hand. He licked his lips as he leaned close for a kiss.

Sophia's eyes went wide. Her fluid movements shut down.

That had been when Brooke flew across the room and

barreled into Brancusi. She knocked the man off his feet, leaned over him and spoke in what she hoped was a menacing voice: "Touch her again. And you go to jail."

She turned to Sloan. "He's lying. Sophia would probably talk to him, and she might think a new documentary could help her acting career. But she'd never thank that pedophile."

"What did you call him?"

"Let's just say that there's a reason he liked hanging around with six young women who had been traumatized." Sloan could put that in his profile and smoke it. "I wouldn't be the least tiny bit surprised to find out that he made those harassing phone calls to Franny."

Keller had been making further headway with Brancusi's alibi for Wednesday and Thursday, gathering names and the places Brancusi had been in Vegas. He promised to contact the FBI office in Las Vegas and have them verify the facts.

"Knock yourself out," Brancusi said.

"When did you drive to Denver?"

"I left on Thursday, stopped in Grand Junction for the night and got into town on Friday before noon. That motel in Grand Junction is proof. I paid for it with my credit card."

Keller asked, "What made you decide to come to Denver?"

"I figured that if I could talk to the gals in person, they might change their minds."

"Had you spoken to any of them on the phone?"

"Not exactly, but I've been talking to Tom Lancaster, and he said they might be amenable."

What the hell was Lancaster thinking? Staring through

the two-way mirror, Brooke curled her fingers into fists. Why hadn't the lawyer mentioned Brancusi to her?

When Sloan touched her back, she inadvertently flinched. "What?"

"How much longer do you want to stay?" he asked.

If she had been conducting the interrogation, she would have wanted to stay longer and delve deeper. After her crystal-clear memory, she knew Brancusi had been inappropriate with Sophia. And he excelled at manipulating people, tricking them into doing what he wanted. But was he a murderer?

Though she didn't want to let him off the hook, she had to admit that he had a lot of proof for his alibi. He couldn't be in Denver, Grand Junction and Las Vegas at the same time.

She whispered to Sloan, "I don't think we'll learn much more from Brancusi."

"Not likely."

"I don't suppose you know if Peter Channing has been taken into custody."

"No."

She sensed that he was holding back. There was more he could tell her, but she'd need a crowbar to pry it out of him. In his own way, Sloan was almost as secretive as SAC Keller.

She shrugged. "We can leave."

There were things she needed to take care of at home, but she wasn't done with her role in this investigation. Not by a long shot.

Chapter Eleven

After only a few hours of sleep, Sloan drove to Brooke's house the next morning. It was early, before seven o'clock, and he hoped to avoid the circus that would swing into gear as soon as the media figured out Layla's identity and her past. In Colorado, a few horrific crimes had captured the public imagination and stuck in the collective memory: the murder of JonBenét Ramsey, the shooting at Columbine High School and the kidnapping of the Hardy Dolls.

When he turned onto her block, he saw the beginning of chaos. The single police car that had been stationed outside the house to provide protection had been joined by three other DPD vehicles. Uniformed officers were doing their best to control the news trucks and teams of camera operators and TV reporters angling for a shot with Brooke's front door in the background. A news chopper circled overhead.

Nothing about this day was going to be easy. Without leaving his car, Sloan showed his FBI credentials to the cops, dodged around the reporter teams, parked in the driveway and texted Brooke, telling her that he'd arrived.

She texted back, GET IN HERE. NOW.

He strode quickly toward the house, grateful that she opened the door immediately and even more pleased that she slammed it behind him. Noise from the street was audible inside the house, but the mood felt less chaotic. Not that it was calm. Franny and the twins joined Brooke. Four sets of piercing blue eyes stared at him accusingly.

He straightened his necktie. "I wish I could tell you that the killer is in jail."

"But you can't," Megan said. "What am I going to do? I can't hide in Brooke's house forever. Is there any way I can safely take Emily to her soccer practice?"

If he remembered correctly, Megan's daughter was four years old. Skipping a soccer practice didn't seem like a big deal. "We can't guarantee protection at a public park."

Megan stamped her foot. "Emily can't even watch regular TV because there's too much stuff about the Hardy Dolls. She'll have questions."

He realized that Megan hadn't told her daughter about her traumatic past, and he didn't blame her. How could she explain being held captive for several months by a sadist who pretended she was his family? A young kid couldn't be expected to understand, but stories about the Hardy Dolls were going to be hard to avoid. "If you want, I can suggest the name of a child psychologist."

"You can do better than that," Brooke said as she stepped up to his side. "Megan already has a therapist for her daughter. Maybe the FBI can escort her to the house so she can talk to Emily."

When he agreed, she gave him a quick thumbs-up. Brooke played the mother role in this little pack. She cleaned up messes and got things done.

"In the meantime," Moira said as she twirled her long braid between her fingers, "you need to chill, sis. Grab some inner peace. I can show you breathing exercises and yoga poses that'll help you relax."

Megan scoffed. "It'll take more than downward-facing dog to make me calmer."

Franny giggled. "I like yoga. Ommmmmm."

"Ommmm." Moira placed her palms together and lowered her head as though praying. "One more time. Ommmm."

"Namaste," Franny said.

"That's enough from you two." Megan turned the spotlight on him again. "I want to hear what Agent Sloan has to say about the investigation."

Sharing information with Brooke was far different from opening up to the whole group. A straightforward, honest conversation might open old wounds and do more harm than good. "Is there coffee?"

"I made it myself," Franny said as she linked her arm through his. "It's really good. I added a pinch of cinnamon and a tiny bit of vanilla bean for flavor."

He'd never been one for fancy coffee, but he didn't want to disappoint this bright-eyed creature who was wearing her crown of roses again. "I'm sure it's delicious."

They trooped into the kitchen and took positions at the large central island. Though there were stools, nobody sat. They were too wired.

Franny handed him a steaming mug of coffee and asked, "Has the FBI arrested Peter Channing yet?"

The directness of her question surprised him. Typically Franny danced around an issue, unable to hold focus. He recalled their conversation from last night and wasn't sure whether she considered Channing to be her hero or a worse villain than Martin Hardy. "He's not in custody."

"Where is he?" Franny's voice held an unmistakable note of fear.

"We're looking for him." Sloan sipped his coffee and shot a glance toward Brooke. Locating Peter Channing was the main reason he'd come to her house, but he couldn't discuss his idea with the rest of the women listening. He needed to get Brooke alone.

She stepped up to the center island and addressed them. "Whether Peter is in custody or not, we have to remember that the killer is still at large. I hired a security team, and our bodyguards will be arriving shortly. Megan and Moira, you each have a guard assigned to you. Franny, you're staying with me, and we'll have one guy at the house. We need to take every precaution, and I mean it. Nobody goes out alone. Don't answer your door. Don't drive yourself."

The other three women nodded.

"These bodyguards," Moira said. "Are they single?"

"I didn't make that a requirement for hiring," Brooke said as she pulled out her phone. "But I have pictures."

She set the phone with the photos on the countertop and stepped back while the other women crowded around, making claims on the bodyguards who were coming to protect them. A healthy response, Sloan thought, though maybe a tiny bit sexist.

It pleased him that Brooke wasn't ogling the body-guards. She looked pretty today in a black blouse and shorts with her hair brushed to a shine and hanging loose to her shoulders. He pulled her aside. "Can we go some-where private?"

"I've got just the place."

After telling the others that she'd be back in a minute, she directed him down the stairs to the basement. They passed the door to the shooting range and stopped outside another closed door with a keypad lock.

"What's in here?" he asked.

"Panic room."

BROOKE OPENED THE LOCKS, ushered him inside and closed the reinforced steel door behind them. As soon as the high-tech latch clicked into place, the twenty-two-foot-square room filled with pure, blissful silence. The temperature remained at a constant sixty-five degrees, which was too warm for a wine cellar but energy smart and comfortable enough when she wore the sweater she kept on a hook by the door. She slipped the soft blue cardigan over her black shirt. When she'd designed this room—her favorite place in the house, maybe her favorite place in the whole world—she'd used several different technologies, from bomb shelter to wine cellar to a place to ride out a tornado.

At six feet two inches, Sloan seemed gigantic in the small room, which was crowded by the survival supplies she'd packed inside. He flipped down the double bed that she'd adapted from a railroad Pullman car. "Nice."

"The mattress is fairly decent."

He pointed to the computer screens mounted on the wall by the door that showed views of the interior and exterior of the house. "How do you get electricity in here?"

"Conduits running through the air vents in the ceiling. If I need to close those off, you know, in case somebody tries to drive me out with gas, I have a small battery-powered generator and an oxygen condenser."

Without stretching, he reached up and touched the ceiling. "This room isn't part of the original house."

"I hired a security firm to add three-inch reinforcement to the walls, floor and ceiling. This space is nearly impenetrable."

Being locked in her panic room with him was having an effect on her. He took up a lot of space, and she felt like the walls were closing in…not in a scary way, but intimately wrapping around her, as though she was being squeezed in a gentle embrace. She imagined that she could feel him breathing and hear the steady beat of his heart. No one could find them in here. There would be no interruptions.

Turning away from her, he checked out the stockpile of nonperishable food, water and medical equipment. "You can stay locked up in here for a long time."

"Not really," she said. "If there are two occupants, my supplies won't last more than a week, and that would require rationing. This room isn't meant to be a long-term bomb shelter."

He stood directly in front of her. "What is it meant for?"

"Safety. It's a place to hide."

"From what?"

In light of what had happened to Layla and the media assault taking place on her front lawn, she hardly felt that an explanation was necessary. "Can't you see what it's like? If I let my guard down, I'm exposed. People are always approaching, wanting a hug or to hold my hand or take a selfie. All they really want is to hear the gruesome details."

"Or they might just want to comfort you."

"It's none of their business," she said, more vehemently than intended. The scrutiny reminded her of the past. "I want to be left alone."

"That's not altogether true. You don't mind being with the women upstairs."

"Don't get me wrong, I love Franny and the twins. But sometimes they make me crazy. Always calling or showing up on the doorstep, wanting me to help them. You saw how nervous Franny got when she couldn't reach Layla on the phone."

"As it turned out," he said, "her fears were justified."

"Let's call that another really good reason for me to have a panic room."

He engaged her with a smile. "You make me think of those tricky little bunny rabbits that set up several hidey-holes they can duck into to evade their enemies. You have this room and the cabin that you and Layla had in the mountains. Anywhere else?"

"If I told you, it wouldn't be a hidey-hole, would it?"

"No need to worry about me. I'm not a predator."

When she gazed into his breathtaking gray eyes, she saw an edge of danger. *Watch out for him!* Not that Sloan would physically harm her, but he had the power to tantalize and mesmerize until she let her guard down. She didn't want to be vulnerable. "There's nothing wrong with taking precautions."

"You're right. The world is a dangerous place. It's smart to be vigilant. As for this panic room, well, I've got to tell you that I love it. If this hideout was mine, I'd be in here all the time. It's like a secret fortress."

"You sound like a kid. Did you have a clubhouse when you were growing up?"

"Me and my brother built a tree house. We had a bunch of comic books, baseball cards, candy and toys. And binoculars. We could see over the fence into the neighbor's yard."

She wished her childhood held such pleasant memories. Brooke had never really been a kid. She'd grown up too soon. "I was a loner, the kind of kid who sits by herself in the lunchroom. That might be why Hardy selected me. Even someone like him could see that I wouldn't be missed."

"But you weren't shy. You were the leader."

"Not right away. At first, my job was to clean and make sure everybody got fed. Then, they started calling me 'Mama,' and I grew into that role. What a joke!" The irony pained her, and she talked fast to cover the ache in her heart. "I didn't know what a mother should be. My birth mom was gone before I even knew her name."

"According to your records, you were adopted as an infant."

"By the Josephson family." She had a photo of them holding her at a baptism. "They named me Brooke because my eyes were as blue as a mountain stream. They seemed like nice people, and I wish I could remember them. Mrs. Josephson passed away from cancer when I was four, and Mister couldn't take care of me. After that, it was welcome to foster care."

"When you were four?"

"And I wasn't a cutie-pie. Mr. Josephson didn't know how to feed me or keep me clean. My hair was chopped short, and the kids at the first home teased me about looking like a boy. One of them called me a scrawny mongrel."

"Not a happy memory."

"I didn't know what the words meant. I remembered them so I could find out." She didn't usually talk so much about herself. "Tell me about you."

"There's nothing too exciting. I grew up in the burbs outside Chicago, did okay in school, went into the navy and ended up at Quantico for FBI training."

"There's something more." Without touching him, she scooted around the room and sat on the edge of the Murphy bed. She wrapped her sweater more tightly around her. "Your life hasn't been all sunshine. I've seen glimpses of a shadow."

"A shadow, huh?" He sat beside her. "You sound like Moira."

"Oh, I hope not. I can't keep up with her yoga and Wicca and chanting."

"This room makes you feel safe," he said. "Are there people who reassure you in the same way? Maybe Gimbel?"

Though she noticed that Sloan had cleverly deflected

her inquiry into his personal life, she didn't push. His question intrigued her. Who made her feel safe? "I trust Gimbel, but I wouldn't expect him to have my back in a moment of danger. He's not as energetic as he used to be, and I'm probably a better shot."

"To feel safe, you need to be with someone who can physically protect you."

"I do." She looked down at her hands in her lap. "There are plenty of people who are supportive of me, like Franny, Sophia and the twins. And I have a therapist, Dr. Joan, who I can tell anything. But when I'm scared, really scared, I need muscles—somebody who's kick-ass."

"Not what I was expecting to hear."

"I kind of surprised myself," she said. "I don't want you to think that I'm a dopey damsel in distress who needs to be rescued."

"I would never think of you as helpless."

"I'm a little bit kick-ass myself."

"More than a little bit."

She shifted position but didn't put more distance between them. Being close to him, alone with him, was surprisingly comfy. Never before had she felt so warm and cozy in this room. She looked down at his right hand resting on the bed between them. Acting on impulse, she glided her fingers across his knuckles.

As soon as she touched him, he reacted. Nothing obvious, just a twitch, but it was enough to cause her to look up. She studied his lips, his cheekbones and his clean-shaven jaw, looking for a reason why he appealed to her. His features projected masculinity. Sloan was strong enough to fight off any predator. He could keep her safe. *At what cost?* The shimmer from his fascinating gray-green eyes enticed her. Did she feel safe with him? Definitely, she felt something. Her sensation of cozy warmth turned to excitement. Her vision blurred around the edges. Her heart thumped, and butterflies did pirouettes in her stomach.

Somehow, they were holding hands. She swallowed hard. *What does this mean?* They were alone, sitting on the bed in her panic room. Instead of overthinking and considering every alternative, she leaned toward him. They kissed.

Sensations cascaded through her body. She was confused but delighted. How could she be shivering and sweating at the same time? Neon lights flared behind her closed eyelids. Her rigid grasp on self-control relaxed, and she was amazed.

His lips parted. He probed with his tongue, and she opened her mouth to draw him inside. Gentle at first, he teased her with his passion, and she returned the favor, tasting the slick surface of his teeth and pressing her mouth hard against his, kissing him ravenously. She heard someone moaning. *Oh, it's me.*

Their physical contact broke the rules. He was an FBI agent and, therefore, could get into big trouble for this indiscretion. She ought to make him stop.

But it was Sloan who ended the kiss. "Are you okay?"

So much better than okay—she'd caught a hint of what sex ought to be about. Her prior experiences were obviously mistakes. "You said you wanted to be alone with me. Is this the reason why?"

"I'm glad we went down this road," he said.

"Me, too."

"But it's not the reason I wanted a private moment. We have a problem with Peter Channing."

His words fell with heavy thuds. With reluctance, she rose from the bed and returned to the real world.

Chapter Twelve

Given a choice, Sloan would have kept the reinforced steel door to the panic room locked and put that pull-down bed to good use. Brooke's kiss surprised him, even though he'd been imagining her as his lover from the first moment they met. Maybe it wasn't the first moment, when she blasted him with the pepper spray, but shortly thereafter. He'd been intrigued.

Who was this lady? Brooke was beautiful, with her soft lips, creamy complexion and shiny black hair curling around the perfect oval of her face. Also, she was sexy. Her kiss had started as a tentative taste but quickly jumpstarted a whole different level of arousal. An incredible woman, she was smart, brave and had a sense of humor. He even liked the way she focused on being well organized, probably because he had a few OCD issues of his own. He liked rules and preferred to have things neat and tidy, which made the proposal he was about to suggest more difficult. He watched her pace in a very small circle.

"What about Channing?" she asked. "You said you hadn't located him."

"We have a phone number, address, license plate number and all the other basic data. But we haven't been able to make contact."

"What about the girlfriend, the woman he's supposed to marry?" she asked. "He could be staying with her."

"One of our agents went to her place. She said she hadn't seen Channing since he went to work at about nine o'clock yesterday. Before that, he'd been with her."

"Where does he work?"

"A food truck called Taco Guac. Our agent talked to the guys who worked there yesterday. They said the truck was parked in Civic Center from ten o'clock to two, and Channing was there the whole time. According to our timeline, that gives him an alibi." They'd figured that the murderer had brought Layla's body to the cabin between eleven thirty and two. "He's in the clear, unless the Taco Guac guys are lying."

Her nervous pacing came to an abrupt halt as she pulled off her blue sweater and tossed it onto a hook by the door. Her flushed cheeks emphasized the blue of her eyes as she stared at him. "Why would the Guac guys lie?"

"He could have paid them off. They could be good buddies. Or they might just hate the FBI. You'd be shocked by how many people lie to us."

Her eyebrows arched. "I hope you're being sarcastic."

"Yeah, I am. In the old days, the FBI got more respect than now," he said. "Anyway, Channing won't answer his phone and hasn't gone back to his apartment."

"But that doesn't make sense," she said. "If he's not the killer, why would he go on the run? What does he have to hide?"

"We need to interrogate him. His emails to Layla must have some significance." After he'd handed over the thumb drive, Keller had wasted no time picking out the emails and printing them. The contents seemed innocent enough. Channing was reaching out to Layla, telling her about his upcoming wedding and hinting that he'd like to see her.

The person he really wanted to meet again was Franny. "Did you read them?"

She nodded. "He referred to us as his sisters and said that he missed us. When he was playing with us at the cabin, he somehow didn't notice the chains on our ankles and didn't hear Franny sobbing after his uncle mutilated her finger. Was he so desperately lonely that he actually thought we were his family?"

"It's possible."

"I don't know whether to hate him or pity him."

"His life must have gotten worse after his uncle was convicted and sent away to a federal prison. Channing was part of a notorious family, probably shunned by the other kids."

She wrapped her arms around her middle, looked down for a long moment and frowned. "Nope, I don't feel sorry for him. He could have helped us escape."

Sloan had to agree with her. As a trained psychologist, he could dredge up a raggedy chunk of empathy for Channing, but the kid had been eleven at the time, and that was old enough to know right from wrong. He'd enjoyed his trips to the cabin too much—probably had a sadistic streak. Still, his behavior didn't fit the profile for a killer.

His emails to Layla were polite and friendly. As Brooke pointed out, his memories were delusional. But he wasn't lewd or hostile. It was hard to imagine him making threatening phone calls to Franny, whom he genuinely liked. If he'd managed to reach his favorite girl from long ago, he would have invited her to a movie. In his mind, they were friends.

"He doesn't have a rap sheet," he said. "A couple of speeding tickets, but that's all. He never went to college. Mostly, he's been working in restaurants and has been employed by Taco Guac for six months."

She sank down on the bed beside him. "It doesn't seem like Channing is the killer."

"But I still need to talk to him. Layla's murder has too many connections to the past to ignore. Channing might refer us to someone else." He turned his head toward her. "That's where you come in."

"I'll do whatever it takes to help."

"Channing hasn't gone back to his apartment, and his phone is turned off, so we can't trace him. He's not answering messages from the FBI, but he'd probably listen if the call came from you."

"Seriously?" Her eyes popped wide. "You want me to call the twerp?"

"Maybe don't start by calling him names."

"Twerp is exactly right," she said. "That was my nickname for him."

"You'd send him a message on a throwaway phone, assure him that everything is okay and tell him to call you back. When he responds, you set up a meeting. Not with you, but with me."

"This plan sounds flaky to me. Has Keller signed off on it?"

"Surprisingly, he has. We're having no luck with Channing, and it's making Keller furious. He's willing to bend the rules if it means getting this investigation moving. It's a high-profile case. If he solves it, he looks good."

She held out her hand. "Give me the phone. I'll leave a message and send a text."

He took a cell phone from his jacket pocket. "Do you get reception down here?"

"It's specially wired. I don't want to get trapped in my panic room with no way to contact the outside world."

"Before you make the phone call, take a breath. Your voice needs to sound welcoming, not threatening."

"Got it." After he punched in the number, she held the phone while it rang and went to voice mail. She cleared her throat and talked to the phone. "Hello, twerp. It's me, Brooke. I want to talk. Call me back on this number."

She tapped a text message in a similar tone, and then handed him the phone. "Now what?"

"Now we wait," he said.

BROOKE LED SLOAN from the panic room to the kitchen, where they rejoined the others. They were just in time to greet the three bodyguards, who were—as their photos promised—muscular, well-groomed and studly. These guys would give Sloan a run for his money, but she still thought the FBI special agent had the bodyguards beat, even though he was wearing a sedate dark gray suit and they were dressed in three different versions of cargo pants and form-hugging T-shirts. She supposed they were trying to look casual, as if these guys could blend in with the crowd.

Sloan kept the cell phone in his possession. As soon as it rang or got a response to her text, they'd go down the hall to her office for the conversation with Channing. Since he was no longer a viable suspect, her attitude toward the twerp had mellowed. She hadn't forgiven him and never would. But she didn't despise him.

Though she was happily married, Megan flirted with enthusiasm as little Emily linked hands with the bodyguard assigned to them and pulled him toward the upstairs bedroom where she'd been playing with coloring books. When they left the kitchen, Megan gave Brooke a wink. "If I take him with us to soccer practice, I'll be the most popular mom on the field."

Brooke didn't want her to be scared, but she didn't want

her to be stupid, either. "He's a bodyguard, not an accessory. You need to follow his rules to stay safe."

"I'm sure I won't mind having him tell me exactly what to do."

Moira consulted a computer program with an astrological ephemeris to make sure that she and her assigned guard were compatible. Franny chatted cheerfully with her bodyguard, who was her new best friend.

Sloan took a position beside Brooke at the kitchen island. "You seem to have everything under control."

"It's what I do."

When there was another knock at the door, the bodyguard assigned to her house checked the camera surveillance and held the computer tablet so she could see. One of the cops had escorted Tom Lancaster to her doorstep. He was more formal than usual, wearing a suit and carrying an attaché. He probably wanted to impress the media.

Brooke gave the security code to the bodyguard and told him to open the door. Though she wasn't real happy with Lancaster for having a chat with Icky Nicky Brancusi, she was relieved that he was here. Layla's death would generate a lot of paperwork, and—since she had no family—the arrangements would be Brooke's responsibility. She knew what Layla wanted—one night, they'd shared a bottle of wine and their conversation turned morbid. They'd talked about what they wanted for their funerals. Both preferred cremation. Layla had specifically said she didn't want a gravestone and hoped her ashes could be scattered in the mountains near their cabin.

Not there. That cabin was where the killer left her body. Even in the supposed safety of their hideaway, their past had found them. The irony enraged her. Brooke found herself gripping Sloan's hand and squeezing his fingers hard.

Quietly, he murmured, "Are you okay?"

"I'll be fine."

When Lancaster entered, he greeted one of the bodyguards by name and told him that he was glad Brooke had gone with his firm, which was the one he'd recommended. He turned to Brooke and said, "We have paperwork and other details to work through. Maybe we should go to your office."

"Of course." She didn't make the mistake of thinking that Lancaster was being sensitive to the feelings of the other women and trying to avoid upsetting them with talk of Layla's death. The lawyer had worked with them long enough to know that they wouldn't get business done in a group setting. He was being efficient.

In her office, she took the chair behind the desk, the power position. Lancaster stood on the opposite side, and Sloan was by the door. He checked the burner phone she'd used to call Channing and put it back into his pocket. She hoped the twerp would contact her soon. Thus far, the investigation had gone from one dead end to another. They desperately needed some kind of direction.

Before Lancaster took a seat, he scowled at Sloan and muttered an unintelligible comment under his breath. Brooke knew they'd argued last night. "Gentlemen, is there a problem?"

"This is confidential information," the lawyer said. "We don't need him."

"Special Agent Sloan and I are working together on the investigation," she said. "Anything you say to me, you can say to him."

"You? You're playing detective for the FBI?"

"I'm a consultant."

"I don't approve. It's dangerous."

"And it's my decision."

What gave him the right to tell her what to do? Sloan

had characterized Lancaster as a narcissist. Though she'd never really thought about it before, she had to agree. In her transcription work, she frequently came into contact with lawyers and doctors. Many of them had egos as vast as Montana. It was no surprise that Lancaster fit that profile.

"We'll get started," he said as he placed his attaché on the desktop and opened it. "As soon as I have official copies of the death certificate, I'll deal with Layla's creditors, debts and insurance policies. The deed for the cabin should be transferred to your name only."

"I'm not sure I want to keep it," she said. "I wasn't aware that there were insurance policies."

"One she got through the college and another for student loans. There might be more. She kept me up-to-date on her business dealings, but I'm not sure I have everything. The explosion destroyed a lot of information."

She glanced toward Sloan. "I believe the FBI has accessed the data on her personal computer, which I would have grabbed off her desk if I'd been thinking properly."

"We were right to run," Sloan said. "The computer was plugged in to other devices, and we would have wasted precious minutes disconnecting. As it was, we barely escaped in time."

"What a mess!" Lancaster shook his bald head in disbelief. "Why on earth would the killer blow up her office?"

"To hide something," she said.

"How did you know the bomb was in the office?" Sloan asked.

"Must have heard it on the news. And Brooke just mentioned the desk."

She wasn't exactly sure what was going on with these two men. Either Sloan was suspicious of Lancaster or he really didn't like the lawyer…or a bit of both.

"Anyway," she said, "when we first came into her apartment, I could tell that it had been searched. Layla must have had evidence that pointed to the identity of the killer. And when he couldn't find it…"

"He blew the place up," Lancaster said, "to cover his tracks."

That theory made as much sense as anything else. Maybe Channing had placed the bomb to hide his correspondence with Layla, but she didn't think the twerp was clever enough to rig a specialized trigger. Not to mention that he had a fairly good alibi. Who could have set a bomb? "The explosive device was sophisticated."

"Something like that can be bought." Lancaster tilted his head back and looked down his nose at Sloan. "Does the FBI have any leads about the bomber?"

"No arrests have been made."

She appreciated his noncommittal attitude. He wasn't spilling information but wasn't being rude to her lawyer.

Lancaster took a typed sheet of paper from a file folder inside his briefcase and placed it on the desk in front of her. "This is the first draft of the obituary. You'll need to add details about the funeral home, memorial services and where people should send flowers."

"Cremation. No burial. No flowers. Layla did pro bono work for a homeless shelter and for foster kids. Those would be good places for donations. As for a memorial? I don't know."

She hated the idea of weeping mourners who had never known her friend. At the same time, she understood how people were touched by Layla's story and needed to express their grief. Memorials were supposed to give closure, but she wasn't so sure. Before she presented the plan to the others, she wanted to talk it over with someone…with Sloan. He'd listen and give good advice.

"A suggestion," Lancaster said. "Since we already have

the fund set up and ready to accept donations, we could ask people to send money there. Later, we'll disperse various amounts to Layla's favorite causes."

"I'd rather start a different fund using her name. She had a separate life that wasn't part of our combined tragedy. She was special."

"Okay, okay, consider it done. What about Layla's will? We ought to set an appointment for the reading."

"No need to rush," she said, "unless there's a time-sensitive issue."

"Not really, but—"

"I have to interrupt," Sloan said. "Brooke has a text that needs to be answered right away."

Excitement rushed through her. Channing was returning her message. Their plan was working. She bounded to her feet. "We're done here, Mr. Lancaster. Please leave."

The lawyer shuffled to his feet and grumbled, moving slowly until Sloan grabbed his attaché, snapped the latch and tossed it into the hallway. Grumbling louder, the lawyer followed his paperwork out the door.

When they were alone, Sloan showed her the screen on the burner phone with the text message from Peter Channing. Not a twerp. Call in five minutes. Use this number.

Though she'd been hoping for a contact, a shiver of apprehension went through her. "What should I do?"

"Have you ever seen that phone number before?"

"I don't think so."

"He must have picked up a burner phone of his own. Maybe he's not as dumb as we thought. The FBI is monitoring the number that belongs to him and can use it to track his location." He came around the desk and stood in front of her. "Put the phone on speaker and call the twerp."

"What do I say?"

"Set up a meeting for me. Tell him he's not in trouble, and I just want to talk. Whatever you do, don't make promises you can't keep—don't get yourself involved." He placed the phone on the desk and turned his attention back to her. Gently, he grasped her upper arms and made eye contact. "You can handle this."

She wished for a ton more confidence. "What if he refuses?"

"You'll convince him. He'll listen to you. They all listen to you." He guided her to the desk chair and got her seated. "You're the boss."

She reminded herself that the twerp probably wasn't the killer. Could she be certain of that? Was it possible for Channing to have killed Layla? If she arranged a meeting, would she be sending Sloan into a trap?

She punched in the numbers. The phone rang twice before a man's voice answered, "Hi, Brooke. Long time, no see."

He didn't sound at all like the preadolescent kid who'd come to the cabin and played with Franny. He was a grown man, twenty-three years old. "I could say the same to you."

"I'm sorry, like, really sorry, about what happened to Layla. She was always nice to me. Not like you. Layla never, ever called me a twerp."

He had the deep voice of an adult, but his words were childish. She could have been talking to an eleven-year-old, chastising him for tracking mud into the cabin. "I'm helping the FBI investigate. They want to talk to you."

"No way. I won't let them arrest me. I won't. This isn't my fault. I didn't do anything wrong. You can't trick me, Brooke. Not like when I was a kid. I know what the FBI is after. They want to lock me up and throw away the key."

"They only want information. You're not a suspect."

"I don't believe you. Damn, Brooke, you don't know what it was like after Uncle Martin got arrested. When people heard my name, they'd run away. I didn't have any friends. All I wanted was to talk to Franny. I missed her so much. She was my best little buddy. Do you know how I can find her?"

His tirade worried her. She'd never tell him how to reach Franny, and she needed to change the subject. "Things are better for you now. You have a girlfriend. You're going to get married."

"So what?"

"You have a happy, decent life ahead of you. All you need to do is talk to this one FBI agent and get it over with."

There was a long pause. She looked up at Sloan. He gave her an encouraging grin.

"Peter, are you there?"

"Ten minutes from right now. Tell him to go to Molly May's Café on Colfax and sit in one of the booths by the front window."

Success! "Thanks, Peter."

"There's one more thing, Brooke. You need to come with the FBI guy. If you're not sitting in the booth at the window where I can see you, I won't come inside."

How could she say no? Peter Channing could play cat-and-mouse games with the FBI for days while the evidence evaporated and the leads turned icy cold. "I'll be there."

"Good."

"Now I have a question for you. Molly May's is close to my house. How did you know I could get there in ten minutes?"

"Check your local news. They're broadcasting from your front yard, and I've been watching since six o'clock this morning. See you in ten, Brooke."

Her heart stopped. He'd been watching? She swiveled in her desk chair and stared through the window at the backyard. Was Channing out there? Hiding behind the tall, cedar privacy fence or lurking in shadow of a big-leafed catalpa tree?

Her house—her sanctuary—was being broadcast on television sets all over Denver. She might never feel safe again.

Chapter Thirteen

Brooke expected Sloan to be annoyed with her. She'd disregarded his instruction about not getting involved. When Channing said she had to attend the meeting, she'd been quick to agree. Not a single attempt at negotiating. No objections, none at all.

Rationalizing, she told herself that she hadn't wanted to scare him off. The twerp might have details about Layla's death, and they needed all the information they could get. "I didn't have a choice," she said.

"No, you did not."

Whew! "I guess I'm coming with you."

"Much as I'd rather have you tucked away in your panic room with a bodyguard keeping watch, you made a promise. If you're not there, Channing will take off like a white-tailed jackrabbit. He shouldn't be a problem. I don't believe this guy poses much of a threat."

"Me neither." Talking to him hadn't scared her. The thought of him sneaking around and peeping into her house made her uneasy but not panicked. If she'd spotted him, she wouldn't have hesitated to pull her Glock from her desk drawer and take aim.

"The way I figure," Sloan said, "if he wanted to hurt you, he would have chosen a more clandestine spot than Molly May's Café."

"Let me grab my fanny pack, and we'll go."

"We're going to need help from the cops on duty to get past the media. Do what I say, move fast and don't tell the others where we're headed."

She strapped on her fanny pack. "Should I take my gun?"

"No."

He ushered her through the house, made excuses for why they needed to rush and promised to be back soon. Megan pressed a "while you're out" shopping list into her hand. And Franny gave her a hug.

After a speedy switcheroo with the cops, they were in his SUV, headed toward Molly May's, a cute little café with plastic daisies on the tables and gingham curtains. Though the checkered pattern was red, it reminded her of the apron she had to wear at the cabin. They sat at one of the three booths by the front window. Because they were side by side instead of opposite each other, she rearranged the silverware so they each had their separate knife, fork and spoon at their right hand. A waitress in a white uniform with an apron that matched the curtains served coffee. If she spilled, would she be forced to scrub at the stain until her fingers were raw? Had Channing known about the gingham?

Brooke looked down at her hands in her lap and realized that she'd shredded her paper napkin. Squeezing the tattered napkin into a ball, she looked out the window, watching the sidewalk and the cars on Colfax—a long, straight street that always had traffic, even at ten o'clock on a Saturday.

In spite of Sloan's assurance that they were in no danger, she noticed that he'd positioned himself so his right side was free. He had easy access to his handgun.

"Do you see him?" he asked.

"I'm not sure I'd recognize him if I did."

As she watched a red truck slow down as it passed the café, her tension level ratcheted up higher. What if he didn't show? *What would she do when he did?* A couple of other cars cruised slowly with the drivers watching. Then she saw a guy shuffling along the sidewalk. A backward Bronco cap covered his close-cropped hair, and his baggy brown shorts flapped around his skinny legs. His posture was dreadful. His feet seemed too big for the rest of him. She wasn't surprised when he waved.

"That's him." Waving back, she felt her mouth curling into a smile. *Why?* Channing was part of her captivity, complicit with his uncle. She ought to hate him.

He picked his way through the café, twice bumping into chairs, and joined them at their table. A dopey grin spread across his face, and she squeezed her lips together so she wouldn't smile back at him.

"Stop staring, Peter. It's rude."

He chuckled. "You're still trying to boss everybody around."

"Allow me to introduce Special Agent Sloan, and then sit down."

After the two men shook hands, Channing scooted into the booth opposite her and Sloan. Like his big feet, his overlarge hands dangled from bony wrists. She noticed several scars from burns and cuts that must have come from his work in the food truck. Considering how clumsy he was walking through a mostly vacant restaurant, she expected worse.

"Do you like working at Taco Guac?" she asked.

"Yep." His head bobbed. "Did you recognize me right away?"

"I knew it was you when I saw—" she pointed to the

corner of her mouth "—your dimple. Do you still have the scar on your leg?"

"You bet." He started to hoist his leg onto the table. "Want to see?"

"I'll take your word."

"I would have known you anywhere, Brooke. You're so pretty. All you dolls were pretty, especially Franny. I think about her all the time. Should I invite her to my wedding? Would she come?"

"I can't speak for Franny." His expression was open, innocent and alarmingly immature. Channing had a man's body but acted like a little boy. How could he forget that when he knew them, they were prisoners? Shackled to their beds, brutalized by his uncle, they weren't his cheerful playmates. She didn't want to bond with him, and she sure as hell wouldn't put him in touch with Franny.

"I tried to get ahold of you and the other dolls. Just to talk, but no. No way. You were hiding behind unlisted phone numbers and computer firewalls and secret addresses. There were restraining orders."

"But you managed to send Layla a couple of emails. How did that happen?"

"She's a new lawyer, looking for business. Her email address was on a flyer for a homeless shelter."

"Pro bono." Her services were free to people who were down on their luck. Layla wanted to help. Instead, she'd attracted Channing, which was a perfect example of how no good deed went unpunished.

"It's cool that she's a lawyer." He wiped a hand over his face to erase his grin. "I'm sorry about what happened to her, really sorry."

Sloan cleared his throat. "I have a few questions."

"First, let me order."

Channing waved the waitress over to their table. It was

a few minutes after ten o'clock, early enough for break-fast. He ordered waffles and bacon. Sloan did the same. Brooke didn't want food. Her easygoing chat with Channing wasn't sitting well in her stomach.

While she sipped her coffee, Sloan ran through Channing's whereabouts for the week. He worked every day and spent most of his downtime with his fiancée, but there were gaps in his activities on Wednesday and Thursday when he could have met with Layla. Yesterday's alibi for eleven thirty until two gave him an out.

The longer they talked, the less she believed he was the killer. Channing was too clumsy to have performed the surgical search at Layla's apartment. He didn't have the smarts to build a bomb or the money to hire someone else to do it.

After their food was served, she asked, "Why were you avoiding the FBI?"

"I've had bad experiences with cops. No offense, Sloan."

"None taken," Sloan said as he drenched his waffles with syrup. "What kind of bad experience?"

"As soon as they figure out who I am and how I was connected to the dolls, they get mean. They slap me around, zap me with Tasers and call me a pedophile. It wasn't my fault. I tried to help, but I was only eleven."

"Old enough to know right from wrong," she said. There was a limited amount of time that she could hold back her resentment.

"Don't start." He shoveled a forkful of waffles into his mouth, chewed fast and swallowed with a gulp. He vacu-umed up another bite. Preparing fast food on a truck had apparently turned him into a speedy eater. "I've got to tell you, Brooke, you didn't make things easy?"

"Seriously? You're blaming me for your problems?"

"You hurt me." She heard a disturbing edge in his voice

and reminded herself that just because he appeared boyish, he could still be dangerous. "You and Franny. You hurt my feelings."

"I don't believe you."

"You were a mean girl. You had all these rules about keeping quiet and not making a mess. I always tried to bring food with me. Don't you remember the jars of peanut butter? My girlfriend says I was trying to buy your love."

She glanced toward Sloan. "Does this make sense to you?"

He gave a brief nod.

As if she should feel responsible for any way that Channing had messed up his life? He wasn't her responsibility. "Your uncle never should have brought you to the cabin."

"But he did, and I wanted to be nice to you. After Halloween, I gave the dolls all my candy. At least Franny was happy."

"Stop saying *dolls*," she said.

"But that's what everybody calls you." His narrow shoulders rose and fell in a shrug. For a few minutes, he ate. The food on his plate disappeared at a startling rate. "You always were touchy and bossy. You had secrets."

Sloan asked, "What kind of secrets?"

"She was like the magpies I saw on a nature show. They're always hopping around, stealing shiny things and tucking them away in secret nests."

Sloan glanced down at her. His unspoken message was clear. She still had secrets and hiding places. So what if that was true? She had nothing to feel bad about.

Channing continued, "One time, she took nail clippers from my uncle and when he noticed and got mad, she pretended like she'd just found them so nobody would get punished."

These sad, pathetic memories disgusted her. She'd

started with stealing loose change from Hardy, thinking that she'd have enough to buy her way to freedom—a plan that made no sense whatsoever. Who did she intend to pay? "I did what I had to do to survive."

"Do you remember when I gave you the key?"

A wave of guilt splashed over her, and she covered her feelings by taking a long sip from her nearly empty coffee cup. Though she wished she could forget, the memory was horrible and clear. She hadn't known how long they'd been at the cabin because there was no good way to keep track, but the weather was warmer, almost like spring. Channing had come through with a useful gift. He regularly brought trinkets for Franny, but this was for her: a key that would unlock the metal shackle fastened to her ankle.

Channing had whispered that he needed the key back before he left, and he'd told her to do what she needed to do. She could have escaped but had been paralyzed by fear. What if Hardy caught her? She'd already seen him cut off the tip of Franny's finger. He regularly raped Layla. She'd felt the force of his wrath when he beat her. Did she dare to run? Where would she go?

Sitting in a booth at Molly May's, she shuddered. A painful heat rose from her belly and spread through her body. She was sweating. Her throat felt dry. Some wounds never healed. She was crazy to think she could make this better.

Her captivity had been more than physical. Hardy had imprisoned her soul. She'd been afraid to use the key, terrified of the consequences. Everybody, including Sloan, thought she was brave, but they were wrong. She was a coward who didn't deserve to be in charge. Because she was too scared to act, they'd been in captivity for two more months, Layla had been raped many more times, and Sophia, too. Brooke had let them down. And it was happening again. Layla's killer was outsmarting her. She wasn't smart or courageous enough to stop him. He was getting away with his heinous crimes.

Her insights provided no help at all. It was time for her to step away before she messed up this investigation.

Channing and Sloan continued talking while they finished their breakfast. The twerp apologized for avoiding the cops and took Sloan's business card, promising to call him if anything else occurred to him. All in all, he wasn't a bad kid. It wasn't his fault that his uncle was a monster.

When they left the booth, Channing tried to give her a hug. *Not yet.* She wasn't ready to forgive him, but she kept smiling. "This wasn't too bad," she said.

"Same to you."

Sloan paid, and they followed Channing out the door, where they saw Brancusi step out from behind a dark brown van with a gold stripe on the side. He held a small camera to his eye and was videotaping them.

"Don't pay any attention to me," he said. "Keep doing what you were doing."

"Who the hell is this guy?" Channing demanded.

Sloan stalked toward the filmmaker and held the flat of his hand in front of the lens. "You don't have permission to film us."

"A technicality." Brancusi lowered the camera and called to Channing, "Hey, kid, do you want to make a couple hundred bucks?"

Though his eyes lit up at the mention of easy money, he shook his head. "You stay away from me."

"Your fiancée was more cooperative," Brancusi said with a sleazy leer. "A whole lot more cooperative."

Channing charged the few yards across the asphalt parking lot and lunged at Brancusi, who pivoted to protect his camera equipment. It wouldn't be a fair confrontation.

Channing had youth on his side, but the documentarian had experience. Though Brancusi dressed like a bearded hipster, he moved like a street fighter. Darting back to the driver's side of his van, he whipped open the door and emerged with a tire iron.

Sloan drew his weapon and aimed. "Put it down."

"He started it," Brancusi said. "He came at me."

"If you disarm yourself, get in your van and drive away, I won't arrest you," Sloan said. "Do us all a favor—don't be an ass."

The threat of being arrested made a difference. Brancusi backed off. Before he closed the door to his van, he said, "Here's a favor for you, Sloan. If you want to solve this, meet with the kid's fiancée."

Dismissively, Sloan turned away from him and spoke to Channing. "Are you okay?"

"I don't like that guy."

"Nobody does," Brooke said.

He gave her a dimpled grin and checked his wristwatch. "If I hustle, I can make my shift at Taco Guac. Call me if there's anything I can do to help."

"I will." Maybe she would.

"And tell Franny to give me a call. Any time."

She watched him walk to the end of the parking lot and climb into his car. Seeing Channing hadn't been what she expected. She'd thought she'd be hostile toward him. Instead, her anger and tension came from inside. Her head ached with memories of her mistakes and bad decisions. The guilt crushed her spirit. She had no business being involved in the investigation. She should step aside and let the FBI do their job.

"I'm done," she said. "Take me back to the house."

"So far, the guy who best fits the profile for a murderer is Brancusi," Sloan said as he walked her back to his SUV and opened the passenger-side door for her. "The film-maker is a typical sociopath."

"What does that mean?"

"His grasp on right and wrong is tenuous. His morality is based on self-interest. Whatever's right for him is the course he chooses."

"That sounds like a lot of businessmen I've known."

"Sociopaths can be very successful. They're capable of being charming when it suits them, but they have almost zero empathy. I can easily imagine Brancusi making cruel phone calls to Franny, not caring that he hurt her."

"Is that the profile for a killer?"

"It could be."

His information tantalized her. Psychology was interesting, and sometimes her sessions with Dr. Joan helped… but not right now. The clearer her memories got, the worse she felt about herself. She needed to go home and clean out a drawer or straighten the dishes in the kitchen. In this situation, she was blinded by emotion. Her intelligence was worthless. There was no way she could help solve this murder. She should bow out now.

She climbed into the SUV and fastened her seat belt. "It sounds like you've got it all figured out."

"I haven't." He went around to the driver's side and slid behind the steering wheel. "Brancusi has an alibi. He was in Las Vegas when the murder took place. Do you think he was working with somebody else?"

She shook her head. "You should be talking to somebody who understands these things."

"I want your insights and your help." He fired up the engine. "What's going on, Brooke? You're not a quitter."

"How do you know? We've only been together a couple of days."

"I know you'll do anything to catch Layla's murderer."

Dammit, he was right. "Fine. What do we do next?"

"Follow up on a clue from Brancusi. While Channing is at work on the food truck, we're going to pay a visit to his fiancée."

Chapter Fourteen

Sloan's job was to profile and apprehend the killer, but he had other motivations. Right now, he was worried about Brooke. The memories triggered by her conversation with Channing must have been dark and heavy. It wasn't the mention of secret hidey-holes that upset her. She was aware of that glitch in her personality. When they were alone in her panic room, she'd admitted to a penchant for secret stashes and hiding places.

He'd noticed a different reaction when Channing recalled a specific incident involving a key. The symbolism of a key, especially to someone who was being held captive, was huge. Had he thwarted her escape? Was she unable to flee when offered an opportunity? Later, they'd talk about it. First, he needed to assess her behavior and decide if she'd be able to help as they moved forward.

"I hope you'll stay with the investigation." He checked the address for Channing's girlfriend in his spiral notebook before he drove the SUV through the parking lot beside Molly May's and exited onto Colfax Avenue. "If you've changed your mind and don't want to be involved, I'll understand."

"I doubt that."

"Give me a break. I understand a lot."

"Do you really?"

She wasn't ready to be open, but he heard a shift in her tone of voice. The darkness might be receding. "You're not a total woman of mystery."

She turned her head away, staring through the windshield. "Why do you need me?"

Determined to lighten the mood, he said, "For one thing, you're not bad to look at."

"That's a terrible, unprofessional reason."

"I'd be lying if I told you that you aren't the prettiest partner I've ever had. I guess that's kind of a backhanded compliment."

"How so?"

"All my other partners have been guys who'd knock my teeth down my throat if I called them pretty."

She scoffed. "Typical guys."

"Bottom line, I enjoy being with you."

Her voice lightened. "I'm still waiting to hear a rational reason for why I should tag along with you."

"You aren't tagging along. You're a consultant, and you've already helped a lot. If you hadn't lured Channing to this meeting, I would have wasted time trying to get the kid to sit down for a talk. Your secret camera at the cabin provided an invaluable parameter for alibis. You're doing great. I'm the one who can't zero in on a profile."

"What about Channing?"

He was an unlikely suspect. His immaturity and indecisiveness might get him into a bar fight. But murder? Sloan doubted the kid would be capable of planning the complexities of Layla's murder. She'd been drugged and her body hidden before she was strangled, then the killer transported her to the cabin and arranged her in a pose. Not to mention the sophistication needed to set the bomb and the trigger.

At Monaco Street, Sloan turned right. Channing's girlfriend lived a couple of miles to the south. Even though they were engaged, she hadn't moved in with him. Sloan had to wonder if it was because Peter Channing idolized the "dolls." When he'd gazed at Brooke, his eyes were reverent. Every time he mentioned Franny, his voice oozed with emotion. He didn't want to kill these women. He wanted to worship them.

"On the surface, Channing is a typical kid. I don't see him committing murder, but he has a fixation on all of you, especially Franny."

"I know. It's weird, huh?"

"His engagement is a sign of recovery. There's another woman in his life, and he loves her. That should indicate he's ready to move on."

Sloan checked his rearview mirror and groaned. "I don't believe this. That idiot Brancusi is tailing us."

She turned in her seat and peered through the back window. "I don't see him."

"In the left lane, two cars back. He's trying to be subtle." Sloan didn't want the filmmaker following them, mostly because Brancusi would think he'd influenced them by mentioning Channing's girlfriend. "Change of plans. We're going to FBI headquarters."

"Fine." She exhaled a sigh, an indication that she still wasn't one hundred percent on board with him.

"I wanted to go there, anyway. There's new evidence. It's about Zachary Doyle, the neighbor."

"The peeper," she said bitterly. "I hope you have him locked up."

"He's not able to travel." Though the peeper was a bad man, Sloan wouldn't wish this fate on anyone. "He has ALS. Most of the time, he's in a wheelchair, but he can move around enough to take care of himself and insists on staying alone at his cabin in the mountains. A home-care nurse comes by twice a week to help him with basic cleaning, cooking and supplies. He can't drive."

"Was he brought in to FBI headquarters?"

"We didn't think it was necessary. He's not a viable suspect because he's not physically capable of committing the crime. One of our agents went to his cabin and videotaped an interview with him."

He paused at a stoplight and studied her profile, trying to figure out how this information affected her. Signs of agitation were apparent. Her brow creased in a frown, and she chewed her lower lip. If viewing the video of Doyle would cause her to withdraw even more, he didn't want her to watch it.

"I hated him," she said quietly. "The man was a nightmare. He took a perverse pleasure in scaring me. But I'm sorry he's suffering."

"Is it worthwhile for you to watch the videotape?"

"I don't know," she said. "I never actually spoke to him. Apart from his leering at me through the window, I had no contact with him whatsoever."

At the next intersection, he made a U-turn and reversed his route—a move he hoped would help him evade Brancusi. "We need a new direction. Our initial premise was that the killer was someone who took part in the events from twelve years ago. Our suspects were Channing, Doyle and Brancusi."

"All of them have credible alibis."

"We have to break those alibis or find new suspects," he said.

"How do we do that?"

"Do you want a list?"

"Of course."

Her tidiness was adorably predictable. "First, I already mentioned needing info about Layla's current friends, professors and associates. Second, I want to take a look at other people who knew her twelve years ago."

"Number one is already done." She took her phone from her fanny pack and flipped through the screens. "I made a list of people she talked about and added some of her email contacts from her computer thumb drive."

"Any standouts?"

"She was close to a couple of her law professors and the other students in her study group. Their relationships were friendly. She and her last boyfriend broke up over a year ago. Layla had been completely focused on completing her degree. Nothing else was on the radar."

He'd expected as much. "Let's move on to my number two concern. What about other people from your past?"

"What about them?"

"I want to know about your memories, your subconscious thoughts. I want to climb inside your head and wander around."

"You might not like what you find, but okay. As long as it doesn't involve truth serum or hypnosis, I'll do it. For Layla."

If the videotape of the peeper didn't rattle her too much, Sloan had another plan for the day. He could spark Brooke's memories by going to the source, setting up a line of communication with the man who had destroyed her life—Martin Hardy.

INSIDE FBI HEADQUARTERS, Brooke felt safe but not comfortable. She didn't expect to be physically assaulted. However—as she well knew—there were other ways to be hurt. Prepared for trouble, her guard was up.

Sloan escorted her past the cubicles to a small office where SAC Keller sat behind the desk. He rose immediately, shook her hand and thanked her for helping in their investigation. The only personal touches in the room were a tall, large-leafed philodendron lurking in the corner and a photograph of Keller and a shiny blonde woman on the ski slopes. Keller's desktop was clean, with a minimum of supplies, a design choice that Brooke appreciated.

After they shook hands, she took a seat. "We don't seem to be having much luck with our suspects."

"Zachary Doyle turned out to be a dead end." Keller laced his fingers neatly on the desktop. "Doyle claimed that he lived alone when Hardy held you captive at the cabin. Is that true?"

"I don't know, but I didn't see anyone else."

"From time to time, Hardy brought other men with him to the cabin."

"Yes."

Her fingers twisted together on her lap, not reaching for the memory but not pushing it away. When Hardy showed up with his "friends," she wasn't allowed to look at them. She served the beer and whatever food they brought with them, and then she faded away.

The same was true for Layla and Sophia, who had been blindfolded and restrained while these strangers did unspeakable things. She dreaded the nights when she heard several car doors slam outside the cabin and Hardy burst through the door with his "friends." He showed an odd degree of loyalty to them, never giving their names to the court.

"At the time," Keller said, "you were unable to identify these men, not even to work with a sketch artist. Has your memory improved over the years? Do you recall any names or identifying marks? Maybe you saw a tattoo or a scar?"

"No."

"Concentrate, Brooke. Did any of them have an accent? Was there anything unusual about their voices?"

"If I had remembered," she said crisply, "I would have reported that information to Special Agent Gimbel."

Keeping his gaze fixed on her, he nodded slowly. Though he didn't aim the finger of guilt in her direction, she had the distinct impression that he didn't believe her, even though she'd done nothing to earn his distrust. She had no reason to hide information from the FBI. The opposite was true.

Determined not to speak first and break their silence, she locked eyes with him and straightened her shoulders, mimicking his erect posture. If he wanted a stare-down, she'd give it to him. Brooke was nothing if not patient. She could sit here for a solid five minutes without blinking.

Sloan interrupted, "Excuse me, sir. Is there new evidence about the other men who went to the cabin, maybe something on Layla's computer?"

"Only hints," he said, ending their showdown to look down at the pristine surface of his desk. "There's nothing substantial, but their existence opens many possibilities."

She shot a meaningful glance at Sloan. She'd also reviewed much of the data on Layla's thumb drives and found nothing to incriminate those faceless, nameless men.

"I agree about the possibilities," Sloan said. "Supposedly, these unknown subjects are out in the world, living their lives. How many were there, Brooke?"

"Over a period of seven months, Hardy must have brought friends home with him six or seven times." This was a fact she knew. Her therapist had talked with her about the stranger rapes a lot and found it hard to believe that Brooke hadn't been sexually assaulted. "I can't tell you how many men, because I don't know if they were different each time."

"I know what you're thinking," Sloan said to Keller, "and it's an elegant theory. Layla might have recognized one of these men and confronted him. That would make a strong motive for murder. She could accuse him of rape."

"Would her murder fit the profile for one of those men?"

"Not a good fit," Sloan said. "When her murderer attacked, she wasn't sexually assaulted or brutalized, which is what I'd expect from a rapist. Postmortem, Layla's body was posed and handled with extreme care."

Keller cleared his throat. "Profiling isn't an exact science."

"Which is why we'll look into your theory, and I'll talk to the other women," Sloan said. "In the meantime, I'd like to show Brooke the video of Zachary Doyle so she can verify his statements."

"If his statement triggers any memories…"

"You'll be the first to know," she said as she rose from the chair. "Technically, you'll be the second, because Sloan will be with me, and I'll tell him first."

She gave him a friendly grin, hoping to call a truce between them. But SAC Keller didn't crack a smile. He issued an order. "Sloan, have one of the techs set up the video. And I'll want a full report on Peter Channing before the end of the day."

"You got it."

As he hustled her down the corridor, she asked, "What a pill! How can you stand to work with him?"

"We're not pals, but Keller isn't a bad guy. He's ambitious and wants results. When he doesn't get answers, he tends to be cranky."

To say the least. She followed him through the maze of hallways and staircases to a small room with a table, a credenza, a couple of chairs and a thirty-six-inch video screen hanging on the wall. Sloan left for a few moments, which gave her time to take a deep breath and consider whether or not she was doing the smart thing by watching the video of Doyle.

Dr. Joan would say no. Seeing Doyle would reopen a lot of old wounds. Delving deeper into the past was a terrifying prospect. For twelve years she'd tried her hardest to forget. But if staring into the face of the peeper would help solve the crime, she had to do it.

Sloan returned with a friendly tech guy who loaded the video, handed a remote to Sloan and asked him to return it when they were done. The tech guy closed the door.

Taking a seat beside her at a small table, Sloan aimed the remote at the screen. "I can turn off the video any time you want, just let me know."

"I can take it." At least, she thought she could.

A silent image appeared frozen on the screen. Though he wasn't seen below the waist, she could tell that Zachary Doyle was sitting in a wheelchair. He was still ugly, and the disease had taken a toll. He was gaunt to the point of emaciation. Deep furrows scored his brow and circled his mouth. His lips pulled back from his yellowed teeth.

She leaned way back in her chair, wanting to be as far away from the image on the screen as possible. Twelve years ago, he terrified her in the night. On purpose, he chose to behave like a monster. The horrific consequences of his disease weren't his fault, but she couldn't help thinking that his outer deterioration reflected the evil inside him.

When Sloan placed a steadying hand on her arm, she flinched.

"Should I start the video?" he asked.

She nodded. "Go ahead."

"Are you sure? You don't have to watch this."

"For Layla's sake, I do."

The vivid image on the screen moved slowly and with

great effort. His entire body shook with a violent cough that made it sound like death was near, but when he started talking, he sounded stronger. Who knew that he had a nice voice?

Doyle repeated the interviewer's question, "What's that? Did you want to know who watched those little monkeys when Hardy went out? It wasn't me. I can tell you that. We weren't close neighbors, no, sir, not me. I can't even see his cabin from my place."

"Did you consider him a friend?" the interviewer asked.

"I kept to myself, and he did the same. A couple of times he asked me to watch over his cabin while he went into town, but I never went inside. Even if I'd wanted to, I couldn't. All the doors were locked up tight. The windows, too. Nobody could get in."

She whispered, "And nobody could get out."

When the media rolled out their story, people asked why it took so long for them to break away from the cabin. After all, there were six of them and only one of him. Couldn't they have overpowered him?

Those people didn't know what it was like. The physical restraints and locks were only part of their captivity. They were trapped by terror—a bone-deep fear of punishment and Hardy's cruel threats. She was still held back by the terror of her memories. Until she could forget, she was in a cage.

Chapter Fifteen

Brooke suppressed the urge to flee from the room. Gripping the arms of her chair, she forced herself to watch the videotape of Zachary Doyle, who talked about how Hardy was almost always at the cabin, never gone for more than a day or two.

The interviewer asked, "Did you ever see the girls?"

His rheumy eyes glanced away as though to evade that question. Brooke knew what he'd done. His face appeared in her window late at night, and he'd laughed at her. But that wasn't what he told the FBI interviewer.

"Can't recall," he said. "Maybe I caught a glimpse now and again."

Brooke was pleased when the interviewer didn't let him off the hook. "Did you ever look in the windows?"

"Like a peeping Tom?" His bony hand wiped spittle from the corner of his mouth. "I'm a God-fearing man. I'd never do such a thing."

"Yes, you did," she shouted at the screen. "Again and again and again, you stared in the window. You did it."

The interviewer continued, "One of the women reported seeing your face."

"I'm not surprised that she'd lie. Those girls were real messed up." He poked his ugly face closer to the camera. "I'm a good person."

A blinding rage exploded in her head. How could this monster claim to be decent? Whether or not he denied it, Doyle had known what Hardy was doing to them. Doyle had seen the shackles and chains. He could have rescued them at any time.

"I've got references, plenty of people think highly of me," he said. "I used to sing in the choir at church, and the reverend will stand up for me. Hey, that reminds me. One of the church ladies brought an armload of girls' clothes to Hardy's cabin. Another time, she left some food on the porch."

"Do you remember her name?"

"Don't know."

Brooke reined in her anger. "He's not lying about the woman."

"Did you ever see the church lady?" Sloan asked.

"No, but I remember the cast-off clothing and a huge pan of lasagna. We rationed the slices, ate it for days."

They watched the interview for another fifteen minutes until Doyle suffered a severe coughing attack, and it was over. When the screen went dark, she hoped she would never see his face again.

Sloan lightly stroked her shoulder. "Are you all right?"

"I wish we'd gotten more from the interview. He never mentioned the other men."

"But he talked about his good buddy the reverend. And a woman from the church. We'll check them out."

She gazed up at him. "I don't even know where the church is. This is so frustrating. What kind of evidence can we get from a church lady who was blind enough to drop off lasagna and not come inside?"

"She might have noticed something."

"It was twelve years ago. How will you track her down?"

"That's the job." The warmth of his smile lifted her spirits. When he leaned close, she could smell the clean scent of sandalwood soap. He whispered in her ear, "Try to believe what I'm telling you. We usually nab the bad guy."

"I hope so."

She needed justice to be done.

SLOAN CHECKED THE address for Channing's girlfriend again before driving away from FBI headquarters. He slipped the SUV into gear and headed toward the exit. In his opinion, the "unknown subject" theory favored by Keller didn't have much traction. He suspected that if Layla had recognized one of her abusers, she would have told Brooke or one of the other women. That seemed to be the pattern. When talking to him, Franny had described how she saw Peter Channing in the grocery store. But she'd given a similar version of that story to Brooke a long time ago.

These women were close. They watched out for each other and didn't keep secrets. The only real conflict he'd seen was between the twins, who didn't really dislike each other. They were born to be best friends. If there was a threat to one, the others would know about it, with the possible exception of Sophia, because she lived in Las Vegas. He made a mental note to put through another call to her.

And he'd talk to the others. He'd already contacted Gimbel and asked him to help pry open any hidden memories the women might have about the men who occasionally came home with Hardy.

Leaving headquarters, he drove from the underground parking lot, passed the gatehouse, where he waved to the armed men inside, and merged into traffic. It was another beautiful, sunny day, filled with light and a view of the distant mountains. After turning on the air-conditioning, he glanced over at Brooke. The fury she'd displayed when watching Doyle had passed. She seemed relaxed.

"What does the FBI know about Channing's fiancée?" she asked.

"Her name is Karen Galloway," he said. "She goes by Kiki."

"How long have they been dating?"

"I don't have many details. Ms. Galloway was interviewed by a cop who did us a favor by stopping at her house and having her verify Channing's alibi. All I have are the basics from her driver's license. She's blonde with hazel eyes and older than him, pushing forty."

"I've got to wonder what she sees in the kid. Channing is so immature."

"I've heard that women like the boyish type."

"Not me. Little boys are unpredictable and boring at the same time. I know that doesn't sound possible, but it is. I've seen a little boy try to stick an unpeeled banana up his nose. Totally unpredictable. Who would think of such a thing? Then he peeled it and tried again. After that, the boy spent ten minutes telling me what he'd just done. Boring, very boring."

He was glad to hear her talking about something other than murder. He wanted to build a relationship that went beyond their shared interest in the investigation. "What do you like in a man?"

"He needs to be an adult who is responsible and smart, capable of holding up his end of an intelligent conversation. Also, a gentleman."

"You like a guy who holds the door for you?"

"Sure." She flashed a grin. "You almost always open my car door."

He'd take that as a compliment. "What about physically?"

"Agent Sloan, are you asking what turns me on?"

He braked for a stoplight, cocked his head in her direction and studied her beautiful face. Her eyes weren't visible because she'd put on a pair of sunglasses from her fanny pack, but her smile encouraged him to tease. "Do you prefer tall men who wear suits?"

"Definitely tall," she said, "but not big and muscle-bound. And I'm fond of a well-fitted suit—better yet, a tuxedo."

"I don't have a tux, but I own a US Navy dress white uniform."

"A man in uniform, very nice." She lowered her glasses and looked over the rims. Her fluttering eyelashes were meant as a joke but were sexy all the same. "And what do you like in a woman?"

"I could say black hair and blue eyes. Under the current circumstances, that doesn't exactly narrow the field, so I'll be more specific." He paused, aware that he was crossing boundaries. The safe move would be to back off, but he wanted to be honest with her. "You have everything I look for in a woman."

She flipped her sunglasses over her eyes and stared through the windshield. Quietly, she said something he couldn't quite make out.

It could have been "you're bad" or "I'm sad." He wanted to believe she said "I'm glad" but decided not to push for an explanation. They were too close to Kiki Galloway's house to engage in a complicated conversation. "We're almost there."

The older neighborhood was typical of those built during Denver's post-WWII housing boom. A row of two-bedroom brick houses was set back from the street. The lawns had begun to yellow due to watering restrictions. Ms. Galloway's bungalow was midway down the block.

When he parked at the curb, Brooke made a tsk-tsk noise. "This could be a nice place, but it's been neglected.

The gutters are falling off, the paint on the trim is chipped and the sidewalk is cracked. I'm surprised she hasn't recruited Channing to make repairs."

"Could be she's waiting until after they're married." When Brooke put her hand on the door handle, he reached across her. "Don't open it. That's my job."

"Being a gentleman?"

"And a bodyguard."

He jumped out of the SUV and circled to her side. After he opened her car door, he escorted her up the sidewalk to meet Kiki Galloway.

STANDING AT THE screen door, Brooke noticed that Kiki wasn't much of a gardener, and she didn't put away her tools. Her car—in need of a wash—was parked in the driveway outside the garage, not unusual for a Saturday. Brooke wondered what she did for a living. Was she expecting her young fiancé to step up and support her?

When Kiki opened the door, Brooke was dumbfounded. Instead of meeting a hazel-eyed blonde, Brooke shook hands with a woman whose black hair and blue eyes matched her own. "You must be Peter Channing's fiancée."

"And you're Brooke Josephson. Please come in."

Unable to take her eyes off the woman who looked younger than the age on her driver's license, Brooke barely noticed the furnishings. There was no central air-conditioning and two fans whirred ineffectively, which was probably why Kiki was dressed in scanty shorts and a tube top. She was an attractive lady in good physical condition with muscular arms and legs. Why had she dyed her hair and put on blue contact lenses?

They sat at a dining room table that was cluttered but nowhere near as messy as the table at Franny's place. Sloan took his spiral notebook from his jacket pocket and started asking her questions about Channing's actions since Tuesday. Other than his job at Taco Guac, he seemed to have spent all his time with Kiki.

She pointed to a big, empty cardboard box in the middle of the living room and said, "We went shopping on Wednesday and bought a nightstand that needed to be put together. It was hot, sweaty work, and I rewarded my man with a big glass of fresh lemonade."

"Two lemons and a cup of sugar," Brooke said.

"That's right," Kiki said. "How did you know?"

She'd followed that simple recipe frequently when they were in the cabin. "I used to make it that way. Channing liked it."

"You were the little mama." She rolled her fake blue eyes. "My sweetie said you were bossy."

Seven months of captivity hadn't been a game of playing house. She'd never wanted to be in charge and take care of them. Any person with a drop of sensitivity would understand that she did whatever necessary to survive. By calling her bossy, Kiki was trying to provoke her.

Sloan moved on to his questions about the next day. "On Friday, you told the police that you and Channing were together in the morning. He went to work from nine until two. Is that correct?"

"That's what I told them. I felt bad for Peter. His taco truck gets so hot." She tossed her shoulder-length black hair. "Are you hot, Agent Sloan? You can take off your jacket."

"Where were you from nine until two?"

"I can't remember."

"Oh, come on," Brooke said. "It was only yesterday."

"You should know. That's when your friend got herself killed, right?"

Anger surged through her, but Brooke held herself in

check. This woman's crazy, deep connection to Channing cast doubt on his alibi. And there was another possibility—they could have been working together.

While Channing was at work, Kiki could have made the drive to the cabin. She had the muscles that would have been needed to carry Layla, who was thin. When it came right down to it, Kiki could have done the murder all by herself.

"What do you do for a living?" Brooke hoped she had a job with access to bomb-making materials, maybe in an electronics store.

"I used to be a checkout clerk at the supermarket, but I've been out of work for a couple of months. It's just as well. Planning a wedding takes a lot of time."

"Why did Channing make you dye your hair?"

"He didn't." She rolled her eyes, again. "He's my fiancé, not my boss."

"You did it yourself? To look like us?"

"You make it sound so weird."

Because it was. "Can you explain?"

"Peter always talked about you girls like you were his sisters. He especially liked little Franny. And I thought it would be funny to dress up like a little girl and do my hair. I liked the way it turned out, and then I added the contacts. When Peter saw me, he was over the moon. Best sex ever."

"You had to know the illusion wouldn't last," Brooke said. "You could never truly replace Franny in his affections."

"He tried to get ahold of you gals for years. He told me that after the trial you disappeared, and nobody would help him find you. When he asked for an address, the FBI threatened him. He was only twelve years old and being pushed around by the feds. No wonder he took off when he heard they wanted to contact him. So sorry, Agent Sloan, but Peter's experiences with the FBI have been all bad."

He acknowledged her words with a quick nod but didn't bother to apologize or defend the actions of other agents. "He was corresponding with Layla via email."

"He wasn't looking for her but stumbled across her address when he was looking for a cheapo lawyer."

"Why? Was he having legal problems?"

"I told him we should sue my landlord because Peter tripped on a broken piece of the sidewalk and sprained his ankle. But he forgot all about the lawyer when he found Layla's name. He was so happy when he sent that first email."

"And she never responded," Brooke said. "That must have upset him."

"He'd never get mad at any of you. His perfect little dolls, the Hardy Dolls." This time she didn't bother to cover her hostility with the cutesy eye roll. "You think you're so special, but you're not."

"You must have hated Layla."

"I never met her," Kiki said.

"Were you jealous?"

"Ha! My sweetie is completely devoted to me. I'm his whole world. You girls are just figments from the past."

Sloan rose from his chair at the table. "I'll only ask one more time, Kiki. Where were you on Friday after Channing left?"

"Seriously, do I need an alibi?"

"It wouldn't hurt."

"No big deal. I did a couple of errands and went to the gym. Talk to my personal trainer."

"His name?"

"Is this really necessary? He probably won't be around. You can talk to somebody at the front desk."

"Give me his name or you're under arrest."

She muttered, "Shane Waters."

Brooke knew that Sloan would verify that alibi. He must be having the same suspicions about this phony Hardy Doll. She was jealous and nasty enough that Brooke felt a glimmer of sympathy for Channing. The feeling passed quickly. He could have been working with Kiki to hurt Layla and take his revenge for years of being ignored.

Chapter Sixteen

When they returned to the SUV, Brooke blurted, "What a horrible woman! She's got to be a suspect, right?"

"Oh, yeah." Sloan slipped the car into gear and mentally mapped out the route to her house, which was about five miles away—ironically close, considering Channing's supposedly desperate search for the women he considered sisters. "I'll arrange with Keller to have Kiki's alibi verified. A visit to the gym is hard to prove. She might have checked in and then left."

"To dispose of the body. Oh, no, how could I say that? The body?" Her hands flew up and covered her face. "Layla was so much more than a murder victim, more than a collection of tissue, organs and blood. She was my best friend."

He reached across the console to rub her shoulder. She'd been going through hell. Not only was she mourning her friend, but Brooke had been hammered by experiences that reopened the past and retraumatized her. He didn't know how much more she could take before she shattered.

Earlier today, he'd considered putting her in touch with Martin Hardy via live video feed from the prison, but that might be a step too far. She hadn't seen him for twelve years, but that might not be long enough. Was there a set amount of time to pass before she could face the devil who had tormented her and scarred her for life?

Sloan knew that if he asked, she'd agree to the interview with Hardy, no matter how much it might hurt. Her overriding concern was to find Layla's killer. That was her mantra. She'd told him a half dozen times that she'd do anything for Layla. *Anything!* Always putting the needs of others ahead of her own, she wasn't great at protecting herself. He wanted to keep her safe, but this wasn't his decision.

She stiffened her spine and hid her expressive eyes behind her sunglasses. "I'm okay."

You're not fooling me. "If you say so."

"So, Mr. Profiler, does Kiki fit the bill?"

"As you mentioned, she's a horrible human being. Nice guns, though."

"Are you talking about her muscular arms? I can't believe you focused on that."

"Her physical assets were hard to miss. She put it all on display." He was a man. Of course, he noticed. "Oddly enough, I don't think her purpose was seduction. All that posing was meant to intimidate."

"Did it work?"

He shrugged. "I could take her."

Though he hadn't altogether been joking, he appreciated Brooke's chuckle. Her mood was returning to something less intense. "Let's get back to Kiki's profile," she said. "Could she be the murderer?"

"You can't put much stock in a quickie analysis, but here goes." He cleared his throat. "Kiki Galloway is a master manipulator, very competitive and demanding. These traits make her the perfect mate for an immature guy like Channing. He needs to be told what to do, and she's happy to give the orders."

"That makes logical sense," she said. "But I don't believe he'd obey a command to murder a woman he cared about."

"Very true, and murder wouldn't be her first choice when it came to besting an opponent. She'd prefer a competition for her man's affection. She might even arrange a meeting between Layla and Channing."

"And then what?"

"I have no basis for further speculation," he said. "Everything I'm saying is pure fiction and can't be acted upon legally."

"I still want to hear it."

While they were sitting at Kiki's messy table, he had envisioned a possible scenario. "Suppose Channing arranges to meet Layla or he ambushes her. She freaks out and he drugs her. That's when Kiki steps in. Using information stolen from Layla, she makes the threatening phone calls to Franny and does the weird stalking stuff."

"And the honking car in my garage," she reminded.

"A woman like Kiki would enjoy the chance to terrorize all of you. At some point, she'd realize that she couldn't let Layla go free to identify her. Then, Kiki might strangle Layla, cover the ligature mark and tell Channing that she didn't know how Layla died. All the unusual moving of Layla from place to place and finally taking her to the cabin would fit with Kiki's manipulative patterns. The weird machinations make me suspect her."

"Like you said, there's no proof. It's just a hunch, but better than nothing."

As they came nearer to her house, he shifted to a different topic. "This afternoon, I'll spend some time at your house, talking to the others. But I need to return to headquarters."

"To arrange for surveillance on Kiki?"

"And to file my reports. Then I need to dig through some fairly tedious police work, reviewing potential suspects."

"How do you decide who's a suspect?"

"Keller has been coordinating interviews with professors, neighbors and associates who had a connection with Layla. If any of them have criminal records or other suspicious leanings, I'll go deeper, see if they fit a profile and maybe pay them a visit."

"Like we did with Kiki," she said. "What else?"

"After a comprehensive computer search, I'll review every person who visited or corresponded with Martin Hardy during the last twelve years. Beyond that, I'll study possible copycat crimes and unsolved murders that fit the profile for this investigation."

"Why would anyone want to copy a scum bucket like Hardy?"

Her innocence touched him. In spite of everything she'd been through, Brooke still had a hard time imaging the sick and twisted motives that drove some people. The world was populated by monsters: sadists, pedophiles, predators and abusers. A confrontation with Hardy via video feed would be traumatic for her. He should forget about it, concentrate instead on keeping her safe. But he felt there might be something to be gained from talking to Hardy. "Do you ever think of him?"

"Every day." A muscle in her jaw twitched. "Sometimes, I think I see him in the distance or hear his voice, even when I'm alone at night."

"Last night?"

"I fell into bed and slept like a log, and that's unusual for me. I often lie awake with a myriad of details rushing across my brain. I think I was too overwhelmed to dream. Yesterday I learned that my best friend was dead, went to the murder scene and nearly got blown up." Her head cocked to one side as she turned toward him. "I'm guessing that you see terrible things on a daily basis. Does it ever get to you?"

Sometimes he wished he could pull the covers over his head and not get out of bed, but he knew firsthand that he couldn't hide from injustice. "It's my job."

When he heard the *thwap-thwap* of helicopter blades, he looked up at a news chopper that should have been reporting traffic jams on the highway. Instead, the helo hovered over Brooke's house. What the hell did they expect to see? On her street, the media trucks and reporters formed a perimeter around her property.

A barricade blocked the end of the street. Sloan showed his shield to a cop, who cleared the way after a brief exchange on his walkie-talkie. As they drove through the crowd, Brooke scrunched down in the passenger seat and held up her hand to shield her face from the cameras.

"You've done this before," he said.

"Sadly, yes."

No wonder she'd chosen an occupation that allowed her to work from home. This kind of scrutiny would make anybody want to lock the doors and throw away the keys. Though he drove into the driveway and parked as close to the house as possible, there was a ten-yard distance between his SUV and the front door.

"Give me your jacket," she said. "I'm going to put it over my head so they can't get a clear photo."

When they left the car, he heard the media people calling her name, trying to get her to turn around. He walked in front of her, shielding her from their view. With every step, he was more and more grateful to be anonymous.

Inside the house, they joined Franny, Lancaster and Gimbel, who were sitting at the dining room table. Franny left her seat, dashed toward them and threw her arms around Brooke.

"Are you okay?" she asked. "Where have you been?"

Brooke cast him a sidelong glance. "Can I tell her everything?"

"I don't see why not."

She faced her perky friend and said, "I talked to Peter Channing."

"Omigod, omigod, omigod." She ran to the front staircase and shouted up, "Moira and Megan, get down here. Brooke has news."

Sloan needed to get back to headquarters. He pulled Gimbel aside and asked him to talk to each of the women about their memories of the unknown men that Hardy had brought to the cabin.

"Twelve years ago," Gimbel said, "I asked a million questions about those guys and got nothing that would identify them. But it doesn't hurt to ask again. Memories change."

"If they come up with anything significant—"

"I'll give you a full report," the retired agent said. "This isn't my first rodeo."

His comment was fitting. In his jeans, boots and battered hat, he looked like an old cowhand. "I appreciate your help."

"I'd do anything for these ladies."

"So would I," Lancaster said, unapologetic about eavesdropping and intruding on a private conversation. "Is there anything I can do?"

In spite of the offer to be useful, Sloan didn't like or trust this guy. "Why are you here?"

"I thought I could be their spokesperson with the reporters. I just want to help."

To help his career. With the bevy of media in attendance, Lancaster was dying to step up to the microphones and make sure everybody saw his shiny bald head on the evening news. More than likely, he'd been waiting for Brooke to come home and give the okay. "If you make a statement, you need to state clearly that your pronouncements are not sanctioned by the FBI."

Before Sloan left, he spoke to Brooke and promised he would return later tonight. If she thought of anything, she should call him. He wanted to pose the question about doing the video feed conversation with Hardy, but he still wasn't sure what to say.

It was a big risk, and he didn't want to hurt her.

HOURS LATER, BROOKE sat behind her desk in her office. She had considered going through files on the thumb drives to look at photos but decided she couldn't bear the images of Layla smiling and laughing. The sorrow was too raw, too new. She didn't want to face the pain.

Instead, she watched the clock and waited for Sloan to return. He'd called, said he'd be over at about nine o'clock—which was in seven minutes—and he'd asked if that was too late. She was okay with having him show up at nine, ten or midnight. Last night she'd been exhausted, but not tonight. Tonight, she was wired.

Today had been productive. They'd eliminated Zachary Doyle as a suspect. Peter Channing seemed to be in the clear until they met his fiancée and started considering them as a team. Since Brancusi's alibi had already cleared, the only suspects connected with the past were the sick, depraved, nameless men who had come to the cabin with Hardy.

Evidence was leading Sloan in different directions. He had to consider Layla's friends and colleagues as well as people who might have visited Hardy in prison and the vast general population of copycats who wanted to emulate Hardy's cruelty. The further afield the investigation went, the less Sloan would be able to use her assistance.

Brooke knew their time together was limited, but she wasn't ready to say goodbye. Their kiss this morning had opened a window of possibility that she hadn't considered for years. Not only was she attracted to the tall, lean federal agent with the intriguing gray-silver-green eyes, but he also aroused her. The unsatisfying sexual experiences she'd had in the past might no longer define her as a woman. Sloan might be the key.

Her memory skipped to thoughts of another key—the one Channing had given her. When she closed her eyes, she imagined the feel of the cold metal in the palm of her hand. She could have used that key to escape, but she'd been too scared to take a chance.

So much of her life had been spent being safe, taking precautions and avoiding danger. It might be time to take a chance. Tonight, she'd arrange for privacy for her and Sloan. And she would make the advances on him. Was that manipulative? Was she turning into Kiki?

There was a knock on the door. Lancaster poked his head inside and asked, "Are you working on anything?"

"No." She hadn't even turned on her computer.

"I'm getting ready to leave. Is there anything you want me to tell the reporters?"

"There's nothing to say."

"Decisions have been made," he pointed out. "Moira, Megan and her daughter will be leaving tomorrow and staying at Megan's house."

"I don't think it's a good idea to say where we are or where we might be going."

"If Gimbel had allowed me to listen while he was talking to all of you, I'd have better information to pass along.

When he was leaving, I asked him if there was anything new, and he brushed me off. The big news is that you talked to Peter Channing."

"Any information about suspects should come from the FBI." From what Sloan had told her, SAC Keller enjoyed seeing his face on the news almost as much as her lawyer. "Please respect our privacy."

"You have bodyguards. You'll be fine."

Safety was a virtue. She'd believed in that rule for most of her life. She gave him a nod and glanced toward her blank computer screen. "I'll have to say good-night."

"Don't worry. I'll be back tomorrow."

She didn't really want to see him again, but his expertise was useful. The clock on her wall said four minutes past nine. Had Sloan changed his mind about coming here? Maybe he'd found a promising lead and needed to follow up. That would be good news, of course—she wanted the killer caught. But she didn't want her time with Sloan to end.

Leaving the office, she went into the entryway, where one of the bodyguards had stationed himself. He sat on a lower step of the staircase. When he saw her, he held up the computer tablet with the camera surveillance so she could see the view of the front door. With a grin, he said, "Looks like you have a visitor."

In enhanced night vision, she watched the screen as Sloan crossed from his SUV to her porch. His loosened necktie was the only sign of disarray after this long, stressful day. An unfamiliar but pleasant sensation fluttered inside her rib cage.

Her heart jumped. Filled with hope, she forgot all else.

Chapter Seventeen

Brooke wasn't exactly sure how she and Sloan had gotten from the entryway to the basement. Floating on air wasn't literally possible, but she lacked awareness of movement and physical sensation. She couldn't feel her bare feet touching the floor or her muscles flexing as she walked. Her vision blurred. Though inhaling and exhaling, she wasn't aware of breathing and hadn't heard her voice as she welcomed him into her home and suggested they go somewhere private to talk.

Inside the panic room, she closed and locked the door. They were alone.

In her mind, she'd built up this moment when they would be together to such an extent that her brain fogged. *What came next?* She should say something brilliant, reveal a hidden talent or twirl like a fidget spinner. But she was frozen. When he pulled down the wall bed and reclined upon it, she couldn't think of one single reason why she should be hyperventilating. And yet, she was gasping.

"Are you okay?" he asked.

"Uh-huh." On stiff legs, she crossed the tiny room and plunked down beside him.

"Gimbel gave me his preliminary report over the phone. He didn't learn anything new."

"Uh-huh." She couldn't think. *What's wrong with my*

brain? Was this what happened to people who got sexually aroused? Did they turn into drooling morons?

"Franny and the twins told him they never saw the men Hardy brought by. He locked the younger girls up in their room."

"That's right." She dug her fingernails into the palm of her hand, thinking that the resulting pain would wake her up.

"Gimbel really likes all of you, and he's deeply concerned about your safety, both physical and psychological. Layla's murder and the threats are traumatic. You know that."

"Uh-huh." She had to stop mumbling. *Snap out of it!* The time had come to untangle her tongue and start making sense. "When things settle down, we'll make appointments with our therapists. I need grounding. Believe me, Sloan, that's an understatement. And I'll make sure the others are okay."

"I'm worried, too," he said. "I don't want to do anything to make this harder for you."

"Great!" Inhaling a breath, she tried her best to find her center and pull herself together. Her psychological issues were *not* what she wanted to talk about with Sloan. Diverting his focus away from her glaring problems, she asked, "What about your afternoon? Did you learn anything new at headquarters?"

"There's stuff I should follow up on. I should schedule personal interviews with people from your list of Layla's associates. As for the database of possible copycats, I never really bought into that profile, not for this case. Martin Hardy never killed anybody. If somebody really wanted to copy him, they'd be staging abductions."

"Speaking of the devil," she said, referring to Hardy, "did you discover any suspicious people who visited the prison?"

"A few, and there were people who wrote him letters." A frown tugged at the corners of his mouth. "There's something we need to talk about. It concerns Hardy."

On a scale of one to ten, a discussion about Hardy was ten times ten in the negative. Not something she wanted to chat about. "Right now, I just want to relax. You know, Sloan, it's just you and me in this room. It's okay for you to take off your necktie."

"Yeah?" He cocked an eyebrow.

"Please."

"It's funny. I never thought I'd grow up to be a guy who wore a suit every day." After he removed his holster and gun, he took off his jacket and neatly draped it on a chair beside the bed. He tugged the knot on his tie, unfastened the patterned fabric from his neck and rolled it into a ball that he tucked into his jacket pocket.

Watching him undress in such a tidy manner excited her so much that her throat constricted. Her voice was as a whisper, which she hoped sounded sexy. "Better?"

"A little." He loosened his collar button and a few more, enough to give her a glimpse of his dark, curly chest hair. A moment of quiet enveloped them. There was nothing more to say. Action was required.

He scanned the supplies that packed her panic room. "You did a good job in here. It looks like you've got all the basics covered."

"And some of the luxuries."

She reached into a woven picnic hamper beside the bed and took out a bottle of merlot, which she handed to him along with a corkscrew. Her hands were trembling too much to open the bottle. This move was brazen, forward and not like her at all. She couldn't believe she'd thought ahead and brought the wine down here.

While he applied the corkscrew, she produced two crystal wineglasses from the basket. They came from an expensive set that she seldom had a chance to use. After tapping them lightly together to hear the ping, she met his gaze. "Too obvious?"

"Your intentions are clear." He pulled the cork. "And I'll be equally transparent. I want to share this wine with you. I want to kiss you again. Frankly, I want more than a kiss. But it's not possible."

"That's too bad." Her soaring spirits took a nosedive. "I don't put on this kind of show for just anybody."

"I'm a federal officer, and you're part of the case that I'm investigating. It's wrong for me to use my position to start a relationship."

She knew the rules and limitations but had hoped they could ignore them. For once in her life, she wanted to color outside the lines, but she understood the restrictions. In a small voice, she asked, "If we'd met under different circumstances, would you be interested in me?"

"Hell, yes. I'd send you a dozen red roses and a pound of chocolate truffles. If things were different, I'd hire a carriage and take you to a five-star hotel, where we'd order oysters and strawberries from room service and make love all night." He poured the shimmering red wine. "Cheers."

They clinked glasses and sipped. Though she wasn't much of a drinker, she liked the crisp, fruity flavor. She drank more deeply as she considered the seductive fantasy that had rolled off his tongue so easily. "Have you ever done that before? Taken a carriage ride and feasted on room service?"

"Never." His lips curved in a grin that was sexier than it ought to be. "You inspire me."

She hadn't intended to be an ethereal muse. Her plan had been to get down and dirty. Holding her wineglass up to the light, she swirled the ruby liquid. "This comes from a winery on the western slope."

"I like it."

She drained her glass and held it out to be refilled. "I have a serious question for you, Agent Sloan."

"Shoot."

"You're good at profiling everybody else. What about yourself?"

"Self-analysis is a part of psychology training. I've heard it said that the reason people go into this field is to deal with their own mental and emotional issues."

"Let me guess," she said. "You're obsessive-compulsive, like me."

"I like to think I'm efficient and neat."

"So do I." She took another glug of wine, aware that she was drinking too fast. "And you're super empathetic. It's like you have your own personal traumatic stress to deal with."

"Right again," he said, too quickly.

"What happened to you, Sloan?"

He peered into his crystal glass as though looking for answers. "We'll talk about it another time."

Avoiding an uncomfortable situation was a tactic she knew well. She understood the wall he put up and his unwillingness to talk about how his life had been forever changed by a terrible experience. Like her, he was still struggling with the aftermath. She stepped away from the topic. There was no point in banging her head against an unbreakable wall of defense.

She contented herself with conversation. Mostly, they talked about food. Though he was relatively new in Denver, he'd been to more restaurants than she had. He confided that he wanted to learn how to ski this winter, and she offered to join him. All the while, they continued drinking the wine.

"Do you know what I want?" She gave him a loose-lipped smile. "I want to stop calling you Agent Sloan. It's too formal, and we're friends."

"Friends? Yes." He tapped the last drop of wine from the bottle.

"Justin?"

"What is it, Brooke?"

Saying his name felt so familiar, as though she knew a secret. Justin Sloan reclined against the pillows on her pull-down bed with his collar buttons unfastened and a wineglass in his hand, looking like an advertisement for pheromone-based cologne. "You know how the firemen have those sexy calendars? Does the FBI have an Agent of the Month?"

"It's not really our thing."

"It should be. I'd buy a hundred copies and use them for wallpaper."

She tilted sideways and set her empty glass on the floor. She'd need both hands free for what she had planned. Though he'd told her, in straightforward terms, that nothing was going to happen, she figured she might as well try to change his mind. Looking down, she unfastened the buttons on her pale blue blouse. Underneath, she wore a black lace bra. With her blouse open, she pushed the fabric aside to give him a clear view.

"Beautiful," he said.

She was pleased to note that his voice sounded as strangled as hers had been when she first came into the panic room. She should have elegantly and silently accepted the compliment, but the wine made her chatty. "About a year ago, I got this bra when I set out to seduce the man I'd been dating. The seduction didn't end well. The guy turned out to be a dud."

"He didn't deserve you."

"Thank you, Justin. That was precisely the right thing to say."

He set down his own wineglass and moved closer to her on the bed. With the back of his hand, he stroked the line of her jaw and throat. His hand glided lower. Gently, he caressed the swell of her breasts above her lace bra.

His touch ignited a million sensations, from the tingling across her skin to the hard throbbing of her heart. Excitement spiraled inside her. This excitement was the start of what she wanted, and she was greedy for more. When she touched him, she didn't use as much finesse. As quickly as possible, she unbuttoned his shirt and yanked it off. She savored the sight of his bared chest.

"When I first met you," she said, "I never thought we'd end up like this."

"I don't believe that. Within five minutes of saying hello, you had my shirt off."

"Not intentionally."

When he slipped her blouse off her shoulders, he held her upper arms so she couldn't move away while he kissed the line of her collarbone. Slowly, he eased her down on the bed beneath him. The subtle pressure of his mouth created a wave of pleasure that surged and ebbed through her body. She arched her back. Her breasts thrust closer to his chest, and she felt her nipples tighten into hard nubs.

She tried to break away from him, not because she wanted to escape but so she could tear off her bra and press her naked flesh against him. He restrained her. The moment of struggle against his superior strength was even more pleasurable when he released his hold and she flung her arms around him, pulling him down on top of her.

Her mouth joined with his for a burning kiss. For the first time in her life, she knew what real passion felt like. She spread her thighs, needing to be closer to him. And he wanted her, too. When his erection rubbed against her, she reached down and stroked his hard shaft.

He made a sound deep in his throat that was midway between a growl and a sigh. And then he pushed himself upright, putting distance between them. Breathing hard, he sat on the edge of the bed. "This isn't right, Brooke."

She lay back on the pillows, humiliated. What had she been thinking? She crossed her arms over her chest to hide her fancy lace bra. She wished she could blame her behavior on the wine, but that wasn't exactly true. Her inhibitions were lowered, but she hadn't gone unconscious. Brooke had known what she was doing.

She rolled onto her side with her back to him. "Agent Sloan, would you please leave."

The bed creaked when he stood. Though she wasn't watching, she knew he was walking toward the door. The last time they were in this room, she'd explained how to open the lock. Like many of her secrets, she'd willingly shared that with him.

Her attempted seduction was a mistake, foolish. All that was left was to pick up the shreds of her pride and try to weave them into whole cloth. She sat on the bed and put on her blouse. "Why are you still here?"

"There's something I need to tell you," he said. "Not many people know about this, and I'd appreciate if you'd keep the information to yourself."

"Sure thing." She infused her tone with sarcasm. "It must be awful to have everyone know the most private details of your life. But wait, I know exactly what that's like."

"Look at me, Brooke."

With the final button on her shirt fastened, she turned

her gaze toward the tall man standing beside the door to the panic room. She wanted to be angry at him, but it was impossible to hate this guy. He meant to do the right thing. He was trying to follow the rules…and he was still so very handsome. With his hair mussed, his shirt open and his silvery eyes shining a spotlight on her, he appealed to her on so many levels.

Averting her eyes, she scooted around the bed and sat primly on the edge with her knees together. "Go ahead with what you need to say."

"After high school, I enlisted in the navy, mostly because I wanted to take advantage of the benefits, especially the college tuition. My original plan had been to get a football scholarship like my big brother, but I blew out my knee in senior year."

Was that the trauma that scarred him for life? A football injury? She was careful not to sneer. Different things were vitally important to different people. "Losing the scholarship must have been a huge disappointment."

"It wasn't that big a deal. I liked the navy, the idea of serving and giving back to the country that was my home. I had a good life and a happy family. We did okay. In the military, the training taught me a lot about myself."

The more she learned about him, the more she liked the guy. His rejection still stung, but she was already beginning to forgive him. "Where were you stationed?"

"My first tour was on a battleship in the South Pacific, where we were diverted on a mission of humanitarian aid after earthquakes and mudslides on an Indonesian island. The devastation was unbelievable. Houses and buildings were collapsed. The surrounding forest was laid waste. Our mission was search and rescue."

The catch in his voice caught her attention. His usual open expression took on a somber aspect. His eyes darkened as he looked inside himself and remembered what had happened on that island.

She assured him. "You don't have to tell me."

"I want you to know what happened. We were dragging people from wreckage, some dead and some alive. I had gashes on my hand and didn't even feel them." He held up his hand and looked at the faded scars. "We saw a barracks-type building still standing. Somebody told us it was a school. For a minute, we began to hope. Maybe the kids inside had survived. They might be okay."

She had a bad feeling about his story and didn't really want to hear the ending. But she couldn't stop listening.

He continued, "Inside the schoolhouse, we discovered the dead bodies of fourteen kids, ranging in age from six to twelve. They weren't victims of the quakes. These children had been murdered by a warlord who used the natural disaster to take over this tiny, devastated town. The wounds these innocent kids suffered were horrible, unbelievable. It was sheer evil. Who could do this to children? The inhumanity tore a piece from my soul."

Unable to hold back, she crossed the room to stand beside him. In the past few minutes, the bond between them had been stretched to near breaking but now was strong again. She held his hand in hers and traced the fine outline of his scars. "I'm so sorry."

"Classic war-related PTSD," he said. "My case could go into a textbook."

"Was that the moment you decided to go into law enforcement?"

He nodded. "Following the rules isn't easy, but it's who I am. It's what I do."

She went up on tiptoe to kiss his cheek. "You're a good man, Justin."

Her passion would have to wait, but she had reason for hope. Whether he wanted it or not, they had a relationship.

"When I came here tonight," he said, "I had something I intended to ask you. This plan might produce evidence that's useful to our investigation. But maybe not."

"I'll do it," she said.

"Not so fast. Facing my own memories gave me a glimpse of what the trauma of your past has done to you. If you're at all uncomfortable with the idea, I'll find another way."

"Ask me, already."

"I don't need your answer tonight. Tell me tomorrow." He paused. "We've arranged a live video feed with Martin Hardy in prison. He's agreed to talk to you."

Seeing Hardy face-to-face after all these years? It would take all her strength and courage to survive. Before she could give Sloan an answer, she heard a hammering at the door to the panic room, and her cell phone rang. An emergency?

When she answered, she heard Franny's panicky voice. "You have to come, Brooke. Right away."

"What's wrong?"

"It's like looking in a mirror. Hurry!"

Franny disconnected the call. Her friend was prone to dramatic outbursts, but this sounded like she had a real cause to be concerned. "Like looking in a mirror? What's that supposed to mean?"

Sloan plugged in the code and opened the door. "Think about it. We might know what she's talking about."

In the hall outside the panic room, Franny stood with her phone in her hand. "Follow me."

They raced up the staircase and into the entryway where two of the three bodyguards had gathered. One of them held up the tablet showing the camera feed for the front yard.

A black-haired woman waved her arms and shouted at the police who were trying to get close enough to subdue her. Brooke could hear her muffled shouts from outside, and she knew what Franny had been talking about. "It's Kiki Galloway."

One of the bodyguards asked, "Should we let the police handle this?"

Though Brooke didn't think Kiki had come here to confess, she might have valuable information. "Open the door and let her in."

"Who is she?" Franny asked.

"Channing's girlfriend."

"No way! Seeing her is like looking in a mirror."

"Not when you get close," Brooke said.

Sloan stepped up beside her. "This might be my fault. When I contacted Kiki's personal trainer, I also discovered that he's her lover."

"Did you tell her?"

"No, but the trainer wasn't real happy about being questioned by the FBI."

Kiki stalked through the door. Her black hair flared around her head. Her mouth twisted in a snarl. "I hope you're happy," she said to Brooke. "He broke up with me."

"Who?" Franny squeaked.

"Peter." Kiki shouted his name. "I never should have cheated on him, especially not with that idiot. He showed up at the house and told me the affair was over. He told me in front of Peter."

It sounded to Brooke that Kiki had gotten what she deserved. "I have one question for you."

"Go to hell."

"Did you have anything to do with Layla's murder?"

"I didn't care about her or you or even this little punk. Franny? Peter loved me. And now he's gone."

"Good for him," Brooke said.

When Kiki lunged at her, Sloan stepped in and grabbed her. With a little help from the bodyguards, he got her wrists fastened behind her back. "You're under arrest, Kiki."

Brooke was almost sad to see her being hauled away by the police. Kiki's personal life was a wreck, but her alibi with her former lover was solid. Her name had to be crossed off the list of viable suspects.

Chapter Eighteen

Another bomb! This time the killer struck closer to home—Brooke's home.

At twenty minutes past four in the morning, Sloan was behind the wheel of his SUV. With the red-and-blue lights in the grille flashing, he broke every speed limit as he raced across town. The message from Keller had come through on his phone ten minutes earlier. An explosive device had detonated in Brooke's attached garage and started a fire. No injuries. The women and the security guards had been taken to FBI headquarters.

"Call Brooke," he ordered his phone.

After five rings, it went to voice mail, and he left a third message for her. "I'm on my way. Call me back."

At the most, it would take ten more minutes to get to headquarters. Not soon enough! He needed to know that she was all right. A fire at her house represented one of the worst things that could happen to Brooke. She loved that place and had carefully arranged every detail, from the triple-pane windows and the marble-topped island in the kitchen to the panic room in the basement. How had her security failed? The house was wired with protective sensors and monitored by cameras. When he first met her at Franny's place, Brooke had mentioned the unexplained honking in her garage. But she'd dealt with the problem, contacting the company that installed her security. Supposedly, they'd checked the system and found no cause for alarm.

Suspicious, he recalled that she'd hired bodyguards from the same company she'd used to install her security system. Had they set the bomb? It was unlikely that the installers and the office people and the bodyguards were all conspiring. A connection to Layla's murder was even more improbable. Sloan clenched his fist on the steering wheel. Why the hell wasn't she calling him back?

Last night in the panic room, he'd been crazy to turn down her sweet, adorable, sexy advances. Sure, the seduction went against his principles. Dedication to his job came first. But she was beautiful, smart and funny. He'd never find another woman who suited him so perfectly. Why had he said no? Clearly, he was an idiot. As soon as this investigation was over, he'd book a penthouse suite in an excellent hotel, fill it with roses and carry her over the threshold. That day couldn't come soon enough.

His phone rang and told him that he had a call from an unknown person. He answered.

A male voice said, "It's me. Don't hang up."

"Who the hell is this?" He swerved around a bread truck on the highway. Two more exits, and he'd be at headquarters.

"Nick Brancusi," the caller said. "I've got something important to tell you."

"Did you hear about the bomb?"

"You bet I did. Sometimes I monitor the police scanner," he said. "And there's already a breaking news segment on the local television stations. There were dozens of trucks and cameramen outside Brooke's house. Most of them were asleep but they were in the right place at the right time to get the story."

Taking pictures of a burning house was an odd idea of being in the right place. "Why did you call me?"

"I've done projects with some of the local film people. You know how it is with us professionals. Anyway, I've been researching experts with fireworks and explosives. It's amazing what these guys can do with timers. I can give you names."

Brancusi was an ass. How could he think that his resources were equivalent to those of the FBI? Though tempted to tell this jerk to bug off, Sloan knew better than to slam the door on anybody offering information. "Text me the names."

"Let's meet. I need a little something from you."

"Kind of busy here." He spun onto the exit ramp at seventy-five miles per hour.

"First, I want to know if the girls are going to Megan's house."

"I don't have that information," Sloan said.

"So you don't think they're headed there. They could be taken to an FBI safe house," Brancusi said with a note of triumph. "Give me an idea where it is."

"Seriously? Do you expect me to give you the address of a safe house?"

"Never hurts to ask. You're on your way to headquarters, right?"

"How do you know?"

"I've been tailing you for the past couple of miles. You're not a great driver."

"I'm hanging up," Sloan said. "Text me the names or not, it's up to you."

Sloan disconnected the call. At headquarters, he used his pass to get past the guardhouse at the entry and access the underground parking, where he pulled into a slot.

Brooke still hadn't called him back, and he couldn't help worrying as he ducked into an elevator.

From the glass-walled conference room near SAC Keller's office, he heard several people talking at once. Peeking around the corner, he saw little Emily sitting cross-legged outside the room with a coloring book open on the carpet in front of her. She sighted him, waved, bounced to her feet and charged in his direction. Sloan caught her under the arms, lifted her in the air and whirled in a circle.

After her giggles subsided, Emily stayed in his arms. She rested her head on his shoulder and nuzzled her curly black hair against his chin. "There was a fire," she said, "and firemen."

"Are you okay?"

"I guess so." She frowned. "My mommy is really mad, though. She wants to go home to our house and the agent man says no."

"What do you want, Emily?"

"A Dalmatian puppy with spots."

"Like the dogs that ride on fire trucks," he said.

"Cartoon doggies."

He didn't know much about four-year-olds, but Emily didn't seem to be traumatized by the bomb and the fire. Long-term effects were possible, but this little girl wasn't exhibiting the typical symptoms of fear. It wouldn't hurt to check in with a child psychologist, but Emily seemed like a smart, secure kid.

Still holding her, he walked along the corridor outside the glass room where four women with black hair and blue eyes confronted Keller and two other agents. The three bodyguards from the security firm stood against the far wall. Though Sloan hadn't made a peep, Brooke spun around as though she sensed him. Their gazes linked through the glass, and a quick smile slid across her mouth.

His tension eased. His worries abated. She was okay. He grinned back at Brooke and spoke to the child in his arms. "Should we go in there and straighten those people out?"

"Yes," she said with a huge nod of her head. "They are all talking at one time."

"And that's got to stop."

When he entered the room, Franny approached and wrapped them both in a hug. In contrast to Emily, Franny's insecurities were painfully evident. Her eyes darted, and her hands trembled. When she spoke, her voice was more high-pitched than usual. "I talked to Peter Channing," she said. "I told him I was sorry about his wedding falling apart."

He hadn't erased Channing's name from the list of suspects. In spite of his alibis, he seemed like the most likely person to make the weird phone calls to Franny. "Did you talk about anything else?"

"He told me he didn't call and upset me. Crossed his heart and hoped to die."

"Did you believe him?"

"Maybe." She took Emily from his arms. "I'm going to take this one and find something to eat. Would you like that, Em?"

"Aunt Franny is the best."

Sloan was glad to see one of the agents follow them, making sure that Franny didn't get lost and start setting off alarms. He edged into a vigorous three-way conversation with Brooke, Megan and SAC Keller. Megan wanted to go home, taking one of the bodyguards with her. Keller pushed for a safe house where he could keep track of all of them. Brooke tried politely to interrupt these two opinionated adversaries but was clearly at the end of her patience.

"Quiet," she said. "Both of you."

"You're not the boss," Megan said. "We're grown-up now."

"I have two reasons why going to your house is a bad idea. Number one should be obvious, but I'll say it anyway. My security is far better than yours, but someone managed to plant a bomb. Your house might also be booby-trapped."

Megan started to speak but closed her mouth.

"Number two," Brooke said in her organized fashion, "we need new bodyguards."

"Why?" Megan demanded.

"Sorry, guys," Brooke said to the three men standing by the wall. "I have no complaints about your work. When the bomb exploded, you acted quickly and efficiently to evacuate all of us. Your driving skills are excellent. And you're friendly, which is a bonus."

"What's the problem?" Megan asked.

"I hired them through the same security firm that set up the system in my house. That system was breached and a bomb planted, which means they must have made a number of errors. We won't know for sure until we have forensic reports from the bomb squad." She asked Keller, "How long will that take?"

"Several hours," he said. "At the moment, all we know is that the device was located in the garage. The room that was most severely damaged by the fire was the office."

Another bomb in an office? Sloan began to see a pattern forming. The bomber seemed to focus more on destroying paperwork than on hurting anyone. He remembered Brooke's quick actions when the bomb exploded in Layla's apartment. Had she done the same this time?

He leaned close to her and quietly said, "Did you manage to save anything?"

"Thumb drives, a laptop and my gun."

She gestured toward a large leather briefcase on the table. Apparently, she needed something more substantial than her fanny pack to carry her Glock. If the gun was in the briefcase, he had to give her credit for bullying her way past security at the FBI headquarters. Brooke was a force to be reckoned with.

She addressed Keller. "As you know, we have experience with staying in safe houses, and I speak for all of us when I say that we'd rather not do that again. We've found the accommodations to be adequate, but a safe house—by its very nature—is restrictive."

"I hate those places," Moira said, speaking up for the first time. "There's no privacy. And I can't come and go when I want."

"It's a terrible environment for my daughter," Megan said. "I want her to be in the safest place possible. But she needs to feel free. A little girl needs—"

"Ladies, please," Keller interrupted. "I appreciate your issues. And Brooke makes some very cogent arguments. Now, I need solutions."

Brooke made eye contact with him. "A hotel."

While the twins enthusiastically confirmed her idea, Sloan held her gaze. In the midst of chaos, they communicated on a secret, sensual level. In his imagination, he was already in that hotel room with Brooke. Her black hair fanned out across a gleaming white pillowcase. She wore nothing but a lacy bra and a smile, and then he'd unfasten the bra.

"It's settled," Keller said. "I can recommend several hotels that we work with, but you'll have to pick up the tab."

"No problem," Megan said. "Brooke will pay up front, and our attorney will reimburse her."

Brooke lowered her gaze and nodded agreement. As they left the conference room, she stopped and stood beside him. It took all his willpower not to gather her into his arms and taste her lips.

"I was worried," he said. "When you listen to your phone messages, you're going to hear me begging—over and over—for you to call."

"You must have been really upset." She stroked his bare arm. "Just a T-shirt? You didn't stop to put on a suit."

On his way out the door of his apartment, he'd grabbed what was handy, which meant jeans and a T-shirt. "I'm glad I remembered to put on any clothes at all."

"I wouldn't mind if you showed up nude, but the guard at the door probably would have stopped you."

"Or not. If I was naked, he'd be able to see that I wasn't carrying a weapon."

She took a step toward the exit. "Here's the deal, Sloan. I want this monster caught and locked up. And I'll do anything to help. Last night, you asked me to make a decision."

He waited for her answer.

"I'll do it," she said. "As soon as you can arrange it, I'll talk to Martin Hardy."

AFTER A SURPRISINGLY relaxing morning at the hotel, Brooke returned to FBI headquarters with Sloan. They were seated side by side in an anonymous beige room with a table. The large screen on the wall in front of them showed the FBI logo with the striped shield, the scales of justice and the banner with three words: fidelity, bravery and integrity. Four technicians were also in the room, and she was aware of at least one camera lens pointed at her.

"Do you like the hotel?" Sloan asked, making an obvious attempt to get her to relax.

"It's not five stars," she replied, "but it's nice, clean and more luxurious than places I usually stay. We have a suite with four separate bedrooms that open into a central space with a table and sitting area."

"Room service?"

"We're taking advantage of all the amenities. We haven't placed an order for oysters and strawberries—not yet, anyway—but we're well fed and everybody gets exactly what they want. It's easier than being at my house, but I miss my kitchen. I can't wait to get back there and put my life back in order."

The images of the fire shown on television had been an appalling vision of leaping flames and gushing black smoke against the thinning darkness of a predawn sky. The fire department had responded quickly, and it looked like the north end of the house had been spared. Her office had been destroyed, and she'd lost many of the projects she'd been working on.

"There's a pool at the hotel," he said. "Did you go for a swim?"

"You don't have to make small talk to comfort me. I had a massage this morning and a manicure. I'm as calm as I'm going to be." Not exactly Zen, but she wasn't hysterical. Facing Martin Hardy was a nightmare that might launch her into a panic attack. "Have you heard anything from the bomb squad investigating the explosion?"

"The device was hidden in the ceiling above the garage, and it could have been placed there at any time. The bomber might have reached the ceiling by standing on the hood of your car."

"That would cause the car alarm to engage and the beeping to start." She should have been more thorough when she checked her car. Her first thought had been a malfunction of the vehicle. She'd called the security service to take a look at the garage, but they hadn't found anything. "What else?"

"The device was triggered by a call from a cell phone."

No help in pinpointing the location of the bomber. "He could have made the call from anywhere."

"Preliminary findings from the investigators indicate that this device and the one in Layla's office were different designs but made by the same individual. They don't know the identity of the technician who created these bombs, but he or she is skilled, professional and probably expensive."

"Peter Channing probably couldn't afford to hire a bomb maker. I don't know much about Doyle's finances, but he might be secretly rich. Brancusi could afford it."

"He called me this morning," Sloan said. "He said he had leads on bomb makers."

"A guilty admission?"

"Or a stupid one."

One of the technicians took off his earphones and said, "We can start the live feed as soon as you're ready."

Her stomach dropped. She glanced at Sloan and whispered, "Don't leave me."

"I'm right here. Whenever you want to end the session, just say so."

"Ready," she said.

The FBI logo disappeared. The face of Martin Hardy filled the screen. He wore a muddy gray jumpsuit over a white T-shirt. His uniform must have been jumbo, because he'd gained enough weight to be an elephant. He had four chins, all covered with smudgy gray stubble. His close-set eyes squinted at the camera as though he could see her through the lens.

He licked his lips. "Are you there, Brooke? Did you miss me?"

"I am here." She considered each word before she spoke. "No, I most certainly do not miss you."

"You're the most tidy and precise girl in my family.

That's what I liked most about you. Tell them to turn on the camera. I want to see you."

She shook her head. "No."

"Please, Brooke."

"If you ask again, the interview is over."

"Fine, we'll do it your way. Now, tell me what you like most about me."

Though it might be smart to flatter him so he'd open up and spill more information, she couldn't force herself to pander to this monster. "Here's what I like most," she said, "the fact that you're in prison and will stay locked up for the rest of your life."

"Don't be so sure, my pretty dolly. There's only a hundred and twenty-eight years left on my sentence."

When he laughed at his sick joke, his entire body jiggled. He'd always been a big man. With the extra poundage, he was mountainous. His beefy hands rested on his belly. She remembered those hands.

Hurtling backward in time, she was a skinny fourteen-year-old girl facing Martin Hardy and making excuses about why she couldn't find his silver money clip. There were plenty of little objects she'd swiped from him, but not the money clip. He didn't believe her. With one casual swipe of his hand, he knocked her across the room. She struggled to get up, but her head was spinning. He kicked her, and she passed out.

Anger mingled with fear as she stared at her tormentor. "You need to answer my questions."

"Ask away," he said.

"You brought other men to the cabin. Tell me their names."

"What for? Are you expanding your Christmas card list?"

"Layla," she said. Speaking her friend's name gave her

strength. She needed to make Hardy talk so they could avenge Layla's murder. "She's dead, and one of those men might have killed her."

"Poor Layla. Not as pretty as Sophia, but so loving."

How could he say such a thing? Layla despised him. They all did. Her fists clenched on the table. Every muscle in her body tensed as she fought the terrible heat burning inside her. On the outside, she was sweating. "She might have recognized one of them, and he came after her."

"Not possible," Hardy said. "Layla was always blind-folded, as was Sophia. The men I brought to the cabin were dangerous. That's why I never revealed their identities."

"Why did you bring them?"

"Money, my dear. They paid a nice fee to spend the night with Layla, even more for Sophia, who was also blindfolded. Taking care of our little family was expensive. I needed the dough-re-mi." He leaned toward the camera and raised his forefinger to make a point. "I protected you girls from those men, kept the little ones locked away and made sure Layla and Sophia were masked."

"What about me?"

His mouth stretched, and he bared his teeth in a hideous sneer. "I told you not to look, and I knew you wouldn't. You never broke the rules, Brooke. In many ways, you liked our little family. You would have been happy to stay together forever."

"But I escaped." It had taken her a long time to get up the courage to defy him, but she'd done it. "I helped the others go free."

"Do you regret that decision? Think about it, my dear little lady. Aren't there times when you wished your life was as organized as it was at the cabin? You knew exactly what was expected, and you fulfilled every task."

She'd tried to please him because she was protecting

herself and the others. There had been no choice. "I despise you."

"If that's true, why did it take you so long to make your break? You had other opportunities to go. But you stayed."

But she'd finally broken free from his control. Using a kitchen knife, she'd spent weeks and weeks prying apart the chain fastened to her shackle. When she was free, she didn't tell the others. Leaving them behind was the hardest thing she'd ever done, but she couldn't risk having them all caught.

She crawled out through a hole under the linoleum and she ran. With every step, she felt him coming closer. Never in a million years could she re-trace the route of her escape. But she'd made it.

"You liked our life," Hardy said.

"Never."

"Admit it, Brooke, you liked me."

He'd gotten inside her head and twisted her memories to suit his vision of a perfect family of loving girls who looked alike. She'd never wanted that. There were so many ways she defied him. She'd poisoned his food, rubbed garlic on his clothing and stolen little trinkets from him whenever she could.

Rising behind the table, she said, "Go to hell, Martin Hardy."

She'd stolen not only from him but also from the men he brought with him. She'd taken personal items. The memory hit her like a bolt of lightning. This was the first time she'd recalled taking those trinkets that might betray the identities of the men. She hid her treasures in places where no one could find them.

She stalked from the room with her head held high. They needed to go to the cabin. Even now after all these years, the hidden evidence might still be there.

Chapter Nineteen

Sloan wasn't troubled when Brooke insisted on taking her briefcase with her on their drive to Martin Hardy's cabin. She wanted to have her gun, and he understood her need to feel like she could defend herself after her brutal conversation with Hardy. The guy was sheer evil. He'd slithered inside her head and made her feel like she was complicit in her captivity.

Hardy was a manipulator, a psychopath and, most of all, a sadist. He derived pleasure from the misery of those six young women.

On a Sunday afternoon in August, taking a drive into the mountains should have been a pleasure. In a week or so, the aspens would turn gold, and the weather would be crisp and cool, a relief from summer's heat. He drove the SUV on a recommended back route to avoid traffic. The cabin wasn't located in any of the trendy, popular mountain communities. There wasn't easy access to skiing or white-water rafting or craft shops. It was no surprise that after Hardy was arrested and the house abandoned, it hadn't sold. Who'd want to live in a notorious place where women had been held captive?

He glanced over at Brooke, who sat stiffly in the passenger seat and stared through the windshield. Her former attitude of calm was no longer in evidence.

"You did a good job," he said. "When you talked to Hardy, you didn't let him hear fear in your voice."

"I could have done better."

"He's a cruel bastard. None of his inferences that you liked him or were trying to help him are true."

"I know." But he could hear the disappointment in her tone. "On a rational level, I'm aware that there was nothing I could have done differently. I don't blame myself. And yet…there's a niggling doubt in my mind."

"You protected yourself and the others."

"But he picked up on my weakness. There were times when I was cleaning and polishing that I took pleasure in the order I was able to create. Some of my compulsive habits started then."

"Or earlier," he suggested. "When you were in foster care, did you organize your surroundings?"

"Obsessively." She gave a short, humorless laugh. "When life hands you chaos, it feels good to exert some control."

"Franny might not agree with you."

Brooke leaned back in the passenger seat and exhaled a sigh. Mentioning her friend had been just the thing to bring her peace. "If she knew I was coming to this house, she'd throw a tantrum. As far as I know, none of us ever returned. If you weren't driving, I wouldn't know how to find the place."

"Lucky for you, I'm FBI. I know everything."

"What happened to the jeans you were wearing this morning? You're back in your suit."

"Back on the job," he said. "But today, I'm casual. Did you notice? No necktie."

"You're a wild man." This time, her laughter was genuine. "I hope we actually uncover some evidence on this trip. Do you think the idea of an unknown subject is valid?"

"It's a long shot," he admitted. "The subtlety of the murder and the subsequent bombings don't fit the profile of a guy who was so vicious that he scared Hardy. That's the type of man who kills quick and dirty if he feels threatened."

She wondered aloud. "Why would he plant the explosives? Two bombed-out offices make me think that our killer wants to destroy data. Layla might have run across incriminating information of some sort. She was a lawyer."

A thought had been playing in the back of his mind. "So is Tom Lancaster."

Instead of protesting that her attorney was beyond suspicion, she nodded slowly. "I hate to say that I thought about him when we learned that the bomb was planted in my garage. Lancaster recommended the security firm that did the work. He might have had an inside edge, a way he could circumvent the cameras and gain access to the garage."

"It also makes sense that he'd take Layla's body to the mountain hideaway you shared. Lancaster knew the location. I heard him tell you that he'd have the title transferred to your name alone."

"He handles a lot of our affairs," she said. "We've known him for twelve years, and he's gone through a lot with us. Why would he hurt Layla? There's no motive."

"You have a significant amount of money in that joint account of yours." The first time he'd seen the women with Lancaster, they were complaining about how he was stingy with their money. "Your attorney is the one who holds the purse strings."

"We have regularly scheduled audits," she said. "Layla handled all that."

Layla had been shopping for an office, going through the accounts. She might have found something, an anomaly. If Lancaster had been cooking the books, she'd be the first to know. "We'll turn the information over to the FBI forensic accountants. They're good at finding crooks."

"Lancaster isn't an idiot. He'd never do anything so obvious."

"And he doesn't have the skills to be a bomb maker." He remembered the phone call from Brancusi. "Explosives are big drama. Who does that remind you of?"

"Our favorite documentarian. I can easily imagine a scenario where he's setting a dramatic death scene." She frowned. "Too bad his alibi is solid gold."

They rode in silence for a while. Neither of them had mentioned the near seduction in the panic room. There was really nothing to say. Until the investigation was over, she was off-limits.

He kept focus on the case. "Franny mentioned that she talked to Channing on the phone."

"They have a very strange relationship. When they were kids, they played together all the time. A bond was formed. After we escaped, she refused to say his name. On two occasions in the courthouse, we saw him. Franny wept."

"Did he make those phone calls? It seems like something a kid would do."

"Like crank calls," she said. "It fits his personality, but I don't think he's clever enough to maintain the lie. Somebody else could have been framing the twerp."

The final turn on the way to Hardy's house was onto a two-lane graded gravel road that followed the winding path of a small creek. The dwellings were few and far between.

"Do you recognize the area?" he asked.

She shook her head. "I didn't go outside. As far as I was concerned, we could have been on the moon."

She pointed at a rustic cabin with a covered porch.

It was a distance off the road, tucked back in the trees. "There. That's Doyle's place. Pull over."

He parked on the shoulder and squinted through the trees. The old man sat on the porch in his wheelchair. As they watched, he laboriously got to his feet and walked to the banister. Not spry and healthy, but Doyle was capable of moving around. "Should he go back onto the suspect list?"

"I just don't know anymore." She exhaled a sigh. "Everybody looks guilty. But nobody could have done it."

About half a mile farther down the road, there was a gravel driveway that led past a clump of boulders. Beyond that was Martin Hardy's two-story house. Signs of deterioration were obvious in the broken windows, the ramshackle porch and the front door hanging open on the hinge, but that wasn't what caught Sloan's attention. Parked in front of the porch was a brown van with a gold stripe.

Brooke opened her briefcase, took out her Glock and shucked off the holster. "I'm not walking in there unarmed."

"I'm going first."

"I'm right behind you," she said. "Don't even think about telling me to stay in the car."

He approached with extreme caution, opening the door to the van and peeking inside before stepping onto the porch. "Nick Brancusi."

Camera in hand, the filmmaker stepped outside. "You've got to go into that house. It's grotesque, dripping with horror. Even without knowing the history, you can feel that something terrible happened here."

"I know," she said. "I lived it."

BROOKE RECOGNIZED BRANCUSI'S flamboyant approach as a documentary maker. He was gathering bits and pieces of setting to beef up his story. No doubt he'd want to follow her through the house, filming every moment, as she searched for the trinkets that might be evidence.

Sloan growled, "What the hell are you doing here?"

"I had a lead, somebody who might have hinted that you were coming here." He lowered the camera and adjusted his fedora. Still in skinny jeans, he wore a brightly colored Hawaiian shirt. "In case you haven't figured it out, I'm good at ferreting out information. In fact, I have something that I'm sure you'll want to know."

"I'm not listening," Sloan said. "You never texted the list of explosive experts."

"And there's a reason for that."

Sloan gestured to the open door. "Why don't you go inside, Brooke? I'll stay out here and keep an eye on Steven Spielberg."

Before entering through the open doorway, she tucked her weapon into the belt of her fanny pack. It was too heavy. She should have brought the holster, but she hadn't. Inside, she noticed the scuffing noise that her sneakers made on the filthy, sticky hardwood floor. Twelve years ago, she'd scrubbed these floors until they gleamed. The walls were marked with graffiti. Upholstery on the furniture was ripped and stained. The house was utterly different, yet she recognized it all.

Memories came at her from all directions. Battered by the past, she wanted to curl up in a ball and hide from the remembered hurt and anger and soul-crushing guilt. Martin Hardy had done terrible things to them, but they'd survived.

I survived.

If the past hadn't killed her by now, she was going to make it. In the disgusting kitchen, she went to the hiding place behind a cabinet where she'd secreted the shiny trinkets she'd stolen from Hardy and the other men. Channing had said that she was like a magpie, and she had to agree. After she took these objects and hid them, she forgot about them, except for the coins. She'd remembered the money and taken it with her when she made her escape.

The trinkets in her hiding place were pathetic: a paper clip, a couple of buttons, a pen and a thumbtack. Not evidence. These things were useless, which she must have realized at the time or she would have come back for them. Another dead end.

From the front porch, she heard Brancusi talking about his proposed documentary on the Hardy Dolls, part two. Instead of facing him, she went through the dining room and past the small bedroom near the kitchen, where she'd slept. The back door—like the front—hung open.

Outside, she gazed into the surrounding hillside with grasses, shrubs and pine trees—a lovely natural setting for Hardy's unnatural acts. A flash of sunlight caught her attention. She saw the barrel of a rifle.

Brooke stumbled backward into the house. Had she really seen a shooter? She drew her Glock and held the weapon in both hands. For years and years, she'd regularly engaged in target practice, but she wasn't a hunter and had never fired upon another human being.

She peeked around the edge of the door. The man with the gun hadn't shifted position or moved. He was bald. Tom Lancaster. All the clues she hadn't wanted to believe made sense. He'd used the security company to plant the bomb in her house. His phone calls to Franny were a way to frame Channing. Lancaster had killed Layla so she wouldn't tell anybody about the money.

When she looked again, Lancaster had moved. Was he coming around to the front? Looking for Sloan? Without thinking of her own safety, she charged through the door and darted up the hill. She raised her gun and fired a single warning shot.

Her motion attracted Lancaster's attention. He stood and turned toward her. She had the drop on him but couldn't bring herself to shoot. Before he raised the rifle, she dodged behind the trunk of a pine tree. Not a very good shield—she ducked behind a boulder. At almost the same time, she fired her weapon.

"How could you do it?" she shouted. "How could you murder Layla?"

"I tried to reason with her." His voice was so familiar, so reasonable. "Put the gun down, Brooke. We'll talk."

"The time for talking is over."

She peered over the top of the boulder. She had a shot, a clear shot. But she couldn't force herself to pull the trigger.

"You can't do it," Lancaster said. "You're a good person, Brooke."

"But I'm not," Sloan growled.

His first shot echoed through the rocks and trees, then came another. As she watched, Lancaster slumped to the ground. Sloan went directly to him, took the rifle and felt for a pulse in his throat.

He waved to her. "Get over here. I need your help."

There was a lot of blood, but Sloan said Lancaster was going to live, and she believed him. She followed his instructions, calling nine-one-one and gathering materials that Sloan used to fashion a makeshift tourniquet.

All the while, Brancusi kept on filming. She told him to stop. This wasn't a movie. Lancaster might die.

The documentarian responded, "I'm in the right place at the right time. Can't stop now."

"Don't give him a hard time," Sloan said. "He has the last, most important piece of evidence."

"That's right," Brancusi said. "I tracked down the explosives expert Lancaster hired to build his bombs. And get this! The guy didn't want to do it, but Lancaster is his lawyer."

They had proof.

Their investigation was over.

She fired a meaningful glance at Sloan. What did this mean for them?

EXACTLY THREE WEEKS LATER, the paperwork on the investigation was filed. Lancaster had survived the shooting. Charged with the murder of Layla, he confessed and was in the process of making a deal with the district attorney. Brooke had been assured that he'd be sentenced to life in prison.

The other women—Franny, Megan and Moira—had returned to their respective homes. As a result of the publicity, Sophia had auditions for several movie and television roles. She was planning a visit to Denver. Most importantly to Brooke, the repairs on her house were underway.

Sloan had made a date for tonight, and she'd bought a sleek, fashionable new dress in her favorite shade of blue. Standing in the front entryway, she watched for him on her newly installed security cameras.

When he arrived, he wasn't driving the SUV. A white limousine pulled into her driveway. Sloan emerged from the back, carrying a dozen roses in each arm. He wore his white navy uniform.

She opened the door, pulled him inside and took the roses into the kitchen. "They're lovely."

"You're lovely," he said.

"Thank you, Justin."

After she put the roses in water, they returned to the front door. He lifted her in his arms and carried her to the limo. This was the start of a beautiful relationship.

* * * * *

LET'S TALK
Romance

For exclusive extracts, competitions
and special offers, find us online:

COMING SOON!

We really hope you enjoyed reading this book. If you're looking for more romance, be sure to head to the shops when new books are available on

Thursday 7th March

To see which titles are coming soon, please visit
millsandboon.co.uk/nextmonth

MILLS & BOON